Empress Gold

Jeffrey Whittam was born in Lancashire, England in 1947. His formative years in Southern Rhodesia were spent fishing, hunting and exploring the wilderness. Still in his early twenties, Jeffrey became a prospector of note and sold his first gold claims in 1973. For the best part of the bush war, he fought with the Rhodesia Regiment's 10th Battalion. He now lives in the wilder reaches of Lancashire's fell country with his wife, children and three dogs.

Also available in paperback:

Sons of Africa

JEFFREY WHITTAM

EMPRESS GOLD

COCOPAN

First published by Jeffrey Whittam as an eBook in 2013
ISBN: 978-0-9573665-1-0

This edition published by Cocopan Publishing in 2013
ISBN: 978-0-9573665-3-4

A CIP catalogue record for this book is available from the British Library

Cover and logo design by Lon Chan Design & Illustration, Brighton

For Victoria

Without whose love I could not have come

this far

ZIMBABWE, 1996

The Empress Deep Gold Mine

'Lee. Call for you on line one. Here or your office?'

'Who is it?'

'Wouldn't say. Sounds official, though. Could be government.'

'My office, Byron. Hold them off till I get there.'

Lee Goddard handed back the phone to the shaft onsetter, nodded his thanks and made for the office steps, his rubber boots still half-filled with drill slurry from long-hole exploration rigs on 587 Level. He unclipped a Willard cap lamp battery from the nylon belt at his waist and lowered it to the grass outside the lamp room. The attendant acknowledged the Empress Deep's managing director with a wide grin and an appreciative bob of his grey, peppercorn-covered head.

'Good evening, sir.'

'David.' Lee smiled back at him. 'Put my lamp on charge, will you. I'll need it first thing tomorrow.' He dragged off his boots and socks and left them where they fell. The old man muttered something indiscernible, retrieved the lamp, ignored the boots and sodden socks and disappeared inside his lamp room. He had been with Lee since the end of the bush war and though now close to retirement, his limbs were still trim and taut as those of a lowland meerkat.

Barefooted, Lee jogged up the steps to his office and made straight for the phone.

'Goddard.'

'Don't talk. Just listen.'

'Who is this?' The connection was poor. Zimbabwe's telephone lines were in a permanent state of disrepair. Again, the distorted voice crackled from the earpiece.

3

'Friday. They want you out.'

'Who the hell are you? What are you talking about?'

'Comrade Pasviri will be with them. Prepare yourself.'
The phone went dead.

Lee stood up from his desk, his mind raced, trying to
tie the voice to one of a hundred faces and while
filtering through the possibilities he projected his anger
beyond the office window.

'Bastards,' he cursed, 'thieving, bloody bastards.' Hoax
or otherwise, like a mental leech the caller's voice had
already worked its teeth beneath his skin.

Twenty-plus years had come and gone since the death
of his father, from then on he had run the Empress
Deep on his own. *Pedal your own bicycle* his old man
always insisted. Lee frowned sharply and the crow's feet
at his temples puckered with annoyance. He was forty-
seven, most men would have already slipped sedately
into middle age, but still his stomach was iron-flat and
his resolve was that of a rebellious thirty year old.

A dark foreboding sky hung above the Empress Deep,
a mating pair of Martial eagles soared in close to the
cloud's edge. The late shift had assembled at the shaft
head, one by one the miners stepped inside the
conveyance, then the banksman drew down the steel
door and for the umpteenth time, Lee heard the shrill
ring of the shaft signal bell and watched the metal cage
with its thirty men drop like a stone to the dark throat of
the mine. Reluctantly, he brought his anger under
control and again, picked up the phone – he dialled an
outside number.

'Gerard?'

'Give me a second. Just spilled coffee all over the
phone. The idiot who designed this cup deserves to be
keelhauled.'

Lee waited for him to calm down. Retired naval
officers didn't allow themselves the luxury of making

mistakes. Seconds later, a more composed Gerard Brownlee came back on the line.

'Sorry about that. What can I do for you, old chap?'

'Karen's chairing a meeting with the Ancient Ruins people so I'll be on my own for a few hours. Come down to the house about seven o'clock. I'll have cook knock up a fillet to go with your Rioja.'

Gerard sensed the underlying concern in Lee's voice.

'You sound a little tense old boy, what's up?'

'Tell you tonight. Just be there.'

He tapped the cradle with his finger and dialled zero three for the lamp room.

'David. Bring a fully charged lamp to my office, and grab me a pair of size eleven boots and some clean socks from the visitors' change house. I'm going back down.'

The banksman waited for Lee to secure the galvanised roll-down door from the inside before ringing the conveyance away. Lee resisted the natural urge to turn on his lamp; instead, he stood with his back pressed hard to the steelwork. Again, his mind raced through a hundred intangible possibilities. His company was being sucked head first into the jaws of Mugabe's decolonisation machine. Zimbabwe's baying fraternity of so-called war veterans were already ripping apart the lion's share of the country's agricultural assets — now, motivated by that same perverse, self-styled power complex and openly backed by Mugabe's despotic government, they were moving in on the mines.

The ground fell away beneath him; at more than six metres per second into an abyss of total darkness. The speed exhilarated him — heightened his senses. The damp, the fouled air and smell of roaring diesels rushed inside the cage. Rubber jockey wheels rumbled against their guides and when the conveyance slowed, his knees flexed to cope with the downward thrust of his own momentum – then the conveyance came to a halt and he heard the station signal bell ring out twice for him to disembark.

A single string of fluorescent haulage lights lit the immediate area, though at thirty yards from the shaft gates the darkness was total; within that first minute even the roar of a three ton, loaded rock hoist had faded behind him. His were the only footprints in the dust. Painted in rough red lettering, *Danger – Explosives Store* loomed through the beam from his cap lamp. He pushed a key into the Chubb security lock and cranked the mechanism.

The steel blast-door swung inwards – months had passed since he had accessed the stone vault; the air inside was stale and though he stepped in carefully was soon knee-deep in swirling dust. Another steel-clad door and second key opened the way to a smaller chamber. Cut from the living rock there was a mingling of atmospheres – marginally cleaner air from the haulage behind him with that of uncountable hours of total isolation.

He moved through the silence and then locked the steel door behind him. Raised on blocks of reinforced concrete, a steel box, painted with rust inhibiting red paint stood as an ominous centrepiece. Again, the barrier was double locked against intruders. Both recessed locking points had been smeared with heavy duty bearing grease, for in that labyrinth of underground workings, intricate mechanisms fell as easy victims to moisture-laden ventilation currents.

Both keys slid in unopposed. Both locks operated first time – lifting the heavy lid took all of Lee's strength.

From inside the box the accumulated wealth of twenty years stared up at him. Though he had seen it a hundred times before, under that yellow glare from his cap lamp, the buttery glint of raw metal took his breath away.

2

With that same, expert eye of the appreciative critic for the sublimity of William Turner's watercolours, Gerard Brownlee appraised the cook's interpretation of his most favoured dish; a twelve ounce fillet steak, medium rare, the only way he liked it. His mouth flooded and the taste of Lee's '82 Rioja was quickly overwhelmed by garlic, succulent beef and black pepper over wild mushrooms. Whilst he gazed upon the masterpiece, from a stone and iron hearth in the far wall, a generously laid log fire shot his hair with flickering silver lights. Wiry and tanned, prominent ridges of fine muscle stood out along the full length of Gerard's forearms, for those first debilitating tremors of old age still had not caught up with him. When he cut deeply into the beef it was with steady hands, backed by that eager, unrestrained gusto of a much younger man – swift and businesslike. However, this healthy outward appearance masked a sinister affliction; the specialist's discovery of a malignant cancer was now his personal black cloud and like some evil harbinger, permanently it hovered over him, its talons deeply buried within the remaining months of his life. With a total disregard for his predicament, Gerard shook off the inevitability of his own death and as an old friend and avid mentor looked at the man sat across from him with concerned affection.

'So what's bothering you, old boy, woman problems?'

'Not that simple, Gerard. A little more sinister; our friendly government jackals are after the Empress Deep.'

'Bastards!' Gerard spluttered. 'They can't do that?'

'Had a phone call this morning,' said Lee. 'Mugabe's mob will be here on Friday, bright-eyed and bushy-tailed along with their bully boys.' He smiled, but the act was weak and unreal. 'A hundred years of investment, Gerard; lock, stock and every hard-won bloody barrel down the proverbial.'

Gerard's pair of waxed moustaches lay almost flat against his cheeks; adding poignancy to his mood they were now the lion's teeth.

'I'm flabbergasted, old boy. What will you do?'

'If I had the guts, blow the mine to hell, but I haven't – too many memories – too many good people depending on it for their livelihood.'

Gerard's eyes flashed, his mood thickened, a mutual need for revenge had already darkened his face.

'Who told you?'

'Didn't give me his name.'

'Could be a hoax?' Gerard growled and lunged at his steak. 'Some sick son of a bitch ex-employee with an axe to grind?'

Lee gave up on his steak and pushed his plate away.

'Contingency plans are already in place, but I need your help.'

Gerard's face lit up. He dropped his fork and grasped the table's edge as though bracing himself for the imminent sideways pitch of a wild sea.

'Twenty-five years with Her Majesty's destroyers, old boy. Whatever it is you want, I'm your man.'

They discussed Lee's plans in minute detail, breaking into small talk when they heard Karen's Mercedes crunch across the gravel driveway.

Karen came in through the patio doorway, her expression terse. She smiled thinly at Lee and dropped a kiss on Gerard's balding pate as she brushed past for the kitchen. Though a little plump around the middle, Lee's wife was every inch the attractive woman. As she walked, aggravated by her mood, her honey-blonde hair lashed as a lion's tail about her shoulders.

8

'I need a drink. Anyone else want a top-up?'

Lee shook his head. 'Would I be right in saying your meeting didn't go down very well, my darling?'

'Understatement of the century,' she snarled and like a spear hurled for the heart of an adversary, her shoulder bag slapped against the fireside chesterfield. 'Had only just got to grips with your mystery phone call and now this. The government's so called, ancient ruins preservation business is just total bullshit.'

Gerard grinned across the table at Lee. 'Fiery wench, this woman of yours; straight out fist fight and I'm sure she'll wipe the floor with the both of us, old boy.'

'Sorry, Gerard, that was the venomous me coming out – I shouldn't have said that. Put it down to an overblown, double dose of stress. The hotel's lounge bar catered for more inbreeds than a seaside freak show.'

Gerard roared at her comparison.

'Sounds more like a battlefield than the venue for a preservation meeting.' He swivelled in his chair. 'Let me guess, old girl; Mugabe's lot were more in favour of plundering than preserving. Museum displays put precious little money in their overseas bank accounts, my sweetheart. The future doesn't fit in with their bigger picture. They want it now, as hard cash, not as artefacts gathering dust in some rickety display cabinet.'

'You must have been earwigging, Gerard, that's exactly what happened. Chizarai was there, the minister for tourism; him and that thieving bastard, Jonas Masasiri, the museum curator. Thick as thieves. Their personal interest in our most recent excavations was just a tad more than obvious.'

'As in, you will please hand over all the good bits?'

Karen nodded her head. 'The pot shards, copper beads and all the boring stuff we can display in the museum. Any precious metals and anything remotely collectable go to a government courier to be taken back to Harare, supposedly for safe keeping.'

'And we all know by whom,' Gerard chuckled, 'some Far Eastern collector with a bottomless bank account and an insatiable appetite for African antiquities.'

Karen left them to it. Another empty Rioja bottle followed the first and both men thickened the air with lakes of blue cigar smoke. Absentmindedly, Gerard watched Lee select two more logs of seasoned mopani and drop them onto the fire. He swung their conversation back on line.

'So you'll be up at the mine when they get here?'

'Have to be,' said Lee. 'We've only got a couple of days left to get things organised, by then I'll be needing you south of the border, ready to move at a moment's notice.'

'When?'

'Soon. Will let you know. Tendai will be going with you. He knows my boat inside-out, been with me since my father died – ex-guerrilla fighter, strong as an ox and loyal to the death. You'll need him. Even with your experience and the both of you on board, *Isabella* will be a tough old girl to get through the channel.'

'*Isabella*?' Gerard's interest sparked. 'What channel? Where on God's earth are you sending us?'

'For an old sea dog like you, a mere walk in the park.' He smiled at the look of disbelief on Gerard's face. 'The mouth of the Rio Save – a hundred miles south of the Sofala Banks.'

3

Lee saw Gerard out through the homestead gates; the old man's tail lights flickered and then disappeared around that first bend in the track. Roused from a fitful sleep, Karen came outside and stood alongside her husband. Still only half awake, her mood, like his, was melancholic. She rested her head against Lee's shoulder and closed her eyes, and for those next few minutes pushed aside all those thoughts which troubled her.

Beneath that star-filled sky, what breeze there was whispered amongst the branches of mountain acacia and planted jacarandas, with it came the smell of warm, night earth. From that same small breeze, Karen drank in the characteristic potato-like scents of the wild Phyllanthus flower, but her peace of mind was short-lived. Since that symbolic telephone call, her head was filled to the brim with moody suppositions. Now, almost in ruins, her future plans threatened to flounder against a rocky shore of disbelief, baiting her with absurdities and that looming government threat to her husband's mining company.

Thankfully, both their sons were abroad. Being educated in England had so far left them untouched by what was going on; they were, through Karen's purposeful engineering kept in a blissful state of not knowing. She knew that the deception could not be maintained for much longer, the way things were deteriorating, seeing the boys would happen sooner than she had anticipated.

Though blessed with his mother's easy temperament, James, the eldest, was more like his father. The comparative physical attributes of both man and boy were obvious, and though only sixteen, James had already reached and bettered his father's height by almost an inch. Shoulder to shoulder they had worked the darkest parts of the Empress Deep; with the miner's pick and fourteen pound hammer they had broken and loaded rock, matching the best of his father's lashing crews, ton for ton. Doted on by his mother, James Michael Goddard could do no wrong, and from the lowliest labourer to the highest paid employees, all who met him quickly fell prey to that infectious smile and prince-like panache of the company's future shareholder.

Broad-shouldered and indeterminably confident, James was equally at ease with college life in England as he was with working the face of the Empress Deep's hardest reef, and whatever the challenge, like a falcon to some high-flying prey, always, James would rise to it with gladiatorial commitment.

When the boys were at home, Karen found herself swamped with admiration for both her offspring, watching without their knowing she would revel in the masculinity of her sons.

Descendent of that same wild mould, Karen's youngest and brightest had taken the world of learning head-on. Blessed by his father's choice, or as some might argue, cursed by the gift of his middle name, Mitchell Rhodes Goddard dedicated the bulk of his spare time to learning and the betterment of his understanding for complex natural problems, though like his brother, he had long since realised the benefits of hard labour and regular physical training. Never once, unless incapacitated by illness, in those last two years since his twelfth birthday had he shirked the call to daily exercise. In a more secluded part of the family homestead, the entire floor space of a spare room had been given over to iron weights and elaborate pulley systems. From five in the morning and for two continuous hours there could be heard the sound of

12

both him and his brother benching and dead-lifting Weider iron; like steam from a locomotive's pistons their exhalations would echo along the corridor.

However, his bedroom was his sanctuary, as in-roads to another world the walls were shelved from floor to ceiling and crammed to overflowing with books. Though most were centred on geology, others embraced anthropology and metallurgy, the universe and its embodiment, but his favourites were those with direct reference to colonial pioneering and the archaeological exploration of southern Africa. Robert Moffat's, Matabele Journals and Richard Hall's, Ancient Ruins of Rhodesia. All of these he treasured and guarded their authors' opinions fiercely.

Being the youngest, rather than what some might regard as a hindrance, had driven him on to excel in everything he took to. Academically, he was a full year ahead of his class. Physically, though slightly smaller in stature than his older sibling, Mitchell Rhodes resembled the sculpted fighter – naturally portrayed as the classically endowed, blonde-haired, blue-eyed young athlete. To Karen, Mitchell was still her little boy, the golden apple of her eye.

Karen shook herself free of the lassitude and opened her eyes. From behind the homestead the Empress Deep's headgear warning lights blinked down to her from a pitch-black hillside.

'Hard to believe that all of this could soon be gone, my darling, don't know if I could cope with starting from scratch again.'

Lee drew her in closer. 'Hopefully you won't have to, but if that's what it comes to, top of our priority list will be the boys' schooling; Stonyhurst College may well be the best choice for them but it certainly isn't the cheapest.'

'Remember that day at the ruins; when you first spoke

to me?'

Lee nodded his head; the memory was still vivid, as if they had met that very day.

'Got to be fifteen years now?'

'More like twenty,' she corrected him. 'You were so full of yourself – strutting about my dig like a bantam cockerel around a farmyard.'

'My gran was still alive.' He smiled at the memory. 'I miss her. That was the start of it; when Bella went, the entire era seemed to fall apart. Mugabe's never-never land, that's what we're left with. Valuable, but immovable assets and lorry loads of sad memories.'

Karen didn't hear him; again she was swamped by her own regrets, so much effort, so much time, all of it would have been for nothing if they were forced into leaving Zimbabwe. Their roots were here, driven deeply inside Zimbabwe's stone heart, beyond her borders there existed a thousand things that Karen abhorred.

'Tell me you have a plan,' Karen implored, 'your infamous get-out-of-jail card that you always come up with.' Through a mixture of hope and humour, Karen looked up at him.' Right now would be a good time to pull that magical card out of your hat, Goddard.'

'We sit tight,' said Lee. 'Once Mugabe's cronies have had their say, either way we'll know what to do.' He turned for the veranda steps and from the length of his stride, Karen knew exactly where he was going.

4

The key was where it had always been, ever since Lee was old enough to remember, *behind that ridiculous stone hippo* Isabella Goddard, Lee's grandmother, always made a point of commenting; 'their little joke' she had called it.

To Lee, following the death of his grandmother, the storeroom had become his own private sanctuary, a place where he could escape reality when the pressure piled on. Where he could revel in the past and rightly or wrongly, through the media of old pictures and precious family antiquities, where he could walk and talk with those who were long dead.

He turned the key and pushed back the door; nostalgia flooded over him. That night, eighteen years ago – Isabella and Rex Khumalo were there with him. That same, sixty watt lamp lit the furthest wall; the smell of dust, old dust and the swish of dust sheets against his legs.

'Brought you a coffee.' Karen set it down on the desk top. 'I'll leave you alone if you like?'

Lee shook his head. 'No – stay with me. Right now I need some company, too many ghosts in here.'

Karen looked around the room; from that fateful day when Bella died, hardly anything had been moved. From front to back, the store was crammed with antique furniture and family paraphernalia. Neither she nor her husband could conjure up the will to clear it, 'The Goddard Museum' they called it. Only on one occasion had she sat alone in the midst of it all, but the ghosts were too overbearing – the imagined whispers too loud for her reasoning to cope with.

She dropped the sheet from the standard lamp and, knowing that it was still connected to a wall socket, depressed the switch at the base of the lamp-holder. More light spread over the storeroom. Haphazardly hung portraits looked down at her; those with a sterner, Victorian countenance made her shiver. She avoided their eyes, afraid the characters they belonged to might come alive and step out from their world behind the walls.

'We've come so far,' Lee growled, 'so much work, so many peoples' lives have gone into putting together what we've achieved.' He focused on his favourite portrait, that of Mhlangana Khumalo, a Matabele Induna of high standing and cousin to Lobengula Jando Khumalo, last king of the Matabele. A set of wooden steps were still there, propped against the wall. 'I remember my gran getting all excited when I climbed up for the grand unveiling. Rex hadn't a clue as to what was behind the dust sheet.'

'Bella said he almost freaked out when she explained his lineage; maybe that's what did it?' Karen recalled.

'Maybe you're right,' said Lee. 'Finding out you are the only surviving grandson of a Matabele king would be enough to freak out even the best of us.'

'I often think about him,' said Karen. 'What makes a man change so radically?'

'That magical call to arms,' Lee mused, 'men do strange things when they're convinced their destiny lies on some far-off battlefield.'

He lit a cigarette and leant back in his chair. 'Genghis Khan, Cecil Rhodes or Adolf Hitler – all of them land-hungry warlords; all of them believed they were key players in some honourable, bigger picture. Problem is Mugabe and his ministerial vampires have taken it one step further. Besides placating the masses with false promises, they've done little more than bleed the country of its assets and whisk them off to foreign bank accounts.'

Karen smiled at his bitterness. 'Your hatred knows no bounds, my darling.'

'And it will get me nowhere,' Lee mused. 'I know that, but at this stage my abhorrence for what the government's doing is all that keeps me going.'

He stood up from the desk. The coffee had chilled and he pushed it away. Inside his chest, cold hands groped for his heart, the fear of total loss. Rex Khumalo, once his friend and closest ally was now the predacious government puppet; together with Comrade Julius Pasviri, like starving lions they were waiting close to the water hole for Lee to drop his guard and drink.

-5-

Three identical, bullet-proof black Mercedes drew up in front of the Empress Deep's General Office, the lead pair were decoy cars filled with dark-suited security personnel, in the event of an attack on the ministerial convoy they would bear the brunt and deal with any aggression. Lee stood at the boardroom window and watched the cars disgorge their passengers. It was happening. Like jackals, government ministers and their flock of vulture-like followers were homing in for their share of the kill.

Behind him, across the east wall and purposely arranged in chronological order were early, monochromatic photographs of the Empress Deep's last one hundred year progression. From the first small inkling of its inception in the eighteen nineties, through to that present day – this present moment when the chances were suddenly sixty-forty in favour of him losing it all. He stood with his hands clasped behind his back; the phone warbled.

'Mister Goddard, sir?'

'I've seen them Byron. Send them up.'

He dropped the phone back in its cradle, drew out a cigarette from an opened pack of twenty and thumbed the wheel on a battered Dunhill. His hand was shaking, but not through fear. Lee curtailed his anger; aggressive indignation would serve only to aggravate his situation.

'Mister Goddard?'

Lee nodded his head to Rex Khumalo, Minister of Mines. His neutral expression feigned any sign of recognition. Many years had lapsed since their last meeting. Rex was more or less how Lee remembered him, perhaps the smallest change in hair colour about the temples; signs of early silvering. Beside Rex, an indifferent Philip Gomo, the Reserve Bank Governor peered at him like a black owl through thick-rimmed glasses. The room flooded with men in dark suits and aviator sunglasses. Lee knew they were CIO men; Mugabe's equivalent of England's MI5, but far more sinister. None of them smiled. Side arms made their jackets bulge; stoically, as mafia lookalikes they positioned themselves around the room. Julius Pasviri, Permanent Secretary for Indigenization and Empowerment was last through the doorway. Dressed in a light grey suit and burgundy tie he stopped directly in front of Lee.

'My government's apologies for its unintended lack of protocol, Mister Goddard, I was sure you would have been warned in advance.' Though mentally he was wide awake, the whites of his eyes had been adversely dulled by years of heavy drinking. The sour smell of old whisky bled from his mouth when he spoke.

Lee shook his head. 'You have me at a disadvantage, comrade minister.'

Pasviri took his time lighting a cigarette and then crossed to the boardroom's picture window. His gaze fell upon the shaft collar, like a thief about to reach inside the earth for the treasures it contained, he gloated openly.

'You have of course been informed of my government's indigenization portfolio?'

'I've heard of it,' Lee admitted, 'though I wasn't aware of it having been implemented.'

'One month, Mister Goddard.' He turned and smiled, but in his eyes the threat of confrontation was always there, a sinister flame flickering in the background. 'That is your deadline. Though government will be flexible in its approach, in essence, you will be expected to submit plans of transfer, for an agreed sum of up to fifty-one percent of your stake in the Empress Deep to certain, government accredited entrepreneurs.'

Lee held his composure. Inside, his hatred for Julius Pasviri had already uncoiled. Like an adder it writhed and fought for release. The men in dark suits watched him intently; the slightest hint of provocation and Pasviri would slip their chains.

'And I have no choice?'

'None whatsoever.'

'So my being a home-grown Zimbabwean stands for nothing?'

Pasviri shook his head and stubbed out his cigarette. There was little need for comment. White colonists and their offspring had long since been selected for marginalisation. There would be few, if any exceptions; black empowerment was to him, a dear and prized obsession.

'Zimbabwe has huge mineral wealth: gold, chrome, coal and iron to name but a few. The second largest platinum reserves in the known world, Mister Goddard and now, as I'm sure you are well aware, there is the small matter of our recently discovered Marange diamond field along our border with Mozambique; a

19

deposit of precious stones equivalent to one quarter of our planet's total reserves.' He lit another cigarette and let the smoke trickle out from between full lips. 'However, the mining sector is starved of capital and is at the moment in a state of decline. Investors have been put off by our, shall we say, uncertain investment climate. In short, my government needs upwards of five billion US dollars to ensure the more positive development of its mining ambitions.'

'Fifty-one percent is a big piece of anyone's pie, companies will lose control of their own assets – you'll have disinvestment on a massive scale. Investors will run with their money. Taking away the incentive for international companies to make money in Zimbabwe will destroy, rather than rejuvenate the mining sector.'

'Then let them run, Mister Goddard.' Pasviri's eyes glittered. 'There are always other investors ready to take up the baton.'

'The Chinese,' Lee growled. The temptation for full-on confrontation now stronger than ever.

'A possibility,' Pasviri agreed, 'or India perhaps. As we speak, their Essar investors are set to take majority control of our troubled ZISCO steel. The deal will more than double foreign investment in Zimbabwe for the current year. Fifty-four percent to Essar; thirty-six retained by our government.'

'And should I object?'

Pasviri's eyes narrowed. 'Only a foolish man would risk everything, Mister Goddard. When the time comes, our government's Comrade Minister for Mines will work in close liaison with you.' He looked across the room at Rex Khumalo. 'As a qualified mining engineer he is better equipped than me to discuss our... how should I put it? Impending partnership.'

Lee ground his cigarette into the green eye of a malachite ashtray. Outside, the waiting ministerial motorcade shimmered under the heat of late morning. Each driver stood alongside his respective car; ominously over-engineered, the matched and heavily armoured black Mercedes appeared more warlike than iconic symbols of Zimbabwe's ruling elite.

Lee made up his mind. Gerard was waiting for his instructions. Time was running out for him. The government's black empowerment program was underway – unstoppable. In a country where western values were looked upon as overly sympathetic, laws were passed on a whim and if need be, quickly enforced with violence. Any company seen as to be out of kilter with Mugabe's ZANU PF ideologies would be mercilessly stripped of its assets.

'One month,' Lee acknowledged and like a leopard, fixed his eyes on Pasviri. Again his loathing for what Pasviri stood for threatened to spill out. He was losing control of the Deep. Everything his family stood for was being torn apart; dismembered and swallowed. Chopped up and flung to the Party elite for them to squabble over. 'What about recompense? Financial compensation for lost interests?'

'You're alive, Mister Goddard.' Pasviri's eyes narrowed. 'In our new Zimbabwe, most men would regard that fact as recompense enough.' He nodded to his entourage. 'Leave us. I will join you shortly.'

In the quiet, two men, both of different origins stood just metres apart. Had it been a hundred years previous, rather than the surroundings of a plush boardroom there would have been thick forest and the discomfort of cold *guti* rain to contend with. Their dress, as decreed by historical circumstance, would have been for Pasviri, fashioned from the skins of jackal and leopard and for Lee, a uniform of roughly woven calico, topped with slouch hat; across his chest would hang a soldier's bandoliers, loaded with British South Africa Company's

.44 calibre, Boxer-Henry ammunition.

'In our grandfathers' day,' said Pasviri, 'forgive me for quoting the Bible, but *kaffirs*, as we were referred to were tolerated only under sufferance, the proverbial hewers of wood and carriers of water.' He took his time lighting another cigarette. 'Not any more, comrade. Along with your infamous Mister Rhodes, the heady days of white supremacy are well and truly buried – forever.'

From outside came the sound of heavy, armoured doors being latched closed and the soft growl of powerful engines.

'My department will be in touch. The Empress Deep will run as normal. Anything seen to be detrimental to its production capabilities will be vigorously contested.' On reaching the door, Pasviri paused and looked back; his gaze even, but menacing. 'On my word, comrade, you will be watched. Any evidence of sabotage or subversive activity and I will make sure you lose it all.'

Lee watched him cross from the reception foyer to the car park. Rex Khumalo followed Pasviri into the shade; from his vantage point it was obvious to Lee that Pasviri was passing on his concerns to the Minister of Mines.

'You will stay in Masvingo, comrade. Reservations have already been made for you at the Flamboyant Motel. Stay close to Goddard. He's going to run, I can sense it.'

Rex nodded his head and looked up at the boardroom window. Lee was watching them; as a raptor guarding its nest he stared down at the goings-on in the car park, his features hard set and hawk-like. The wheels were turning; contingency plans were already in place. Pasviri was right; Rex sensed the truth in what he had said. Lee would not give in easily, his fight to maintain control of the Empress Deep would be long and more than likely, bloody.

6

Lee parked his Land Rover between a twelve-seater minibus and his wife's Mercedes. The Great Zimbabwe Hotel car park was almost full. Karen was waiting in reception for him. From the way he walked she knew something was wrong.

'What's happened, reception said it was urgent?'

He leaned over and kissed her cheek.

'Walk with me.'

Lee took hold of her arm and steered her out of the foyer.

'They were up at the mine; three car loads. The Reserve Bank Governor, a half dozen CIO goons and Julius Pasviri, Mugabe's Indigenization and Empowerment minister. Rex was with them.'

'Did he speak to you?'

Lee shook his head. 'Made as if he didn't know me, just watched and listened – stayed out of it.'

They followed a gravel avenue lined with musasa and mahobohobo trees. The road was thickly flecked with mica, as shredded Christmas tinsel it glittered wildly under that direct angle of high sun. Minibuses loaded with backpackers rumbled past for the ruins' car park and from a half mile distant it was easy enough for Lee make out antlike columns of eager tourists swarming upwards for the ancient stone portals of the hill fortress. Below the granite fortification, strewn across a park-like valley were the tumbled dwellings of that vanished civilisation. Amongst the trees, as though some mythical giant had nested there, the elliptical outer wall of a vast and ancient temple reared defiantly before the skyline – towering over it all.

Karen led him away from the main road to where a narrow path wound between the trees. She pondered over their most recent run-in with the authorities. Meagrely funded via the Department of Antiquities and anonymous donations, her work, meticulously executed over the past twenty years was all that supported her own unbiased ideas as to the origins of that ancient city. Many of her theories, though backed by solid finds had been scoffed at – her writing scorned, often looked upon by Party extremists as pro-colonial, her theorising intently aligned with those of R.N. Hall, a widely renowned Victorian explorer and archaeologist. Her suggestions based on her findings, discredited any indigenous involvement with the original building of Great Zimbabwe, but these were openly ridiculed; only through her prolific unearthing of precious artefacts had the position of resident archaeologist been left open to her. The ruling Shona- controlled ZANU PF had claimed the ruins as their own, a creation of their Rozwi forebears – conveniently heralded by The Party as the ancestral heartland of a Mashona-ruled Zimbabwe.

They stopped alongside the small museum. An old jacaranda held off the sunlight. The ground beneath the tree was now nondescript, left uncared for. Only those who knew would pause and linger there, those unable to stop themselves from searching out the smallest signs of what had been.

'Hard to imagine,' said Lee, 'that my great-great-grandfather's remains were buried here.'

'Thirty-three men,' Karen recalled. 'Just as well Rhodes had them moved to the Matopos. At least now they stand a chance of being left alone, hopefully under the protection of World Heritage.' She touched his hand. 'Depression won't get us through this my darling.'

'I know,' said Lee and squared his shoulders. 'I guess the penny has only just started to drop, but I'm okay.' He watched a dozen tourists haul themselves out from a cramped minibus. To them the disembowelment of

24

Zimbabwe or the Empress Deep just didn't matter and he envied them for it. 'What I need to know are your views on what I have in mind. It's important. Once the ball is rolling, there'll be no going back.'

'And would it make any difference if I disagreed?' Karen's smile was wistful – that of someone betrayed by all they had believed in. Her hair, though still that pale colour of winter grass, was finely strung with silver. At the corners of her eyes where the sun had burned her that deep and lasting brown, there showed the indelible lines of continuous working in open sunlight. Years of excavating, carrying and cataloguing had preserved her resilience to hard work, though her nails were worn like a man's and her hands were calloused. As were her feelings for the man who stood beside her, so was her love for the ruined city obsessive, that and her deepest desire to prove its origins were all that had kept her sane. With soft fingers, Lee brushed a strand of loose hair from her cheek.

Karen looked around her, for half a mile in any direction the ground showed signs of prolific excavation, years of patient dedication committed to finding the key to that lost and unrecorded civilisation. Leaving it all behind would stand as the hardest decision she had ever made. Walking away would break her heart, but through that one, sadistic twist of fate the decision to leave had been made for her. There was no way out. She had sons to educate and the surety of a sound future for them took precedence over everything else. A nondescript beige Toyota pulled up alongside them. The driver's window went down.

Rex Khumalo had rid himself of jacket and tie; his shirt sleeves were rolled up to the elbows, the aviator sunglasses were still in place.

'Climb aboard, we need to talk.'

'What do you want?'

'Nothing sinister, I swear to it. Please, get in the car; both of you.'

Rex turned the Toyota back on its tracks, in less than five minutes they were parked up outside the hotel.

Detached from the main building, the dining room's sugar-white outer wall was partially covered with thatch shadow and in the high, pinnate leaves of wild date palms, male weaver birds squabbled for the attention of females. Like brightly coloured fruits they clung beneath intricately woven nests; raucous consorts in yellow suits and black masks.

Vervet monkeys peered from roofs and leafy jacarandas. Children watched the monkeys; parents watched their children and ordered cold beers, gin and tonics – cokes for the kids. The swimming pool was full. For the wealthy, life was good.

Rex turned off the engine.

'My wife is holding a lunch reservation for us – like I said, we need to talk. Over a thick steak and glass of house red our meeting will seem less conspicuous.' He smiled at Karen. 'Bear with me, I know a lot of water has gone under the bridge and that not all of it was clean; an hour of your time, no more.'

Inside, the dining area ran full length of the building, out of the forty or so tables most were already filled with tourists. A stream of waiters in white linen suits flowed from the kitchen; the smells that followed them out through swing doors, tantalising.

Sally Khumalo had dressed simply, in Armani jeans and white cotton blouse. Her hair, cropped in close to her skull reminded Karen of Roshumba Williams; she was obviously unsure of what to expect. Somewhat ill at ease she rose from her chair and held out her hand to Karen.

'Sally Khumalo, wish we could have met under better circumstances. I'm an avid follower of your work; bold and dangerously out of vogue with popular thinking and I love it.'

Karen warmed to her. 'I'll take support from any quarter, not many people are reckless enough to agree with my theories.' She accepted Sally's hand, her grip was firm yet welcoming; her nails, though cut short, were immaculately finished in clear lacquer. Above that easy smile her eyes were catlike, almond shaped, dark and soft as brown silk, but alert like those of a startled bushbuck doe. Sally was the shorter of the two, but only by a few centimetres. Rex ordered from the wine list and though his mood seemed light, the assertive, ministerial Rex Khumalo was still very much in control.

'About this morning,' he spoke directly to Lee, 'I had no involvement with my government's choosing your Empress Deep for their indigenization program.'

'It was you who phoned me?'

'It was.' Rex nodded. 'There is no love lost between myself and Julius Pasviri.'

'Whatever your differences, you're still a colleague of his.'

Rex shook his head. 'No hidden agenda, Lee. You have my word on it. There are others in government, besides myself who harbour views different to Pasviri's. We do not agree with disenfranchising successful businesses in favour of placating overzealous, corrupt so-called war veterans.'

'Bullshit, Rex, you're up to your neck in it.' Lee looked around the room. 'How many CIO monkeys have you brought with you?'

Sally Khumalo rounded on him, now those almond eyes were wide and threatening, those of a leopardess protective of her mate.

'My husband does not associate with murderers, Mister Goddard. What he is telling you now is borne of truth. If the CIO had been here, all four of us would already be on our way to Chikarubi Prison.'

Everyone fell silent. Karen squeezed Lee's hand, urging him to stay calm. He looked at Rex and then straightened up as though he was going to carry the argument forwards then changed his mind. For a moment he saw the Rex Khumalo of old. The man who, until that fateful night of eighteen years ago had been the Empress Deep's mining engineer, as well as a close family friend. The war had changed all that; they had fought on opposite sides. Habitually, Lee fingered the scar inside his hairline, half an inch lower and the bullet from Rex's Kalashnikov rifle would have taken his head off.

'My apologies.' Lee sat back in his chair. 'Fresh start. Take it from the beginning.'

Sally ordered for everyone; fillet steaks with fresh spring salads from the buffet table. Rex went on with his explanation.

'Pasviri is convinced you're involved in something subversive. Moving funds abroad – financial subterfuge.'

'Then the comrade minister has a problem,' Lee countered. 'Everything I have is tied up in the Deep.'

Rex sat back whilst the food was brought to the table and let the waiter drift out of earshot before carrying on.

'Gold, Lee, not cash. Native Africans are cursed with the gift of paranoid pre-emption; they expect nothing less than to be ripped off. Pasviri now sees you quite literally as the holder of his golden chalice – the gatekeeper to his own private store of gold bullion. Having a white, ex-Rhodesian army captain at the helm of the Empress Deep brings out the worst in him.'

Lee shook his head and smiled at the supposition.

'When he's worked out where all this gold will be coming from and how to get it out of the country, tell Pasviri to let me know. I might well have a crack at it.'

'We fought the same war, captain.' Rex's face broke

with a wry smile. 'You cannot deny the thought had crossed your mind.'

'And what about you? You think I'll do it?'

Rex shook his head. 'Didn't say that, but I know you all too well. Zero retaliation is definitely not your style.'

'Even if I had the gold,' Lee countered, 'I would never get it across the border. Any move I make within of fifty miles of Beit Bridge and Pasviri will have his pet CIO boys breathing down my neck.'

'There are always alternatives,' said Rex. 'But you are right. Already your details have been passed to our border posts. Try to leave Zimbabwe without prior emigration clearance and you will be detained.'

'Pasviri would like that.'

'More than you realise, one wrong move on your part and Pasviri's jackals will take the Empress Deep away from you – in its entirety.'

'Why do my instincts tell me that's what will happen anyway? I can't fight your government, Rex. The older your comrade president, the more paranoid he becomes. Being white and owning a productive gold mine puts me right at the top of Mugabe's favourite foods list.'

'Half a mine is better than none, captain; ideas change, even misguided government officials can learn from their errors. It is widely accepted throughout western governments that we Africans discard mistakes as quickly as some would discard their women. Socialism or capitalism, it matters not. On the day, what matters is a positive return for our efforts.'

Rex leaned against the table, his smile warm, but in his eyes the warning was there.

'Don't do anything stupid. Pasviri is watching your every move, nothing would pleasure him more than walking away with the keys to your Empress Deep.'

'Then I have no choice,' said Lee, 'at least for the time being.'

7

Karen weighted the map with fruit from the coffee table then sat back against her heels. Unnerved by the uncertainty and danger of Lee's plans, her mind was still in a state of flux.

With the palm of his hand, Lee smoothed down creases and fold lines that criss-crossed the map of Zimbabwe's south-eastern border area. Swiftly, he picked up on the River Save and traced its meanderings with his fingertip. Like a black snake the river wound its way from Zimbabwe's Eastern highlands, down to the border country where it merged with its largest tributary, the Lundi before crossing into Mozambique.

'Gonarezhou Reserve.' Lee tapped his index finger at a pre-selected spot on the map, and then marginally, slid his finger sideways to a more exact position. 'Below the falls at Mahenya, there's an old fishing camp on the east bank; plenty of room to launch the inflatable.'

'What about border security?'

Lee shook his head. 'Same side, but further upstream; close to the old Hippo tungsten mine. Mugabe's personalised Fifth Brigade has a base camp there – our road in passes right through it, but as long as we play the innocent fishermen there shouldn't be a problem.'

Karen looked up from the map.

'I thought the Fifth Brigade had been disbanded?'

'All is not as it seems. On paper, it has been.'

Karen watched him write down distances and work out how much fuel they would need for the outboard motor. Lee noted places where they might encounter difficulties, where the river narrowed, or broke up into shallow, unnavigable rivulets.

'The rains are imminent,' he went on. 'As soon as the river rises we can drift with the current. That way we can save on fuel – use the outboard only when we have to.'

'We must be mad,' said Karen. 'If Pasviri tumbles to our running gold across the border, half the army will be after us.'

The phone rang. Karen snatched it up. She recognised the voice.

'Gerard. One second, I'll hand you over to Lee.'

'Lee! Are we still hooked in to plan A, or are you having second thoughts?'

'Nothing's changed, old-timer. Stick to the original plan.'

Fate was closing the door behind him, the opportunity to change course now hardly an option; fast approaching the tipping point there was little chance of him turning back. The noose was tightening; Pasviri's determination to take over the Empress Deep was now obsessive.

'Will do old chap. Might need one or two extras, just to be on the safe side.'

'No worries; get what you want from Jose at the marina. My credit's good and he knows my boat. I've had *Isabella* kitted out for long-range fishing safaris. Make sure both her tanks are full and she'll do the thousand mile round trip without refuelling.'

'Will do, Lee. If all goes well, will be ready to leave as planned. You stay safe old boy.'

'Sleep on board, Gerard. Stay with the boat or the locals will strip her bare. Unlock the forward stowage locker. A bit of muscle in there should you need it.'

'Got that, old boy. This damned line's getting worse. Will try the phone again tomorrow. If no joy will wait for comms via the radio. Make contact as soon as you're in range. Any nonsense your end and make sure you give 'em hell!'

Lee dropped the phone back in its cradle. 'It's on.

Gerard's ready to go.'

'I feel sick,' said Karen. 'All our belongings, the house. What happens to it?'

The smile on Lee's face turned bitter and he took his time in lighting a cigarette, forestalling his answer, but Karen's unwavering stare drew the answer from him.

'If it all goes pear-shaped we lose everything. If we make it to Maputo, we refuel and head for Madagascar. I already have a buyer for ten percent above current market value – paid into the bank of my choice, anywhere in the world.'

'Either way,' Karen pointed out, 'we can't come back to Zimbabwe.'

'Depends on how well I've judged Rex,' Lee said.

'Why should he care?'

'Rex is a Matabele. He hates Pasviri's mob more than I do; and he loves his country. Rex will do his damnedest to keep the mine running for as long as possible. If anyone can clear the way for us to climb back under the radar, it's Rex Khumalo.'

Some of the tension eased from Karen's face.

'How long before we leave?'

'We'll give Gerard a few days start and then we move.'

'Byron – have you told him?'

'Not yet. He knows nothing about the gold. We're fishing, drinking and watching the sun go down, that's all he needs to know. David, my lamp room superintendent will be coming with us, only as far as the camp at Mahenya. Byron has directions and map location of my camp – any emergency and he'll find it.'

'You still have to get the gold back to the homestead without attracting attention.'

'Tomorrow,' said Lee, 'sparrow fart – as soon as the dayshift men are underground.'

8

As a growling giant the winding engine slowed to creep-speed and gently lifted the conveyance from its hole in the earth; in the early sunlight the cage sparkled with water. The call bells crashed out twice. The door rolled open and under Lee's watchful eye, a flatbed jumper car was pushed out onto the shaft bank. Immediately, a diesel forklift powered up and on Lee's command slid its lifting forks through open access channels at the base of a steel box.

'Back of my Land Rover. Take your time, the box is filled with core samples from deep reef so don't drop it.'

Expertly, the driver tilted his forks and gradually increased hydraulic pressure to raise the load. With his heart racing, Lee supervised the transportation and loading of the heavy, steel container. The Land Rover's rear end settled lower into the springs as it took on board the total, three hundred kilogram weight. The forklift driver withdrew and Lee, with apparent lack of concern, closed the Rover's tailgate. It was then he sensed the cold scrutiny of the watcher. It fell upon him like a chill wind.

He drove away and maintaining second gear, slowly he nursed the Land Rover over rough ground and resisted the urge to look back over his shoulder. Using his rear view mirror, constantly his eyes flicked between the road he had left behind and that up ahead; the road stayed empty, but that sickening feeling of being followed never left him.

Karen was waiting for him; urgently she waved him into the car park and closed the gates, her nerves already stretched to breaking point.

'David just phoned from the lamp room. The police are up at the mine.'

'When did they get there?'

'Five minutes ago, they just missed you; they're questioning the shaft onsetter. David overheard them talking about you bringing something heavy and bulky out from underground.'

Lee switched off the engine and climbed out.

'We have to move quickly; help me.' He vaulted up over the tailgate and unlocked the steel lid. He gave Karen a hand up. 'On my count of three... lift.'

Together, they prised open the steel lid and laid it back against the Rover's cab.

'My God, Lee!'

'The wheelbarrow, as quick as you can, but stay calm. Bar at a time; I'll hand them down to you.'

Karen vaulted over the side and ran for the gardener's metal barrow, by the time she came back with it, Lee had the first, ten kilo bar balanced on the top edge of the tailgate.

'Don't be fooled by the physical size – feel for the weight before you lift.'

Karen dragged the bullion against her chest; with her legs braced she took up the weight and then slowly lowered the gold bar inside the barrow.

'Keep them coming, Lee, I can manage.'

Five times they manoeuvred the laden wheelbarrow back inside the garden. Covered in rotting leaves, the stacked gold was now an inconspicuous heap of garden waste.

Lee glanced at his watch; five more minutes at the outside before Pasviri's men were throwing questions at him.

'The last batch of core samples from the mine; where did you put them?'

'Kitchen floor – right hand side as you walk in.'

'Help me bring them out; Pasviri's goons will be here any minute.'

34

The steel box was re-filled, this time with core samples from long-hole exploration drilling; all of them neatly stacked and partitioned in moulded plastic trays. Between them, Lee and Karen lowered the lid. Lee threw the locks and dropped the keys inside his pocket.

'Back inside,' Lee warned her, 'I can hear a car. Get some bacon on the go, make the little darlings feel as though they're welcome; quickest way to get rid.'

Within minutes of Lee and Karen going inside, two nondescript Mazda saloons parked up side by side on the gravel driveway.

'Stay calm,' said Lee, and planted a hurried kiss on Karen's cheek. 'Keep your smile sweet and the bacon hot, my sweetheart.'

Lee watched their approach from the dining room window; four men, athletically built; the usual dark suits and aviator sunglasses. The smell of bacon was already inside the room.

He stood up from a hurriedly laid breakfast table, breathed in deeply and crossed to the veranda door. The government's CIO men were halfway up the steps.

'I'm flattered.' Lee kept up the pretence. 'Two visits in one week, Comrade Pasviri is really keeping you guys busy.' He waved them into the dining room. 'Sit yourselves down, Karen's pouring tea and knocking up bacon sandwiches, no trouble for her to make a couple extra.'

'No breakfast, Mister Goddard.' The tallest of the four removed his glasses, his voice, though even, was laced with undertones. 'The metal box you removed from your mine this morning.'

Lee feigned surprise. 'You're referring to the red box on the back of my Land Rover?'

'I believe that is the one.'

'Core samples from exploration drilling on 587 Level. What seems to be the problem?'

'I need to inspect the contents.'

'Why?' Lee asked and then to save himself from any aggravation, he capitulated. 'Doesn't matter; give me a moment to hunt down the keys.'

He took his time, exaggerating the pretence of searching through kitchen drawers. If David hadn't phoned from the lamp room, Lee's plans, by now, would have been compromised, the gold he had taken so long to accumulate would have been impounded and the CIO would be well advanced with their horrific interrogation methods. The Empress Deep, as a family business enterprise would have already ceased to exist.

Waving the supposedly, elusive bunch of keys, Lee led the men back outside. Karen looked on from the patio window. Unable to help herself, constantly her eyes flew back to the compost heap, convinced the soil had moved. There would be that slight glint of yellow metal. The sun would find it. Unable to cope with her rampaging apprehension, she turned her back on the window and went back inside her kitchen.

The CIO men waited for Lee to throw the locks. High on adrenalin, without asking for help he swung up the heavy lid and backed off to make room.

The drill cores were laid out in orderly rows; ten to each plastic tray, each stone core labelled with black ink as to when and where the sample came from.

'Help yourselves, gentlemen, but please don't mix them up, puzzles are not my forte.'

The top two trays were lifted out. Pasviri's men peered inside, eager to find something.

'Drill samples taken from deep reef,' Lee explained. The fact that he was telling the truth made it sound even more convincing. 'They'll eventually be handed over to the bank for assaying. Correct sampling is critical for the mine's future development, without these we would be digging in the dark.' Again, he feigned confusion. 'I don't understand? What did you expect to find?'

Orders were given in Shona; within minutes the box was abandoned and both government vehicles were nothing more than clouds of dust heading for Masvingo.

'Close but no cigar.' Lee smiled at Karen. 'One in the eye for Pasviri's indigenization plans.'

'They might come back,' said Karen.

'Not much chance of that happening, sweetheart. State security doesn't take kindly to being made a fool of twice in one day.' He linked arms with Karen. 'Now what about that breakfast?'

'Bacon rolls?'

He rolled his eyes in protest. 'As long as there are fried eggs, tea and toast to go with them, my love. We'll need all the strength we can muster if we're to excavate the world's richest compost heap.'

-9-

Rex Khumalo rolled his eyes in wonderment. 'Your entire livelihood is under threat and now you tell me you're going fishing?'

'Byron can run the show without me,' Lee insisted, 'he's done it several times in the past; it's no big deal. With the pair of you on site things will tick along just fine. I need time to sort myself out.'

Rex shook his head. 'Bullshit, Lee. Doesn't make sense; what about Karen? Is she going with you?'

Lee nodded. 'She's my wife, remember. We have a sort of old fashioned, western style hand-in-glove arrangement. Call it a white man's weakness, one woman apiece. Where I go, my wife goes with me; at least for most of the time. A week – ten days at most and we'll be back.'

37

Rex ignored the sarcasm. 'What you're planning is totally irrational. Pasviri won't buy it; he'll pick up on you not being here to protect your interests. Where exactly are you supposed to be going?'

'Mahenya – Save Lundi junction. An old fishing camp. Pasviri can go to hell, he doesn't own me. Gas lamps, open fires and a distinct lack of government interference are all that I need right now.'

'The army has a base near there.'

'Bully for them.'

'Don't get flip, captain.'

'Not flip comrade, try pissed off. Short of being born with a white skin, I've done nothing wrong. Why not drop in on our camp with half a dozen of your trained wolves. They could join me for a barbecue and couple of drinks before getting blood on their Aviators from pulling out my fingernails.' He ground a half-finished cigarette into the ashtray. 'Who knows, you might catch me fishing without a licence. I can see the front page of The Herald: Mugabe hangs colonial fisherman for breach of conservation laws. Should go down well at your next impromptu, PF party get-together.'

'Don't make things difficult for me, captain. I'm doing my best to stay neutral. Work with me and perhaps we'll both come out of this better than expected.'

Lee stood up from his desk. Both men stared through the boardroom's picture window, Lee with his hands thrust deep inside his pockets.

'Everything's changed, not sure I want to be a part of it anymore. We shared some good times; that day in the old workings when we found the mural, do you remember?'

'As if it were yesterday,' Rex smiled. 'Once this mayhem has settled down, perhaps we could take another look. Renew old friendships even. That is, if by then you are still a free man.'

From an open packet in his jacket pocket, Rex shook out two cigarettes. Lee took one. Outside, beyond the mine headgear a vibrant forest clung to the hillside; emerald green, mauves and a hundred shades of terracotta. Rex held out his Zippo for him.

'How's your friend, Gerard these days?'

Lee felt his heart skip.

'Getting older like the rest of us, I should imagine.'

'Two days ago he left the country through our border post at Beit Bridge. One of your employees, a Shangaan miner was with him.' Rex turned away from the window. 'A retired navy man and a lowly mine labourer? Doesn't add up. An unlikely pairing for a successful holiday; or am I reading things wrong?'

'Get to the point, Rex, where is all this leading? I'm not his keeper. The old man goes where he wants.'

Rex pulled hard on his cigarette. A few random raindrops splattered against the window. The rainy season was still in its infancy; occasional thunderheads threatened, but dissipated just as quickly.

'Don't play games with me, captain, I know about your boat.' He inclined his head at Lee. 'Your grandmother's name lives on, I believe. The *Isabella*; you chose well, captain. I'm sure your boat is just as reliable and equally as feisty.'

He turned his attention back to the rain. Smoke from his cigarette pressed against the window.

'Made a few phone calls. Did a little private snooping of my own and purely by chance, found out that a boat called the *Isabella* slipped her moorings in Durban marina and headed north for Maputo. I have it on good authority that the man at her helm was Portuguese. The *Isabella* has not yet returned to her regular moorings. That was a month ago.'

Rex pushed home the advantage, determined to make Lee see sense.

'Brownlee crossed the South African border at Komatipoort at around twelve thirty yesterday afternoon, final destination, Maputo. Called in a favour and persuaded an associate of mine do some checking for me.'

He paused to let the information sink in.

'It's pretty much obvious, captain. Your boat is waiting for Brownlee at some local marina. Fitted with long range tanks her cruising range can easily cope with a round trip of eight, nine hundred miles. When Pasviri finds out that your associate is sailing north along the Mozambique coastline he'll bottle up your camp on the Save and pull you in before you cross the border.' He stared at Lee, his expression one of deep concern. 'I'm pretty sure I know what you have planned, captain. Fortunately for you, at present, I'm the only person who does. However, I give you a week at the most before Pasviri and the CIO pick up on your scheme. From Maputo, your boat can return trip the mouth of the Rio Save within a matter of days. With the right craft, shall we say an inflatable like the one you have in your outbuilding, rendezvousing with Gerard Brownlee at the mouth of the Rio Save would not be impossible.'

'You're guessing, Rex. You can't prove any of this.'

'Neither can you prove otherwise, captain. Go through with this and the knock-on effect could prove more far-reaching than you can ever imagine. Fail and you will never see your home, your wife and children or your Empress Deep again.'

Lee pulled hard on the cigarette and kept his eyes to the front.

'So Gerard uses my boat, he knows the coast up there like the back of his hand. At least a couple of times a year he takes her out as and when; where's the mystery in that?'

Rex's eyes glittered. 'More fishing stories, captain.

Come on, Lee, what do you take me for?'

Lee stubbed out his cigarette. 'This time of year big Marlin run the channel and head for their breeding grounds off Mauritius. No law against fishing. Leave the man alone, he's enjoying himself.'

'I am not your immediate problem, captain.'

Lee stared at him; cold realization had stepped inside the room. Rex knew him too well; he had worked things out for himself. Within those last few seconds, Lee's world had moved in close to disaster – his plans were falling apart. He gave up on the charade; Rex was one step ahead, the towel already ripped from his hands and thrown into the ring.

'So what would you have me do? Hand Pasviri the keys to the Empress Deep?'

Rex smiled, relieved by the change of heart.

'As one old soldier to another, I can only hope you stick to catching fish. Up to now you're in the clear. We can work this out, stay within the law and our friend Pasviri will leave us both alone. Make a break for the ocean and we will be forced to come after you; pray I reach you first, captain.' He lit another cigarette and watched the smoke spiral upwards to the ceiling. 'Believe me when I say Pasviri's CIO men will not be quite as understanding.'

Karen swung up a packed cooler box and manoeuvred it down amongst the other provisions. Fully loaded, the Land Rover stood low to its springs. Behind the tailgate and already coupled to the tow bar, Lee's fourteen foot Zodiac inflatable sat crammed full to its trailer; a twenty-five horsepower Yamaha outboard lay full width across the Zodiac's floor.

'This is suicidal.' Karen stopped for a breather; sweat ran down from her hairline and her face was flushed bright red from continuous exertion in hot sunlight. Fuelled by her growing paranoia, a multitude of different scenarios now swirled inside her head. 'If they suspect what we're up to, Lee, why in God's name are we doing this?'

Lee finished checking off their provisions against the list in his hand.

'Because the gold's ours. Not the government's, not comrade bloody Pasviri's, ours. This is our only chance.'

He dropped the list and climbed on top of the Zodiac.

'Because I sweated for nearly twenty years to get it, in conditions that would terrify most men half to death; two broken legs, half buried alive by mud rushes and rock falls and almost blown to hell by my own dynamite – that's why I'm taking what's mine out of Zimbabwe. I would sooner tip it into the river than let our comrade minister, money grabbing bastard Pasviri get his thieving hands on it.'

'We could both be killed.'

'Then so be it; rather that than live with Mugabe's boot on our neck.' He picked up an ex-army, 7.62mm FN rifle and checked the action of its cocking lever. The breech still smelled of oil. 'This baby and five hundred rounds of ball might convince them to stay back long enough for us to reach Gerard. Once aboard the *Isabella* we're home and dry. If nothing else comes of this, at least the bastards will have a fight on their hands and they'll never forget us.' He shook his head and grinned at Karen. 'No siree. For the next ten years, anyone mentions the name Goddard and every comrade minister in Mugabe's government will chuck their portfolios in the air and run for cover.'

Karen stared at the military issue rifle. Lee recognised that look.

'Yes, it's illegal; a knock-off job from my last stint with Smithy's army.'

She forgot about the weapon, even though the war had ended a long time ago, guns had been a part of her life for as far back as she could remember.

'Anything more from Gerard?'

'Not yet,' said Lee. He zipped the rifle back inside its canvas carrier. 'Depends on the tides; Maputo's right at the head of the Lusutfu river mouth and at this time of year the currents are unpredictable, but *Isabella* is more than powerful enough to cope.'

'How long will it take for us to reach the mouth of the Rio Save?'

Lee had scaled off the distance from the ordinance survey map, then, applied it to a fair estimation of the Zodiac's average speed. Having considered the need for them to sometimes drift with the current in order to conserve fuel, he had approximated the time needed to reach the Indian Ocean.

'From below the rapids? Three days at best; hundred and fifty miles to the mouth, give or take.'

Karen shuddered at the thought of them getting caught.

'Why don't we just bury the gold and sit this out?'

'Because the longer we wait the more paranoid Pasviri will become and the more people he'll have watching

43

me. If the bubble bursts completely we'll either end up living out our lives in Chikarubi or thrown out of the country with nothing. It will take money to put our boys through university, my sweet, a lot of it. Besides a couple of thousand pounds of standby holiday money in the UK, the gold is all we have.'

The phone rang; Karen ran inside and picked it up. Gerard's voice piped through the earpiece.

'We're ready to go! Can you hear me?'

'I hear you Gerard, hang on for Lee.'

'That was quick; you must have damn near gone without sleep.'

'Almost, old boy – worked through most of last night. No cloud for most of the time and a good moon. Might have a bit of bother getting around the headland; currents look damned powerful and there's a fair amount of debris coming down. Must have had some rain inland, with half a dozen rivers emptying into the bay things are really starting to move down here.'

'Where are you, exactly?'

'Still at Jose's marina. Good old stick, he's checking out *Isabella*'s working parts as we speak. Will be ready to push on first thing tomorrow. Confirm no radio contact until I reach the mouth of the Save?'

'Channel four. Leave her switched on once you're into the estuary. I need to be within a thirty mile radius of your position before my radio falls within usable transmission range. Locate the Save's main channel before the estuary floods or we'll have a devil of a job finding one another.'

'Roger that, will keep a listen out. Any hint of trouble your end?'

'Some, but it's sorted. Watch yourself in the estuary, take your time or you'll run aground. How's my boat holding up?'

'Sweet as a nut, old chap – gave her a test run this

morning to blow out the cobwebs. At three quarter speed the old girl planes like a ski boat. Oil pressure, engine temp and diesel consumption are right on the number.'

'One last thing, old-timer. Two weeks, no longer; if you haven't heard from me by then, turn my boat around and head for home.'

'Will do, Lee.'

'Safe journey, old friend. Remember to listen out for me once you reach the river mouth – and watch your fuel, it's a long walk back to Maputo.'

'God Speed, old boy and keep your powder dry! Give the bastards hell if they come after you. Will leave the marina at ten tomorrow; reach me via Jose if you need to talk before I leave Maputo.'

The phone went dead. Lee nodded his head to Karen.

'Gerard leaves for the Save river mouth on tomorrow's tide.'

'I gathered that,' said Karen. 'I still think this is sheer madness, Gerard's an old man.'

'Don't underestimate him, your grey-haired old man's on the high of his life. He knows the Mozambique coastline better than most and Tendai will look out for him. Between the four of us we'll see this through.'

For a long moment, Karen looked at him. Lee had already come to terms with the game he was playing, she knew that through his eyes the alternative was unacceptable, he had long since become addicted to the game of winner takes all; getting a fortune in gold out of Zimbabwe had become that all.

'So, tomorrow it all begins?'

'Early,' said Lee, 'four o'clock.' He lit a cigarette. 'I want us fully encamped at the Save Lundi junction before dark.'

Slowly at first, the inklings of a genuine smile formed on Karen's lips, her eyes brightened and the weight that had for days hung as a heavy chain about her shoulders fell away.

'All hell will break loose if Pasviri finds out what we're up to. Highly pissed off won't cover the half of it.'

Lee sensed the change in her; new excitement had taken a hold, he saw in front of him the old, vivacious Karen. Like old times the anticipated thrill of a deadly chase-and-run had buoyed her spirits; now her eyes glittered.

'We'll make it.' She hooked her arms about his waist and stared up at the man who had long since become the very reason for her existence. 'No more pessimism, Mister Goddard, we're unbeatable. Pasviri's thugs don't stand a chance.' She stood on tiptoe and kissed him full on the mouth.

*

By sunrise, they were well south of Masvingo and deep inside Zimbabwe's south-eastern corner. Mopani trees, those natural, hardy stalwarts of the lowveld spread as thick forest for as far as the eye could see. It was an area of intense summertime temperatures, gravel roads and the malaria-carrying, anopheles mosquito. Rising to no more than seven hundred metres above sea level, ancient basalt lava flows appeared as barren, castellated ramparts between the granites. From the junction of two great rivers, for the next hundred and fifty miles there was little more than ancient flood plains, mangrove forest and that single riverine highway reaching out for Africa's eastern shoreline. Beyond the border, the land had been ravaged by civil war and though the fighting had almost totally dissipated, Lee knew the Shangaan people had been brought to their knees by starvation, disease and wanton banditry.

It was mid-morning before they reached the road bridge below the Chisumbanje agricultural research station. Now on the Save's eastern bank, Lee swung south-easterly along a potholed gravel road that for most part hugged the river line. From thirty years ago, Lee remembered bouncing over that same track in his father's old Series one Land Rover. Karen picked up on his nostalgia.

'Judging by your smile I'd say you are back on one of your old stomping grounds?' Sweat slid from her hairline; down inside her collar, but in the lowveld, sweating was par for the course and she ignored it.

'It was a long time ago,' said Lee and his brow furrowed from frustrated attempts at searching out familiar landmarks. 'The valley was wilder then, more big trees, more elephant and fewer people.' He looked in the rear view mirror, David was asleep, his head of silvery peppercorn hair bobbed up and down between the cooler boxes. Snaking behind on its lightly sprung trailer, the inflatable bounced and jinked over rough ground.

'How much further?' asked Karen.

'Couple of hours, at least.' He moved his foot to the brake and cursed under his breath. 'Army road block. Stay calm and don't forget, we're on a fishing trip.'

Karen froze in her seat. 'They have guns, Lee.'

Lee coasted the Land Rover to within a few metres of the army checkpoint. He recognized the red berets of Mugabe's elite Fifth Brigade. He kept his smile even, the tone of his voice placatory. He slid back the window and smiled.

'Good morning, sergeant. Comforting to know our country's elite armed forces are out and about looking for bad guys.' He switched off the engine.

'Identification.' The usual lack of please and thank you – no smile. The sergeant took Lee's paperwork and gave the contents a cursory going over. 'You are both from Masvingo?'

Lee nodded. The introductory humour wasted; the first inklings of doubt crawled inside his collar.

'Fishing trip. Below the rapids. We camp there every year for the tiger fish and game viewing.'

David had woken up and now watched with big eyes from his redoubt of camping gear behind the cab.

'The man sitting in the back? Where is he from?'

'An employee,' said Lee. 'A good man, has worked for me for more than twenty years.'

Lee adjusted his vision to suit the surrounding forest. From a camouflaged, sandbagged bunker, a light RPD machine gun covered the checkpoint. Lee's FN rifle was buried with a four man tent in a canvas carry-all. Knowing it was so close goosed the back of his neck.

The soldier hung on to the paperwork, his eyes now fixed to the over-generous load of equipment – even the Zodiac inflatable was filled to the brink with provisions and spare fuel tanks. Silently, Lee cursed his own stupidity for not covering the extra fuel.

'You are well stocked with provisions, Mister Goddard. You have obviously planned for a long stay at your fishing camp?'

'At least ten days, but only if the fish are biting. If you like, I can drop some off for your mess kitchen on our way home.'

The sergeant seemed reluctant to return their identification papers. Lee sensed his hesitancy; an astute decision to search their vehicle and the game would be up. He went for broke and played his trump card.

'Comrade Rex Khumalo, Minister for Mines will be joining us shortly, once the camp is ready.' He paused to let what he had said take effect. 'Gives us chance to get our fridges working properly; doesn't like his beer served up warm.'

48

'You know Comrade Khumalo?'

'Close friend of the family,' Lee exaggerated and seized upon the opportunity, 'known each other for years, sergeant; damn good mining engineer. Bit of a waste, really.'

'You work on a mine?'

'The Empress Deep gold mine,' said Lee, the conversation now less antagonistic; even Karen appeared relaxed. 'Family run business,' Lee went on. 'I'm the owner – hence the greying hair and stress lines. Rex was my chief mining engineer before the government snatched him.'

The first showings of a smile; the papers came back through the window.

'I will tell the comrade minister you are waiting for him.' He raised his hand, the checkpoint boom lifted. 'Good luck with the fishing, Mister Goddard. Stay with this road, but beware of wild animals. Elephant sometimes can be a problem.'

Lee started the engine and casually pulled away from the checkpoint. Before they had travelled fifty yards, David was banging on the cab roof for his attention. Karen looked back through the window and her heart leapt. A soldier armed with a Kalashnikov assault rifle was waving his arms for them to pull over.

Lee engaged reverse gear and backed up.

'You should have carried on driving,' Karen hissed.

'They would have come after us,' Lee countered, 'keep the smile going.' They drew level with the soldier. 'What's the problem corporal?'

'You must come back – the sergeant will speak with you.'

Lee released the clutch and pulled up with the trailer almost touching the boom. The sergeant lowered his face to the open window.

'On my advice, Mister Goddard, stay within sight of

your camp. Where you are going is within a few kilometres of the border; crossing into Mozambique without proper authority would not be looked on merely as an indiscretion.'

'No chance of that happening,' said Lee.

The sergeant nodded his head; his eyes unblinking. 'Ten days, then. Hopefully the fishing at Mahenya will live up to your expectations.'

-11-

Karen hung her gas lamps in the trees surrounding their camp and just as soon as the sun dipped below the horizon, David went from one to the next with his matches until the entire site was pleasantly bathed in soft, yellow light. He built a fire of thick mopani; it lit up the shoreline and as a yellow aura spread upon the surface of the river. The sky above the forest changed from blue to vivid shades of orange and vermilion and from the forest, the wake-up calls of nocturnal creatures screeched and barked, all of them keen for the dark to come quickly.

'Sky's clear and the river's quiet as a lamb,' said Lee. 'We've timed it right. No excessive rain; hopefully not for at least another couple of days. A stroll in the park, my lovely. Before you know it we'll be in Maputo, washing down tiger prawns with copious quantities of cold Manica beer.'

'What about the soldiers?'

Lee shook his head. 'Forget about them. We'll cope with being followed as and when. Ten to one they won't spare us a second thought.'

He switched on a powerful hunting lantern and panned the beam in a wide arc over the water. The sun had gone. The moon had already risen and the stars were bright above the forest canopy, scattered as silver coins across the firmament.

'Over there on that sandbank; about a six-footer, I would say.'

The eyes were coloured discs, turned almost red by the torchlight.

'Learn to judge their size by the distance between the eyes; the further apart, the bigger the croc.'

On the far bank, as grey ghosts, hippos foraged amongst the reed beds, by morning they would have ingested half their own weight in riverine plant growth.

David pulled out a length of steel mesh from behind the Land Rover's cab; on four prearranged river stones he balanced the makeshift barbecue grill and spread the coals as an even, glowing blanket beneath it.

'Will you be needing me for anything else, sir?'

'Thank you, but no, David. Grab yourself a couple of beers and a pack of meat from the cooler box. I'll see you tomorrow morning at first light.'

'Goodnight, madam.' David smiled at Karen. 'Do not forget to close the zip on your tent; there are many crocodiles.'

'Goodnight, David.' She returned the smile. 'What about you? Where will you be sleeping?'

'Back of the Land Rover, madam – crocodiles do not have wings.'

They drank Zambezi lager; ice cold bottles from the cooler box. Karen stared at the moon; so big and yellow it appeared close enough for her to touch.

'How much have you told David?'

'As much as necessary,' Lee answered flatly. 'That we're looking to get some good stills of big jumbo and if we're lucky enough, pick up a tiger fish or two further downstream. Might well be away from camp for a couple of days.'

'And if we're not back at camp within our allotted total of ten days?'

'Then Byron will come and pick him up; kept things on a need-to-know basis.'

They ate straight from the barbecue, inch-thick rump steaks barely seared and still running with juice. Fat dripped through the grill and tugged out spitting, smoky flames from the embers.

'We're looking at three days to reach Gerard. Once we're in range of *Isabella*'s radio, he'll talk us in. As long as he stays inside the Save's main channel we'll find him.' Lee looked up at the sky and searched for signs of a change in the weather. 'What we don't want at this stage is heavy rain. A flooding river would not be good right now. Twenty miles in from the coast, the Save runs over ten miles wide at peak flood.'

Absentmindedly, Karen prodded the fire with a stick. The warmth, a full stomach and flickering firelight made her sleepy.

'Why do I get the feeling, Rex knows exactly what we're up to?'

'He's got a fair idea,' Lee finally admitted, 'but he won't do anything, not unless he knows for certain that we've crossed the border.'

'My husband's a madman.' Karen shook her head. 'Why didn't you tell me? Confirm our friend Comrade Pasviri will be waiting just around the first bend in the river; with open arms?' The glow vanished from her face. Now she was wide awake. 'I thought we at least had a chance of pulling this off, but now you tell me that everyone short of the Pope knows exactly what we're up to?'

'Pasviri doesn't know, neither do the CIO.'

Karen found the opener and wrenched the top off another bottle of lager.

'This is not one of your war games, Lee; this is the real

deal Africa, not some kid's interpretation of cops and robbers around Centenary Park. People just disappear out here and no one is ever the wiser. And quit staring at me when I'm angry, it's bad manners.'

Lee sliced the last succulent piece of steak in half and offered some to Karen.

'You're all fired up, chew on this while I attempt to redeem myself.'

Karen snatched up the meat and like a cat with a luckless mouse, chewed off a corner.

'You could have told me before we left home.'

'You wouldn't have gone for it.'

She nodded vigorously. Steak juice dribbled from her chin.

'You're damn right buster.'

'Then at least hear me out.'

Karen swallowed the mouthful of steak and followed it down with beer.

'You have two minutes, Lee Goddard, and it had better be good or I'm packing up and going home.' She belched unashamedly. 'With or without you.'

Lee grinned at her. 'You'd let me go it alone?'

She cocked her head at him. 'After what you've just told me? In a flash, mister.'

'I had no choice,' Lee told her. 'Rex knows about the *Isabella*. He started piecing things together. Any time he wanted he could have told Pasviri and the CIO would have been all over us.'

'And you trust him enough for him not to have a change of heart? How can you be so sure he won't turn on us?'

'He won't,' said Lee and his mind flew back to those final days of the bush war; the thickly forested hill country along Rhodesia's eastern border with Mozambique. For twelve hours he had lain in thick mud, semi-conscious and disorientated. Rex could have finished him there and then. 'Rex will keep his mouth shut. None of what I've told you will reach Pasviri.'

'Don't be so damned trusting; spilling out what he knows would put a thousand PF Party feathers in his cap.'

'I can't answer for him. But he won't rat on us – not unless his life depends on it.'

Lee kicked aside the empty grill and covered the embers with more logs. They burnt up fiercely; tongues of green fire. Both Lee and Karen stared into the flames, too comfortable to move. Relentlessly, flames threaded their way between the logs. Piece by piece the timber succumbed to the heat and fell away as red ash.

'Okay,' she held up her arms in mock surrender, 'this is our family's future we're talking about. Every penny we own will be riding on this so I'm still in, but no more hidden agendas, Goddard; no more keeping me in the dark. Hypothetically though, what happens when Pasviri's lot eventually wipe the sleep out their eyes?'

'We have to get clear of the river mouth before they reach us.'

Karen countered his explanation.

'Obviously, but what if he sends out helicopters? A couple of hours flying time will be all that they need.'

'That's why it's imperative we find Gerard before Pasviri's goons beat us to it. Once we're mobile and out at sea their pilots won't risk following; they'll run out of fuel.'

Karen shook her head. The cold reality of what they were doing washed over her.

'We're both crazy. Especially me for agreeing with you, this whole escapade is suicidal; what about bandits? Mozambique is crawling with gangs of Renamo renegades. They'll kill us just for the hell of it.'

'The inflatable is our ace in the hole,' said Lee, 'as long as we keep to the main channel we'll get through. Only one sticking point...'

'Why don't I like this,' said Karen. In fear of the answer she focused her frustration on the fire. 'Go for it; get the bad bits over and done with. What are you saying?'

'Ponte Sobre.'

Karen's brow furrowed. 'What in hell's name is Ponte Sobre?'

'Steel suspension bridge across the Save some fifty miles or so up from the estuary. The Portuguese army maintained a forward base there during their run-in with Frelimo. I think there's an airstrip.'

Karen rolled her eyes at him. 'An airstrip? It gets better by the minute. Why not send Pasviri some holiday brochures? He might want to wave at us when we float past. Half the damned army will be waiting for us.'

'We'll be through before they realise what we're up to.'

'Like you can be so sure. Pasviri might well be cleverer than you think.'

'They won't pre-empt anything, not unless Rex throws a wobbler and chucks a spanner in the works.'

Karen drained her beer and dropped the empty bottle on the sand.

'Sensible Karen says go back home. Crazy Karen says go for it. I suppose you're planning on passing the bridge at night? What about the moon?' She looked at the river. 'It's bright as day out there. All we're short of are flashing lights and loud music for Christ's sake.'

'We'll get through,' he said and stood up from his place at the fire. Reassuringly, he brushed Karen's cheek with his fingertips. 'I have no intention of letting Pasviri get his grubby hands on our pension fund, my sweetheart. Moon or no moon, in three days' time we'll be aboard the *Isabella* swapping stories with Gerard Brownlee and heading south for Maputo.'

By sunrise, Lee and David were up and about; by half seven the trailer had been reversed into shallow water and stripped of its cargo. Tethered to the sandbank, the fourteen foot Zodiac inflatable slewed gently with the current and though fully laden, sat comfortably high in the water. Her twenty-five horsepower Yamaha outboard, less than a month old, had already been fuelled and primed; a single, firm pull on its starting handle would be all that was needed. While Lee carefully balanced the dinghy's load, Karen prepared a breakfast of steak and eggs on a skillet slung above the fire. The extra portions of cooked meat were wrapped in foil and crammed into her cooler box.

'Just about enough food to see us through,' she told Lee.

'That's all we should need, if everything works out smoothly, three days from now and our illustrious Comrade Julius Pasviri can go whistle Dixie for his gold.'

'Our gold,' Karen corrected him. 'Providing we make it through.'

'We will. Provisos don't come into it. Gerard should be close to the river mouth by now. Today, we'll push as far as we can; fifty miles would be good. The same tomorrow, then we'll fire up the radio and see if Gerard's listening in.'

Lee poured coffee and sweetened both mugs with brown sugar. He lit a cigarette and sat down facing the river. The hippos were back in the water; bellies filled from that last night's foraging, eyes and ears primed for movement and any alien sounds that floated across from the sandbank. He stood up from the fire and swilled his cup in the river.

'We'd best get moving before our friends at the checkpoint decide to pay us a visit.'

-13-

Comrade Minister Julius Pasviri pulled a chair out from the head of the boardroom table and placed one foot on it, draping an arm across his knee. Air conditioning hummed in the background. Byron dropped his pen and stared up at him, startled and owl-like from behind a section by section printed account of the Empress Deep's current production figures. For almost a minute, Pasviri said nothing; the silence alone was powerful and intimidating, powerful enough for it to have already initiated that first exposé of Byron's Achilles' heel.

'You're shaking, Mister Fuller? I find it strange that a mere courtesy call from a government minister can evoke so much fear in a man.' He lit a Kingsgate filter and with the cigarette clamped between his teeth, pointed it at Byron as though it were the barrel of a gun. Reluctantly, he suppressed a need for his usual, more preferred methods of interrogation. For the moment, Pasviri was openly titillated by the ease in which he was able to manipulate the white man's lack of self-control. He took pleasure from Byron's paranoid fear of government authority.

Behind Pasviri, three CIO men leaned against the wall; they stared impassively at the Empress Deep's acting General Manager. As a blatant act of disregard, Pasviri shook the ash off his cigarette and let it fall to the boardroom's perfectly waxed tabletop.

'I will ask you one more time, Mister Fuller. Where is your employer?'

Though fifty yards away from the office windows, the sudden jangling of shaft call bell signals touched a nerve; Byron's cheeks twitched and Pasviri was quick to pick up on the phobia.

'I take it you steer well clear of any actual mining operations?'

Byron nodded his head, relieved by Pasviri's apparent change of tack. Memories of that fateful day came back to him; that sudden, downwards lurch of a runaway conveyance, the sound of his own screaming and those of thirty other terrified men hurtling into the abyss. Only after long, agonising moments had their uncontrolled drop for shaft bottom been picked up on by the engine's over-speed safety circuits, and only then had the winder's massive brakes been slammed on.

'My forte lies with the admin side of things – that's my job, comrade minister. The thought of going underground positively abhors me.'

Pasviri slid his foot from the chair.

'Walk with me.' He beckoned to him. 'A guided tour of your shaft headgear and surrounding area would prove enlightening, Mister Fuller. We can discuss the whereabouts of Goddard as we walk.'

Begrudgingly, Byron took on the mantle of ministerial tour guide and though apprehensive of Pasviri's persistent questioning he was grateful of the fresh air and bright sunlight. He detested dark places; the claustrophobic effects of total darkness terrified him. Every night for as far back as he could remember he had slept with his bedside lamp switched on. However, with the warm breath of an illicit lover, the dark throat of the Empress Deep's main shaft beckoned to him.

As a man tormented by vertigo, Byron sensed a strange, irrepressible urge to peer into the abyss. He glowered up at the headgear, its great sheave wheel now motionless. To him, the iron wheel was symbolic of some nightmarish iron beast; the living, beating heart of all his fears. From it hung the winding engine's steel rope, thick and serpent-like. Fixed to the rope, as a hanged man, the steel conveyance trembled and shuddered. Pasviri studied the change in Byron, fascinated by a sudden hatred for the very thing that succoured him. He left Byron alone and made his way across the shaft collar to where the banksman supervised the stripping out of equipment recently brought out from underground. Broken shovels and other damaged mining paraphernalia had been wired together in bundles, ready for the salvage yard.

'The top of the conveyance, bring it level with the bank.'

Without looking up from the morning's log sheet, the banksman shook his head, unaware of who he was engaging with.

'You'll have to wait. The shaft's locked. We'll be pulling out material for at least another hour.'

'I will try again, comrade. Lower the cage, or I will kill you.' Pasviri held a Tokarev pistol on a line with the banksman's forehead; the man's eyes fluttered wildly and he dropped the log sheet. Pasviri snicked off the Tokarev's safety catch. 'I will give you one minute, comrade; disappoint me again and I will blow your brains out.'

Terrified, the banksman fumbled the 'shaft open' signal through to the engine room. The driver acknowledged by mimicking the call.

'Now lower the conveyance.'

The banksman pulled down the roller shutter door and kicked in the locking bolt. Again the bell clamoured out new instructions and after a short pause the conveyance obeyed, inching downwards. The banksman pulled once on the triangular shaped signal actuator and the cage came to a standstill, its steel roof now level with the edge of the shaft bank.

'Leave the gates open,' Pasviri held the gun on him. 'What is the depth of your furthest level?'

'587 Level,' spluttered the banksman.

'That is five hundred and eighty-seven metres?'

The banksman nodded his head. 'One thousand seven hundred feet, comrade minister, give or take two hundred feet to shaft bottom.' His hands were shaking. Sweat stood out from his forehead.

'Signal your driver,' Pasviri ordered him. 'The cage will go to 587 Level, but only when I tell you.'

The banksman reached for the signal box and rang the relevant code through to the winding engine driver. Without his final lock signal, the conveyance would not move away from the bank. Pasviri looked over his shoulder and beckoned to the CIO men.

'Bring me our Mister Fuller. I have an interesting treat for him.'

Byron realised Pasviri's intentions and had already turned back for the office block. The CIO men caught up with him and steered him back towards the shaft. Pasviri stood with his hands clasped behind his back. A fresh cigarette hung from the corner of his mouth.

'Come now, Mister Fuller. Every mine manager should avail himself of the opportunity to check his main access shaft for unsafe working conditions.' He smiled easily, but his stare was that of the fox for the rabbit. 'I asked you for the whereabouts of your employer, comrade. Perhaps the first thousand feet of oblivion will loosen your tongue.'

'Don't do this,' pleaded Byron. Choked by fear his voice came through as barely more than a child's whisper. 'I'll tell you where they are. For God's sake don't do this to me.'

Pasviri's eyes glittered. 'Indulge me, Mister Fuller.' He levelled the Tokarev. 'Please climb aboard, your carriage awaits.'

Shepherded by CIO men, Byron stumbled onto the cage maintenance platform. Without a safety harness, should he lose his footing there would be nothing to hold him.

'They're at a fishing camp; somewhere near Mahenya. The Save River. On my life, comrade minister, I swear it.'

'That is what you would have me believe, comrade. However, your little ride will give you adequate time to think of the consequences should I choose to disagree. Lie to me at your peril Mister Fuller. Mislead me, and I will send you back down – without the cage.'

Byron dropped in close to the steel humble-hook, the point at which the winding engine's steel hoisting cable terminated; a multi-stranded steel umbilical cord that, for over a thousand feet into nothingness would be his only link with the world outside. Apart from Byron's pathetic mewling there was silence. Men who had been unloading the cage watched the spectacle unfold, like a crowd gathered about the hangman's gibbet, their faces were expressionless. Pasviri nodded his head at the banksman.

'587 level, banksman. Maximum speed, if you would be so kind.'

The shaft safety gates were closed. The locking bar engaged.

The banksman looked piteously at his superior, then, fearful for his own life he rang the conveyance away.

Huddled down to his nest of cold steelwork, Byron locked his arms about the humble-hook. Warm grease squeezed from between his fingers and like a rat to the wreckage of some doomed ship he clung there, alone and terrified. A slight trickle of bright blood showed at his brow and behind his grease-covered glasses his eyes were those of a man pushed to the very limits of all his fears.

As a wintering snake, silently and slowly at first, the conveyance slid below the surface. Byron shut his eyes and clenched his teeth in anticipation of that sudden stomach-wrenching rush of downwards velocity; that first, terrifying, Big Dipper fall into oblivion. The shaft was his nemesis, his personal earth-bound black hole and now it was closing around him; eagerly it sucked him down beneath the ground.

His screaming, when it came, quickly succumbed to the roar of displaced air. Now at maximum speed the cage was little more than a blur to those on the lower levels who saw it pass, then as suddenly as it had begun, the speed was brought in check; gradually, the driver slowed the conveyance – at creep-speed the cage nudged in square to the station lip on 587 Level.

'Now bring it back,' Pasviri ordered and the banksman rang his surface bank call signal through to the driver.

Two minutes later, Byron felt the sun on his face. Unable to use his legs, he lay in a miasma of grease, water and his own faeces. His glasses had been torn from his face and sent to shaft bottom.

'Bring him out,' Pasviri ordered. The banksman flung open the shaft gates and stepped onto the cage roof.

'Can you hear me, Mister Fuller, sir?'

Like a bullied child for its father, Byron stretched out his arms; his face smeared in grease and blood, his clothing soaked through with filth and shaft slurry. The fear from what had happened was still in him and he whimpered pathetically.

The banksman, broad-shouldered, lifted him easily. He stepped clear of the shaft collar and set his superior down in open sunlight.

'Can you stand, sir?'

Byron nodded his head; thankfully he turned to face the full-on warmth of the sun.

Pasviri watched them, openly amused by the spectacle. From the stub of his cigarette he lit another, giving Byron time to contemplate what might have happened.

'You didn't really believe that I would have allowed you to sweep our little contretemps under the carpet, did you, Mister Fuller?'

Byron stared at him and as if steeled by the nearness of his own death he projected the full venom of what he felt for the man responsible.

'You've got what you came for, now leave me alone.' His whole body trembled. Greenbottle flies were drawn to the smell of his soiled clothing. They clung to him, the way they would cling to the rank hide of an old buffalo. Pasviri smiled at the white man's uncharacteristic show of bravado.

'I will be in touch, Mister Fuller. You have a direct line through to my office, should you hear of a change in your employer's intentions you are to phone me immediately.'

Byron didn't reply. He started for the shower block; before he reached the door he peeled off his shirt and flung it away in disgust. Three black ministerial cars growled awake and sped away from the car park.

-14-

Lee looked at David through the eyes of an old friend; any attempt at hiding his affection would have come across as a lie.

'Help yourself to what there is, David. If something goes wrong and we're not back in a week, just sit tight. Byron will be down with a driver to bring you home.' He handed David the keys to the Land Rover. 'Look after them. Chances are you'll be getting a visit from our army friends; just play dumb, all you know is that we're fishing and taking pictures of elephant further down the river.'

David reached for Lee's hand and squeezed it gently.

'The people will wait for you. Once you have found your elephant do what must be done and then come back to us.'

Lee gritted his teeth; saying goodbye was never easy for him. His eyes filled and he did his utmost to make light of leaving David behind. Even though he had disclosed nothing of his plans to the old man, the reality of what was taking place was obvious.

'Just need some time to sort things out. I've left instructions with Mister Fuller. As from the end of this month, if for some reason I haven't made it back, your full pension will be there for you, as and when you want it.'

'Pensions are for old men. I will watch the road for your return.' Again he reached for Lee's hand. There was a compelling firmness to his grip. 'You will come back; there is much for you to do. *Hamba gashle*, captain. Go in peace.'

From the inflatable, Lee and Karen looked back at the lone figure of a man on the sandbank, and for a long time neither one of them spoke, not until the current took the Zodiac beyond the apex of that first bend. For Lee, it was the final letting go; blindly, they were drifting into the unknown. Karen sat alongside him, her mood sombre.

'There's still time to change your mind?'

Lee shook his head. 'We passed that marker two days ago, there's no going back, my love.'

'He called you captain?'

'Must have got it from Rex,' he smiled sardonically and left it where it belonged – in the past.

The Zodiac drifted easily with the central current;

compared to the previous day, the water was a different colour. Though now only slightly darker it was enough for Lee to recognize the changing beat of Africa's heart. Somewhere, upstream from Mahenya, rain had fallen. Soon, more would follow. In the foothills of Zimbabwe's eastern districts, great cumulus clouds were gathering over the watershed.

'The rains are starting,' said Lee. 'Another day and we'll see a marked rise in the water level.'

Karen made a rough guess at their present speed; comparing it to a fast walk she made her calculations.

'Five miles an hour at best. Maybe we should use the outboard?'

Lee concurred and reached behind him for the starter handle. The motor fired first time; he climbed back into the driver's seat and engaged the forward drive.

Though heavily laden, the Zodiac responded valiantly; with the favouring current she crested the swirls and dark eddies.

'We have twenty gallons of spare fuel,' Lee spoke above the engine noise, 'plus the eight we have in the tank.' Gradually, he eased back on the throttle, gauging the engine's slackening speed as he did so. 'I'll run her at half speed; about three thousand rpm. With the current helping us, that should give us a good twelve miles to every gallon of fuel used.'

Again, Karen measured their rate of travel between pre-selected natural markers on the river bank, using the second hand on her watch as her yard stick.

'Twelve miles an hour, give or take. Depends on how many obstacles we come up against as to how far we travel before dark.'

'Sandbanks,' said Lee, 'keep your eyes peeled, we need the deeper channels. Running aground is not an option.'

'What about rapids or waterfalls?'

Lee shook his head. 'Aren't any. The closer we get to

the coast, the flatter the terrain. You're sailing where Arab traders brought their boat-loads of trade goods upstream from Sofala on the Indian Ocean over nine hundred years ago.'

'Only as far as Mahenya,' Karen reminded. 'We archaeological diggers up of ancient antiquities tend to know these things.'

'Oops! Sorry, *Herr Doktor* – slipped my mind.'

Karen smiled at the platitude.

'The iron rings, you mentioned last night? How come you know about them?'

'An ex-BSAP man showed them to me. Ted Dowling, he's retired now and living in Australia. We still keep in touch. Two iron rings grouted into the rock – some sort of ancient mooring site. Not many people know about them.'

'Ex-policeman?'

Lee nodded his head. 'Man and boy, spent most of his career patrolling the valley for poachers. Tough old guy, hunted lion back in the forties. Remembers the old Hippo Mine in its heyday.' He swung the wheel to avoid a part-submerged tree; a remnant of last year's floodwater. In the distance, flocks of cattle egrets rose as flurries of white thread to a blue sky.

'An unusual name – the Hippo Mine. Definite romantic overtones.' Karen smiled, sidetracked by her own imagination. 'So what did they mine? And don't say hippos or I'll shove you overboard.'

'Tungsten. More commonly known as, Scheelite. Used for hardening steel. Hacksaw blades, parting tools, specialist armaments. Very heavy mineral, fluoresces under ultra violet light; turns a blue-white colour.'

'You're pretty clued up on the subject?'

'It's interesting, love talking about it. Apparently they mined right under the Save river bed, blanket reef; sort of flat. Parallel to the surface rather than going down at a steep angle, as is the norm.'

They both fell silent and for the next few minutes watched the forest slide by. Lee was first to break the mood and picked up where they had left off.

'Back in forty-three, the men who owned the mine did exactly what we're doing now.'

Karen looked at him, captivated by the mysterious titbit. 'Go on then, don't leave me hanging – what happened?'

'They rafted a load of raw tungsten down to the river mouth. A British destroyer took it on board and paid the miners way over the odds for their trouble. Over five tons of the stuff for the war effort. That's all I know, but apparently a true story.'

'And that's where you got the idea from?'

'Yes siree. One big difference though, they weren't running from anything.'

Karen refocused her concentration on the river ahead. For two hours they held the Zodiac to half of her full speed and Karen guessed they had already passed the first twenty-five mile point from Mahenya. On both banks the forest thinned, most trees were confined to higher ground by the wide expanse of the Save's natural flood plain; the undergrowth was heavily laced with game paths and hippo tunnels. Crocodiles lay in the sun with their mouths wide open, their colourful throats that familiar, eye-catching deep orange. Apart from the sibilance of moving water and the drumming of the Yamaha outboard, there were no other sounds. Zimbabwe's bricks and mortar infrastructure seemed now an entire lifetime away.

Lee's paranoia shuffled backwards and forwards through a dozen possible scenarios; from personal experience, he knew that by helicopter it would take only a matter of an hour at the outside for Pasviri's men to be up with them. He looked down at the throttle

67

lever, sorely tempted to push it hard over for full speed, but the act would prove foolhardy, gallons of precious fuel would be quickly wasted away.

<h1 style="text-align:center">-15-</h1>

The Flamboyant Motel's receptionist handed Rex the office phone.

'The caller is holding for you.' She smiled politely then left him alone; gently, she pulled the door closed.

Rex knew who it was.

'Comrade Pasviri.'

'When did you last see Goddard?'

'Two days ago. He and his wife are away. Fishing trip, I believe.'

'And did he tell you where they were going?'

'No comrade, they left without notification. Goddard's personal assistant is standing in for him, a Mister Byron Fuller.'

'Ah yes – Fuller. Goddard's personal, Mister Timidity. The Empress Deep's acting mine manager, and yet a man so loathsome of its workings.'

'Comrade Minister?'

'A helicopter will up-lift you from the airport at Buffalo Range. Three o'clock this afternoon, comrade. Do not be late.'

Rex glanced up at the clock on the wall.

'Why Buffalo Range?'

'Mister Fuller was kind enough to give me the whereabouts of Goddard's supposed fishing camp. They were stopped by one of our military checkpoints some fifty miles south of Chisumbanje research station. I need you to find out why someone threatened with astronomical financial losses suddenly decides to go fishing.'

Though they were over a hundred miles apart, Rex sensed Pasviri's increasing need for his full control of the Empress Deep. The situation was rapidly becoming untenable. His influence over Pasviri's decision-making had already weakened; he was now the jackal, threatened with losing his place at the kill.

'I'll be there,' Rex confirmed. 'Destination? Where exactly am I going?'

'The pilot has been instructed to fly you out to the old Hippo Mine, a few miles upstream from Goddard's camp. The Brigade has established a border control base there; the man in charge is a Major Ephraim Thebisa. He is expecting you.'

Rex went back to his room and dragged out an overnight bag from the wardrobe, cursing Pasviri for his lack of timing. He selected clothing that would be more suited to the hot, clammy conditions of the lowveld. From a bottle in his toiletries bag he emptied out two, anti-malaria tablets and swallowed them both without water. Two hours later, sweated up and dust- ridden he was swinging a government 4X4 Nissan Patrol into Buffalo Range airport car park.

'Comrade Minister Khumalo?'

Rex nodded; the young pilot officer had appeared from nowhere. Dressed in loose-fitting army coveralls he took up Rex's bag.

'Follow me please. Two minutes' walk, comrade minister that is all.'

The landing zone was merely a whitewashed circle, emblazoned with a central cross; it was a remnant of the war days. Walking towards the Alouette gunship evoked in Rex, simultaneous feelings of apprehension and déjà vu. He felt the hairs at the back of his neck rise. Twin .303 Browning machine guns had been left in place;

perhaps the same guns that on many occasions had almost robbed him of his life. He threw the canvas carry-all inside and pulled himself into the vacant flight tech's seat. Along the fuselage, another remnant of the bush war; a coat of grey, anti-missile paint.

'About thirty minutes flying time, comrade minister.'

Rex, without dropping his eyes from the gun nodded his head to the pilot. The howl of the Alouette's Artouste engine fell upon him wild and wolf-like. For long minutes, again he was there on a remote hillside, almost twenty years younger, twenty pounds lighter, with the weight of a lethal Strela missile launcher balanced across his shoulder. In the sky above him, linked to where he stood by a mile-long vaporous thread from the rocket's motor, a Rhodesian Fireforce helicopter crumpled and fell to some far-off forest canopy; bursting into flames when it struck. His brow furrowed from the recollection.

'Are you alright sir?' The pilot had been watching him. 'In a few minutes we'll be overflying the Save River.'

'I'm fine, thank you.' He smiled at the pilot. Below, forests of spring mopani flowed as a single, bronze-coloured carpet in all directions; the Alouette's shape, as a stark shadow leapfrogged trees and rocky buttresses surrounding the river line. A minute out from the defunct Hippo Mine, the pilot put the Alouette into a tight turn; like its counterpart at Buffalo Range, the helicopter landing zone stood out from between the trees as a whitewashed circle and cross.

The brigade's company commander turned his back on the dust and waited for the Alouette to power down.

'Welcome to the lowveld, comrade minister.' He shifted a leather-bound swagger stick into his left hand and extended his right to Rex. 'Major Ephraim Thebisa, your host for the next few days.'

Rex accepted the hand. To the millimetre they were

equal in height; Rex, slightly broader across the shoulders, Ephraim Thebisa, slightly smaller at the waist. At first, both were suspicious of each other and like bare-knuckle prize fighters were unwilling to drop their eyes. Around the landing zone, camouflaged canvas tents had been erected at random amongst the trees.

'Comrade Pasviri said you would explain my being here, major.'

'All in good time, comrade. First a little something to wash the dust from your throat.' He looked to a young Subaltern. 'Take the comrade minister's bag to his quarters. Make sure the fridge is well stocked and that everything is as it should be.' The Subaltern saluted and went away at the double. Thebisa relaxed his guard.

'How do I call you? Or would you prefer that I abide by our government's socialist protocol?'

'Rex will do just fine.'

'Then, Rex it shall be.' He appeared at ease with the decision and was silent for a few moments; Rex could see that he was piecing together information given to him by Pasviri. 'Mining Engineer, war hero and now Minister for Mines.' He slapped the swagger stick against his calf. 'Impressive. No, I stand corrected. Meteoric, I think would be a much better way of putting it.'

'Or merely a victim of convenience, major. I had the qualifications; the government needed a caretaker to oversee their future mining acquisitions. Right place, right time. I just happened to fit the bill.'

'Over there.' Thebisa used his stick as a pointer and led the way towards a thatched rondavel. Large enough to accommodate several people, the open-sided roundhouse overlooked a deep cleft in the country rock; at the valley's lowest point the Save River meandered as a slack, earthy ribbon of quiet water.

The rondavel's waist-high, semi-circular wall was of

71

rough natural stone taken from the Hippo Mine's waste dumps. Pitted with weathered calcite and flecks of copper pyrite, in that late sunlight the stone structure stood attractively iridescent to a background of rocky knolls and ancient baobabs.

Thebisa encouraged Rex to join him. 'Sundowner time I think the colonists called it. A practical tradition, one that I have adopted as my own and as some would be quick to point out, one that I perhaps support a little too avidly.'

Upwards from the metre-high wall, poles of iron-hard mopani rose in support of the structure's thatched roof; sculpted by local Shangaan craftsmen, the grass had been laid to a full twelve inches in thickness, still that African gold in colour, for even that vicious lowveld sun had not yet found sufficient time to dull it. Cooling air flowed naturally through the seating area, and unrestricted, the view across the valley remained magnificent.

With an artist's passion, Ephraim Thebisa, with a single sweep of his swagger stick encompassed the full extent of the panorama.

'To a painter of pictures, the ultimate canvas – and yet no one has ever committed their skills to its reproduction.' He looked to Rex for an opinion. 'Why do you think that is, comrade? Why does no one chance to record for posterity this magnificent image of our own, mother Africa?'

Before Rex could reply, Thebisa cut back in.

'Because they are afraid, comrade – frightened off by the damning sneer of our own brutality. Every democratic country beyond our borders is sick of the subterfuge. That Zimbabwe has propagated a monster is a powerful, God-given truth. Western governments look upon our way of governing the masses as an impossible, dictatorial dream; repugnant even.' He threw the swagger stick onto a chair and without looking up finished off the drama of his introduction. 'The sad thing is, comrade, we have no say in what is happening. We do what is asked of us or like the conjurer's assistant, we will simply be made to disappear.'

Rex pulled a chair over and sat with his legs outstretched, the sun still warm on his face. To the wrong ears, Thebisa's ideology would come across as insightful – anti-government, treacherous even, though deep down, Rex found himself in agreement.

'Things will change, major, but Africa was never the faithful lover; she moves from one to another as and when it pleases her. The British, Americans, Chinese – all of them eager suitors queuing at our borders.' He smiled up at Thebisa. 'We learn as we go along, major. One day, there will be peace. Your artists will flock in their thousands for a chance to see what we in Zimbabwe take for granted.'

'Ice with your scotch?'

Rex Nodded and shook out a cigarette from a twenty pack of Kingsgate.

'Half scotch, half water.'

Below where Rex was sitting, as a slothful child the Save, though stirred by first rains appeared loath to move. However, the now quiescent river would soon be forced to boil and growl its way to the Indian Ocean. Thebisa handed Rex his drink and pulled out another chair from beneath the table.

'Julius Pasviri. How do you view the man?'

'Through hooded eyes,' said Rex, 'a corrupt bigot, on a par with Adolph Hitler.'

Thebisa nodded his head. 'Not your favourite Party colleague, then?'

'Given the choice, major, I would rather share my food with a crocodile.'

Ephraim Thebisa smiled at the comparison; nursing

his scotch he watched a final flare of late sunlight burn itself out and slip below the horizon.

'He doesn't trust you.'

'On what do you base your assumptions, major? Why are you telling me this?'

'Because like you, comrade I detest the man. Julius Pasviri is my brother-in-law. Through my inherent lacking in the common sense department I was coerced into marrying his wild-eyed sister. Why do you think I live in the back of beyond?'

'Thrown out by your wife?' Rex grinned.

Thebisa shook his head and laughed. 'No my friend, I volunteered. I take little pleasure from being accosted by a woman cursed with the sexual appetite of a lactating gorilla. Julia is an incorrigible alcoholic. Being straddled at every opportunity by some amorous drunk does not, as the English say, blow my hair back.' He took Rex's glass and re-charged it with scotch and ice.

'This Goddard fellow? Two days ago. He and his wife passed through our road block. How well do you know him?'

'Since before the war,' said Rex. 'I worked for him as his resident Mining Engineer.'

'But you parted company?'

'I was borrowed,' Rex mused, 'ZANLA made me an offer I couldn't refuse.'

'Forcibly recruited?'

Rex nodded. 'Fought with them right up to independence. I was glad when the war ended. There are better things for a man to do than blow other peoples' brains out.'

They were still there after dark. Rex welcomed the chance to unwind; the iced scotch and warm night air drew heavily at his eyelids. By seven o'clock, Thebisa's bottle of Famous Grouse had dropped to well below the one third full mark.

In compliance with the major's earlier instructions, the cook sent food directly from his kitchen; pliant maize-meal porridge and thick steaks – barely seared, the meat still ran with fat and was heavily spiced with salt and black pepper. Strategically placed bowls of hot water and crisply laundered hand towels were left on the low wall. Thebisa lit only one of the lamps, leaving it far enough from the table to draw away any invading insects. Both men rinsed and dried their hands and then set about the banquet. Rex's stomach growled; he had eaten nothing since breakfast.

A rich sauce had been cooked in a three-legged iron pot, for an hour over a slow fire. From it breathed the peppery smells of old Africa, those of fiery dwarf chillies, sliced onion and over-ripe oxheart tomatoes, big as a man's fist. In a separate enamel bowl, *muriwo*, the valley's wild spinach steamed emerald green in the lamplight.

In the African tradition, both men took up food with bare hands, kneading the maize porridge between fingers and palm before dousing it with sauce. Neither one of them spoke until the last slivers of beef had been consumed.

'More than enough, major.' Rex glanced down at his stomach. 'You have killed me with your hospitality.'

Again they washed their hands and settled back in their chairs, Rex with that first after dinner cigarette wedged between his lips. The moon was bright and from the valley the river shone out as a silver road from behind the Chamfute trees. Thebisa stared up at the firmament – the sky, now totally black, a far off celestial show of tiny lights.

'Pasviri wants your friend checked out. Tomorrow morning. An hour's drive downstream. He's convinced Mister Goddard is up to no good.'

'Pasviri is paranoid; the idiot is wasting your time.'

'Then we will establish the fact and have you back here ready to fly out by lunchtime.'

*

By first light, dressed in a pair of loaned army fatigues and fortified with coffee brewed from the cook's special reserve, Rex now sat outside that same thatched roundhouse. Through narrowed eyes he looked down on the river, his head ached from that last night's binge on imported scotch, but his hand was rock steady when he lifted the cup to his lips.

'Thought I might find you here.'

Rex slid his cup onto the table and looked over his shoulder.

'A curse on you, major.'

'Headache?'

'The mother of them all,' Rex admitted. 'You are in the presence of near death. No sudden noises or I swear my head will explode.'

Thebisa pulled up a chair alongside him. 'Relief is on its way; full English breakfast,' he slumped down, 'another colonial trait I have taken a liking to.'

Rex felt his stomach heave.

'Toast, major – and more coffee. Going off the noises coming from my insides that will be more than enough.'

'Nonsense, comrade. No man, not even a battle-hardened, ex-guerrilla like you can survive the day on an empty stomach.'

The cook brought out their food, piping hot and steaming from the kitchen skillets. Oval shaped porcelain breakfast plates had been stacked to the brim with everything Rex was fearful of – greasy bacon, glassy eggs and fat, unguinous pork sausages.

'I've decided to take the helicopter,' Thebisa spoke

through a full mouth. 'We can complete our assignment and be back here in a couple of hours, depending on what we find. My brother-in-law has already been on to me for results; the man never sleeps.'

Rex ate in silence; crisp slices of toast and after relenting to Thebisa's insistence, one small portion of bacon. The sausages were ignored. Thebisa appeared none the worse for his debauchery and cleared his plate. The sun came up; Africa's first colours bled from along the horizon. Rex pushed his plate away and took solace from black coffee and a cigarette.

'Mozambique, comrade,' Thebisa pointed eastwards, the same direction taken by the ancient river, 'just a few miles downstream from where we are sitting; so easy for a man of dubious intent to slip unseen from the country.'

Rex noticed a change in the officer's mannerisms; his outlook was now more guarded and the over-the-top cordiality he had shown Rex that previous night had been toned down. Thebisa turned in his seat and from that faraway glint in his eyes, Rex was reminded of the awakening jackal.

'Last night, my brother-in-law radioed me from Harare. Most excited, seems he's convinced your friend Goddard is set to jump the border – something about an illegal cache of gold bullion?'

Rex showed no surprise, Thebisa's raising the subject of Lee's supposed attempts at smuggling gold bullion was long overdue; since his arrival in the camp, every minute of the day he had expected it.

'Pasviri's paranoia is infecting us all, major. Only a fool would move a cargo of that nature through Mozambique.'

Rex ground out his cigarette and dropped the butt in the ashtray.

'Why would he do it? Goddard owns one of the

largest, privately run gold mines in Zimbabwe. Both his sons have yet to finish their schooling in England and three generations of his family are buried in the back garden for God's sake; he was born and raised here, the man has nowhere to go.'

Thebisa smiled at Rex's sudden show of concern.

'Then he will have nothing to fear, comrade. We leave for Goddard's camp at Mahenya in half an hour; for his sake, pray that we find him there.'

-16-

Major Ephraim Thebisa sat in the tech's seat, whenever he turned his face to the front, the silver Zimbabwe bird brigade motif on his beret caught at the sunlight. Holstered against his left side, a 7.62mm Tokarev pistol favoured the reach of his right hand.

Rex sat directly behind Thebisa, along with two, fully armed Fifth Brigade troopers – both stared down at the ground through permanently open doorways, eyes locked to the river bank. Neither one of them spoke.

'Down there!' Thebisa shouted above the noise. The pilot gave the standard 'thumbs-up'; he had already seen the beige-coloured tent and swung the Alouette close in to the campsite. From adjacent sandbanks a dozen or so Nile crocodiles bolted for the water. The pilot cut power from the engine as soon as the wheels touched down. Both troopers stayed with the helicopter. Rex didn't need to be told that Lee wasn't there – the inflatable had gone. Thebisa looked at him and smiled thinly.

'Looks like your friend might well have disappointed us, comrade.'

Rex understood from Thebisa's sarcasm that the pleasantries of their earlier first name relationship had been withdrawn; from now on, any exchange of words would be executed formally.

'He's out on the river, fishing, major. That's why they came here.' Rex held is voice steady. Through his position as government minister, he still commanded top seat at the table.

David approached from behind the Land Rover. He recognised Rex from his earlier visits to the Empress Deep.

'Comrade Minister, sir – it is good to see you again.'

'And you, David. Mister Goddard – where is he?'

David's smile faltered – his eyes suddenly fearful.

'Mister Goddard and his wife went out on the river yesterday morning, comrade minister. They take pictures of big elephant and look for *mucheni*, the tiger fish.'

Rex felt his stomach tighten, what he had feared most was happening. Lee had blatantly disregarded his warning and made for the coast with a load of smuggled bullion and Karen was with him.

Thebisa knelt alongside the remains of Lee's campfire; the ashes were cold and he picked up on the camp's atmosphere of abandonment. The fire would have been kept alive for when the occupants returned. Stony-faced, he stood up. To David, Thebisa's eyes were those of a lion about to tear out his entrails.

'You are lying, old man. Think carefully before you speak again. Where is your employer?'

'I have not seen them since yesterday, comrade. On my life, I give you my word.'

Thebisa's patience evaporated, he smiled at David, but it was that thin, deathlike smile of a forest adder.

'And your life it may well come to, old man. When will Goddard be back?'

He only had to look sideways for the troopers to come to him at the double.

'Our friend here has never flown before. We must

enlighten him.'

Words froze in David's throat; his face took on the ashen hue of a man having glimpsed the inevitable; that of someone forced to climb those final half-dozen steps to the gallows' upper platform.

'Bind his hands and feet,' growled Thebisa, 'you know what has to be done.'

They seized the old man by both arms and dragged him bodily towards the Alouette. David stayed silent, but his eyes spoke for him, the terror of what was happening robbed him of his legs and involuntarily his bladder emptied.

Powerless to intervene, Rex watched the Alouette uplift and come about. He could make out the powerful shape of Ephraim Thebisa gesticulating for the benefit of the pilot.

Like some predacious metal insect, the Alouette hovered midstream, no more than a metre above the Save's deepest channel. Hammered by turbulent downdrafts the surface water shuddered and broke into frantic eddies. Bound securely and held in the helicopter's open doorway, David stared down into what seemed to him as the very jaws of hell.

Thebisa tapped the pilot's shoulder and shouted over the noise.

'Take us in close to the water!'

Totally helpless, Rex stood at the water's edge and watched the drama unfold. Even if he were up there with David, in the face of three, fully armed soldiers, taking sides would prove suicidal.

Thebisa now stood in the Alouette's bulkhead doorway; held securely by his safety harness he was allowed complete freedom of movement so that he leaned out into the void with his hands tightly locked about David's ankles.

Trussed with lengths of nylon cord, as some grotesque

human pendulum, David was lowered head first to within inches of the water. Terrified beyond his understanding, he thrashed and screamed. Easily, Thebisa held the old man's weight and even from that distance out from the sandbank, Rex was reminded of the untouchable perversity wielded by the military. To Thebisa, other than meat at the end of a rope, David meant nothing.

'Give me what I am after you Matabele dog and I will pull you up!'

'I swear to you, comrade major, all I know is that they took their boat downriver!'

David's voice was swept away by the downdraft; his eyes were wide with raw fear; twenty yards away dark shapes amassed in the shallows, confused by the noise, some slid silently into deeper water. From where they lay on the riverbed they watched the plight of the creature above them. Though most were wary of the disturbance, some, titillated by the floundering, watched the creature in a way the voracious barracuda would watch the fisherman's lure cavort and twitch on the surface of the ocean.

'When did they leave? Hurry old man, my arms grow weary from holding you. When did you see them leave the camp?'

'Yesterday. I swear I have not seen them since, comrade major. They took their boat down river. They told me nothing!'

Thebisa nodded his head at the pilot. 'Take us back to the shore.'

Ten metres out from the sandbank, Thebisa released his grip on David's ankles. Like a half-filled sack of maize he slapped belly first into the river. Rex waded out to where the old man floundered and dragged him spluttering and terrified onto the sandbank.

Karen lowered herself waist-deep into the shallows; with her elbows wedged against the rocks she let the water rush over her.

'My first bath in two days.' She breathed in the freshness of the water, but overpowering it was the rank odour of her own body. 'I smell like a goat.'

Watching from higher up, Lee sat with the FN rifle rested across his knees, even in fast, shallow water crocodiles were still a real threat.

'*Eau d'Afrique*,' he joked. 'Josephine, Napoleon's mistress purposely eased off on the hygiene department for when lover boy got back home from playing soldiers. He liked his women ripe and heady. Bottle the stuff and we'll make a fortune.'

'Perverts, the lot of you.' Karen waved a bottle of shampoo at him. 'You can wash my hair. And easy on with those horny hands, Goddard, this is your wife you're soaping down, not your Land Rover.'

She leaned back for him, tilting her head to touch the water. The action forced back her shoulders; water flurried inside her shirt and as cool insistent fingers, gently stroked her breasts.

Lee propped the FN against the rocks and moved in behind her, the shampoo, a blue pearlescent pool in the palm of his hand.

Silky smooth and smelling of wild flowers, her hair sparkled; enlivened by shampoo and sunlight. Bright, iridescent bubbles ran from her face and sped away with the current.

'I could fall asleep,' she said softly, and without him knowing studied his face through half-closed eyelids. Reaching for his hand, she drew his fingers to the topmost button of her shirt.

'I want you to make love to me.'

'In the river?'

'In the river. Right now. The way we used to.'

With her free hand she drew his head down; her kiss was savagely urgent.

'Quickly,' she breathed huskily and drove the tip of her tongue deep inside his mouth. With one hand on the riverbed for support, he rolled to face her. She helped him with the buttons and with her shirt opened to the waist, urged his head lower.

Her nipples, excited by the river coming over them, were now hard and dark as wild rosehip; covering one with his mouth he gently took the tip between his teeth.

'Oh God, Lee – yes there; don't you dare stop. It's been so long, my darling.' She reached out for his chest and with finger and thumb, tugged out his own small nipple until it hardened berry-like from his arousal. Karen heard him curse the fastenings of his khaki bush shorts and pushed his hands aside.

'Let me do it!'

'You've done this before,' he teased and traced the line of her throat with his tongue.

'Not often enough – something you'll have to think about, mister.' She grinned back at him. 'Best you get on with it before our bearded friend down here changes his mind and goes back to sleep.'

Carefully, he found footholds on the riverbed and with extended arms raised himself directly over her. Hot sun burned his back and buttocks, and when he edged between her legs the water rushed about him, sensuous and strangely invigorating.

For long seconds he stayed there, motionless, just the tip of him brushing the inside of Karen's thigh. Through narrowed eyes Karen glowered up at him.

'What are you waiting for?'

Lee twisted his face to the sky.

'Listen.'

Karen froze – shampoo running down her face.

'What's wrong?'

'Engine noise – light aircraft.'

Her eagerness dissipated; in its place, as some spiteful creature, a wave of apprehension skittered along her spine.

'What is it?'

'Don't know yet; fixed-wing job – single engine.'

'Shit and bugger, bugger.' Karen cursed the disruption and pushed herself upright; hurriedly she re-buttoned her clothes.

Lee zipped up his shorts and grabbed his rifle. 'Hurry up. Could be a reconnaissance plane. Help me pull the Zodiac into the reeds before they see us.'

Karen scrambled out from between the rocks; between them they managed to drag the heavy Zodiac round to where the reeds stood twelve feet high above the water. Bowed by the wind, as a lattice work of natural camouflage, a thick curtain of green stems wrapped itself around the inflatable.

'Keep still,' Lee warned and together they crouched down and watched the horizon for that tell-tale crucifix shape of the light aircraft.

They did not have long to wait; from the west, low to the horizon, a small two-seater Cessna stood out against the blue sky. Liveried with that familiar, yellow Zimbabwe bird air force insignia, it bore down on their hiding place.

Through a gap in the reeds, Lee glimpsed the pilot's face. Now almost down at treetop level the Cessna altered course and hugged the river line; it soon disappeared – the urgent drum of its engine slacked to a soft drone.

'Got to be us they're looking for,' Lee cursed and checked the time on his watch. 'Two hours of daylight

84

left. We'll stay here till dark then drift with the moonlight, by that time our nosey friend up there will be back at Buffalo Range.'

'David must have told them,' Karen realised. 'Oh my God, Lee, what if they've hurt him?'

He had hoped for more time before Pasviri found out what they were up to. David would have done his best to hold them off, but Lee knew firsthand what Mugabe's men were capable of. From here on, it would be an all-out race for the estuary.

The river had started to take on more colour. Fine silt, that uppermost covering of loose earth had been swept from far hillsides and stirred in with the run-off. Those who had experienced it before would recognise subtle changes in the river's temperament. Lee looked over his shoulder, back towards the north-west.

'Now would be as good a time as any for a two foot rise in the water level.'

The sky above the far horizon was now the colour of burnt iron. On the breeze, though the storms were still many miles away, Lee found what he was looking for. The air had moistened, that parched, tail-end of the dry season was over. He climbed back in the inflatable and from the equipment stacked in the Zodiac, dug out an ex-army A63 radio.

'Let's see if we can listen in on our pilot friend.' He freed the aerial from its canvas sleeve in the rucksack, powered up and saw the radio's battery indicator swing to 'full'. In turn, he started searching through each of the twenty-four VHF channels. At first, the only sounds from the telehand were those generated by static interference. Karen looked on, an ear cocked for the returning Cessna. The voice, when it came through was gin-clear, uncluttered by incumbent radio procedure, a direct one to one conversation between the pilot and control tower at Buffalo Range.

'So far I have seen nothing of them, comrade minister.'

'They have to be there!' Irritated by the pilot's failure, Julius Pasviri's voice barked from the handset. 'You idiot, Goddard is hiding from you. Where are you now?'

'Directly above the bridge at Ponte Sobre, comrade minister.'

'The north side of the bridge – there's an airstrip – can you see it?'

A tense moment of silence, then an acknowledgement.

'I see it, comrade minister.'

'Land your aircraft and await further instructions.'

'What about clearance, sir?'

'I said land your plane, lieutenant. Mozambique authorities already know that you're there. I have spoken with their military, should anyone question the reasoning behind your appearance you will complain of instrument failure and confirm my personal contact with our technicians in Harare. Tell them that at our earliest opportunity our repair crew will be with you; at the latest by midday tomorrow.'

-18-

Propelled by strengthening currents they drifted far out from dry land; taking in turn a half hour of precious sleep whenever the opportunity presented itself. Lee was thankful of the river's gradual drop in altitude and for its bed of soft, forgiving sand that sometimes brushed against the Zodiac's hull. Every hour, more miles were put behind them, precious fuel saved by their drifting with the current. Doused in moonlight the river showed up as a great meandering highway; everything protruding above its surface was marked indelibly – jammed logs from that last year's floodwaters, mid-stream reed beds and humpbacked sandbanks, all were sharply outlined, black as pit coal. With continued vigilance and by using the Zodiac's paddles for steerage, they kept the inflatable well inside the safer, central channel.

Because of the clean air, any noise, natural or otherwise carried over vast distances. From villages more than a day's walk away, sharp sounds, the crack of an axe to firewood or the shout of a mother chastising her child, all of them were to Lee and Karen, but a stone's throw back from the riverbank.

'Are you awake?' Gently, he touched Karen's shoulder. 'The river's coming up fast. I need an extra pair of eyes.'

Karen forced herself to sit upright; with her back pressed to the Zodiac's side she stretched out her legs to ease the pain from cramped calf muscles. Now the current was stronger, deeper and more vibrant where the channel narrowed, pushing the Zodiac with greater urgency.

'How far do you think we are from the bridge?'

'Not sure,' said Lee, 'five, maybe ten miles – hard to tell.'

As he spoke, the Zodiac swung out wide from a tight, right hand bend in the river; pinpricks of bright artificial light appeared through the trees and reed beds. 'There's your answer, my sweetheart; more lights than the Thames embankment. Looks like Pasviri has organised a Welcome to Mozambique committee in our honour.'

Karen rolled onto her feet, holding tightly to the forward mooring rope and with feet apart she balanced her weight like that of a water-skier. She measured their speed against the distance to the bridge.

'Half an hour at the outside. Don your thinking cap, Goddard, we're running out of time.'

'We have no choice. With that amount of light they'll see us coming a mile out from the bridge. We'll never make it through.' He felt for the binoculars and soon the harsh reality of what was waiting for them showed as urgent, floodlit images along the entire span of Ponte Sobre. 'The whole bridge is crawling with troops – light machine gun emplacements and another thirty or so men armed with rifles. Pasviri's upped his game plan; he has no intention of letting us slip past without him knowing.'

'We're too close in to use the motor,' said Karen.

Lee dropped the binoculars and reached for the outboard motor, he disengaged the latching mechanism and tilted it clear of the water. With the propeller lifted above the surface, fifteen inches was all that the Zodiac needed to keep her hull clear of the bottom.

'Grab a paddle and go for all your worth at our starboard-side. Once we get closer in to the left bank I'll use the anchor rope to swing us in to the shallows.'

Gradually, more by luck and conflicting surface eddies, the Zodiac was swept in closer to the northern side of the river. Urgent activity clattered back from the bridge. The river was picking up speed. Driven by heavy rains about its source it hissed between the sandbanks; some it covered quickly, those more stubborn were slowly being eaten away by rising floodwater.

'Over there.' Lee pointed to where the moonlight lit up gaps between half submerged vegetation. 'The lowest parts of the bank – through that break in the trees.'

Skeletal fingers of white tungsten light groped upstream from the bridge; illuminating islands and sandbanks they skimmed the river's surface for shapes or movement at odds with that natural stretch of water.

'He knows we're carrying gold,' hissed Karen.'

'And he will never get his hands on it,' Lee growled. 'By this time tomorrow, Comrade Pasviri and company will be left with egg on their faces.'

Lee waited for the distance between them and dry land to narrow considerably before abandoning the paddle.

With his feet apart and sixty feet of loose rope coiled alongside him, he swung the three-pronged anchor in a widening circle about his head. Slowly he increased the momentum. Though made from tempered steel, the small, lightweight anchor had been designed solely for use in slack water; now with the full weight of his shoulders behind it, the improvised grappling hook hummed above his head.

'Stay down!' he warned Karen, and at the same time prayed that his voice had not carried to the soldiers on the bridge.

The hook shot out in a high parabola above the water; losing sight of it, Lee willed all twenty yards of ski-rope to pay out before a sudden jolt to his hands told him the line was fully extended. He braced his weight against the bulkhead and readied himself for the river's powerful sideways drag on the inflatable.

The anchor held and the Zodiac started a wide swinging arc for the riverbank. In the moonlight, Lee used his paddle to probe for the riverbed; within forty feet of the bank he struck sand. He slid over the side and with the water up to his thighs he waded for dry land.

'Be careful,' Karen called to him. Now in slack water, the Zodiac followed behind like a dog on a leash. Lee pulled it as close as he dared to the bank and lashed the rope to a partly submerged bush.

'Sit tight. I want to get a closer look at that bridge.'

Karen looked up apprehensively. 'Where are you going?'

'I won't be long,' he assured her and looked sideways to where the land sloped upwards from the riverbank. 'Top of that rise, I need a clear view of what's out there.' He leaned across and kissed her forehead. 'I'll be back before you know it, a chance for me to play soldiers again; it's been a long time.'

'Take the rifle,' Karen pleaded with him, but he shook his head and reached past her for the binoculars.

'Don't need it. If I get lost I'll whistle and you will have to talk me in.'

Before Karen had chance to reply he had disappeared amongst the shadows.

From higher ground, Lee had unrestricted views of the road in and out of Ponte Sobre. He checked his watch; four hours to sunrise. Thick cloud was coming in from the west, another hour and the moon would be gone, apart from Pasviri's illuminated blockade, the entire surrounding area would be thrown into complete darkness. He strained his ears for sound; other than the hubbub of soldiers equipping the bridge there was total silence.

The incoming track wove in and out of moonlit groves of scrub and malala palm; with his binoculars he traced the lie of the land to either side of it and soon found what he was looking for. High tension overhead power lines ran as parallel metallic threads in close conjunction to the eastern edge of the access road.

'That will be the main, eleven kilovolt electricity supply for the whole area,' Lee noted. 'Our comrade minister is using mains power. Big mistake, comrade – huge.'

Again, he listened for the throaty growl of diesel generators, giving his hearing time to adjust before committing himself.

'Definitely no generators,' Lee whispered, and smiled at Pasviri's folly. Behind him, lightning, though still some miles away, rumbled its way through growing banks of black cloud.

Rex Khumalo leaned with his elbows braced against the trestle table. He spoke with conviction, aware that others seated opposite were listening closely – assessing his loyalty.

'What makes you so sure Goddard won't turn back when he sees the lights?'

Pasviri smiled at the inference, then, from an oval mouth expelled a perfect smoke ring; above the table it hovered just inches from Rex's face.

'Either way, comrade, it does not matter.' In the light from a forty watt lamp his teeth were startlingly white – the pupils of his eyes black as the night outside the tent. He tapped the ash from his cigarette. 'As we speak, the river is rising. By tomorrow night the Rio Save will be in spate. Goddard's option for turning back has already been taken from him. He has neither the power nor the fuel for an upstream fight with a flooding river.'

He glanced outside the tent, a bank of heavy thunderheads gathered as monstrous hills to the western horizon.

'Major Thebisa here has men patrolling both sides of the river, downstream from Mahenya. Should Goddard choose to abandon his subversive act of anti-government entrepreneurialism and return on foot, he will be quickly apprehended and taken to Buffalo Range.' He paused for effect and watched for their appreciation.

'He could have already made it through and be thirty miles downstream by now?' Rex countered.

Pasviri shook his head. 'Highly unlikely. He would have been seen. Only a suicidal fool would risk using an outboard motor.'

'Do not underestimate him, Goddard is nobody's fool.

He's a risk taker.'

'And a desperate man,' Major Thebisa cut in. 'Goddard will not turn back, comrade. Nor will he risk losing his boat to a flooding river.'

Pasviri lit another cigarette.

'So we are all in agreement. The Empress Mine's managing director is, as we speak, committed to reaching and passing beyond our bridge defences. He has therefore left the country without proper authorisation and with his boat loaded with what I suspect to be a sizeable, illegal exportation of gold bullion. Mister Goddard, gentlemen, is determined to rendezvous with his accomplice, Gerard Brownlee. I would hazard a guess at their meeting place as somewhere near to where the Rio Save reaches the ocean.'

'A stab in the dark,' said Rex, 'how could you know this?'

Pasviri scowled at the unwanted variance. 'For what other reason would he risk imprisonment and the total loss of his assets?'

'He may well be still be in Zimbabwe – is it not possible that we have misjudged him?'

'No more than our expecting Ian Smith to return as Prime Minister, Comrade Khumalo.' Both Thebisa and Pasviri laughed at Rex's implications. 'No, my friend, Gerard Brownlee left Maputo harbour several days ago at the helm of Goddard's cherished, ocean-going, *Isabella*.' He had seized the upper hand; from the look on Thebisa's face he knew they were both in agreement. 'The boat is kitted out with long range tanks and VHF radio. We must therefore also assume that Goddard has the ability make radio contact with his associates, though I have been informed by my own communications people that until he is within a range of thirty miles or so this will not be possible.'

'How much gold do you suppose he is carrying?' Thebisa asked.

Pasviri shrugged his shoulders. Light from the single incandescent lamp fluttered momentarily; thunder rolled through the smoke-filled ops tent as if to underline the magnitude of what he was about to say. He smiled thinly, relishing the attention.

'My estimations are upwards of a million American dollars. Our colonial friends would not risk being caught for anything less.'

'Straight to the Party coffers?' smiled Thebisa.

'But of course, major. Where else would I have in mind?'

'And what about Goddard and his woman?' Rex asked, but already he knew the answer to that.

'Flooding rivers are fraught with danger, comrade.' Another perfectly formed ring of grey smoke crossed the space between them. Pasviri watched it break into wisps; again the light faltered then steadied. 'The river is deep, my friend – the currents powerful. Goddard should have known better. A wiser man would have heeded my warning.'

-20-

Lee found his way back to the Zodiac easily enough. However, within that last hour the river had risen high enough for it to reach above his waist when he waded out to Karen. The main channel, swollen with fresh run-off had started to clutter with debris, though not as yet with those dangerous, half submerged trees and hull-ripping logs of the imminent peak floodwater. Lee pulled himself back aboard the inflatable.

'We haven't much time. Three hours of dark and we're

going to need every minute of it.'

'And there's the mother of all storms coming,' added Karen. 'Did you find what you were looking for?'

Lee nodded his head. 'We at least have a chance; as long as I can make it back before the river really gets moving.' He pointed to the outboard motor. 'The security chain – unhook it both ends, I need to take it with me.'

Karen unclipped the three metre length of lightweight steel chain and looped it into a loose coil for ease of carrying. She tried her utmost to remain calm and make light of what he was doing.

'So what's the plan, Mister Bond?'

'Keep your eyes on the bridge.' Lee slung the chain over his shoulder, and slipped back over the side. 'Watch the lights. Twenty minutes after I convince our friends down there to switch them off, I'll be back. If the rain beats me to it, keep our equipment covered and pump water; we don't need excess weight.'

'Please be careful,' Karen pleaded and reached out to touch his arm. Only once more did she catch sight of him; a dark shadow moving low through the moonlight, then the wild silence of Mozambique engulfed the Zodiac and reluctantly, Karen settled down to wait.

At a fast walk Lee took all of fifteen minutes to reach the north south gravel highway. He avoided the open road, making his way instead along a latticework of goat trails running alongside it; periodically he paused to watch and listen.

The going was flat, the vegetation thinly grouped, at no one time did the aura of light surrounding the bridge disappear from view. Ten minutes later he found what he was looking for.

Highlighted by the moonlight, a second, high tension supply branched away from the main power line. At a sharp angle, the secondary, small gauge conductors ran

94

as silver lines straight for the Ponte Sobre Bridge.

'Time for some fun,' Lee whispered, and then using what shadows there were, followed the smaller branch line away from the road.

A hundred yards out from the junction he recognised the shapes of three, fused, isolator links. Silhouetted against the sky, the D-links were mounted horizontally below their respective main line insulators. A small pole-mounted transformer hummed compliantly in step with the power demands of Pasviri's bridge lighting.

'It's now or never, Goddard.' Lee uncoiled the steel chain from his shoulder. First clouds; storm forerunners, started to eat at the moonlight. At less than ten metres from the line, Lee focused his aim on three high tension dropper wires linking the fused D-links with the high voltage terminals on the transformer. In the stilled air the whirling chain made an eerie sound.

'Fly straight, my beauty,' Lee prayed for his aim to be true, then loosed his grip on the chain and watched it cartwheel upwards through the moonlight.

Though protected by low amperage fuses, the sudden surge of current from short circuiting two of the eleven kilovolt lines blew the chain into a hundred molten pieces. Belatedly, Lee covered his eyes from the flash and the noise from it was that of a high-powered rifle crashing in at his eardrums. He looked away to his right; where once he had seen a bridge bathed in brilliant white light, now there was only darkness.

'Time you weren't here, laddie.'

His return bearing was along a direct line with the three bright stars of Orion's Belt; at a fast jog he set off for where he had moored the Zodiac. From the bridge, the shouts from cursing NCO's and other chaotic clamouring of human confusion followed after him. Diesel engines turned and fired. The soldiers were using their vehicles' head lights in a desperate attempt to reilluminate the river, but compared to mains-powered floodlights, the effects were pitiful.

Lee guessed the distance between him and the Zodiac at a little over one kilometre. Raindrops soaked through his shirt and directly above him dark impatient clouds were rolling back the moonlight. The earth gave off its smells of mud and Africa and some ten or so miles away lightning jumped the gaps between sky and rocky kopjes. He turned on the speed, exhilarated by his success and the increasing beat of warm rain.

Crouched amongst their equipment, with the precious A63 radio and Lee's rifle closest to her, Karen pulled a waterproof canvas sheet over as much of the Zodiac's cargo as she could manage, then closed her eyes and braced herself for those first, closing growls of wild thunder.

Lightening illuminated the river and within minutes, Lee was back in the water. Urgently, he wielded the knife like it was a small machete, hacking away lighter, younger growth from bushes on the riverbank. After a third trip, loaded with reeds and saplings, the Zodiac appeared more as a floating raft of flood debris than a man-made rubber inflatable. He handed over one last bundle of thick camouflage then pulled himself back on board. The storm was close now, the moonlight was fading, ten more minutes and navigating the main channel would prove almost impossible; they would be forced to rely on chance to take the inflatable between the bridge's massive concrete stanchions.

'You ready for this?'

Karen nodded her head. 'As I'll ever be. What about the anchor?'

'Already cut the rope,' he told her. 'Couldn't free it – stuck fast.' Lee picked up a paddle then pushed the Zodiac away from its mooring. 'Once the current takes a hold there'll be no turning back, not even if we use the motor.'

'I love you,' said Karen, 'just in case it all goes wrong.'

'It won't.' He leaned over and kissed her cheek. 'We're going shopping in Maputo, sweetheart and Pasviri won't be coming with us.' Lee hooked his paddle deep inside the water and soon felt the powerful pull of rising floodwater draw them away from the bank.

-21-

Standing beneath the canvas awning, Comrade Julius Pasviri focused all his anger on the darkness outside, and though the thunder rolled and crashed above his head he resisted the natural urge to move further back inside the tent. He gestured to Major Thebisa.

'Where is your Land Rover?'

'Behind the tent, comrade minister.'

'Bring it around; we're going down to the bridge. Goddard is close, I can sense his cunning, now is the time he will take his chances. The dark will flush him out from his hiding place.' He smiled thinly. 'When it does, I want to be there on the bridge to welcome him.' He flicked his cigarette stub at the dark and saw it die, then looked back over his shoulder. Backlight from a standby hurricane lamp picked Rex out from the shadows. 'If this power cut is Goddard's doing, he will be made to pay, comrade. I do not like being made a fool of – especially by some settler colonist.'

Thebisa disappeared around the side of the tent and within that same minute, returned at the wheel of a buff-coloured military Land Rover, he pulled up close to where Pasviri waited.

Pasviri held the door and gestured to Rex.

'Get in. I want you to see the look on Goddard's face when we drag him from the water.'

-22-

Minutes away from reaching the bridge, Lee did his best to estimate their rate of drift and the strengthening, sideways swing of the main current. Ponte Sobre stood as a modern-day giant above the Save River. Six steel suspension towers rose vertically from their concrete support stanchions, thick steel cables drooped from one tower to the next and from them to the bridge itself hung a web of smaller, high tensile steel suspension ropes.

From the north bank, projected outwards by Land Rover headlamps, beams of light criss-crossed the river's surface; light from the moon was slowly being overpowered by a fifty mile rolling redoubt of storm clouds. Lee made final adjustments to the inflatable's camouflage, making certain that nothing abnormal stood out from amongst the leaves. The deception had to work. To those on the bridge the Zodiac had to appear as natural flood debris – a raft of flotsam swept from submerging islands.

'Stay down,' he told Karen. 'Another five minutes and we'll be right under their noses.'

'I'm frightened,' said Karen, and was glad when Lee crouched down beside her. Leaves covered their heads, leaving only a small opening through which they could watch the bridge. Lee hooked his arm around Karen's waist and, holding her close, tried his best to control her trembling.

Rain flailed the river's surface and leapt angrily from the Zodiac's canvas buck sail. Lee peered out through a gap in the camouflage, his line of sight to just above the rubber prow; momentarily, the bridge had disappeared, swallowed by the storm. However, from within that frantic drumming of rain and thunder, Lee picked out the vague clamour of men's voices; those of higher authority screaming orders to their subordinates. Then, as if the Zodiac had found a corridor between the squalls, the rain lessened enough for Lee to glimpse the confusion now sweeping the full length of the bridge. Karen lifted her head and for the first time realised the immensity of the structure their tiny craft was bearing down on.

Powerful beams of bright tungsten light panned back and forth across the surface of the river.

'They'll see us, Lee!' Karen felt that first rush of wild panic. 'For the love of God we'll never make it.' She looked up at the sky and willed the storm to shut them off from the bridge. 'Come on rain, damn you to hell we're sticking out like a sore thumb.'

Fingers of white light closed about the camouflaged inflatable. On the bridge, Major Thebisa's radio sprang into life. Purely through chance, a soldier had picked out an unnatural shape from the murk.

'I have found something, comrade major, but I am not sure.'

'Description and position?' Thebisa snapped.

'Two, maybe three hundred yards – close to the north bank. I am holding my light on it.'

Thebisa reached out and quickly selected a switch on the dashboard. From the Land Rover's roof-mounted spotlight, powerful white light shot through the darkness. Thebisa manipulated the lamp from inside the cab and swung the beam directly onto the flotsam.

'Debris,' growled Thebisa. 'Rubbish washed in from the riverbank; you have wasted my time.' Then, seconds before his fingers again found the switch he caught the faintest glimmer of bright silver. 'Wait! Hold your lamp steady, there's something there.'

Steadying the spotlight, Thebisa tracked the supposed island of broken vegetation into those last one hundred yards of wild water; here the current swung wide and fast for a way between the stanchions.

'They've seen us,' Lee warned and braced himself for the boom of a loudhailer.

Light breached the Zodiac's outer camouflage. Karen held her breath; terrified of being raked by gunfire she steeled herself and dropped in low behind the port-side bulkhead. She closed her eyes, but the nightmare persisted. Voices screamed at them from the bridge; a second spotlight locked on to the inflatable and the metallic clatter of weapons being cocked and loaded forced her down against the flooring. Now, like a wild rodeo bronco the Zodiac reared and plunged, gripped by the full force of the flood.

'Only another fifty yards!' Lee shouted. 'Keep your head down, there's nothing they can do now.'

'We know you are there!'

Lee recognised Pasviri's falsetto voice screeching out from the bullhorn.

'Bring your boat to the side or I will give the order to open fire!'

'Trust me, he's bluffing! He won't do it!'

Karen opened her eyes; every available lamp had been turned on them. They were helpless; at the mercy of pure chance, their efforts trashed – escaping prisoners caught in the harsh glare of perimeter searchlights. The Zodiac was picking up speed; parted from the main stream by a massive concrete stanchion, the channel swung the inflatable hard over. Like a toboggan gripped by those violent twists and turns of the Cresta Run, the inflatable gave in to the enormity of force driving it forwards. Now, totally out of control, spinning and bucking it shot below the bridge. For a moment, total dark swept over them, and then once again the lights were there, tracking the Zodiac's course as it sped away from Ponte Sobre.

The first shots were sporadic; a half-hearted warning for them to pull the Zodiac into the bank – then Pasviri pushed aside a young machine-gunner and took his place at the bridge railing. Leaning into the weapon he sighted along the barrel and squeezed the trigger.

Seconds before the sound of gunfire reached them, Lee recognised the flash tempo of the RPD light machine gun. He pulled Karen down against the floor of the inflatable and shielded her with his body.

Mesmerised by incoming blips of phosphorescent light, Lee braced himself for that first, fatal slap from a high velocity bullet. It was then that the fear of being hit left him. The gunner was guessing. His shooting was that of an untrained amateur, his aim erratic and indecisive. Tracer raked the sky, but far out to their left and more than a hundred feet above the surface of the river.

Within that same minute the gun fell silent and as quickly as the rain had eased off, so it came back. This time, with renewed vengeance the tropical deluge completely blanketed the bridge.

'It's over! We're through – they can't see us!' Lee whooped above the noise of rain. Ahead, the sky had cleared, the change was almost magical; dry air and moonlight covered the river.

Karen raised herself on one elbow and peered above the level of the Zodiac's stern. A quarter mile to their rear and faintly edged in moonlight, the rain appeared as an ominous black wall. Spellbound, she watched the storm swing back on the bridge. With a vindictive smile on her lips she willed the lightning on to the steelwork and through her mind's eye imagined the chaos it might inflict.

Lee cleared the Zodiac of her redundant camouflage, then unlatched the outboard and lowered the propeller back beneath the water.

'Not quite sure how, but we're past Ponte Sobre, alive and still in one piece.' He looked at Karen and grinned like an errant schoolboy. 'Are you okay?'

She nodded her head. 'Semi-paralysed with fear, but no blood. No thanks to my husband, though. You almost got us killed.'

'But we made it,' he countered, 'and for now we're in the clear.'

He looked eastwards; their speed had eased, but they were drifting blind, at the mercy of the currents. Using what little moonlight was left, thankfully he was able gauge the inflatable's position as central to the river. He glanced at the luminous dial on his watch. 'Half an hour at the outside before the sun comes up; as soon as it's light, Pasviri will have his helicopters on our tail. Twenty minutes flying time from Ponte Sobre and they'll be up with us.'

'So what do we do?'

'Carry on as we are,' Lee said, 'at least until daylight, then we'll fire up the outboard and find somewhere to hole up. We can use the time to make contact with Gerard and grab something to eat; laying low for a few hours might throw Pasviri's bloodhounds off our scent – at least for a while. Keep a paddle handy and look out for logs and sandbanks; yell if you see anything.'

The river was spreading, bursting from its banks to form smaller channels across the flood plains. On slightly higher ground the forest stood thick and lush, its growth encouraged by the permanently high water table. From the air and closer in to the Indian Ocean, the Save's delta would now show up as a silver, many-fingered hand, fanning outwards to a seasonal width of more than fifty miles where it broached the coastal lowlands.

Almost engulfed by deepening floodwater, only the larger sandbanks now stood out above the surface, creating treacherous narrows either side of the main stream. By using their paddles as makeshift rudders, with some trepidation, Lee and Karen were able to hold the Zodiac to the widest part of the river.

'How much further before we reach Gerard?' Karen asked, her voice fraught with exhaustion.

'If he's made it to the estuary – about thirty miles. We could be aboard *Isabella* before nightfall; that's if Pasviri doesn't find us first.'

The sky started to colour. The current had slacked off and now the river seemed content enough to glide sedately above a wide bed of smooth sand. Karen took advantage of the temporary calm and on a small gas cooker, boiled up water for coffee – sweet and strong and laced with red rum. Lee nurtured a filled enamel mug and carefully drew out a dry cigarette from a plastic bag inside his pocket. Shattered from lack of sleep he leaned back against the engine transom and for a few luxurious minutes, through gritty eyes watched the dawn break.

'Wake up.' Karen shook his arm. 'Time for us to get a wriggle on, mister.' She prised the empty mug from his fingers and swilled it with river water. 'We need a place to lay-up and something to eat.'

Lee shook himself fully awake.

'Damn it, I fell asleep.'

'I know, you were snoring your head off.'

'My cigarette?'

'Over the side,' she told him. 'Start the outboard we need to get a move on.'

Lee primed the carburettor and soon had the Yamaha running smoothly. He climbed back behind the wheel and pushed on the throttle lever. The Zodiac surged ahead of the current. Lee cupped his hand over the side and splashed his face with cool water.

'Keep your eyes peeled. Find somewhere safe for a couple of hour's kip.'

'We're too late.' Karen called out and pointed skyward. 'And he's seen us!'

Aided by light from a dozen Land Rovers, the pilot had uplifted from the bridge airstrip whilst it was still dark; a full half hour before the earliest signs of dawn were apparent to anyone on the ground. Following the river downstream soon brought the single engine reconnaissance plane directly onto the Zodiac. The aircraft came in low enough for Lee to make out a look of effusive triumph on the pilot's face.

'He's calling in the wolves,' Lee hissed.

'The swine's laughing at us,' Karen added, and out of frustration shook her fist at him.

On his next pass the pilot brought the Cessna in lower than the bank-side treetops; so close to the Zodiac that Karen lost her footing and fell over backwards. Her head cracked against the outboard's fuel tank.

'Are you alright!' Lee called out to her; unable to leave the wheel he gunned the Zodiac diagonally across the current. Karen pushed herself upright and felt for the injury. The damage was minimal. A smear of bright blood stained her fingertips.

'I'm okay, Lee. Keep going, the swine almost had me in the river.'

'He's coming back – stay down and hang on.'

Lee saw the aircraft turn and then straighten out; again, the plane was dangerously low to the river.

'Son of a bitch is using his wheels as a weapon!'

Lee opened the throttle and swung in close to as he dared to a bed of tall reeds. Once alongside, he jerked the steering hard over, turning the craft's prow upstream he throttled back and held the inflatable into the current.

'He's crazy!' Karen yelled. 'What in hell's name is he doing!'

'Keep your head down.' He abandoned his seat and gestured to Karen. 'Stay focused. Take the wheel from me.'

Lee reached beneath the canvas buck sail for the gun bag; he ran back the zip and dragged out his FN rifle. Standing fully upright, he splayed his feet for balance and faced the incoming aircraft head-on. He brandished the rifle at arm's length above his head and animatedly, he cursed the pilot.

'You want to play rough? Let's see how big your balls are, buster!' He made sure the pilot saw him pull back the weapon's cocking lever.

The pilot's reaction was immediate. The unarmed Cessna yawed violently from side to side as the pilot over-corrected.

Now less than thirty yards from the Zodiac, the roar of the aircraft's engine drowned out Lee's cursing. A split second after the aircraft flashed passed they heard the impact.

Flushed from their roost in deep foliage, flocks of white egrets rose cloud-like above the river. Like a hunting shark through spiralling shoals of sardines, the Cessna bored head-on into the melee. Panicked by his sudden loss of control the pilot fought desperately to pull up the nose, but with her propeller badly damaged and now out of balance, the engine was already shaking violently in its mountings. The pilot was flying blind; the aircraft's Perspex windshield thickly flowered with blood and feathers.

Like a migratory bird sapped of its stamina by ocean headwinds, the Cessna's will to stay aloft gave out and she dropped her nose to below that critical point of the horizontal.

'He's going in!' Karen marvelled, mesmerised by the inevitable death of another human being.

For a moment, the aircraft appeared to make one last, feeble attempt to climb out, then, yawing sideways, her starboard wing tip touched the water. The plane cartwheeled through banks of tall reeds before it was dragged down and flung into the central channel by the force of its own momentum.

'Scratch one spy-in-the-sky,' Lee said dispassionately and handed his rifle to Karen before taking back control of the Zodiac's wheel.

Sickened by what had happened, Karen shuffled sideways and slumped with her back to the port-side bulkhead; unable to tear her eyes away from where the spotter plain had gone under. Only the Cessna's tail section showed above the surface, then, like some stricken animal it twisted and shuddered as the river forced its way inside the fuselage.

Filled with water and now in the grip of powerful currents, as some contrived, theatrical prop from an old movie, the Cessna lifted her tail skyward; momentarily it hovered there before slipping below the surface.

'That was horrific,' Karen gasped.

'Could have been us,' Lee countered, 'don't let it get to you; the bastard wanted us on the bottom. Screw him, along with the perverse bastards who sent him.'

'They aren't going to give up, Lee.'

'Nothing's changed,' he said. 'A lot depends on whether or not our submariner friend out there radioed our position back to the bridge.' He pushed the throttle lever full over. 'Hold tight – we have to find a place to lay-up before Pasviri's boys catch up with us.'

23

Julius Pasviri snatched the telehand away from the radio operator; his eyes were red and glassed over from lack of sleep. He screamed into the mouthpiece, focussing all of his frustration on the Cessna's pilot. Spittle flew from his lips.

'Damn you, lieutenant – I say again, give me your position!'

'I cannot see, comrade minister! They have killed me!'

Pasviri's fingers tightened around the telehand.

'Calm down you fool! How far from the bridge are you now?' He glared at the radio. 'Answer me, lieutenant – give me your position.'

The radio operator shook his head.

'We have lost contact with the pilot, comrade minister.'

Pasviri threw down the telehand in disgust. He beckoned to Rex and stepped outside the ops tent. Unlike the previous day the sky was clear and blue from horizon to horizon.

'Goddard is obviously armed; he has brought down our reconnaissance aircraft.'

'We have no proof of that.'

'Then who else could it be?' Pasviri shrilled. 'You heard the pilot. The plane is down.' He glowered at Rex. 'What is it with you, comrade? Always, you seem overly keen to protect this Goddard fellow?'

'I have my reasons. Goddard is worth more to me alive. His knowledge of the Empress Deep is a most valuable asset, comrade. It would not be to our advantage if he were killed.'

Pasviri clamped a cigarette between his teeth. 'The man is now our enemy and will expect to be treated as such. He mocks me comrade, but I will find him, that I promise you. Our resources are many, other than luck and his woman, Goddard has nothing.'

'There are many ways to win the co-operation of an enemy,' Rex pointed out, 'all men are cursed with a weakness, comrade. It is simply a matter of finding that weakness.'

Pasviri re-opened the cigarette packet and held it out. Rex accepted the peace offering.

'Keep him alive, that way you gain his expertise as well as his gold. The Empress Deep is like a woman, treat her gently and she will give you all that your heart desires.'

Pasviri smiled at the metaphor; like rain on cut coal his eyes glittered. His anger dissipated, replaced by wanton greed.

'How much gold do you think he is carrying?'

Rex relaxed. Pasviri's thoughts had been steered away from killing. Keeping Lee and Karen alive was no longer the impossibility he had feared.

'A million – maybe two. However, compared to what still lies hidden inside the Empress Deep, it is but an insignificant amount – a mere sample of what the mine is worth.'

'Of course, comrade. Obviously our interests are mutually interwoven and I commend you for your insight. Now that we are looking at things from the same window, perhaps we can work together more as a single entity for the benefit of the greater good. With you and Goddard running the Empress Deep, not a single ounce of gold will pass through its gates without me knowing.' He turned on his heels and looked Rex straight in the eye. 'And those I can trust, Comrade Khumalo, will be more than adequately compensated for their efforts.' He blew the ash from his cigarette. 'But first we must find our man; before he reaches his precious *Isabella* and disappears.'

24

Diego Siqueiros brought his binoculars into fine focus. Leaning against the ruined trunk of an old malala palm he guessed the distance between where he was standing and the crash site. His skin was the colour of old leather, that of the Mozambique half-caste or the Malacca pirate, tainted more by genetic descent than the harsh effects of haranguing sunlight. He was dressed in the tiger-striped combat denims of the Renamo guerrilla, and even during the colder, July days of mid-winter, his upper torso was left open to the elements.

Forced to adapt to a nomadic lifestyle, his body stayed wiry and sleek, that of a man who might run for days without the need for food or rest. Across his right shoulder looped the carrying strap of a Kalashnikov rifle and at his waist, the sharp metallic lines of a Tokarev pistol stood out from behind his belt. Drawn tightly back from his forehead and cinched at the nape by a leather cord, a thick scalp lock of dark hair reached almost to his waist – blue-black, like the mane of a king lion.

Women found themselves entranced, sexually enraptured even by that granite-like solidity of muscle. Shielded by the half-dark of a draped room, to the whore's fingers his face would appear as having been scarred perhaps by the bursting of a shell or some chance ricochet, for in the dimness of a single, lighted candle, the healed cicatrises of some dreaded pox were barely noticeable.

Crouched alongside Siqueiros, a man with shoulders almost equal in width to those of the bull buffalo cupped his hand against the sunlight, with the naked eye he struggled to pick out meaningful shapes from between the reed beds.

'The woman, Diego, describe her to me.'

Siqueiros chuckled at the Shangaan's preference for white women.

'Patience, Roberto. Always you think with your balls instead of your brains.'

'*Por favor*, my friend – it has been a long time – tell me what she is like, Diego.'

Siqueiros tore the gold filter from a Russian Sobranie and clamped the remains between his teeth. This time he focused entirely on the woman; the sun shone directly into her face and because of the compressing effects of wind to her front, her breasts showed up as some veiled, erotic artwork upon the fabric of her shirt.

'Her hair is yellow, Roberto – like sunlight,'

'Her face, Diego? That of an angel, or the death mask of some Maputo whore?'

'An angel, my friend. As magnificent as those inside that crazy head of yours.'

Roberto shuffled against his heels; across his knees his arms hung like those of the silverback gorilla. His fingers were thick and calloused and where once there would have been square and powerful nails, now only quarter moons of gnawed cutis remained. He hooked his arm about the malala tree and pulled himself upright; the tree trembled under his weight. From a crude leather strap, Roberto's Kalashnikov hung as a child's toy to the wide bole of his sternum; the stock, aged and oiled with the sweat of its carrier was now the colour of wild honey, the barrel and working parts bright silver, worn to the raw metal by a thousand confrontations. With hungry eyes Roberto stared out across the swamplands.

The inflatable, having found a way through the shallows had reached the cover of overhanging trees on the left bank. Diego heard the engine die. He lowered the binoculars; only minutes earlier, like a hunting fish eagle a light aircraft had repeatedly swooped in low to

the river, harassing the white man and his woman.
Either they were fugitives from the law or were carrying
something precious enough for the pilot to have lost his
life for. Whatever the reasons, Diego was drawn to the
boat with the curiosity of a fox for the open hen coop.

'Time for us to move, Roberto. Gather the men
together; your angel is coming ashore.'

-25-

Close to the flooding river, the sand was warm and dry
beneath the trees. Here the bank edge was veiled in
greenery; reeds grew in lush redoubts along the
waterline, tunnelled through by hippo and wild pig.
Pulled hard into the bank, the Zodiac was almost
impossible to spot from the air. The adrenalin rush from
their encounter with a Zimbabwe spotter plain had
almost subsided; Karen struggled to push the incident
from her mind and as a means of forced distraction kept
herself busy. Rather than light a fire, again she used her
gas cooker to make coffee. The flame was clean – no
smoke.

'Eat what you can of the steak before it goes off,' she
told Lee. 'From here on in, baked beans and stale bread
– plenty of coffee though.'

Whilst they ate, Lee stripped and cleaned the FN
before sliding it back inside the canvas gun bag. He
scowled at the expectant irony of being hunted by what
were once his own gunships. He was the fugitive and
those he had once tracked and fought against were now
the hunters. Pasviri's men would soon be within striking
distance.

He rolled back the canvas sail that covered their
equipment. Even without direct sunlight the air alone

was hot enough to dry out their kit and any remaining storm water was soon pumped overboard. He dragged out the A63 radio, flipped up the aerial and switched on. He watched the power indicator needle swing to 'full' and then turned the channel selector to 'four' before depressing the transmit key on the telehand.

'Gerard, can you hear me? Come in, old-timer we need to know you're out there.'

Karen stared at the radio; her features drawn, with her best effort she willed the old man's voice from the earpiece. Lee tried again and encountered more of the same crackling interference.

'I need more height.' He turned off the radio to conserve battery life and looked about for a more favourable transmission point. He selected a young forty foot mahogany and shrugged on the radio pack. He nodded his head to Karen. 'Up there should do it. Keep an ear out for engine noise and stay out of sight.'

Once inside the lower branches the climb became easier. Karen monitored his progress until the foliage thickened and swallowed him up.

With his legs hooked to the topmost branches he was now head and shoulders clear of the leaves. From the natural platform and by the very nature of the surrounding terrain, Lee was able to look out above the land for thirty miles in any direction. To the west, a blue shadow of distant hills stood as a vague reminder to where he had come from, but to the east the land was flat, patched with green islands of palm and mangrove trees where the Rio Save's delta opened out to coastal flood plains.

'Gerard, are you there?' he felt exposed, perched on top of the tree he presented an easy target, but the extra height had increased the reach of his radio's transmission; the interference was less prolific. Again he tried to contact the *Isabella*.

'Talk to me, Gerard. Come in old-timer or I'll have Tendai feed you to the sharks.'

The radio spluttered to life. The incoming signal was strong; the sender was closer than Lee had estimated.

'Got you strength five old boy! Where in the blue blazes are you? Confirm you are both still in good order?'

'We're fine, pretty sure the authorities have tumbled to what we're up to, though.'

'Good God, old man that's not good. Are you able to give me your position, copied?'

'At a guess, no more than twenty miles from the *Isabella*. We should be up with you by tomorrow night.' He sensed Gerard's agitation. 'Not sure how these next twenty-four hours will pan out. Might get nasty so stay in close to the radio.'

'Got that. Will keep an ear out, old boy. What about fuel?'

'Enough,' said Lee. 'How's my boat holding up?'

'Absolute darling,' Gerard warbled, 'solid as a rock all the way from Maputo. Picked up a few extras from Jose, your marina man; thought they might come in handy if we run into bother.'

'Like what?'

'Just one or two oddments, old boy, nothing to worry about. One never knows when certain undesirables might show themselves. Give the blighters a damned good run for their money is what I always say. Jolly good price; good discount. Jose will buy them back when we're finished if they're still intact – sort of hired them from him.'

Nervously, Lee scanned the horizon. Like the Cessna, the helicopters would follow the river from Ponte Sobre; he sensed they were closing in.

'The river, Gerard, what is it like your end?'

'Rising, old chap. A day or so and I might well have

problems; have run out both our anchors. Suggest you and yours get a move on. Don't relish the thought of being caught out here at night when the river's in spate.'

'Will do our best,' said Lee. The carrier band stuttered; someone else was demanding access to that wavelength. 'Got to go, Gerard. Stay off your radio unless I call you.'

The incoming tone changed slightly and a different voice keened from the earpiece.

'Very resourceful of you, Mister Goddard, your breaching our blockade at the bridge was quite spectacular. However, Comrade Khumalo has assured me that you are a man I can reason with; I look forward to that opportunity. Twenty minutes at the most and we should be dropping in to discuss a matter of compensation. The gold you are carrying should at least cover the cost of a new aircraft. Do not retaliate, comrade, my men have been instructed to return fire. Resisting will only provoke them.'

Lee stifled a sudden urge to reply. Pasviri was drawing him out. He reached back over his shoulder and switched off the radio. The silence bated him. From the air the Zodiac would be difficult to find, but Pasviri was close, like a hawk he would be watching for Lee to break cover.

'We sit tight,' Lee whispered, 'let's see just how good you are at hide-and-seek, comrade.'

From the shadows, Karen's eyes showed up white and owl-like, thrown wide open by fear and the constant pressure of a plate-sized hand across her mouth. Her head was drawn backwards, the flesh about her throat pulled tight; it would take but a slight, downward thrust of Roberto's hand to work the blade and sever her head from her torso. Siqueiros smiled at the look of horror on Lee's face.

'My English is not too good, *senhor*, but it will not matter. Give your word that you will co-operate and I will tell my friend to release your woman.'

Lee's stomach tightened. 'Let her go – you have my word.'

Siqueiros glanced sideways at Roberto. Reluctantly, the Shangaan loosened his grip. Karen stumbled across to Lee and like a frightened child grabbed hold of his arm. The blade had punctured her skin; tiny droplets of blood beaded her throat.

'What do you want with us,' Lee growled; to be obsequious with men like these would earn him only contempt.

Siqueiros lowered his rifle, his focus turned to where Lee had moored the Zodiac.

'A small boat, *senhor*, for such a long journey? And the plane – the pilot, he gave up his life trying to stop you.'

'The pilot was a fool,' said Lee. 'Should have been more aware of what he was doing.'

Siqueiros smiled coldly. 'Then, as you say, he died as a fool, but that does not tell me why he was after you?'

Desperately, Lee cobbled together fictitious reasons for their being in Mozambique.

'We're both writers; the Rio Save was once used as a trade route between Sofala and the ancient gold mines

115

of Monomotapa. We are merely gathering information – taking photographs. Mugabe's ministers believe we are purposely trying to ridicule their claim to Zimbabwe's ancestral heritage. They insist the Shona people built the city of Zimbabwe.'

Siqueiros shook his head. 'And you do not?'

'It has never been proven,' said Lee.

Siqueiros' eyes narrowed. 'You are lying, *senhor*. A man's life and the loss of an aircraft? I do not think so.' He put up his rifle. 'There are things you are not telling me.'

Roberto became agitated; his acute sense of hearing had picked up on the faint rumble of aircraft engines. Siqueiros shouted instructions and within seconds, other than himself and Roberto none of his men were visible. All of them had disappeared into the forest. He turned to Lee.

'Your Shona friends have caught up with you. We will talk again. Stay out of sight until they have passed.'

The Alouettes were tracking the river line; three machines, low to the water. Through a gap in the trees, Lee monitored their movements; their flight paths altered. Now indecisive, kestrel-like they twisted and then hovered above a wide point in the river.

'They've found the plane,' Lee muttered. Karen stood alongside him, aware that Roberto was watching. Like some giant ape ready to pounce, he leered at her through the foliage.

Pasviri looked down at the wrecked aircraft. Brought back to the surface by trapped air, the tail section stood a metre proud of the water. The rest of the aircraft's forward fuselage was out of sight, lodged against the leeward side of a small island. He relayed his findings to Rex and Ephraim Thebisa.

'Our plane is lying directly below me. Goddard has to be close. We will carry on downstream, comrades. The first sign of anything unusual, no matter how insignificant it might seem, you will contact me immediately. Maintain vigilance, Goddard will be armed. You will open fire only in a retaliatory situation. Confirm both call signs copied that?'

Both commanders acknowledged his orders. Pasviri ordered his own pilot back on course; hungry for the final outcome, he guided the pilot through every hidden twist and turn in the riverbank. Since their first confrontation, many nights he had lain awake dreaming up ways to rid himself of the Empress Deep's managing director. Now he sensed that time was close, the consolidation of interests that Rex Khumalo had suggested had already been discarded as unimportant; he wanted nothing short of total control over the Empress Deep's gold output. Both Goddard and his woman would be taken out of the equation, their corpses left in unmarked graves or chopped to pieces and fed to the crocodiles. Either way, as mere statistics they would both be written off, a direct consequence of their own reckless venturing deep inside the bandit controlled, central province of Mozambique. The largest, most productive gold mine in Mashonaland would soon be his. With a wry smile on his lips, he refocused his attention on the job at hand; as a veteran of the bush war against Smith's elite fighters he acted now on that same, gut instinct, every reed-covered island or grove of trees was scrutinised for sign.

From his hide, Lee watched the helicopters fly in single file, breaking formation only when thick, riverine bush necessitated closer inspection. Here, the pilots flew in dangerously close, using the downwash from their rotors to force back the foliage. Many times, wild pig or a water buck broke cover; startled by the noise they crashed away inside the forest.

Crouched against his heels, Lee willed the helicopters

to fly wide of where he had moored the Zodiac. Karen cupped her hands over her ears; the roar of Artouste engines and drum of rotor blades reverberated through the foliage, smaller trees whipped and bent from the hurricane-like downdraft.

Working alone, Siqueiros shunned the cover of trees and stepped out into the open. Rested across his shoulder was the wooden wraparound heat shield of an RPG-7 launcher, a high explosive, rocket-propelled grenade already loaded into its muzzle.

'I see the boat!' The pilot shouted into his headset and for Thebisa's benefit swung the Alouette through ninety degrees. Thebisa now had an unrestricted view of the left bank.

Siqueiros flicked up the launcher's iron sights; aligning his eye he centred his point of aim to the helicopter's open doorway. With committed intent, slowly he squeezed the trigger.

Driven by the initial booster charge to a speed of three hundred and eighty feet per second, the rocket-propelled grenade leapt clear of the launch tube. The abrupt acceleration triggered the rocket's sustainer motor; trailing blue smoke, it made little of the one hundred and sixty yards separating Siqueiros from the Alouette.

Within those final seconds, having seen the rocket leap from its launch tube, the pilot slewed the chopper to starboard, but his reaction proved to be pathetically ineffectual and through his own floundering, brought the Alouette's tail section directly into line with the rocket's flight path.

The grenade detonated against the fuselage, less than half a metre from the aircraft's whirling rear rotor. Like a dog in pursuit of its own tail, the Alouette started to spin out of control. From the crippled rotor hub, black smoke poured through shrapnel holes in the tail section.

Terrier-like the entire tail rotor shook and snarled to be free of its smashed mountings.

'Pull back! Pull back!' Pasviri screamed through his headset, and from a distance looked on in horror as the Alouette cartwheeled into the riverbank; scything back the foliage before the turbine shuddered to a standstill. From behind the cockpit, Avgas pumped as a glittering spray from a foot-long gash in the fuel tank.

'Back off, she's leaking fuel!' Rex ordered his own pilot to keep clear.

The Alouette lay on its side with the open, starboard-side doorway fully submerged. Desperate to evacuate, Thebisa's men fought to exit the wreckage via the port-side doorway. Mercilessly, those too badly injured were used as stepping stones; driven by sheer panic, as savage dogs the soldiers fought each other for access to the remaining exit point.

With quiet determination, as though Siqueiros were enjoying the gentility of some Scottish grouse shoot, he handed the empty launcher to Roberto and took back his rifle. Still with that casual air of the weekend shooter, he chambered a round of phosphor-tipped tracer and sent it boring into the wreckage.

In those final, fateful seconds, Rex caught sight of Thebisa's face. Framed by the doorway, the Fifth Brigade major struggled for a hold on the now, horizontal fuselage stanchion and for a moment appeared as if he might haul himself clear of the wreckage. However, the pilot had just as quickly thrown off his harness and like some desperate, terrified animal had wrapped his arms about Thebisa's neck. Locked together, both men fell back inside the Alouette, just as the very air about the ruined fuselage was engulfed by a terrible inferno of white light; even the river's surface streaked with burning Avgas.

The Alouette, now the soldiers' pyre flamed out

brightly against the backdrop of the riverbank. None had escaped the firestorm. The inhuman sounds from their screaming lasted for what seemed to Karen as an eternity.

Siqueiros shouldered his rifle and moved back from the riverbank. He lit a cigarette and casually he watched the Alouette's dramatic ending from just inside the tree line. At his side, Roberto looked on impassively, watching men burn to death was to him, nothing out of the ordinary.

The breeze turned and carried with it the smell of burning flesh from across the river. Karen covered her face, but the insidious sickly stench of roasting pork was everywhere. On her knees, she retched into the undergrowth

'Go now.' Siqueiros shouted at Roberto. 'Take the men with you.' He swung the Kalashnikov onto Lee. 'Make ready the boat, *senhor*. Do as I say and you will not be harmed, deceive me and I will kill you both.'

'The other helicopters?' Lee questioned his decision to break cover. Two more fully armed Alouettes were still out there. This time they would fire on sight. There would be no chance of their surrendering.

Siqueiros shook his head; victoriously, his eyes glittered.

'They have pulled back. Like women, the Shona dogs are afraid to fight.' He spat the cheroot from his lips and nodded at Lee to uncover the Zodiac. Lee complied, at least they were alive. He helped Karen back on her feet and led her down to where they had moored the inflatable.

'Are you okay?'

She managed a weak smile. 'Where are they taking us?'

'Don't know. Just stay calm and concentrate on getting through this.' He shrugged off the radio's carrying straps and risked turning the channel selector switch away from channel four; his fingers itched for the chance to transmit and forewarn Gerard of what was happening. Siqueiros herded them onto the Zodiac, his rifle in line with Lee's stomach.

'Your woman will sit in the back with me *senhor*. You will drive the boat. Do exactly as I say or the pretty lady goes over the side.'

-27-

Julius Pasviri lashed out with the instep of his leather combat boot and sent Siqueiros' spent cartridge case spinning into the river. Cheated of his quarry he searched amongst his own men for an excuse on which to vent his rage.

'You!' Randomly he selected Rex's pilot. 'Why did you not come to Comrade Thebisa's aid?' He jerked a Tokarev pistol from his webbing belt and aimed directly between the pilot's eyes. 'You let him burn. What is your name, boy? What name will your mother call out when she lies awake and grieves for her son?'

'Ndhlovu, comrade minister. Flight Lieutenant Emerson Ndhlovu.'

'You are Matabele.'

The young pilot nodded. He was shaking. Sweat glittered below his hairline. Pasviri's eyes narrowed; titillated by the terror he had instilled in the young Matabele he prolonged the moment. Slowly, his anger abated.

'That I am forced to entrust my life to a Matabele pup unnerves me.' Reluctantly he lowered the pistol. 'Start your engine. We go back to the bridge for refuelling. You will be ready to follow up at first light.'

Rex intervened. 'Why not follow them now?'

Pasviri shook his head, still with his eyes fixed on the pilot.

'This baboon of a Matabele *mukumana* left the bridge with his fuel tank only three quarters filled. The loss of a helicopter to enemy firepower is bad enough, comrade. Losing a second to lack of fuel will see us both in front of a firing squad. The men who took your friends are bandits, nothing more, but like feral dogs they fight well and are many. Corner them with Alouettes and you will see the boat destroyed and sent to the bottom of the river, the gold along with it.' He lit a cigarette and smiled thinly at Rex. 'My apologies, Comrade Khumalo, I forgot that you are yourself a Matabele, take nothing from my lack of consideration.'

Pasviri waved them back to where the remaining Alouettes waited on open ground. The sun's heat was now a vicious, unrelenting force; shimmering halos encapsulated the helicopters. Within minutes both aircraft were airborne and on a dead reckoning for the temporary military base at Ponte Sobre.

For the umpteenth time, Rex turned the situation over in his mind; Lee and Karen had been abducted by those who were more than likely, ex-Renamo guerrillas; opportunist renegades, leftovers from a war of acquisition. Their lives depended on how well they had hidden the gold, if the renegades found the bullion, the white man and his woman would be quickly disposed of, in the shadow of so much wealth they would be looked upon as mere liabilities – not worth keeping alive.

Momentarily, Rex had caught a glimpse of the man who had fired the rocket-propelled grenade; with that single act of hostility, the half-caste revolutionary had destroyed a multi-million dollar aircraft. Major Ephraim Thebisa, along with his back-up crew had been incinerated. Outwardly, Pasviri appeared unaffected by the death of his sister's husband. 'The fat cow will have to find herself another man', he had gloated; his face devoid of any feeling, it was the measure of a man who would kill without the slightest provocation.

Rex knew he was playing a dangerous game; his family involvement with the Goddards was in Pasviri's eyes, abhorrent and with respect to their mutual camaraderie, had already cost him dearly. However, now there were even bigger stakes to play for. His popularity as the only elected Ndebele minister in Mugabe's, predominantly Shona government was growing fast; nurtured silently by his peoples' deep, longstanding need for a powerful tribal icon. Women averted their eyes and bowed their heads respectfully when passing him in the street; men raised their hand and gave him precedence without the uttering of a single word and with their eyes alone silently they paid homage to their chosen leader. Rex was their phoenix, their salvation from continuous persecution meted out by a self-elected Shona hierarchy. His was the only voice, that of the Matabele nation – He Who Drives like the Wind, they were already calling him; it was the praise name of his antecedent, Lobengula Jando Khumalo.

With a practiced feel for the controls, the young lieutenant touched down. Pasviri was through the doorway almost before the wheels compressed under the weight; from a cupboard in the ops tent he snatched out a bottle of Smirnoff vodka and filled a plastic coffee cup to just below the brim. He cocked an eye at Rex.

'Do you want one?'

Rex shook his head. 'I need an ordinance survey map of all the territory east of the bridge.'

Pasviri waved his glass at the radio operator. 'Find one. Leave your radio on channel four. You will leave it there unless the change is authorised by me.' He lit a cigarette and watched the smoke work its way up to vents in the canvas roof.

Rex spread the map across the table in front of him, it reflected in its entirety the tract of land that interested him. Through it, the Rio Save meandered as an unrestricted line from the border with Zimbabwe to the Mozambique coastline. Rex traced the river with his fingertip, pausing where it broke from a solid single line to the wide fan-shaped spread of its tidal delta. From there to the open sea, a maze of tiny rivulets and sheltered lagoons laced together vast reaches of swamp and mangrove forest. It was the perfect hiding place.

'We found them here,' Rex hazarded, 'roughly thirty miles from the coast.' He circled the chosen area in pencil. 'And this is where I think they will be. There has to be water enough for the inflatable to get through, though only the Maker Himself will know how to root them out from a thousand square miles of swampland.'

Pasviri refilled his cup. Now relaxed he slumped into a canvas camp chair and lassoed the neck of the Smirnoff bottle with smoke rings.

'Perhaps the man he doth protest too much.' He smiled at Rex, contented by the veiling effects of the vodka. 'Shakespeare, comrade. Though having been born a Matabele, perhaps you will not have heard of him.'

Rex ignored the elitism.

'The fact remains, they have slipped through our fingers. We are now at a disadvantage.'

'Only insomuch as it will take a little longer for us to catch up with him.' Pasviri leaned with his elbows against the table. 'We know for a fact that Goddard is carrying a radio. My pilot assures me that from where we made contact to our present location, as the crow flies, is little more than twenty miles.'

'What are you saying?'

Pasviri swivelled in his chair and sat facing the radio. He stared at the glowing power light as though it were alive.

'Before nightfall, comrade, they will make contact with us.' He swung back to Rex. 'Diego Siqueiros. The man who destroyed our gunship.'

'You recognised him?'

Pasviri nodded. 'Mercenary – ex-Renamo. Operates from within the mantle of some imaginary army. Self-appointed General to a band of freebooters and cut-throats. I had the dubious pleasure of working with him through the Rhodesia debacle.' His eyes narrowed. Not so favourable memories of his contretemps with Renamo renegades were still fresh. Absentmindedly, he lifted his hand to a half-moon scar on his cheek. 'He controls the territory north of the Rio Save. Looked upon by the authorities as some untouchable warlord, totally ruthless. For the gold we are after, Siqueiros would gladly slit the throat of his own mother.'

'And you want us to follow them – with two helicopters and a handful of men?'

Pasviri shook his head.

'First, we will talk and bargain with him. We will come to an arrangement Every man has his price and my friend, Diego Siqueiros is no exception.'

He finished his drink and without taking his eyes off Rex, waved the empty glass for the attention of his radio operator.

'Pressure, comrade. Either through pain or greed, squeeze hard enough and even men as hard as Siqueiros will bend.'

Following Siqueiros' instructions, Lee steered the Zodiac deeper inside the mangrove forest, steady on to a northerly bearing, always with the warmth of late sun to his left shoulder. Seemingly at odds with itself, away from the powerful central stream of the Rio Save, the water hung still and heavy with silt between the mangrove roots, for the Indian Ocean's tide was now on the verge of turning. Thick with sea salt this was the domain of the feared estuarine crocodile and the river shark. Always alert, Siqueiros watched the water for sign; always with his forefinger curled inside the Kalashnikov's trigger guard. Half an hour out from the main river he called to Lee above the steady drum of the outboard motor.

'Where the channel splits, you will go to the right.' He turned his attention to Karen and instead of the broken mouth she had expected, his teeth were white and perfectly matched.

'Tonight *senhora*, you will be the guest of honour to a hundred men. They are not accustomed to seeing a white woman, your being in my camp will provoke much interest.'

Karen stayed silent. However, when Siqueiros looked away she found herself watching him, and though terrified by her predicament was unable to distance herself totally from the sheer physical presence of the half-caste. What Siqueiros stood for was against everything she believed in and yet, though morally repelled, she experienced the strange instinctive turning of the sedate and loyal wife for the very devil himself. As if he had sensed her unease, Diego Siqueiros turned his head and smiled.

'What do you want from us?' Karen cut at him,

surprised by her own sudden show of bravado.

At first, Siqueiros made no move to reply; he was the wolf, she the wounded deer. Openly, with his eyes he stripped away her clothing and his smile was languid, that taunting leer of the conqueror.

'Whatever I need,' he told her. 'If you fight me, *senhora*, perhaps even your life. My men are not as cultured as your husband. For blood and money and more so for a beautiful woman they will do anything – anything at all.'

Karen sat in total silence; dark happenings, fuelled by fear and confusion swirled inside her head. Instinctively, her hand moved up to the open neck of her shirt and she buttoned it closed.

'Turn for the high ground.' Siqueiros shouted his orders to Lee.

The mangroves opened up into wide lagoons for now the saltwater forests were at the very limits of the ocean's tidal influence. Transposed from one world to another, Karen marvelled at the change. Gin clear, cleansed of silt and brine by incoming forest seepage, submerged natural gardens were, through that late angle of sunlight, more than spectacular. In their thousands, multi-coloured tilapia, that voracious African bream hunted through banks of hyacinth stems for minnows and young crab. Siqueiros cupped his hand and scooped the water to his lips.

'Here the water is good. No salt.' Like some compliant tourist guide he conversed easily with Karen. 'Without fresh water, *senhora*, not even Diego Siqueiros can survive.'

Lee put the distance they had travelled from the Rio Save at six miles, perhaps four if their journey were measured as a straight line; in their wake and for as far as he could see, the mangroves had closed ranks. To the front the channel opened up, islets of solid ground breached the surface and the vegetation growing upon them was of the type that needed fresh water for its survival. Aligned with the Zodiac's prow, a wide promontory stood out above the lagoon. From the water's edge a beach of cleared earth stretched for sixty yards to a forest edged with ancient hardwoods. At first it seemed as though the landfall would serve only the likes of birds and wild animals; then, grey smoke, spirit-like for lack of wind wove its way through the forest canopy. Again, Siqueiros shouted out directions and from that quarter mile out, Lee steered a new westward course.

'We are close now.' Siqueiros pointed to the mouth of a narrow inlet. 'My men know we are here, they will be waiting.' He made his way forward. Crouched behind Lee he talked him between orderly rows of fishing platforms.

Fashioned from river reeds, cone shaped traps had been fixed to just below the level of the river's surface, expertly strengthened to withstand the constant flow of water, they were held in place by sharpened stakes driven into the riverbed, positioned with their mouths left open-ended to the current. Shangaan women moved from trap to trap; the river reached up to their waist and with slender spears they drew out striped tilapia and the smooth-skinned, whiskered catfish. On the bank, others stood watch; armed with Kalashnikov rifles they guarded those fishing against the threat of attack by crocodiles.

Crowded about a makeshift jetty, Siqueiros' men waited expectantly. All of them were heavily armed, most were dressed in faded, tiger-striped denim and battered combat boots. Silently, they watched their prize come in and without exception their eyes were fixed on the woman. Karen, aware of their intent stared back at them and as her only line of defence, vehemently she projected the anger building inside of

128

her.

Lee cut the motor and drifted the Zodiac into the mooring point. At the pier's head, as a black giant, Roberto leaned out for what was left of the anchor rope and made it fast. Siqueiros stepped onto the wooden planking. He spoke in mixture of Portuguese and Shangaan dialect.

'You made good time, my friend.'

Roberto nodded his head; never once did his eyes leave Karen.

'The men were eager to return, Diego.' Like a child demanding the fulfilment of a promise, he reached out his arm for Karen.

Siqueiros thrust his rifle between them.

'Not yet, my friend. Leave her be, I have much to find out. There are others who know we have them. Clear the boat of their equipment and bring it up to the camp.' He reached inside the Zodiac for the radio and gestured to Lee and Karen for them to follow.

-29-

Driven solely by his instinct to survive, Siqueiros had found the perfect place where his men could build their encampment. With the cunning eyes of the fugitive he had searched it out; a place where men could hide without constant fear of harassment by government soldiers. To the south and east, the vastness of the delta stretched for hundreds of square miles, as a natural barrier its unpalatable waters were filled with man-eating crocodiles, venomous snakes and the mother of all Africa's killers – the anopheles mosquito, carrier of the feared malaria virus and yellow fever. Northwards and to the west, to those who knew the way, a lattice-work of narrow pathways, accessible only during the dry winter months of July and August. However, once the rains came, again these inroads were closed off; the encampment effectively shut away from the outside world by returning floodwater.

From the water's edge, at a slight gradient a narrow path led deeper inside the forest. Both Lee and Karen were silenced by the immense size of the trees. Leadwood and mahoganies, many greater in girth than the fully-laden belly of a bull elephant reared against the skyline; at their base, ten feet in diameter and from vast roots to their topmost branches, mast-like, with their limbs spread, they rose up more than a hundred feet into the air.

'Stay strong,' Lee encouraged and walked with his hand constantly to Karen's shoulder.

Roberto walked behind them, his chest and stomach were thickly covered with body hair; his arms were grotesquely powerful and disproportionate to his height. Periodically, his right hand would seek out the stock of his rifle and with the gentle touch of a lover, tenderly, he would caress it. From his forehead, a single strip of coarse hair had been left to grow in the style of the American Mohican, the rest had been shaved clean, now disfigured by the welts and cicatrises of confrontation. Like those of the raven his eyes were never still, black as any night and like the ape he naturally emulated, protected by that overly thickened brow, his eyes were deeply set within the armour of his skull.

Karen sensed his nearness and the smell of him sometimes caught up with her – that ripened scent of the forest animal mixed with that of gun oil and pungent native tobacco. Not once had Roberto taken his eyes off her; barefooted, he padded behind like some obedient primate. Karen glanced over her shoulder and in the half-light of the forest she saw Roberto smile.

'I'm scared, Lee. That thing behind us hasn't stopped looking at me.'

'Keep your cool,' said Lee, 'don't let him get to you.'

Without warning, the forest opened into a wide clearing, at the highest point a buttress of living rock stood as a natural lookout platform and was thickly ringed by trees. From far-off, looking inwards from the mangrove forests the camp would be impossible to recognise, blending chameleon-like with the canopy it would appear from a distance, nondescript, merely a small part of the surrounding forest. However, from that natural vantage a man might see for thirty miles in all directions, no intruder would get within five miles of the stronghold without being picked out. Just inside the treeline, again, camouflaged by natural growth, typical grass and mud dwellings of the Shangaan people stood unobtrusively below the skyline. Through openings in the foliage, Lee picked out the dark, familiar shape of the Zodiac and he felt his breathing catch. Two, perhaps three days was all that they had before Siqueiros grew bored of having them around. It took all of Lee's self-control to stop himself grabbing a hold of Karen's arm and bolting for the jetty.

-30-

Pasviri studied the survey map in front of him; every minute detail, every sighting, every incident relevant to Lee's clandestine crossing into Mozambique had been logged and charted with coloured markers. A single, white pin marked the position of the crashed Cessna. The loss irritated him and like the burrowing larvae of the maggot fly, constantly the shining pin reminded him of the doomed pilot's voice screaming out from the radio.

'Goddard has already cost our government millions of dollars. The gloves are off; when I catch up with them, both he and his woman will be held to account.' He stabbed the marker with his forefinger. 'This is where the plane went down.' The same finger slid further eastwards, downstream from the crash site. 'And here is where our Renamo friends helped themselves to what by rights, is ours.' Red ink encircled an area within a fifty mile radius of the downed helicopter. 'Our gold, comrade, is now in the hands of my old friend, Diego Siqueiros.'

He lit a cigarette, using the break in conversation to alleviate his anger. 'However, all is not lost, that is if fate sees fit to give us another chance. A second aircraft, another two-seater Cessna has already been deployed and is about to land at Buffalo Range.' He glanced at the young subaltern stood to attention in the doorway to the ops tent. The muscles in Pasviri's jaw flexed as he spoke, those of a Rottweiler gnawing through bone. 'As soon as the replacement aircraft has landed, it will be refuelled and be made ready for take-off. You will notify either me or Comrade Minister Khumalo when the task has been completed. On your life, comrade, you will not fail me.' The subaltern saluted smartly, about turned and left the tent.

Rex stood up from the table and crossed to the map board; dressed in full combat fatigues and red beret of Zimbabwe's elite Fifth Brigade, his presence alone gave credence to the gravity of the mission. The epaulettes on his shoulders carried the black crown insignia of a company major. Like Pasviri, he pieced together the happenings of those last few days.

'The fact that Siqueiros was in the area at the time, and going off the severity of the terrain tells us that his home base won't be far away. I would say, no more than twenty miles from where we lost the Alouette to the rocket attack.'

Pasviri nodded his head in agreement.

'He has taken Goddard's inflatable, we must therefore assume that his base is close to water – somewhere north of the river. South is out of the question, without a boat of sorts the rest of his men could not have crossed the Save's main channel.'

Again, Pasviri took up the board marker and reduced the size of his first choice.

'In here, comrade.' He ringed the smaller objective; confining his attentions to an area ten miles further to the north west of the crash site.

'We start the search at first light?' Rex insisted.

Pasviri nodded and clamped a cigarette between his teeth.

'By midday tomorrow, comrade, I am confident that a sighting will have been made. Diego Siqueiros is not a man who would spend his time rotting away in a mangrove swamp; like a lizard, he will be out in the sunlight, somewhere warm and dry.' Again, he condensed the pilot's search area, reducing it to an even smaller tract of land, adjacent to the swamp's northernmost edge. 'Somewhere along here, I am convinced of it. Once Siqueiros' camp has been identified we will deliver our ultimatum; either he hands over the gold...' he spun the wheel on his lighter and touched the flame to the cigarette, '... or I will deploy every soldier I have at my disposal and take it from him.' He turned to the radio operator. 'Notify me the moment you hear anything. Let us see if our retarded half-caste friend has yet worked out how to make use of Goddard's radio.'

Karen stayed close to Lee, her arm permanently looped with his; purposely she had chosen the place for them to sit, well within a protective aura of firelight. Armed guards watched their every move. To the east of Siqueiros' camp, already the sky had turned that deep and infinite colour of the African night. On the western horizon, the heavens were slashed across by deep vermilion where the sun had already set.

Excluding the Zodiac's outboard motor and inter-connected fuel tank, the boat had been stripped of everything visible. Lee's FN rifle, spare magazines and the A63 radio were laid out on a table in front of Siqueiros. From close in to the makeshift ops tent, Lee and Karen could hear the continuous hiss from the radio's empty carrier band. Behind Siqueiros, barely visible, Roberto's gorilla-like shape blended uncannily with the shadows. Only if Karen made as if she were about to stand up did he threaten to move away from his leader.

With deliberation, Siqueiros switched from one channel to the next; he listened intently to each new bandwidth. From its greater vantage point high above the river delta, the set's transmission range had increased dramatically; any incoming signal from within a thirty mile radius would quickly be picked up on.

Lee counted the clicks and whispered to Karen. 'He's on channel three – one more and all hell will break loose.'

As though Siqueiros had heard him, he moved the selector switch to four.

Lee held his breath; Karen closed her eyes and prayed for another empty side band. Static hissed from the open speaker and then, like a spectre from some other world, Pasviri's reedy voice bled through the silence.

'I do not remember you as a foolish man, comrade. Before it is too late, return what is rightly mine and I will leave you be. I will repeat my more than generous offer on the hour, every hour, Diego. By tomorrow morning, if I have heard nothing, my men will begin their search for your camp. I say again, comrade, do not disappoint me, in the past we have worked well together. However, should you choose to ignore my offer, you will leave me with no alternative; I will destroy you.'

The transmission ended. Siqueiros turned off the power and smiled thinly at Lee.

'As I thought, my friend. Comrade Pasviri already knows that we have you.'

'So let us go.'

Siqueiros shook his head at the ruse. 'You have something, something Pasviri values enough to kill for.' He stood up from the table. 'Though perhaps, if you were to leave it with Diego, then he might let you and your woman go free.'

He knelt on one knee and lit a cigarette from the fire. Expectantly, Roberto moved in closer to his master.

'My friend, Roberto.' Siqueiros clamped the cigarette between his teeth and smiled at Karen. 'His patience is running out, *senhora*. White women are his weakness – I cannot hold him back for long.'

Lee spoke out, attempting to defuse the situation.

'Pasviri is obsessed by his own greed; he's convinced I'm carrying gold. Only a madman would use a rubber boat to smuggle gold through Mozambique.'

'So what are you saying? There is no gold – the treasure Pasviri is after exists only inside his head?'

Lee nodded and Siqueiros' eyes narrowed.

'Then why would Pasviri follow you over the border? You do not strike me as a fool, *senhor*. Why would you run with nothing?'

135

'I have my reasons, comrade. The largest independently owned gold mine in Zimbabwe belongs to me. For the last ten years...'

'You have been stealing your own gold!' Siqueiros interrupted. 'You are a criminal, like me, *senhor*! With the mind of a genius I think you are calling it.' Abruptly he stopped laughing. 'Then you are also crazy – why would you leave all the gold behind and run for the border?'

Now it was Lee's turn to smile. 'Who said anything about leaving it behind? At least, not all of it.'

Siqueiros' eyes turned thin and snake-like.

'Your story changes quicker than the colours of the chameleon's clothes – first there is nothing, now you are saying you have it with you?' He looked over his shoulder. 'The boat, Roberto. Go alone, search every inch of her.' Roberto disappeared; minutes later, Lee caught the glimmer of paraffin lamps from down at the water's edge. Siqueiros stood up from the table and through a gap in the trees looked down on the jetty. For the moment, his mind was distracted.

'My God,' Karen hissed, 'after all that we've been through, the trauma we suffered getting past the bridge, then all of a sudden on some petty, stupid whim you've just given it all away?' She shook her head at him. 'Why, for God's sake? At least tell me why.'

'Keep your voice down. I misled you on purpose. I admit I should have told you.' He lowered his voice. 'But at the time I had no choice. You would not have gone for it otherwise.'

'Gone for what?'

'The deception. Mugabe's CIO men have been watching us for weeks.'

Karen's eyes narrowed. 'You've lost me – what are you talking about?'

Lee took a deep breath and came clean.

'There isn't any gold, at least not on the Zodiac –

136

never has been.'

'Crap,' hissed Karen, 'I helped you load it; damn near crippled me.'

'We unloaded it; later that same day, when you were in Masvingo. Gerard helped me load it into a specially concealed compartment under the Mazda pick-up.'

'You've lost the plot,' she cut back at him, 'I spoke to him in Maputo; he phoned remember?'

'He wasn't in Maputo. We were play acting. Gerard phoned from the Victoria Hotel in Masvingo. Left for the border at Beit Bridge the day before we left for Mahenya. Our supposed fishing trip was to draw Pasviri's attention away from Gerard.'

She stared at him, slack-mouthed. 'All that talk of Jose's marina and the strong currents coming into Maputo harbour...'

'Never happened. *Isabella* was moored at Jose's Marina all along. I paid Jose to bring her up from Durban a month ago.'

'The hotel rooms? The reservations you asked me to make?'

'Decoys. All of it bullshit.'

'All bullshit? You bastard, Lee Goddard. You had me risk my life for an empty boat.'

'Trust me. I need you to play along. Stay calm, once we're out of this mess, then I'll let you kill me.'

Siqueiros came back to the fire. 'I think Roberto has found nothing.'

'I told you the gold is real enough, but it's not on my boat.'

'So it is you, Pasviri is after.' Siqueiros pulled a Tokarev pistol from his belt and clicked off the safety catch. 'Do not play games, *senhor*, here in Mozambique your lives mean nothing.'

'Kill us and Pasviri's men will destroy you. Without us you have nothing left to bargain with. Pasviri will assume you have taken the gold for yourself.'

Siqueiros lowered the pistol. Dead they were worthless. Bargaining with Pasviri for their return was the only option left open to him; any ransom demands, however small would be met with full-blown military retaliation.

'We will talk again in the morning.' He looked directly at Karen. 'Try to escape and this time, *senhora*, it will not be easy for me to stop Roberto.'

-32-

By first light, the air force Cessna reconnaissance plane had been refuelled and its pre-flight checks completed. With the dramatic panache of a Second World War kamikaze pilot, the young lieutenant squared his shoulders and saluted smartly.

'I will find them, comrade minister. I will not fail you.'

'Failure is not one of your options, lieutenant; on your daughter's virginity if you do not succeed.' Pasviri waved him away. 'Now start your engine and the moment you find this dog-eating pig of a half-caste you will call in immediately.'

'As soon as I find them, comrade minister.'

They watched the Cessna take off and then bank away sharply to port; light from a low sun reflected off its wing-tips, the drone of its single engine quickly dwindled to nothing.

'Soon, your man will be over delta,' Rex surmised. 'If your theories hold true, in this angle of sunlight, Siqueiros' camp should be easy enough for him to locate.'

With a customary rubbing together of hands, Pasviri showed his excitement.

'Once we have his position I will radio Siqueiros, if he refuses to co-operate we will take the gold on our terms, comrade. You will lead the men. Thirty of our best troops will accompany you. Siqueiros will die as he lived – like a dog.'

He opened a fresh pack of cigarettes and drew one out with his teeth.

'My interests lie only with what your friends are carrying. You will leave behind no proof of having been there.'

'What about Goddard?'

Pasviri smiled at him, a gloating little smile that left Rex in no doubt of the preferred conclusion to the operation.

'You are a man of infinite resourcefulness, Rex. I am sure you will make the right decisions when the time comes.' He pulled hard on the Kingsgate and watched the smoke rise up through the sunlight. 'I believe his wife to be quite attractive – for a white woman.'

-33-

Roberto was first to hear it, that distant, bass drone of an aircraft engine. He tilted his head and listened intently; like a lemur patiently tracking the movements of some deep wood-boring insect. He touched Siqueiros' arm and within those same few seconds accurately he had pinpointed the Cessna's position.

'They have found us, Diego; Mugabe's jackals have scented our spoor.'

Siqueiros snatched up his binoculars from the table and with Roberto's guidance, quickly he located the aircraft – a tiny spark of reflected sunlight pinned to the sky. Like the morning star it hung there, stationary for a moment and then, unerringly it came on. Diego dropped the glasses against his chest.

'Send men down to the jetty; have them cover the boat with branches. Do it now Roberto.'

Roberto barked out orders; those not quick enough were scattered from their campfires, Roberto's pan-sized hands were balled like hammers and he lashed out indiscriminately as the men fled past him. Diego cursed his own stupidity; he had underestimated Pasviri's dogged determination. He had left it too late. Smoke from cooking fires spiralled out from the forest canopy and as blue, indicting fingers betrayed the whereabouts of his encampment.

From the Cessna's cockpit the pilot quickly picked up on glittering eyelets of bright water. Further to the south, the Rio Save's main channel stood out as a brown, silted highway. However, to the delta's northernmost perimeter the water had lost that acidic green tint proliferated by tidal flood waters; here, there were islands of yellow grassland and bright forests. The pilot reached for the transmit button; being the only operational aircraft aloft and far enough from any civilian, ground-based air traffic control, he dispensed with standard military radio procedure.

'I am approaching the swamps, comrade minister; ten miles east of my present position.'

Pasviri's reply was immediate, his tone laced with agitation.

'There will be smoke, lieutenant. Look for Goddard's boat, anything out of the ordinary.'

The pilot shed altitude. From three thousand feet and bathed in early sunlight, the landscape below showed up bright and sharp as any full colour photograph. Small herds of Cape buffalo fled from the water's edge, stopping only when they reached the protection of tall trees. For ten more minutes the pilot searched unsuccessfully for sign of human habitation, then, on the verge of him swinging further to the south east, the back of his neck flushed with gooseflesh. Like winter mist, smoke from a dozen fires had come together and as a blue and damning flag it hung above a tiny inlet of bright water.

'I have found something, comrade minister.'

'What is it? Tell me what you see, lieutenant – your best description – do you see the boat?' Pasviri's excitement bubbled into the cockpit. 'Go in close, comrade. There will be men, lieutenant – armed mercenaries. Give me the exact position – a map reference.'

The pilot read straight from the map. 'A mile east of that grid reference, where the water ends and the forests begin. Smoke, comrade minister.'

'Cooking fires,' Pasviri realised. 'What else do you see? Goddard's boat – is it there?'

'I see it! The fools are covering it with branches, but they are like ants to an upturned pot of sugar.'

'I knew it!' Pasviri revelled in his own foresight. He pounded the table with his fist. 'I was right, comrade, we have him cornered.' He turned his attention back to the radio. 'How many men, lieutenant?'

'I see no more than twenty.'

A new voice interrupted the transmission.

'You are trying my patience, Julius. Call off your dogs.'

Pasviri's fingers tightened around the handset; expertly, he curtailed his excitement.

'Diego, my friend, at last you have decided to co-operate. There is a small outstanding matter of you returning what is rightfully mine; I give you my word, return your captives and the contents of their boat and I will leave you alone with your snakes and crocodiles. Fail me, and not even your own mother will recognise the pieces we leave behind.'

141

'You flatter me, Julius.' He nodded his head at Roberto, instructing him with his eyes. 'Your men are not welcome here; your friend Goddard is carrying nothing of value. I say again, call off your dogs or prepare to face the consequences.'

Roberto balanced the launcher against his right shoulder and growled at the man stood behind him cradling the high explosive projectile. Purposely, he raised his voice

'Load!'

The loader pushed home the nine point eight kilogram, ground-to-air Strela missile. Roberto felt the missile seat against the launcher's ignition terminals and he adjusted his balance to suit. Again, Siqueiros pressed the transmit key on the handset.

'You have little time, comrade. I give you one more minute to recall your pilot; refuse me and your man will die.'

Rex realised what was happening and tried his utmost to intervene.

'Get your man out of their air space. He's got a portable ground-to-air – a SAM-7'

'They are bluffing.' Pasviri challenged. 'Siqueiros is lying.' He keyed the handset. This time the threat was openly hostile. 'It is you, Diego who has run out of time. I will share your minute, comrade, but that is all – agree to my terms, or I will let loose my soldiers.'

'He's not bluffing,' Rex warned. 'He has nothing to lose – bring back your pilot or Siqueiros will fire the missile.'

'I'm waiting,' Pasviri countered the threat, his words hissed their way through the ether, but it was then that the first zephyr of cold air brushed against his cheek. From the look in Rex's eyes he realised his mistake.

Roberto switched on the launcher's power pack and for one last time looked to Siqueiros for the order to fire.

Diego pressed the transmit lever. There was no going back, in the face of both men that slightly opened door of chance negotiation had just slammed shut – the stand-off would be won and lost within those next few seconds.

'That was your biggest mistake comrade; for your pilot friend, now is his time to die.'

Siqueiros nodded his head to Roberto; through the iron sights the Shangaan locked on to the Cessna's in-bound flight path.

Like a wild goose wearied by long days of arduous flight, the aircraft started shedding altitude. Emboldened by his own success the pilot manoeuvred the Cessna for a final triumphant fly-by, directly above the jetty; with his finger held to the transmit key his excitement bubbled back to Pasviri. On the ground, gunfire showed as tiny, impotent pops of white smoke.

'They run around like monkeys, comrade minister! The fools are shooting at me.' He banked to port for a clear view of the Zodiac. Siqueiros' men were firing their short range assault rifles, putting up a feeble barrage of anti-aircraft fire. Even in bright sunlight the pilot was able to make out blips of green tracer hurtling skywards, but as spent fireworks they fell away, a thousand feet short of their target. He released the transmit button and immediately, Pasviri's voice screamed at him from the panel-mounted speaker.

'Return at once, lieutenant; do not overfly the camp. Bring your aircraft back to the bridge!'

'As you wish, comrade minister.'

Defiantly, the pilot stuck to his flight path, rolling the Cessna sideways-on to the clearing below. At that height, the Zimbabwe air force insignia stood out as a taunting yellow flag to Diego's men.

Roberto held the Cessna's image within the narrow

eyelet of the launcher's sights and he marvelled at the pilot's stupidity. With the aircraft less than a mile out from the clearing, he fully depressed the trigger on the grip stock to uncage the missile's seeker electronics. The infrared tracking sensor picked up the aircraft's heat emissions and illuminated the launcher's red 'locked-on' light. An audible buzzer sounded and Roberto applied slight lead to the oncoming target.

Within that next brief moment, the missile's onboard power supply ignited the throw-out motor and with a thrust speed of over thirty metres per second drove the Strela-2 clear of its launcher. Both the forward steering guidance and four, rear mounted stabilizing fins unfolded as the missile left the tube. At five metres out, the rocket's sustainer motor activated and accelerated the missile to its maximum speed of four hundred and thirty metres per second. Tethered by its thread of silver smoke, the missile lifted phoenix-like above the lagoon, the rumble of its motor dulled by distance and the drone of the approaching aircraft; the harrier for the goose – the falcon for the dove.

Enraptured by his sole possession of an open sky, the pilot again banked steeply, then at a lower altitude he levelled out and dipped the Cessna's wings, first to port and then alternately to starboard. The act itself was inflammatory, another vindictive show of the pilot's growing bravado. He was the conqueror, the victorious hunter pouring scorn upon his aggressors. Comrade Pasviri would reward him personally for his skill as a reconnaissance pilot. From his port-side window the pilot laughed aloud at the confusion being acted out far below him. It was then that he saw the missile and the laughter died in his throat.

With realignment ability of nine degrees per second, the Strela's AM tracking sensor stayed locked on to a powerful source of black heat growling from the aircraft's twin exhaust ports. In a vain attempt to avoid destruction, the pilot rammed the yoke fully forward, forcing the aircraft into a steep dive. That loss of control drained his courage and left him floundering; he had lost sight of the Strela, the roles had been reversed. He was now the prey; the claustrophobic child trapped inside some dark room and he screamed out loud, gripped by insurmountable panic.

The missile wobbled in flight as its on-board seeker momentarily lost that powerful central eye of infrared radiation. However, quickly it made minute alterations to the missile's angle rate tracking system. From beneath, it found the Cessna's downward flight path; as the Peregrine falcon might flush its prey from the sheer sides of some Welsh mountain, so did the Strela rise from below in deadly pursuit of its quarry.

It struck the Cessna's fuselage at its lowest point, amidships of the aircraft's exhaust outlets – detonating the fragmentation warhead just a metre forward from the pilot's feet.

Most of the blast energy was absorbed by the solid mass of the Cessna's engine, but to the rear of its mountings the flimsy metal bulkhead had been ripped through. Fanned by rushing wind, acrid smoke from burning oil and Avgas forced its way inside the cockpit.

Flung against his harness by the explosion, the pilot was left confused and disorientated, then the violent shuddering of his stricken aircraft and the ingress of terrible heat snapped him back to full awareness.

Where once his legs had operated the steerage pedals, now, through a ragged hole in the floor a furnace roared where his feet had been – it was then, like starving wolves to the stumps of both his legs did that gnawing pain engulf him.

Siqueiros saw the missile strike; a small flicker of white light, moments later there followed the sharp explicit crack of detonation. Fascinated by the destructive power wreaked by such a small projectile, Siqueiros steadied the binoculars and followed those final dying moments of the spotter plane.

Wrapped in its own inferno, the aircraft spiralled out of control. With the engine stilled, the only sound was that of far-off rushing wind, barely audible to those who watched spellbound from below. Siqueiros keyed the radio's handset seconds before the forest canopy swallowed the Cessna down.

'A final message from your pilot, comrade.' Siqueiros turned the handset towards the forest, still with the transmit key depressed.

At first, Pasviri and Rex Khumalo heard nothing more than the soulful cry of a fish eagle. Mesmerised by the quiet, they continued to stare at the radio and willed the pilot's voice from the speaker.

Her tanks, still two-thirds filled with volatile aviation fuel blew on impact; a single clap of thunder. At her maximum free-fall speed, the Cessna's nose and forward fuselage drove deep inside the soft earth, the pilot's own crematorium.

Pasviri tightened his grip on the handset.

'I will find you, Diego. Your swamps will not protect you. My men are eager for you, comrade. Like dogs they will hunt you down and tear you to pieces!'

'I will watch for them, my friend. Be sure to send your best. Killing them will make the touch of your Zimbabwe gold seem all the sweeter.' He grinned at Roberto and loaded the bait. 'Fifty kilo's, Julius. How much will that be worth in Maputo? A million US? Who knows, comrade – perhaps two, even?'

'My final offer, Diego. Return my gold – keep the woman if you will, I have no need of her.'

'Nor do I have the need for you, comrade. You forget quickly, already I have them both. Do your worst, my friend. Send your soldiers and as I have done with your aircraft, I will destroy them all.'

-35-

Rex walked alongside Julius Pasviri to where three Alouette helicopters baked in open sunlight; by tomorrow's dawn, they would be fully equipped and refuelled, less than a half hour's flying time would see them over the swamp, his trackers would root out sign and spoor; a slight indentation in soft earth, a broken leaf, disturbed grass, anything at all, no matter how small it would be found – Siqueiros' line of march pin-pointed to within a corridor of a hundred yards. He prayed that he would be the first to catch up with Lee and Karen. He had chosen the men himself, all of them young; men he could trust and would take instruction without question, hardened troopers waiting for the signal to deploy.

Pasviri paused in front of the nearest gunship, he reached out for the twin Browning machine guns and with a lover's touch caressed them, then he looked to Rex for his assurance.

'This entire operation is becoming something of an embarrassment, comrade. Bring Siqueiros back for me – as a whole, or in pieces, it does not matter.'

Losing the gold and three aircraft in as many days had all but pushed Pasviri over the edge. Revenge and anger were to him, volatile bedfellows. Siqueiros was nobody's fool, constantly, he was one step ahead of the game – he would be waiting, more than likely with more portable SAM-7 missiles. Guerrilla warfare had turned Renamo fighters into feral killers; ghost-like they struck from nowhere and always when least expected.

'Thirty men,' continued Pasviri. 'Two waves. Once the first fifteen are down you will hold your position and wait for the second drop.'

'First light.' Rex nodded his head. 'Four days' rations and three hundred rounds per man – anymore and my men will be slowed up.'

'Siqueiros will have a full day's start, perhaps more.' Pasviri shook his head; the reality of the facts now cast that first shadow of doubt over his optimism. 'If he takes to the swamp you might never find him, not without air support.'

'They'll keep to dry ground,' Rex countered. 'Goddard and his woman are precious cargo; Siqueiros will not risk losing his bargaining tool to the crocodiles.'

'The radio.' Pasviri added. 'As long as the batteries hold, Siqueiros can be tempted to change his mind. The woman will slow him down, he will make mistakes and when he does, I will be waiting.'

'Killing Siqueiros will serve no purpose. He will not trust his men with the gold, he will have hidden it. We need him alive, Julius.'

Pasviri nodded his head. 'Regretfully, I have to say that you are right, but only long enough for your less than subtle persuasions to be put to good use – then you will kill him. Siqueiros has played me for the fool for long enough.' He glowered at Rex. Besides recovering the gold, Siqueiros' death was the only thing left that would ease the humiliation of being repeatedly outwitted. 'The outcome lies squarely across your shoulders, Comrade Khumalo – do not fail me. The dog's head on a plate, my friend – nothing less.'

Lee zipped together both their sleeping bags. Plagued by mosquitoes and thickening humidity, he and Karen struggled to find sleep. With her head on his shoulder, they dozed fitfully in deep shadow thrown outwards from the forest's edge; but for him rest was hard won, his awareness of being watched left him permanently on edge. At least four of Siqueiros' men patrolled the camp's perimeter and Karen especially, sensed that Roberto was with them.

Lee turned his face closer to Karen's and kept his voice to a whisper.

'Gerard will be wondering where the hell we are. If I don't contact him within the next couple of days he'll assume the worst and head for Maputo.'

'I'm scared, Lee.'

He stroked her cheek. Directly above them, the Milky Way blazed as a glittering river through the night sky. The dark was Siqueiros' only defence, Lee knew that come first light, Pasviri would send in his helicopter gunships.

'We must be ready. Pasviri will have the pilot's map reference to go by; as soon as its light enough for his chopper pilots to uplift, all hell is going to break loose.'

'The outboard and main fuel tank are both still on the boat,' Karen reminded him. 'All we need from up here is your rifle, spare jerry cans and the radio.'

'You're crazy,' Lee countered, 'Siqueiros' men will kill us.'

'Nothing else on offer; crazy is all we have left. If we don't get away from here they'll kill us anyway.'

He knew that Karen was right; they had little choice. If it came to an all-out battle, Siqueiros' men would not risk their lives to being slowed down by a couple of

149

civilians.

'Try to grab some sleep. There's not a lot we can do before morning.'

Wary of being watched from the forest, Karen closed her eyes. Within minutes her breathing had quietened. A lone satellite tumbled along its north-south orbit and then disappeared.

From where he was lying, Lee had a clear line of sight into the heart of Siqueiros' camp; a military-style ops tent, lit from the inside by smoking oil lamps. A remnant of Portugal's colonial fight with Frelimo guerrillas the tent was patterned with the usual forest camouflage – for the most it had been bleached the colour of old bones by the sun. Lee's FN rifle, the A63 radio and a belt of five, filled magazines were still where Siqueiros had left them. He needed them all; he needed to get himself and Karen away from Siqueiros before the renegade decided to rid himself of the burden; pass them on to his men for their amusement – two, perhaps three days at the most before they were both dead.

To pass the time, Lee calculated the distance they had covered since leaving the Save's main channel. He worked from the jetty; mentally he wound his way in reverse, through those narrow breaks in the mangrove forest to where the first plane had crashed into the river; coupling this with the Zodiac's speed he guessed they had travelled a distance of eight miles in a rough, north-westerly direction. The crossing at Ponte Sobre would be no more than twenty miles west of Siqueiros' stronghold; fifteen minutes flying time for Alouettes. Before the sun was a foot clear of the horizon, Pasviri's gunships would be strafing the camp with light machine guns and cannon fire; then the troops would be deployed. Depending on how fierce the attack and from which side it came, there might just be enough confusion created for Lee and Karen to retake at least

150

some of their equipment and make it back to the Zodiac.

-37-

Rex was awake and fully kitted out an hour before sunrise, he stood outside in the clean air. Mixed emotions fought their war inside his head. On one hand, apprehension did its utmost to hold him back, but stood to the other, the resurgent thrill of a possible firefight excited him, titillating his senses like some eager lover from long ago.

Dressed in loosely fitted combat gear, Julius Pasviri clutched a mug of steaming coffee with both hands, and between his teeth his first cigarette of the day glowed as a red, pernicious eye. Slouched against his Land Rover, he relaxed to the first warm rays of sunlight. After what had happened to his brother-in-law, the serenity of the heavily fortified camp was now his shield; he would leave the fighting to those who were younger and fitter, more expendable.

'Perfect combat weather, comrade. If we are fortunate, the battle will have been fought and won by sundown.'

Helicopter crews and combat ready soldiers were waiting for the order to board the Alouettes.

'Wishful thinking,' Rex warned. 'Don't be fooled into believing Siqueiros' men are idiots. They know we're coming.' He flicked the dregs from his mug.

Pasviri shook his head at the inference.

'Diego's rabble army are no match for our soldiers. Friends in Maputo have given me free rein, they want rid of Siqueiros. He has become an embarrassment. Foreign investors are loath to leave the safety of the city lights.'

151

'Free rein for you to accomplish what they cannot, my friend. Diego's men are like wild dogs, they take what they want and whenever it suits them.'

Before full sun all three Alouettes were airborne. Rex leaned from the doorway of the lead helicopter and watched the camp at Ponte Sobre fall away behind. Already, the character of the land had changed and to the east, coming into view were those first inklings of vast wetlands, the starting point for the Rio Save's ancient delta. Deep channels and eyelets of still water sat jewel-like amongst the mangrove forests. Rex adjusted the speaker-arm on his headset.

'Both call signs – confirm you can hear me?'

The response was immediate. 'Alpha Two, that's affirmative; Alpha Three, strength five.'

Both section commanders had been fully briefed before take-off; there was no need for any further discussion. Siqueiros would be trolling backwards and forwards through the full scope of the radio's bandwidth.

Rex clipped his safety harness to the overhead static line and moved in behind the paired, .303 Brownings. He checked his watch; fifteen more minutes flying time before they reached a supposed rebel camp identified by the ill-fated reconnaissance pilot. He would deplane along with the first group, go to ground and wait for the second wave before moving in on the camp. All his men had been instructed to keep a look-out for Lee and Karen, ordered to bring them in alive.

The unnatural sounds were almost indiscernible, absorbed by those of the forest, but to the bull-like Shangaan that faint though steady beat of Alouette rotors was all powerful – already it was all around him. As some bass reverberation, the drum of inbound aircraft made his skin crawl with anticipation, for his thoughts were now of war.

Lee sensed Roberto's agitation and softly he nudged Karen awake.

'Time to move. Lover boy has heard something.'

Roberto ran between the trees, rousing the men with fist and boot from warm scrapes beside their campfires, and within that same minute, every fire was quickly extinguished. Anything other than the natural was spirited away inside the forest, so that from the air there would be little left for those looking down to pick up on.

Siqueiros came out from the camouflaged ops tent and calmly he called out his instructions to Roberto. He took his time lighting a cigarette and inhaled deeply, as though nothing untoward was happening.

'I see that our Comrade Pasviri has not yet learned his lesson, Roberto. Bring the launcher with you. Quickly, my friend.'

Roberto obeyed without question and lumbered after Siqueiros with the missile tube and pack of three projectiles slung across his shoulders.

*

Rex identified the freshwater lagoon from the Cessna pilot's last sit-rep. He ordered all three aircraft into extended single file flying formation; as a team they hunted close in to the shoreline, nose down, silhouetted against a backdrop of lush greenery. Rex was first to spot the camouflaged jetty; the Zodiac was barely visible. Covered with foliage stripped from the forest, it had been made to mimic a grove of young trees.

'Ten degrees left!' He pointed out the jetty's position. The pilot acknowledged and altered course. Almost touching the lake and now stripped of any cover, Rex took comfort from the recent fitting of anti-Strela shrouds to his Alouette's tailpipe. Deflected by the shrouds, hot exhaust gases would be forced upwards and into the turbulent downdraft created by the rotor. Dissipating gases would deny any inbound missiles a concentrated source of engine heat for their guidance system to feed on.

With his hands locked to the Brownings' firing handles, Rex traversed the twin barrels back and forth to gauge their arc of fire. The guns were loaded with four hundred rounds of belt-fed .303 ball; their combined firepower would be devastating. A single, centrally mounted prismatic sight served both guns.

He looked back across the lagoon, the remaining Alouettes had fallen behind and he cursed the pilots for their stupidity.

From the granite ledge above the camp, Siqueiros positioned himself for an unobstructed view of the entire area. Using the binoculars he quickly found the gunships, the nearest machine some mile and a half ahead of its followers. With the launch tube cradled against his right shoulder, Roberto tracked the lead helicopter. He depressed the trigger, but the approach alert signal buzzed only intermittently before the red, locked-on light extinguished. The aircraft's weak infrared emissions were erratic and inconsistent, forcing him to re-sight the weapon. Siqueiros heard the

Shangaan curse the rocket's failure to activate.

'Wait for the machine to overfly, Roberto. Like a boar with the sow you must take it from behind, she is different to the one you killed yesterday. Be patient my friend and shoot only when I tell you.'

Cold fingers hurried inside Rex's shirt; mindful of Siqueiros' cunning he pulled back the cocking levers and instinctively braced himself for an all-out firefight.

'Bring her in wide!' he shouted to the pilot and immediately the Alouette fell away to starboard.

Siqueiros saw the helicopter swing away from its original flight path. He cursed the pilot for that last minute change in direction.

'Let her go, Roberto, this time she lives. Save your friend for the other two.'

Roberto scanned the open sky for another target. Siqueiros stood at his side, he would act as the Shangaan's loader and in readiness he cradled a second Strela missile across his forearms. Like before, he marvelled at the terrible killing power of such a small projectile. Weighing a little over seven kilograms, within a range of four kilometres the missile could wreak total devastation upon its chosen target.

'I hear them Roberto. Prepare yourself, they are close,' Siqueiros put up the glasses. Both aircraft were flying side-on to where he was standing; both at the same height and from the rear of each Artouste engine, shimmering exhaust gases poured from unprotected tailpipes.

*

Through gaps in the undergrowth, Lee and Karen watched Siqueiros' men swarm like ants from upturned nests, all of them heavily armed with automatic rifles and grenade launchers. What had at first appeared to Lee as a ragtag gathering of leftover's from a protracted war of independence was now the efficient fighting machine, and as a silent wraith it blended with the forest. Each man carried a load equivalent to half of his own weight in armaments and munitions. Like guinea fowl going to roost, in single file Siqueiros' men climbed higher along the hillside.

Lee waited for a last few stragglers to pass and then stood up from the hide. He positioned himself as best he could for a clear view of the ops tent. Light from an abandoned oil lamp was enough for him to make out his FN rifle and webbing belt; straining his eyes he located the A63 radio and his heart leapt.

'This is our only chance; it's now or never.' He looked at Karen. 'Your call, my sweetheart. We make a break for the boat or we sit tight and see what happens?'

'No contest,' said Karen and inflexibly, emphasized her decision. 'No way am I going through a one on one romp with Roberto.' She grasped Lee's arm and urged him back towards the ops tent.

For long minutes they stood in close to the tent and listened. Nothing moved. The forgotten lamp was burning itself dry on the table. The entire camp had been deserted, sporadic bursts of gunfire echoed back from the forest.

'No guards,' Lee whispered.

'I don't like it. Looks too easy, Lee – why the sudden disinterest?'

'Siqueiros has his hands full. Without the gold I guess we're not worth bothering about.'

He went forward and Karen followed his movements between the trees. With her heart in her mouth she watched him enter the makeshift ops tent. Lee beckoned to her and carefully she traced his steps through the undergrowth.

'I'll take the rifle and belt,' Lee told her, 'you get the radio.'

'What about food and water?'

'Grab what you can find. Tinned stuff only; our water bottles if you can find them.'

He buckled on the webbing belt and picked up his rifle. The transformation was immediate. Karen pushed past him for the radio. Her leg brushed against the table, the lamp flared and yellow light filled the tent; it was then that Karen felt a slight whisper of restraint across the front of her ankle. A strand of steel wire had been strung just inches above the ground. As a glittering silken thread it had lodged inside the narrow space above the collar of her boot.

-39-

From the highest point above the camp, through his binoculars, Siqueiros tracked the Alouettes' flight path. Absorbed by deep shadow both he and Roberto were rendered almost invisible from above; to their front, a rapidly darkening sky lay open and unhindered by foliage. The lead Alouette had disappeared behind the eastern treeline, but the remaining pair, after deploying troops, still hunted the forest for a chance encounter with Siqueiros' men.

'Switch on the launcher, Roberto, this time they will not escape us.'

With thick fingers, Roberto activated the launcher's power supply; he shuffled forwards to the very edge of the granite outcrop.

Some eight hundred yards apart, both helicopters were purely by chance now on dead reckoning for Roberto's vantage point. The Shangaan settled the launcher against

157

his shoulder, his recollection of downing the reconnaissance plane still virulently fresh in his mind. He trembled with excitement and like a father encouraging a son on his first hunt, Siqueiros calmed Roberto's nerve with soft words.

'Aim carefully my friend; wait for the bird to turn its tail for you. Do not forget, the light must be red for the missile to find its way.'

Again, the launcher's lock-on warning light flickered intermittently, the audible signal weak and uncertain. However, as the Alouette rose up slightly and veered to starboard, this time, like some glaring, blood-red eye the light illuminated. As angry bees, the audio 'target acquired' signal demanded the missile be set free.

With his legs splayed for good balance, Roberto tracked the Alouette, forced into leaning back on his heels to compensate for the helicopter's awkward flight angle. Then, with the committed eye of a determined hunter he depressed the trigger; holding the aircraft's line of flight, he led the Alouette by only a few metres.

Excited by powerful heat emissions from the Alouette's unshielded tailpipe, it took only seconds for the Strela missile to close the gap. At maximum thrust it slammed into the gaping exhaust portal and with terrible ferocity tore away the engine's metal innards.

Roberto grinned at the devastation he had wreaked. Shrouded in flaming Avgas, the mortally wounded Alouette spiralled out and ripped through the forest canopy.

'Stand as you are.' Siqueiros ordered and slid a second missile into the launch tube. He felt the ignition terminals engage and moved away to avoid the backblast.

Coming from the valley and at a height below that of the granite buttress, the second gunship swung away from its original flight path. Like a shark to a fisherman's chum line, single-minded the pilot followed his gut instinct and pushed the Alouette all out for high ground. He had marked the missile's launch platform and now, fearlessly he closed with it. Flying head-on to the granite lookout meant there was less chance of a second missile strike. However, Siqueiros realised the pilot's tactics and shouted a warning to Roberto.

'They come for us, Roberto. This time you will shoot for our lives my friend.'

At the last moment, the pilot swung the Alouette sideways-on to the granite. From a distance of one hundred yards, the gunner unleashed a solid flail of ball and tracer, strafing the trees and granite for that chance hit from a wild ricochet.

-40-

Karen's eyes flew wide open. The explosion seemed less than a hundred yards away.

'Sweet mother of God, what was that?'

Lee silenced her. 'Don't talk. Keep still or it ends right here. Move your foot and we're both dead.' Then gunfire, long bursts from light machine guns. Lee recognised that sustained roar of twin .303 Brownings.

He shook off what was going on outside and concentrated on what he was doing. Across the bridge of Karen's right foot, hooked between her bare skin and the metal fasteners of her boot, a steel tripwire stretched away diagonally to opposite corners of the tent. The half-caste had cleverly second guessed their attempt to break free. Siqueiros' bizarre trap had caught them off guard; their equipment vindictively left as bait.

'He's played us for fools,' Lee said. 'Siqueiros knew we would try to make a run for it, this is his retaliation for

Pasviri's nonexistent gold; his own sweet way of saying goodbye – permanently.'

With trepidation, Lee crouched down and touched the wire – there was no slack.

'On both our lives, my sweetheart, whatever else happens, for God's sake, do not move your foot.'

Though she had never seen one, Karen knew what it was.

'Booby trap?'

Lee nodded his head. 'Keep still. From now on you do only what I tell you.'

'Please, I need to know what I'm hooked up to.'

'Don't know yet.'

On all fours he moved away from her. The wire had been stretched under and between the legs of folding camp chairs, hurriedly disguised with discarded bits and pieces. The FN rifle and radio had drawn him in; Siqueiros had stripped the tent of what he needed and it was now obvious to Lee that he had no intention of coming back.

'Can you see anything?'

'Stay quiet,' he warned, 'I need a clear head for this.'

The Russian made anti-personnel fragmentation mine nestled between two full, four gallon jerry cans; Roberto had carried up their spare fuel for the Zodiac's outboard motor. Fixed to the ground by an integral wooden spike, the device taunted him from the shadows. Finished in matte green it was no bigger than a can of baked beans – its outer skin chequered with pre-fragmented iron segments. On detonation, these cube-like pieces of iron would be hurled outwards at the speed of high velocity bullets – lethal and totally devastating for anything caught within a five metre radius. Barely visible, the tripwire had been suspended just inches above the earthen floor. Karen's eyes never left it.

'Tell me,' Karen insisted, but now there was fear in her

160

voice, for that ghostly third person had stepped inside the tent. 'Tell me, Lee – I want to know, then I'll leave you be.'

With reluctance, Lee explained the cruel cunning of their adversary.

'Russian-made PomZ, anti-personnel mine, but this one comes with a twist, four gallons of petrol either side of it. Two kilos of drag on that wire is enough to trigger the striker spring. In short, move your foot any further, my lovely and we'll both be blown to hell.'

Karen shivered, chilled through by the terrifying revelation. Besides shrapnel from the mine, within a split second of the trap being sprung, the tent in its entirety would be engulfed by a raging inferno. Neither one of them would survive. There would be nothing left.

'What are you going to do?'

'The mine is a pull-to-detonate type and as long as there are no secondary traps in play, we have a fighting chance of staying alive – providing you keep still. Whatever happens, don't move your foot.'

A faint smile lifted the corners of Karen's mouth. 'Piece of cake then. Why not move the petrol first?'

Lee shook his head. 'Could be rigged, first priority is to get you clear of the tripwire.'

'I love you.' Again she smiled, but now that terrible fear of what might happen was there in her eyes.

'Likewise,' Lee said. 'With all my heart.'

On his hands and knees he crawled in close to the mine. Cutting the wire was out of the question, any sudden coiling motion could be enough to jerk the pin free; in that limited light, Lee could barely make out the PomZ's sensitive striker configuration. The striker retaining pin itself was already two-thirds clear of its insertion pocket, bored horizontally into the ignitor column. Millimetres were all that it needed, one slight tug on the tripwire would be enough to release the spring and send the striker pin crashing into the percussion cap. In turn, this would fire the detonator – then the high explosive core would erupt.

He waited for his eyes to adjust properly and then, with a surgeon's fingers, reached out for the ignitor column.

Karen watched him work; the muscles in her legs already cramped from the awkward angle of her stance. Her breathing skipped and flurried, like that of a bird caught in the hunter's snare. However slight, through every movement Lee made, she was set upon by a sense of cruel anticipation. Often she closed her eyes, convinced that at any moment a terrible hurricane of heavy shrapnel and burning petrol would rip out her life.

'He's taken the make-safe pin,' Lee cursed and shook his head in disbelief. Once more, he moved his fingertips over the full length of the ignitor; double checking every possible contour where the steel pin might have eluded him.

A centimetre of severed cord was all that Siqueiros had left. Had the pin been there it would have been the relatively small matter of a steady nerve for Lee to re-insert it and render the mine safe.

'The sick son of a bitch has cut the retaining cord, the pin's gone.'

Karen's courage, like a chastened child slid away inside the shadows. Her legs began to tremble. Though only slightly, it was enough to show as small vibrations along the full length of the tripwire. Lee discarded the idea of pushing home the half extracted retaining pin, fearful of it being brushed aside by the constant, downwards compression of the striker spring.

'I'll have to improvise. Are you listening?'

Karen nodded her head. 'I'm listening; what do you need?'

'Some sort of pin – strong wire. Anything you can see.'

There was more gunfire now. Lee knew the ground troops were homing in on their targets. Siqueiros' men were fighting running battles with Pasviri's soldiers.

'Your hair.' Lee called up to her. 'Hair grips – there might still be one.'

Karen reached up; slowly, so as not to lose her balance. She worked decisively, her fingertips unsure of finding anything. For the last three days her appearance had meant nothing; her hair was now totally unkempt and covered in filth, personal grooming had been the last things on her mind. However, slightly above her hairline she felt the firm outline of something metallic nestled down amongst the matted strands of her fringe. Carefully, she uncovered the precious clip and drew it out.

'Okay, I've got one.' She held out her hand. Lee shuffled backwards. Gently he touched her arm, encouraging her. His throat was dry; his emotions were running at fever pitch and he was now afraid that talking might weaken his concentration. He took the hairpin from her fingers and for that moment felt a sudden urge to stand up and hold her close. Karen saw the need in his eyes and she nodded her head to him.

'You can do this, my sweetheart. There's still too much to be done with our lives for them to end here like this.'

With his elbows propped against the ground for support, he moved in close as he dared to where the steel tripwire connected with the mine. Again he waited for his eyes to adjust and for his breathing to quieten. One last time he looked over his shoulder; in the soft light, Karen's face, like that of a young girl, appeared ethereal, almost angelic. He turned away from her and forcibly banished her face from his mind.

As a living, breathing entity, the fragmentation mine willed his fingers to make mistakes. Even in that warm atmosphere, the metal felt cold, the unevenness of the iron segments like that of dank, graveyard walling. He prayed that the improvised pin would match the hole and that it would withstand the downwards thrust of the spring; then, with the fingers of his left hand, he steadied the mine against it toppling over from the exertion of his sideways pressure.

More gunfire, closer this time, interspersed with that solid *crump, crump* of mortar bombs on thick forest. Blanketing all of these sounds was that unremitting slog of his own heartbeat.

-41-

Rex picked up on the missile just moments before it struck home. Burnt gases as a tell-tale, silver thread streaked from the rocket motor; then came the all too familiar flash of white light from the stricken Alouette's exhaust vent. Seconds later, held back by sheer distance came that sharp, thunderous clap of the detonation. In the mere blinking of an eye the helicopter, like some wild pheasant flushed from the English field had been expertly gunned from the sky. Mortally wounded and glittering with Avgas from ruptured fuel lines, at a sharp angle, the gunship spiralled into the forest canopy. The explosion, when it reached for Rex's ears was dull and anticlimactic, dampened by the closing over of deep undergrowth. A column of black smoke snaked from the treetops and Rex felt his anger rise up with it. He snatched up the radio's handset and depressed the transmit button.

'Alpha two, do you read?'

'Strength five, comrade major.'

It was then Rex saw the second Alouette rise above

the granite and turn its guns on the missile's launch point. He pictured the SAM launcher being reloaded and readied for another strike. Instinctively, he scanned the open sky for movement.

'Alpha two, disengage. Return to the bridge for refuelling and second uplift. Do it now.'

Immediately, the Alouette broke away from the ridge. Rex watched it leave, but at a mile outward bound, he saw a second missile streak from that same granite outcrop. Almost parallel to the surface of the lake, on its thread of silver sunlight it turned like an arrow caught in a crosswind.

'Alpha two. Evade! Evade! You have missile inbound!'

Out of desperation, the pilot swung eastwards; almost on its side the Alouette slewed hard to starboard. Aligning himself with the sun's radiation the pilot kicked the Alouette's tail round; with the glowing sun now behind him he faced the Strela head-on, and with the bulk of the Alouette's exhaust now hidden from the missile's heat-seeker, he dropped the aircraft's nose and fell like a stone for the surface of the lake. Within yards of touching the water he levelled out; looking upwards through the perspex bubble of his canopy, the pilot watched and prayed.

For those next few seconds the missile jinked through moments of wild indecision, uncertain of its target. Then, like the wild dog to fresh scent it aligned itself to the sun's infinite source of infrared and locked on. Excited by the solar radiation, valiantly the rocket took the missile skywards – at almost four kilometres out from the launch tube, not having reached any solid point of impact, the missile's self-destruct mechanism activated.

-42-

Lee knew they were running out of time, the gunfire was closer now, more intense. Soon the camp would be overrun by Fifth Brigade soldiers; or even worse, Siqueiros would be back and without the slightest hesitation would take great delight in killing them. The game would be over. Their lives snuffed out. His sons would never know what happened; the only reference to their parents would be a casual three-liner in the Herald newspaper, reporting the disappearance of two white fugitives somewhere in Mozambique.

'Stay calm,' he whispered and matched one leg of the hair clip to a hole in the ignitor column.

It went straight in. Surprised by his own luck he smiled reassuringly at Karen.

'Nearly there. Another few seconds and you can move your foot.' He reached for the mine, unclipped the tripwire and pushed home the safety pin.

With the wire now slack, Karen flung it clear of her ankle and stumbled out into the sunlight. Lee picked up his rifle and looped the strap across his shoulder. He carried out the radio and both jerry cans, only then did he go back inside for the mine and trip-wire.

'The mine will buy us time,' he told Karen, sparing only precious seconds to console her. 'They'll be here soon, my sweetheart. Our only hope is to stay one step ahead of them.' Gently, he squeezed her cheeks between finger and thumb. 'Can you make it down to the jetty?'

Karen nodded her head – her eyes fluttered and then her breathing steadied. 'I'll be okay. What do you want me to do?'

'The radio and one jerry can?'

'Should be easy enough,' Karen told him and determinedly she gathered together those last remnants of her courage. Lee resisted his own need to hold her close; mutual sympathy would serve only to sap what little mental strength they had left.

'How're we doing for food and clean water?'

'Baked beans and two litres of water, that's all I could find.'

'Enough to see us through,' Lee said. 'It'll make Gerard's food taste all the more like home cooking.' Without fuss, he leaned over and kissed her cheek. 'Time we got ourselves away from here.'

Karen followed him at a safe distance, the weight of a full jerry can dragged heavily at her shoulder. Twice they heard the closing beat of helicopter rotor blades and they were forced into thicker cover. Sporadic bursts of gunfire pointed to the fighting being confined to thicker forest further back along the hillside. However, they were reminded often enough by the sudden, vicious crack of rifle propelled grenades and the thunder of Browning machine guns.

At the edge of the treeline, Lee set his equipment down and pulled the stake-mounted, anti-personnel mine from behind his belt.

'No more cover from here on in.' He cleaned the grenade's striker column of sand. 'This will slow them down if they come after us.'

A metre from where the path narrowed he pushed the stake into the ground, hooked the tripwire to the safety pin and drew out the slack, then secured the loose end to the base of a small bush. Karen watched him prime the mine and camouflage the area with dry grass.

Through a gap in the trees, they could just make out the Zodiac's hull; still covered in branches it would give them time to load their equipment without being seen.

A lone helicopter bored away above the lake, with its tail up and head down. Karen likened it to a swallow feeding on the wing, just feet from the water.

Exhaustion encouraged her mind to wander; fantasies of safe, uninterrupted sleep weighted her eyelids. Lee realised what was happening and nudged her back to full awareness.

'Stay focused. Our sons need their mother alive.'

A second Alouette howled overhead; through an opening in the canopy, Lee stared straight into the gunner's eyes. A chill wind flooded over him; a small valley, miles to the north-west – sixteen years ago. Karen saw the change in him.

'What's wrong?'

'Nothing,' he lied. 'Trick of the light. The guy behind the Browning looked familiar, for a moment there I thought it was Rex.'

He rubbed the ache of fatigue from his eyes. 'Like you, I'm knackered; we both need rest.' He wrinkled his nose at the breeze. Cloud had thickened the sky above the western rim of the lagoon. 'There's rain coming. Another storm would be good; the choppers won't be able to fly.'

He led Karen away from the path. Slowly, he pushed his way between creeper vines and young saplings, careful not to leave any sign. A single, bruised leaf or the flipping over of small stones would be all that a tracker needed to find them.

He found a place between a matched pair of giant mahogany, as if to form the legs and arms of some fairytale throne, the roots of both trees had intertwined, twisting back on themselves they coiled serpent-like about the base of the great trunks they supported. Amongst the roots the ground was dry and in places thickly covered with soft mosses and fallen leaves. Shielded from the north-westerly winds and elevated to slightly above the surrounding soils, the space was a natural, dry hideaway. There was the scent of wild civet and porcupine, but it was the possibility of him finding something far more sinister that made him hold back.

'Give me a minute,' he told Karen. Rifle first, he shuffled forward into the hide. Using the rifle barrel, he probed amongst the leaves.

The permanence of the forest and deep windrows of fallen leaves made it the ideal habitat for the Gaboon viper; camouflaged by their natural colouring they were adept at nestling in with dried leaves and other forest detritus. By nature, the viper was placid and difficult to provoke, although, if stood upon would in the blinking of an eye drive its two-inch long fangs full length into the leg of its aggressor.

Lee checked the entire hide, then, satisfied that Karen would be safe he called her inside.

'Get some sleep if you can. No one will find you here. I'll be back before the storm breaks.'

Karen baulked at being left alone. 'Where are you going? Why can't I come with you?'

He shook his head. 'You're dead on your feet.' He reached for her and kissed her cheek. 'I like my women fresh-faced, not with blue rings round their eyes. Stay quiet and yell out if anything happens, I won't be far away.'

Before Karen could reply, Lee had disappeared inside the forest.

Screened from below by thick foliage, Lee pressed his back to the firmness of the tree's trunk for balance. With the radio lodged between his knees he switched on the power and prayed for a strong signal. It was imperative that he made contact with Gerard before the old man gave up on them.

The battery indicator rose to just above half full. He switched the selector to channel four and with the radio now on minimal volume, lifted the handset against his ear and listened. With his heart racing, he pressed the transmit key.

'Gerard, can you hear me?' He released the key. The reply was immediate.

'Can hear you, Lee, but your signal is weak – strength three at best. Give me an update, over.'

Again, Lee depressed the transmit switch and hurried out his message.

'Listen carefully. Upstream from your location. Black sky, there's a storm coming. We're about five miles south-east of it and I'd say as the crow flies, directly in line with your loc.'

'Copied that, Lee. Confirm you are north-west of the main river?'

'Affirmative. Too much for me to explain right now. Keep an ear open. Will come back to you before dark.'

'Got that, Lee. Confirm you and Karen are okay?'

'Alive and kicking, old-timer. Got to go. Conserving batteries. We'll talk later.'

He turned off the power and slung the radio across his back. The rain was close now; the wind had dropped and above the sporadic crackle of rifle fire he heard the thunder. Once back on the ground, he retrieved his rifle from the undergrowth and backtracked to where he had left Karen. She woke as soon as he touched her and though he had been gone for less than twenty minutes, she appeared to him as refreshed and fully alert.

'The storm's close,' he told her. 'We move as soon as the rain hits.' He shrugged his shoulders, repositioning the weight of the radio pack. 'I managed to contact Gerard.'

'Thank God for that,' breathed Karen. 'How far do you think we are from the *Isabella*?'

'Give or take, twenty miles, thirty at the outside. First we have to find our way back to the main channel. We'll keep heading south to south-east and pray we make the river before dark.'

'What about the boat?' Karen asked. 'Surely Siqueiros will have people watching for us?'

'We'll find out soon enough, maybe we'll strike lucky and Siqueiros' men are too busy saving their own skins for them to worry about the Zodiac.'

Karen dusted her clothes of leaves; her actions now were quick and her eyes sharp again. Above them, the sky resounded with closing thunder.

Lee found a different way back to where the forest gave way to open ground; the PomZ was still in place, the tripwire exactly as he had left it. They pulled away the grass from where they had concealed the jerry cans and carried them forwards as close as they dared to the bare periphery of the lagoon. Lee knelt on one knee and waved Karen in next to him.

'Keep your eyes on the trees left of the jetty; if there's anyone out there, that's where they'll be watching from.'

They waited for as long as they dared, watching for movement and listening for sound; a man coughing, or out of boredom, talking carelessly to a comrade, but apart from sporadic gunfire and the sibilance of approaching rain there was nothing.

As a vertical moving wall, storm rain cut through the

forest. Where there had once been sunlight and bright colour, now even the shadows had disappeared; all of it swallowed down by that moving eye of low pressure. Lee turned his back to Karen for her to fasten down the canvas flap and secure the radio. A hundred yards to their front, the Zodiac's outboard motor barely showed through the camouflage. Lee knew that to cross the open ground in open sunlight would prove suicidal; they would be spotted within the first twenty yards and gunned down. The storm was their one chance of reaching the inflatable. They needed the rain; solid sheets of it, that first almighty deluge that would for a few precious minutes cover their approach.

'Keep your eyes on the Zodiac; whatever happens, don't stop moving forwards. Blow this chance of getting away and your lover boy, Roberto will be sending out wedding invitations.'

Karen glowered at him. 'Very funny, Goddard.'

'Your incentive not to get caught.' His expression hardened. The chase had started; the clamouring of pursuing men reached to him from the direction of the camp.

'They're on to us.' He flicked off the FN's safety catch and willed the heavens to open. He nodded his head at Karen. 'Pick up your jerry can, sweetheart. Get ready for the longest run of your life.'

-44-

In the face of the oncoming storm, Rex ordered the pilot to put down. Sheltered by the leeward side of a small hill, the pilot landed the Alouette and shut off the turbine; for a minute the silence was total. However, the calm was short-lived. With tempestuous fury, lightning clawed and slashed at the forest canopy; topmost boughs were torn free and sent crashing to the forest floor. Soldiers debussed from both doors and threw a defensive ring about the Alouette; crouched inside the undergrowth they were oblivious to the deluge.

Rex lit a cigarette; smoke curled up to the cockpit canopy, visibility outside was down to five metres and still the sky continued to darken. Toad-like, the helicopter sat to a pad of solid granite, all around the rain lashed and within seconds the ground flooded with run-off. Beyond the clearing, the forest rose up as a tangled, living redoubt; without axes and machetes no one would get through.

'I know how Goddard thinks.' Rex forced his voice above that of the storm. He addressed the young pilot officer. 'Within the next ten minutes he will make his move; he'll use the rain as cover.'

'Providing he is still alive, comrade major.'

Rex nodded his head. The man was astute and forward thinking.

'He's alive; I can sense him,' Rex countered. 'Like an old fox he will take the fowl from under Siqueiros' nose and run for it.'

'You know this, Goddard well, comrade major?'

'Better than most, lieutenant; ex-captain with Smith's colonial army. We fought one another. Captain Goddard is not a man who gives in easily. As long as he sees a slight chance of survival, he will take it.' He leaned over and flicked the spent cigarette out through the port-side doorway. Though still the tropical downpour, the initial fury had eased off. At a steadier rate, incessantly, the rain drummed against the fuselage.

Rex reached out for the Alouette's radio and immediately, Pasviri's voice hissed inside the cockpit.

'I know you are listening, major; give me your sit-rep and for both our sakes, I pray for it to be a good one.'

Rex adjusted his headphones.

'Confirm call sign Alpha two has uplifted from your loc?'

'Several minutes ago, major. Another five troopers and a medic, as you requested. The pilot told me of your errant misfortune.'

'Siqueiros was ready for us; most of his men have taken to the forest. As small groups it will take months to find them.'

'Let them go, they are of little importance. What about Goddard and his woman? Their boat, comrade – have you found their boat?'

'Affirmative, but the area has still to be cleared.'

'Excellent! When will you begin?'

'As soon as this storm blows over; visibility is down to a few metres.'

'Once you have reached Goddard's boat you are to contact me. I am tired of waiting for a result, Comrade Khumalo.'

Rex focused all his hatred on the voice inside his headset.

'Finding Goddard is in both our interests. You will be the first to know.' He flicked off the switch.

The storm was moving away towards the south-east; squalls of grey rain were being dragged across the lake. Rex prayed that Lee and Karen were well out of harm's way. He nodded his head to the pilot.

'The rain is breaking up, lieutenant, ten more minutes

174

and you can take us back across the bay; let's find out if I was right. I'll bet a hundred dollars to your one that our Captain Goddard has cut and run for the Save.'

-45-

Heavily laden, Karen forced herself into keeping pace with Lee. At almost twenty kilo's, the jerry can was now a remorseless, downwards drag on her arm and the muscles in her shoulder screamed for relief. Thunder roared like cannon fire and within seconds of her stepping away from the treeline her clothes were soaked through. Grit and old sweat streaked from her hair, to the front, anything further than ten yards distant was quickly veiled in rain.

Moving over open ground, Lee trusted the line he had taken; at that angle they would have no other option but to come in contact with the shoreline. He glanced over his shoulder and waited for Karen to catch up.

'One minute's rest; that's all we can spare,' Lee told her. 'Any time soon and Siqueiros' men will be breathing down our necks.'

Run-off cleared the ground of debris and to their advantage quickly wiped away any sign of their footprints. Lee slung the rifle across his chest and gestured to Karen for him to take the second jerry can from her. Reluctantly, she gave it up. Now able to travel faster, they closed with the shoreline and within those next few minutes, Karen recognised the misty silhouette of the jetty.

Lee stopped dead in his tracks. He lowered both jerry cans, raised his hand and drew Karen's face close in to his cheek.

'They've posted a guard; in the boat.' He held up a finger. 'One man – I need you to stay put.'

Karen crouched against her heels. Lee disappeared, swallowed up by the storm. Caught by a flash of lightning, for a brief moment the hooded figure of a man showed up through the rain. Sat towards the Zodiac's prow, with both arms draped across the stock of his RPD light machine gun, the Renamo soldier appeared as though he were asleep.

Angling his approach from behind the outboard, Lee moved forward just as another sharp squall of rain thrashed across the inflatable. The noise became his ally and within seconds he was crouched to within a metre of the guard. He engaged the FN's safety catch and raised the rifle to shoulder height. He drove the rifle butt at the base of the guard's skull, where the uppermost vertebrae were most vulnerable and with the full weight of his shoulders behind the strike. Rain and sodden clothing muffled the blow; it found the hollow of his neck, just an inch above the line of his collar, crushing the cervical spine. The guard slumped sideways over the prow and like an otter sliding from its holt, quietly he disappeared beneath the surface of the lagoon.

Lee tore aside Roberto's makeshift camouflage from around the outboard motor and called out to Karen. She dragged over the spare fuel and between them they lowered the jerry cans down inside the Zodiac.

'What if the motor won't start? What then?' An almost paranoid fear of failure fell upon her.

'It will,' Lee insisted, 'one way or another this baby is going to get us out of here.' He pointed to the rear mooring rope. 'You'll have to free the knot – I don't have knife and for Christ's sake hurry up the rain's lifting.'

When it came, the explosion seemed less than a

hundred yards away; a single, sharp report. Though tempered by the storm, the sound swept over them.

'They've triggered the mine!' Lee realised and frantically he fought to free the forward mooring line. Slippery and swollen by rainwater, the knot tore at his fingernails.

'This one's free!' Karen yelled to him and then looked around her, searching desperately for something Lee could use to sever the remaining rope.

'We're out of time,' Lee hissed and thumbed off the rifle's safety catch. He pressed the rifle's flash guard up against the knot, backing it up against the wooden planking of the jetty; he fired a single round through the mooring line. What was left of the knot fell open. He jerked the rope free of the Zodiac and dropped it overboard.

'Grab the paddle!' he shouted instructions at Karen and reached out with his foot to shove the Zodiac away from the jetty.

Karen positioned herself as close as she could to where the bulbous, rubber prow narrowed enough for her to use the paddle. She forced herself to keep an even rhythm, but reluctantly, like some ageing hippopotamus the Zodiac lumbered sideways-on into deeper water.

Lee scrambled over the jerry cans, he opened the shut-off valve and pumped the outboard's rubber priming bulb. He felt the build-up of internal fuel pressure and with a trembling right hand grabbed for a firm hold on the starting handle. He closed his eyes and braced his feet against the transom.

'Start for me, sweetheart – one more time – just take us the hell out of here.'

With commitment, he pulled back on the handle and immediately the engine fired.

'The throttle!' Lee shouted to Karen. 'Push the lever forward – but slowly!'

Karen slid into the driving seat and with even pressure, inched forward on the throttle lever, but the outboard shuddered and died before Lee had chance to adjust the mixture of fuel and air to the carburettor. He reached for the manual choke and fractionally, pushed it further in for a leaner fuel mix. Twice he turned the engine over and on his third attempt it fired up and settled to the familiar steady beat that he was looking for. The Zodiac was less than twenty metres out from the jetty when the first of Siqueiros' men broke clear of the trees.

Dampened by the noise from the outboard motor, the renegade's triumphant bellow echoed across the space between them. He came in low and fast, his eyes were on Karen; with the fixation of a wild beast he committed to that final charge for the water's edge and in a single, fluid moment brought his rifle to bear.

Karen lunged for the orphaned RPD machine gun. For a fleeting moment the need to kill frightened her; since childhood she had conditioned herself to preserve rather than to destroy, but the moment flew and quickly she looped the nylon carrying strap about her shoulder. With her hands locked to the weapon's stock and bipod, she hefted the gun into her right hip.

From the hip and at a full run, the soldier fired his Kalashnikov in long bursts. However, through the folly of his own excitement the shots went high and wide, and in the way that Lee had taught her, Karen lowered her own aim to compensate for the shooter's tendency to over-elevate the barrel.

Oblivious to incoming fire she braced her legs for the recoil, then squeezed the trigger and gave free-rein to the terrible force she had unleashed.

The soldier was driven backwards. The gun's cyclic rate of fire gathered him up, tossed him aside and still Karen held the trigger down, traversing the barrel from left to right while empty cartridge casings clattered about her feet. More than half the gun's four hundred round drum magazine had been expended before Lee reached her and tore it from her grip. She slumped sideways against the bulkhead, and like a drunk in the aftermath of a violent brawl she retched into the water.

Lee dropped the gun and opened the throttle. With her bilges awash with storm water, valiantly the Zodiac surged forward and disappeared inside the rain.

Lee was forced to shout above the engine noise.

'Are you okay?'

Karen nodded her head. The horror of what she had done left her weak in the legs. She had killed someone – another human being. She turned her face to the rain.

'I can't believe what I did back there.'

'You did right. Push it to the back of your mind,' Lee told her. 'Same as our run-in with the Cessna pilot – it was him or us.'

Out of character, Karen found herself marvelling at the efficiency of the weapon. How easy it had been. She reached out and touched the barrel; it was still hot. She pulled her fingers away and trailed them in the water. Thunder growled, this time further away. The storm was abating. Lee looked up at the sky and guessed the longevity of their cover. Once inside the mangrove forest they could kill the engine and hole-up – take stock of their situation.

'Twenty minutes and the rain will be gone. We need rid of the bilge water, the extra weight will burn more fuel than we can spare.'

Whilst Karen worked the pump, Lee strained his eyes at the murk to their front. The horizon opened and closed; rain then mangrove forest, then more rain. As a grey veil it draped from angry clouds, seemingly for fifty miles across the delta. He adjusted the boat's heading and feathered the throttle, running the outboard just above tick over to save on fuel. Half an hour out from the jetty he made out that first sliver of eggshell blue where the sky had opened a crack in the clouds.

-46-

Against a clear sky, two Alouette gunships hovered with impunity above the deserted encampment. Most of Siqueiros' men were already deep inside the forest. Return fire was sporadic and ineffectual, a last, futile showing of armed resistance before it was washed away by the merciless clatter of heavy machine guns. On the ground, a platoon of Fifth Brigade troops swept in extended line formation from the forest's edge and anything living they happened upon was slaughtered indiscriminately – anything man-made, torn down or torched by the deployment of white phosphorous incendiary grenades.

From their vantage point above the stronghold, with indifference, two men looked down upon the devastation. One of them screwed a black Sobranie between his lips and touched a lighted match to the tip.

'Our time will come, Roberto, let the fools do what they will. Did the imbecile, Pasviri think I would stay behind to welcome his soldiers?' Siqueiros shook his head at the Fifth Brigade's supposed, triumphant defeat of his forces and his mouth broke with a wry smile. 'No my friend, what they will find is worthless; scrawny chickens and old men, that is all. Their prize has flown.' He slung his rifle across his chest. 'I will wait for you at the water's edge; get word to the men. Tell them to pull back; they know what must be done, leave Pasviri's baboons to fight amongst their own shadows.'

'What of the white man and his woman?'

Siqueiros smiled at Roberto's angst. 'They are where I

180

want them to be. Patience, my friend – they will not escape us. Your woman is safe.'

He followed Roberto's progress for as long as the undergrowth afforded a glimpse of the Shangaan's whereabouts, then turned on his heels and at a steady jog made his own way through the forest.

For three more hours, Siqueiros followed a ridge of dry ground towards the south-east, only once did he stop to rest, forced to stand silently for a moment where the forest thinned. Pools of open grassland gave him little cover. Upwind of his scent and oblivious to his passing, small herds of red impala grazed in close to the treeline and a family group of white rhino lumbered, heads down for new grass. He marvelled at the length and girth of the rhino's horn; in American dollars, Maputo traders would pay top prices. Moving ivory and horn to the Far East continued to bring fat reward for those who had the nerve to flaunt their disregard for wildlife conservation. Hard cash spoke louder than preservation; the demand was brisker than ever so that traders fought for prime placement at the bidding tables.

The sun was already low in the sky when Siqueiros reached his prearranged rendezvous with Roberto – a small, rocky promontory of dry land. It was a place where fresh water from inland rivers met with the indomitable influences of the tidal delta; a blending of fresh, vibrant growth and clear water with that of the perpetual, acidic green periphery of the mangrove forests. He knew that Lee and Karen would have passed within a hundred yards of where he was standing and instinctively cocked his head and listened intently for any sound drifting back from the Zodiac's outboard motor.

'The body is strong but the legs grow old, Diego. What took you so long?' The Shangaan had pushed all out to get there before him.

Diego took up the challenge, toying with the Shangaan's psyche.

'Goddard's woman was not easily satisfied, Roberto. She slowed me down, her needs were many.' He sensed Roberto's agitation and went on with the charade. 'Many times she called out for the great Roberto, but after that first hour had eyes only for me.' He shook his head. 'She chose the fitter, younger man, Roberto – she had no desire to be crushed between the earth and the belly of an old buffalo.' Again he shook his head and smiled wistfully. 'You missed so much, never have I walked so many times in paradise.'

'And you, Diego, are a man who lies too easily. Your stories are those of a father for his smallest child.' Like a wild animal he sniffed at the air. 'They are already into the swamps; the smell of engine smoke is still here.' He pointed out the widest channel. 'Like the cow hippo their boat is fat and idle, they need wide water for them to reach the river.'

'But we do not, my friend. Uncover the boat; if our luck holds strong we will be up with them before nightfall.'

The boat was a *rua hang yao*, the long-tailed boat – built in the boatyards of Bangkok's heaving waterfront, expertly crafted by Thai boat builders her lines were those of a sleek, eight metre long canoe; barely wide enough to take Roberto's massive girth. However, with his legs braced against the sides and with Siqueiros stood upright to the engine's tiller, the craft sat high and stable to the water, her prow, custom built for maximum speed through Thailand's inland waterways.

Shipped to Maputo aboard a Chinese freighter, the *rua hang yao* had stood as part payment for Diego's last delivery of illicit ivory and rhino horn. Powered by a thirty-five horsepower Vanguard engine mounted high up on the stern transom, the ageing American Go-Devil drive unit was equally as rare as the contraband used for its procurement. Originally developed by a foresighted, Baton Rouge entrepreneur to propel the Louisiana mud boats through shallow water, the powerful outboard motor could drive the needle-like canoe to speeds of almost thirty miles per hour between the mangroves, even water of less than a foot in depth proved to be of little consequence.

Diego stripped away remaining pieces of canvas from around the engine, then took up the weight of its six gallon fuel tank and roughly gauged its contents.

'Almost full.' He reached for the in-line cut-off valve mounted between the tank and carburettor intake. Restricted by the mangrove trees and narrow channels, six gallons would take them no further than thirty miles into the delta. 'The spare tank.' He gestured to Roberto. 'Bring it, or we run out of fuel.'

Roberto slid back in the water and waded to the shoreline. He hefted the spare tank across to the boat; with some trepidation he climbed back inside and crouched to the boat's central point of balance. Nervously he scanned the swamp for any sign of crocodile, then nodded his head to Siqueiros.

'I am ready.'

From a distance, the bridge at Ponte Sobre hung web-like between north and south embankments; passing the giant structure on its southernmost side, nose to tail, both Alouettes changed course and came in wide for the airstrip. Like a signaller's heliograph, their bulbous perspex windshields flashed simultaneously in that late sunlight.

Comrade Julius Pasviri waited for Rex to reach the Land Rover before pushing open the door. He adjusted his aviator sunglasses and screwed up his eyes at the glare. Rex loaded his kit onto the back seat and before Pasviri had chance to speak, climbed in alongside him and first-footed the conversation.

'A direct hit with a SAM-7 and a near miss with a second. Then the mother of all storms prevented follow-up. I swear I have never seen so much rain.'

'So, for the second time our friend, Goddard has given us the slip.' Pasviri scowled. Uncharacteristically he accepted the setback and swung the Land Rover away from the landing zone.

In a matter of minutes they were back inside the ops tent. He slumped into a canvas chair and looked about expectantly for a drink.

'The problems we have incurred from Goddard's escape will be resolved soon enough, comrade.' He took off the Aviators. 'The storm may well have worked in our favour.' A young recruit brought in opened bottles of cold Zambezi lager and set them down on the table. Pasviri dismissed him with a perfunctory wave of his hand. He drained the first bottle before carrying the conversation forwards.

'Whilst you were chasing after Siqueiros, our reconnaissance people located Goddard's charter fishing boat. She is anchored midstream, some twenty miles inland from the river mouth. On board we have a certain, Gerard Brownlee. Obviously, he is waiting for Goddard and his woman; it does not require the brain of a genius to work out their final destination.' He finished a second beer and dropped the bottle next to his chair. 'Finding Goddard is now our prime objective. With regard to the glamorous *Isabella* and her captain elect, neither will be allowed to leave the estuary.'

He lit a cigarette and then tossed the pack to Rex.

'By this time tomorrow, we will both be wealthy men and all of our Goddard related problems will be over.' He flicked the wheel on his lighter and stared outside the tent at the oncoming twilight. A skein of wild, Spur-winged geese caught his attention; cutting westwards for Zimbabwe they held that familiar arrow-like formation. Brought on by the rains, new grass would be growing along the riverbanks. The geese would feed on it, grow fat and make their nests amongst the reed beds. Pasviri watched them change to tiny shifting flecks then disappear into the horizon.

'Ridding Zimbabwe of one more colonial enclave will be, as the white man puts it, the icing on our cake.' He swivelled sideways in his chair and turned his smile on Rex.

'You my friend will be duly installed as manager elect to the Empress Deep. You will take full control of our project. With my influence and your knowledge of mining, nothing can stop us. Ready markets for everything you produce have already been sourced, along with the continuous rise in the gold price and my Far Eastern contacts, within this next year our financial prowess will rival even that of our illustrious prime minister.' His smile widened; expensive dentistry caught the sunlight and like gold from the mine he was about to plunder, it glowed provocatively.

He stood up from the table and pocketed the sunglasses. The entire operation had been thwarted by heavy rain and silently he cursed it. Tomorrow he would take back control of the situation; the weather people had forecast clear skies, there would be no further setbacks – he would make sure of it.

'Sunrise, comrade. I suggest an early night for the both of us. See to it that the helicopters are fuelled and fully armed; our friend's entrepreneurial bid for freedom is about to come to a grinding halt.'

-48-

With the motor throttled back to less than quarter speed, Lee nursed the inflatable away from the main channel; both he and Karen strained their eyes for a safe place to spend the night. Rafts of rotting vegetation beckoned as islands and solid shorelines, though none were substantial enough to take the weight of even a single man. Mangrove trees, as though on tip-toe stood with their roots enmeshed above the waterline and from the paler colours of the high water mark, Lee could tell how much the incoming tide would rise before that next ebb. Robbed of their lanterns by Siqueiros' men, finding somewhere safe and dry to sleep was proving problematic.

Lee kicked the engine into neutral and let the boat glide through a narrow break in the vegetation. Hanging foliage closed the gap behind them.

'This is as good as it's going to get, at least we should be safe here, another half hour and it will be dark.' He cut the engine. From every quarter the silence rushed in at them; for the next twelve hours they could sit out the night. Karen rummaged through her canvas pack and whilst she felt for something to eat, Lee rigged the radio's aerial and turned on the power. The indicator needle shuddered to quarter full; Siqueiros' listening out for military transmissions had all but sucked the life from the battery.

'Gerard, can you hear me?'

As soon as he released the transmit key, Gerard's voice crackled through the handset.

'Had me worried old chap, where the devil are you?'

'We're back on the Zodiac, about three miles north of the main river. We've pulled into cover – got no light and hardly any food but I think we're safe. At least until sunrise. How far in from the coast are you?'

'I'd say fifteen-plus miles. The river's high but holding steady. Any more rain upstream could be dangerous. A lot of debris coming down. Are you clear of trouble, over?'

'Not sure yet. They may well be looking for us. We'll head for the river as soon as it's light. With luck we'll reach your loc sometime tomorrow. Stay close to the radio and keep your eyes peeled. Have to go, Gerard, the battery's almost knackered. Will talk again in the morning.'

-49-

Stressed by the Save's powerful race for the ocean, like telegraph wires in high winds *Isabella*'s anchor ropes thrummed continuously. At the trailing edge of a long island, opposing currents met and broke into confused eddies, creating a narrow though more neutral backwater. It was here that Gerard made his final stand against the river. He switched on the boat's bridge searchlight and swung the beam at right angles to the

Save's central channel. Like monstrous juggernauts, uprooted trees passed no more than thirty metres away from the boat's hull.

Twenty miles downstream where river and ocean conjoined, the Save vented her gut of froth and flotsam. From the air it would be seen as a dark highway; picked up by powerful ocean currents it swung southwards, strengthening an already vast arc of silt and debris sweeping out from the shoreline.

For the past three days the flood level had remained constant, and then fortuitously the sky had cleared of rain clouds. Light from a limpid moon touched to the tops of tall trees.

'If the weather holds, the river should start to slacken off,' Gerard thought aloud and switched off the searchlight; with a damp rag, vainly he tried to stem the flow of sweat from his forehead. Soft lighting cast a yellow glow about *Isabella*'s cockpit. Tendai sat with his back to the bulkhead, unable to find sleep he hummed quietly and listened to the river. The temperature was at a constant high and the humidity, even at night, without the restraint of a cooling breeze had become almost unbearable. Outside, attracted by the light, mosquitoes swarmed in their hundreds of thousands.

Tendai shook a drop of sweat from his nose and leaned forward with his elbows against his knees.

'The river is angry. We cannot move; it will destroy our boat.'

Gerard nodded his head in agreement.

'So we sit tight. Lee will have to do the same. The Zodiac's motor isn't powerful enough to cope with this lot. He'll end up half way to Australia before he knows what's hit him.'

He stared at the radio. Its power-on light glared from the console; every small sound from the speaker plucked at his nerves. He glanced at his watch; four in the

188

morning. Still too early, but boredom and the pressure of not knowing made him reach for the radio's handset.

'Lee – can you hear me?'

He released the key. On his third attempt the carrier band came alive and though heavily laced with static, the voice that hissed from the radio pumped as iced water through Gerard's veins.

'I think your friend is unable to hear you, Mister Brownlee. I had expected him to have reached your loc by now. Where exactly are you?'

'Who is this?'

'Who I am is of no consequence, however, your colleague and I have already made our acquaintance. Perhaps you and I should talk; face to face. Before midday would be to my liking. Watch for me, but make no attempt to prevent our meeting, comrade. At the first sign of any aggression I will destroy your boat and everyone on board.'

The transmission died. Dumbstruck, Gerard dropped the handset back in its cradle. He nodded to Tendai.

'Got to be Pasviri. The bastard knows where we are; he can't be far away, the incoming signal was pretty strong.'

'How can he find us?'

'Helicopters. There's no other way for them to reach us.'

'Then we will fight,' Tendai growled.

'And a fight it may well come to,' Gerard confirmed. His eyes sparkled. 'Pasviri doesn't know what he's up against.' Again, he checked the time. 'An hour till sunrise. Time enough for us to stand to and break out whatever weaponry we've got below.' He stopped himself and grinned at Tendai. 'Not really your fight old boy. No offence if you sit this one out – could get nasty.'

Tendai shook his head and laughed.

'And leave you alone with Mugabe's soldiers? Just not done old boy.'

He swung back the cockpit stowage hatch and disappeared below. He felt for the light switch and a single bulkhead fitting lit up the storage space. Stacked on shelves to either side, still in their wooden shipping crates were six oiled, Lee Enfield .303 calibre rifles. Alongside these, Tendai recognised three innocuous RPG launch tubes and their grenade packs. Two RPD light machine guns had already been threaded up to their gangster-like drum magazines; these he brought out first and one at a time held them up at arm's length for Gerard to lift clear of the stowage.

Gerard's nostrils flared at the smell of gun oil; side by side, on metal bipods, the machine guns evoked in him forgotten feelings. Like a child exploring the contents of some long-abandoned toy box he ran his fingers along the gleaming barrels of both guns. Old memories surfaced, crackled and burned like wildfire. He was the underdog. The very thought of being fired upon by a better-equipped, superior fighting force had come upon the seventy year old as a rush of pure adrenalin. In his mind's eye, the tiny *Isabella* was now the ocean-going destroyer; Her Britannic Majesty's ship of war and from her bridge to her very bowels there echoed the sound of running feet and claxons. His men were clamouring for battle.

Tendai secured the hatch; it was then Gerard pointed out a small doorway. Made from the same marine ply it had been discreetly stained and varnished to match the bulkhead panelling.

'The finishing touch,' he smiled and threw Tendai the key. 'Open her up.'

Tendai worked the latch and looked inside. What appeared to him as an innocuous piece of printed linen had been lovingly folded and placed with reverence

190

upon the shelf.

'Bring her out, man.' Bright with excitement, Gerard's eyes were on fire. 'Brought her along for good luck. Didn't think we would ever need this, but today will be as good a time as any for old *Isabella* to fly her colours.'

With Tendai's help, Gerard opened out the naval battle ensign to its full size.

'So, what do you think sailor? The real thing; not some damned foreign imitation.'

Tendai shook his head. The six by twelve white ensign had him baffled.

'Our battle colours!' Gerard howled indignantly. 'Her Majesty's Royal Navy? Don't you see? Damn it man don't look so bloody nonplussed.'

'You're crazy, old man.'

'Ain't that the truth,' Gerard chuckled, 'but it might just buy us some time; and who knows we might get lucky. Might make them think twice before turning their guns on a boat flying the Queen's flag.'

-50-

Cloud-like and blood-hungry, mosquitoes swarmed from amongst the mangrove trees.

'I'm being eaten alive,' Karen whispered. 'We've had no anti malaria tablets since leaving Mahenya.'

'We'll double-dose once we're on board *Isabella*,' Lee encouraged her quietly. He loosened the fuel pipe from the in-line filter. 'Cup your hand below the filter. Dab some petrol on your arms and cheeks, and a couple of drops in your hair.' He dribbled out precious fuel from the pipe. 'You'll stink like a filling station for a couple of hours, but the petrol fumes should hold the mosquitoes off — at least for a while.' Lee followed suit. The stringent smell of raw petrol appeared to work. 'They pick up on your scent as well as body heat. Only good for non-smokers, though.' He grinned at his own brand of weak humour, then reached for Karen's arm and squeezed it gently. 'We'll get through this, my sweetheart. By this time tomorrow you'll be eating fillet steak and listening to Gerard's stories of derring-do over a bottle or two of cold Zambezi lager.'

It would be a long night. The floor of the Zodiac was still awash with rainwater. Fending off mosquitoes would deny them sleep, but succumbing to it would prove more than foolhardy; at night, the mangrove forests were alive with venomous snakes and though Lee had not seen them, he knew the voracious saltwater crocodiles were well aware of them being there.

'I'm starving,' Karen demurred.

'What about the cans you took from the ops tent?' Lee reminded her. 'Beans would be good right now.'

'Beans *a la* no tin opener,' she countered. 'What about shooting the tops off?'

Lee shook his head. 'Gorilla man might hear the shot; too risky.'

Karen grabbed hold of his hand.

'Listen!'

Lee strained his ears for any unnatural sounds. Creature noises were all around them and sceptically, he dismissed the possibilities of Karen having heard anything unusual.

'Your ears are playing you false, just frogs and stuff.'

'Be quiet and listen!' Karen hissed at him. 'There it is again!'

This time, Lee heard it; that dull, oppressive drone of the outboard motor.

'Didn't count on them having a boat; big mistake.' He stood up and turned to face to the north-west. 'They're looking for us – high-revving, four-stroke engine and they must have lights. Whoever's out there sure as hell isn't dragging his heels.'

Light flickered between the trees.

'About a mile,' he whispered to Karen, 'maybe less; got to be Siqueiros. No one else would have a boat like that.'

'We've got no lamp, Lee. We're sitting ducks for Christ's sake. Without a lamp, we won't stand a cat in hell's chance of getting away.'

'We sit tight and pray they go past us.' Lee dragged over the RPD and hooked the gun's bipod over the stern transom to give it stability. The drum magazine would still be carrying upwards of a hundred rounds. 'If they see us, the shit will hit the fan, but whatever happens we're not going back to Fantasy Island. We stand and fight – whatever the outcome.' He gestured to her. 'Pick up my rifle and lie next to me. Fire when I tell you and aim low. Trust me, in the dark you will shoot too high.'

A breeze sprang up and Lee was thankful of its strong easterly flow. With it went the pungent smell of petrol. No more than a quarter mile stood between the Zodiac and the incoming craft and on the warm night air, Lee recognised the deep bass voice of Roberto.

With the FN into her shoulder, Karen braced herself for a firefight. The remorse had left her. Through her mind's eye she saw her sons; both were watching her, both were stood in the rain, English rain – so far away and she wanted to run to them. For that split second she faltered, then the instinct to protect her young kicked back in and she shrugged aside any last vestiges of uncertainty.

'Wait for me to open fire,' Lee reminded her, then settled himself behind the machine gun. Above them, the sky blackened and the stars were white fluorescent scatterings across the firmament. Formed as some wide and glittering highway, light dispersed by the Milky Way was enough for Lee to differentiate between the mangrove trees and open water. Slowly, sharper outlines came into focus and through a slight break in the foliage he guessed the place where Siqueiros' boat would pass directly across their stern. He traversed the gun's barrel through the available arc of fire; there would be little more than a two second window of opportunity for him to maximise his chances of a clean kill.

The boat was close now, no more than a hundred yards away from the Zodiac. Karen's heart, like a trapped bird, beat against her ribcage. Scared of firing prematurely, she strived to regulate her breathing and withdrew her finger from inside the trigger guard. Praying they would not be discovered, Karen lowered her face below the transom. Inside her head she played out favourite songs, but spitefully they shrivelled and blew away. Now the sound of Siqueiros' boat was close-in.

Torchlight flickered above the mangroves. Though Lee could not decipher the mixture of Shangaan and broken Portuguese, the excitement in Roberto's voice was obvious.

The Shangaan sat astride the knife-like prow, his feet almost touching the water; with his rifle slung across his chest, both hands were free for him to direct the beam from a powerful hunting lamp.

'They are close, Diego, without light they cannot go far.'

'And their boat is slow, my friend, they will not outrun us. When we find them, do not shoot unless I tell you. We want them both alive, Roberto.'

Karen heard the Shangaan's name; her breathing raced and faltered as if she were being held by the ankles to the very edge of some sheer and limitless drop. Her finger found the trigger and the urge to open fire was now compulsive. Rather she would turn the gun on herself than suffer even a single minute of being mauled by the ape-like creature closing in on their hide.

'There, Diego!'

'I have seen them.' Siqueiros throttled back on their speed; from fifty yards, small reflections showed as dull red coins from between the mangrove trees.

'They've found us,' Karen whispered and expectantly she tightened her grip on the rifle. Lee felt her stiffen beside him, but he was still not convinced of them having been seen.

The incoming light flooded past their hide, then committed to another opening in the mangroves. Slowly, Lee reached for Karen's arm.

'Not yet,' he whispered to her, 'hold your fire – there's something else out there.'

-51-

For more than a thousand millennia, like the great killer sharks evolved of limitless oceans they had changed little, perhaps only in size; though the brain remained miniscule and was no bigger than the clenched fist of a newborn child. And yet, as hunter killers they stood easily upon the same predatory platform as the great white and the feared Zambezi river shark. They had survived the breaking up of continents and the mutating of their climates, the geological turmoil of a shifting land mass, the tearing of its surface and through these wounds, the venting of the earth's innermost anger. All these things they had survived and adapted to and were equally adept at hunting down prey from freshwater rivers as they were from the saline vastness of the Indian Ocean.

The first of their kind had walked upon the earth during the age of reptiles; the Jurassic period, and still these ancient saurians were the undisputed champions of all the subcontinents' great tropical rivers. However, this was not of a common freshwater species of Nile crocodile; this was a beast of Africa's lost order, that of *Crocodylus porosus*, a terrible saltwater leviathan of dark inlets and malaria-ridden mangrove swamps.

Through the occurrence of natural disasters, many of these ancient reptiles were torn from their native shores of south-east Asia and India's Andaman Islands by a devastating tsunami. In the grip of powerful ocean currents they were drawn westwards for some distant archipelago and beyond. Most succumbed to starvation and the continuous harassment by sharks, though one such creature, a monster of almost two tons had survived, and over those ensuing months had continued to drift in line with the setting sun, riding the swells and ocean storms on rafts of debris abandoned by the tsunami. The carcasses of cattle and the stench from human cadavers were thickly enmeshed with the flotsam, so that the reptile easily hunted out this plethora of grisly putrefaction on which it could feed.

After more than a thousand miles, the monster reached the outer islands of the Seychelles Archipelago. It dragged itself ashore, the scales along its back thickly encrusted with living barnacles and amongst the dense island forests and tiny inlets the beast had rested. Feeding mainly on fish and crustaceans, it built up new muscle and a store of thick energy-giving fats, and on a night when the moon had reached its fullest quarter and the currents and trade winds were favourable, the reptile once again turned its armoured head towards the western horizon and slid unseen into the surf.

Swimming between a hundred granite islands, driven perhaps by some inexplicable atavistic instinct it came

196

upon the northern tip of Madagascar. However, the need for it to carry on was paramount, but over those next forty days, plagued with hunger and ripping tides it was forced to take respite amongst shallow coral reefs where it gorged on young shark and leatherback turtle. The winds in the Mozambique Channel were now perpetually offshore, howling in from the north-west, and the waves that sprang from them were sometimes taller than the ships that sailed its reaches.

Days strung into weeks until at last the winds abated and having once again regained its strength, with instinctive determination, the reptile powered away from the shore. More than two hundred miles of wild ocean separated Madagascar from mainland Africa, but to the saltwater crocodile such a distance was of little consequence.

Finally, where coastal mangrove forests stood as bastions to the ocean, timed as if by purpose to the breaking of the first seasonal rains, the ancient saurian swam unnoticed between Shangaan fishing boats and the sandbars of a great river mouth. It followed the deeper, darker channels and compared to that of the open ocean the water was somnolent, warm and thick with human scent and sediment washed from Africa's far hinterland.

52

Roberto waved his arm for Siqueiros to him to take them closer to the inlet, but Siqueiros held back on the throttle. If need be, he would force Roberto to wait for first light before risking any confrontation. He wanted them alive. He had missed something and whatever it was that Pasviri sought so vehemently had to be on board the Zodiac, or was being held in safe-keeping by an expectant third party. Pasviri would not have deployed so many men if the reward for the white man's capture was anything less than extensive. Goddard was the key; capturing him alive was the only way of unlocking the conundrum.

Roberto became agitated, Diego's indecision had caused him to lose touch with what he had seen; the reflections had disappeared. Clinging on with his knees, he dragged the beam back and forth across the entrance to the inlet, but saw nothing. The wind direction changed and Roberto turned his face to it.

'Petrol, Diego. I can smell their boat.'

Siqueiros lifted his head to the new wind, but unlike Roberto's, his senses were not as keen. He cut the motor and strained his ears at the silence. The breeze brought with it the soughing of its own movement amongst the mangrove trees, but nothing more.

The boat trembled slightly; wobbled about its centre of gravity. Roberto steadied the hunting lamp and leaned outwards from the prow. Peripheral lamplight skittered about his feet and as a yellow tail the fullest part of the beam struck out over the water – a cord of yellow light from the inlet to his ankles. As the fisherman's lure his feet hovered just inches from the surface of the water.

Like a jack pike taking an unwary duckling from between the lily pads it erupted from the surface. At almost two tons, on that giant tail it powered vertically from deep water directly beneath the boat, jaws flung wide open and those finger-long teeth were things possessed of terrible nightmares. With a bite pressure of more than three thousand five hundred pounds per square inch it engulfed Roberto's head and upper torso, crushing his skull and ribcage before it dragged him from the prow and rolled his already lifeless body away, down amongst the mangrove roots.

Siqueiros fell back against the tiller. Disorientated by the horror of what he had witnessed, he clawed his way forwards. Frantically he searched for a weapon; his chest, still constricted by raw fear prevented his screams from reaching his lips. The hunting lamp, still burning brightly from within its waterproof casing rolled and bobbed some thirty feet from the boat; an ominous yellow marker to where Roberto had disappeared.

Lee and Siqueiros opened fire simultaneously; the half-caste with his foot against the prow and with the Kalashnikov hard into his hip. In one final act of defiance and with his rifle on full-automatic he fired into the water. Lee stroked the RPD's trigger only once, with the weapon aligned as best he could to the Kalashnikov's muzzle flashes. Two rounds slapped against Diego's sternum and flung him backwards over the side. For a short time they could hear him thrashing about in the darkness – then came the quiet; the only sounds were now the click and flirt of hunting bats above the swamplands.

53

They navigated more by instinct than by the ability to see where they were going. Slowly, with the engine at its lowest revs, Lee inched the Zodiac out from their hiding place. Karen held her rifle at the ready, her finger curled against the trigger for she was still in mortal fear of the crocodile reappearing. Siqueiros' boat drifted ahead, pushed by a slight breeze and from some twenty metres beyond, light from the hunting lamp bobbed and beckoned.

'We need the lamp,' Lee insisted, 'then we'll check out Siqueiros' boat for anything useful.'

With trepidation, Karen steeled herself against the horrors of retrieving the lamp; the water was pitch black, only slightly rippled. She found herself reliving scenes from Peter Benchley's, *Jaws* so that even in that humidity of the African rainy season her skin flushed with gooseflesh.

'What if that thing comes back?'

'It won't.' Lee tried to sound convincing, but the chances were well in favour of the reptile being only one of another half-dozen within a hundred metres of the Zodiac. Crocodiles, like sharks were adept at smelling out blood. Sensors along their muzzle would alert the beasts to the smallest of vibrations, those of a floundering fish or careless human being; either way they were well-equipped to hunt.

Lee took the rifle from Karen; gently he eased the Zodiac forward and then nudged the outboard's drive into neutral.

'Once we're alongside, reach down and grab a hold of the lamp.' Momentum took the Zodiac into the open. Lee braced his feet against the prow and hooked the fingers of his free hand inside Karen's belt. The lens was face down, creating an ominous yellow cloud below the waterline. With her heart in her mouth, Karen leaned out from the Zodiac's prow. At the very moment her fingertips found the rubber casing, the water around the boat effervesced with bright bubbles. Disturbed detritus directly below the inflatable had released carbon dioxide gas into the water.

Like a fisherman's cork float, Roberto's severed head bobbed to the surface. Crushed by the monster's powerful jaws it was hideously disfigured – the eyes were blooded sockets and that ruined mouth, compressed at a comical angle leered at Karen through the murk.

With her fingers locked to the lamp's carrying handle she was unable to scream or even tear her face away from the water. The effort needed for her to drag herself back inside the boat was a force that she no longer had control of. Now emptied of buoyant gases the mutilated head filled with water and slowly, slid back beneath the surface.

Lee sensed her horror and wrenched her away from the water. He prised the lamp from her fingers and turned the light on her face. Her eyes were wide open, without blinking she stared directly into the light.

'What happened? What did you see?'

She shuffled away from the prow and locked her arms around his neck. Gradually the terror abated.

'Roberto.' She whispered the Shangaan's name.

'Roberto is dead my sweetheart. It's over.'

'His head,' she whimpered. 'I saw his face – in the water. The rest of him was gone.'

It was then Lee realised what had happened. Roberto had literally been torn apart and his head, like some grotesque air-filled bladder had risen up from the deep.

'Hold the lamp for me,' Lee prompted her. 'Concentrate the light on Siqueiros' boat. We'll take what we need and get the hell away from here.' He glanced at his watch. 'An hour until sunrise.'

Karen steadied the lamp, her head ached and her limbs were leaden weights from her lack of sleep; the urge to curl up on the Zodiac's flooded duckboards was now impossible to ignore.

Lee brought the Zodiac alongside Siqueiros' boat and secured them both amidships. Karen held the lamp for him to climb aboard the river boat.

'A spare fuel tank,' he tested the weight, 'and damn near full to the brim.' He grinned at Karen. 'Just when we needed it, got to be at least eight gallons and with what we have already, enough to get us all the way down to the estuary.' Before passing the fuel tank across to Karen he took the lamp from her and lit up the river boat's outboard motor.

'Bigger than ours. Thirty-five horse, extended shaft. Flies like the wind, I've seen them perform; shame we have to leave her behind.'

'Mekong River,' Karen added. 'Designed to handle flooding rivers – I watched the same documentary.'

They looked at each through the torchlight. Lee got in first. 'So why don't we change boats? The Save will more than likely have maxed out and be running at full flood, this little beauty will cope with anything.'

Karen was already nodding her head. 'Pasviri will be looking for an inflatable; a little ingenuity might go a long way to buying us some time.'

The unexpected lucky break buoyed their spirits. The long-tailed boat could weave its way through debris at high speed whereas the Zodiac, with its smaller engine and bulbous prow would prove to be a lot more cumbersome.

They emptied the Zodiac of fuel, the radio and their meagre supply of fresh water and canned beans. Within that next half hour the long-tail boat had her extra weight evenly re-distributed. Trimmed and well-balanced she sat eagerly to the quiet surface of the lagoon. Lee crouched with his back to the engine transom, a can of baked beans clamped between his feet. Karen watched him lever away at the lid with a screwdriver and pliers from a half-rusted tool kit he had found beneath the transom. Her mouth ached and salivated from the anticipation.

'I can smell the sauce,' she croaked, 'please hurry up before I starve to death watching you.'

The lid tore free and he dropped it overboard.

'Use your fingers to scoop it out; watch out for the ragged edges'

He watched her eat. Sauce ran down her chin and like a starving cat, terrified of leaving even a single drop she reached inside the can with her tongue. She licked her fingers and flung the empty tin into the lagoon.

'I could eat another ten of those, but God that feels better.' She belched unashamedly and took a mouthful of clean water from her bottle. The influx of protein and cool water delighted her senses; now invigorated, she was ready to push all-out for the *Isabella*.

The sky had already started to change and the first faint colours of dawn bled as watery paint from between the stars. A fitful breeze stirred the upper branches of the mangrove forest and from where Lee and Karen watched and waited for those first, usable minutes of daylight, there appeared just enough pale sky for them to make out flocks of snow-white egrets lifting above the horizon.

'The light's coming fast,' Karen whispered, 'time we weren't here.'

54

Two military Alouettes uplifted from the airfield at Ponte Sobre. Comrade Minister Julius Pasviri commanded the lead aircraft and three Fifth Brigade troopers sat with their backs to the pilot, their kit and weaponry stacked at their feet. Pasviri stared determinably into the distance, prepared to fly all the way to Mozambique's coastline, if need be.

Rex sat in the tech's seat of the trailing Alouette; the pilot was the same young Matabele lieutenant from the attack on Siqueiros' encampment. Wind drummed past the permanently open doorways, a legacy of the Rhodesian war; troops could emplane or deploy without encumbrance. To the front, the sun had already risen well clear of the skyline.

Pasviri's voice hissed through Rex's headset.

'Luck is with us, comrade. Goddard's last transmission to his friend on the *Isabella* was intercepted only a few minutes ago. They are on the move. Locating them should not be a problem.'

'He could be armed?'

'Do not engage.' Pasviri warned him. 'When you find them, radio their position to this call sign and that is all. We need them alive, at least until we have what we're after.'

'What about the *Isabella*?'

'When the time comes, comrade, I will decide. They are communicating via channel four. Stay with channel six. Your pilot has already been briefed. That is all.'

Rex's pilot held the Alouette on a dead reckoning for Siqueiros' camp; the lagoon showed up clear and lake-like; the shallows, a pale emerald green, the deeper channels dark to almost black. Where the salinity of the swamplands took over, the water appeared as lifeless and nondescript. Blackened ground showed where Rex had deployed his Fifth Brigade soldiers. Even in the rain, their white phosphorous incendiary grenades had proved effective; Siqueiros' entire encampment had been razed to the ground. Other than scavenging flocks of pied crows, nothing moved. Like busy morticians they hurried amongst the devastation.

Rex picked out the jetty where the Zodiac had been moored, a bloated corpse floated face down, close-in to the wooden staging. From his vantage point above the swamplands, Rex identified an interlinking network of open waterways running in a north to south configuration; he pointed them out to the pilot.

'That's your marker. Go south. Stick to the widest channel and keep your eyes peeled for Goddard's boat.'

The pilot aligned the Alouette with her new course; he levelled at eight hundred feet, high enough to give them the advantage, but low enough for them to cut away in a hurry if they were fired upon.

As a usual sequel to heavy rain, mist boiled off from the open water. Rex leaned sideways and looked down through the port-side doorway. Everywhere, as acid green islands, groves of mangrove trees dominated the delta. A desolate place, fit only for reptiles and birds, for no dry land creature would stand a chance of surviving here. Away to the north-east, where the swamplands ended, Rex picked out vaguely outlined banks of what he thought to be papyrus reeds and the fan-shaped leaves of the lala palm. Where fresh water run-off fed into the delta, groves of wild date stood straight and lank as telegraph poles.

'A boat, comrade major – directly ahead.'

Rex swivelled in his seat; the Zodiac was less than a mile in front and appeared to be drifting. He put up his binoculars.

'She's been abandoned – there's no one on board.

Take us in for a closer look, lieutenant.'

The pilot brought the Alouette in low above the mangroves; downdraft from the rotors pushed the Zodiac up against the trees.

'Empty.' Rex stood in the doorway and communicated with the pilot via his headset. 'Just the motor – everything else has either been stolen or offloaded.'

'Siqueiros could have caught up with them, major?'

'Doesn't make sense,' Rex countered, 'he wouldn't have left the boat.' He leaned out for a better view of the Zodiac's storage, then quickly realised that the engine's primary fuel tank had been removed. Trapped between the motor and its transom and agitated by the rocking motion of the boat, spent cartridge casings reflected the sunlight.

'There's been a fight.' He gestured to the pilot. 'Give me a hundred yard radius and three-sixty of the area around the boat. Let's see what we come up with.'

They were eating up precious fuel. Rex condensed the search area and it was within those last twenty metres of the inflatable that Rex found the answer he was looking for.

Siqueiros' body had surfaced amongst the mangrove roots. Most of the chest area had been shot through and already, crabs and brine shrimp had been feeding on soft tissue parts. The wounds in his sternum were white and bloodless. Air turbulence uplifted the early sign of putrefaction and wafted it inside the helicopter; Rex balked at the stench and stepped back from the doorway. He nodded his head to the pilot.

'Make for the river. Nothing will be gained by our staying here.' He checked the radio's channel selector; it was still on six.

'Julius. Have found their boat; confirm you copied that?'

Pasviri came straight back at him.

'What about Goddard?'

'Gone. Just the Zodiac and going off your description, your friend, Siqueiros. Not far from the boat; shot through the chest.'

'The Zodiac's contents? Did you see anything?'

'Empty, apart from the outboard motor.'

'Where are you now?'

'Four miles out from the river. Goddard must have swapped boats; he's taken the Zodiac's fuel tank.'

'Not very clever your, Captain Goddard. The fool should have sunk the Zodiac. His accomplice is no more than twenty miles from your present position. Brownlee knows we are watching him.'

'Where are you now?'

'Left bank. A mile north of the *Isabella*. The river is dropping fast; make your way to this loc, but I say again, stay well back from the main river. We will wait for them to reach the *Isabella* before moving in. As of this moment, your friend Captain Goddard and his woman are no more than an hour away from losing everything.'

-55-

Lee stood with his legs splayed for balance and with his right hand on the throttle – the nylon cord from the engine's kill-switch clipped behind his belt; should he fall overboard, the thirty-five horsepower Vanguard motor would cut out automatically. Trailing the stern, Lee held the motor's six feet long driveshaft at a shallow depth; if need be, less than a foot of water could be negotiated safely. Karen sat at the prow, her hair slicked back from her face by the wind. At a shade under thirty miles per hour the long-tailed, *rua hang yao* sliced a curling path through chocolate-coloured floodwaters.

Lee shouted above the engine noise for his voice to reach Karen.

'Watch out for sandbanks, the water level's dropping fast!'

Karen gave him a thumbs-up. Invigorated by the speed she kept her face to the front and let the wind rush inside her shirt; she yearned for a hot shower, fresh food and a clean full-sized bed to sleep on, but still she was thankful; they were free of the mangrove forest and only occasionally did she allow her mind to recollect the horrific happenings of that last night.

With his free hand, Lee reached out and powered up the radio. He turned his head to the side, shielding the handset from the wind.

'Gerard, can you hear me?'

Within seconds Gerard's voice came back at him.

'Lee! Been trying to raise you. Pasviri knows I'm waiting for you; got me on the radio last night. He knows the score so watch your back.'

'What's the current like where you are?'

'Strong,' said Gerard, 'but getting better by the hour. Already over a metre down on last night's high water mark.'

'By my reckoning, I'd say an hour at the most before we're up with you. Get Tendai to listen out for us; throw me a line once I'm in close.'

'What about Pasviri? What do you want me to do?'

'Stay calm, old-timer. No heroics. I'll risk the batteries and leave the radio turned on. Listen out for helicopters; that's the only way Pasviri can reach you, copied?'

'Got that. Stay with the central channel; we're moored on the downstream side of a small island.'

'What's your food situation?'

'Plentiful.'

'Bacon?'

'Freezer full.'

'Dig some out, we could eat a sow – and sweet tea, gallons of it.'

'Hang on, Lee. I can hear something.'

Gerard turned his eyes to the sky. It didn't take long for him to spot the Alouettes.

'They've found us – helicopters – two of your old army gunships.'

-56-

Rex was quick to spot where Pasviri had put down. Half a mile to the south, the floodwater had eased back from full spate and now, like humpback whales, a thousand sandbanks shoaled the Save's channels and shallower glides. Only the central, deeper heart of the river was still open. Pasviri's voice hissed from Rex's headset.

'I have you visual, Comrade Khumalo. Do not attempt to land. Once I have uplifted, you will follow me to where Brownlee has moored the *Isabella*.'

'Copied that. What are your intentions?'

'That depends on Brownlee.'

'Goddard has to be close, there may well be confrontation.'

'Then we will deal with it as and when. What happens to Goddard's entourage of white colonists is of little interest to me, comrade. First the gold, then we can do whatever we decide with what is left. Go to channel four, perhaps your Captain Goddard will be listening in, time for him to realise the error of his ways.'

With both Alouettes airborne, Rex followed Pasviri towards the south-east; within minutes they were overflying *Isabella*'s anchorage. Rex shrugged on his safety harness and stood behind the guns. He cocked both weapons and in pretence of something to engage with, peered down through the open doorway. The *Isabella* appeared close enough for him to touch. Sleek and snowy white, unavoidably her colouring stood out in glaring contrast to the surface of the river.

Rex changed channels. Intimidated by that initial radio silence, he held his breath; then, as though they were standing face to face, Lee's voice was there with him, garrulous but authoritative.

'Got them, Gerard. Run out your guns old-timer, looks like these guys have no intention of letting us out of this alive – any trouble and will back you up as best I can from this end.'

Lee glimpsed a first sighting of his pride and joy. White as any Indian Ocean surf, *Isabella* stood out high and proud between the sandbanks.

'I can see you, Gerard! They think I'm carrying bullion. Use the Strela! Knock one of the bastards down and the chances are the other one will turn tail and run for home!' He released the transmit key and Karen stared at him, blank-faced.

'What are you telling him, Lee! Since when for Christ's sake has Gerard been carrying a ground-to-air?'

'Hasn't got one. I know that, but they don't. I'm banking on them listening in. Pasviri won't take any chances – the missile story may buy us some time.'

He swung the *rua hang yao* away from the central channel; single-minded he gunned the powerful Vanguard outboard at peak revs and with his heart in his mouth, knifed through redoubts of silt and barely submerged sandbanks. At less than a foot deep the water boiled and churned as a muddy wake. Mud-skipping the riverbed, he stuck to where the shallows ran at their swiftest; light-coloured arteries of live water. His decision to cut the corner saved them precious minutes. To his front, the *Isabella* rolled sedately with the slacking current and to a moderate wind, Gerard's battle ensign now flew fully unfurled above her stern railing.

Leapfrogging the forest's edge, the leading Alouette fell like an Osprey to the surface of an English lake. Expertly and at maximum speed the pilot dropped to within a few yards of *Isabella*'s wheelhouse and then cut away eastwards. The scream from the Artouste engine was enough to make Gerard and Tendai duck for cover. Tendai looped the carrying strap of the nearest RPD across his right shoulder. Gerard picked out the pre-loaded RPG launcher and nodded his head for Tendai to follow him outside.

Mesmerised by what was happening, Karen tracked the Alouette's flight above the forest; swinging in behind their *rua hang yao*, it was now the howling metal monster locked to their wake. From inside the Alouette's port-side hatchway, the gunner watched impatiently for the pilot to come about; his twin .303 machine guns already cocked and loaded with ball and tracer.

Karen snatched up the FN rifle. The weapon was already armed; all that was needed was for Karen to free the safety catch. However, the Alouette was coming head-on and at that angle her port-side guns were denied a useful arc of fire. Frantically, Lee gestured to Karen to get down below the level of the prow.

'Lie flat!' Lee shouted to her and as soon as she was down, he put the tiller hard over.

Pasviri flinched at the evasive manoeuvre and screamed at the pilot.

'Imbecile! You are losing them!'

'The trees, comrade minister – I cannot follow. The trees are too many!'

Pasviri twisted in behind the tech's seat. He pushed the gunner clear of the Brownings and checked they were ready to fire. He shouted through his headset.

'Take us down! Close as you can to the river.'

The pilot complied and shed height, giving Pasviri the

211

visual access he demanded.

A fan of narrow channels spread between the sandbars, like muddy fingers they felt amongst the flooded foliage and along one of them, Lee jockeyed his long-tailed boat through the shallows – straight for the far side of the island.

Pasviri sighted his guns and depressed both triggers. Ball and tracer lashed the outboard's wake, just inches from the motor. Lee felt the propeller bounce and rip at the mudbanks, then, with spirited determination the Mekong riverboat shook herself free of the shallows. Under full throttle, like a thoroughbred colt released to the open field, the *rua hang yao* leapt for deeper water.

Karen righted herself and again reached for the rifle. From the island's outer edge the Alouette rose port-side on to the main channel with its guns blazing. Karen fired from the shoulder, her aim no more than two metres above the stern so that Lee instinctively ducked his head from the whiplash effect of rapid fire. Karen fired short volleys of twos and threes, but her aim was wild and unfocused, her shooting thrown off target by the boat buffeting diagonally on to the current.

Unable to contain his anger, Rex bellowed into his headset.

'Julius! For Christ's sake are you mad? Back off!'

Pasviri replied with another withering burst from the Brownings. Just yards away from the *rua hang yao* the water boiled.

'Stay out of my way, Khumalo. Goddard fired on a government aircraft and now he will pay the price. Your concerns have been noted.'

Again, Pasviri opened fire; shell casings clattered about his feet and cascaded from the doorway. Hunched over the weapon's prismatic sight, demonically, Pasviri's face contorted with excitement.

Lee put the tiller hard over and swung in close to

Isabella's port-side; he cut the engine, lashed the *rua hang yao*'s stern to *Isabella*'s lowest railing and grabbed the RPD.

'End of the line!' he thrust the gun at Karen. 'If they come in close, shoot for the pilot.'

On the *Isabella*'s small afterdeck, Gerard stood shoulder to shoulder with Tendai. Above them, provocatively, the ensign flew three quarters full to a west wind; two, heavily out-gunned soldiers; a battle scene from some old classic, but here the bullets were real.

Through the launcher's iron sight Gerard zeroed in on the Alouette's open doorway, oblivious to the storm of bullets lashing the air about his head. At just under two hundred yards, Gerard allowed for windage and elevation. Instinctively he led the shot, aware of the rocket's tendency for turning into the wind. The attempt favoured him missing to port; with less than a fifty-fifty chance of the missile striking home, Gerard Brownlee squeezed the trigger.

Watching from the trailing Alouette, Rex shouted orders to his pilot.

'Stay clear of them lieutenant, this is not our fight. That fool of a Shona imbecile will get us all killed.'

The pilot held the Alouette at five hundred feet; far enough back from the *Isabella* so as not to become embroiled in Pasviri's full-on determination to destroy. Rex, for one fleeting moment thought to turn his guns on Pasviri, but the idea was fanciful and quickly he pushed it from his mind. However, as if by magic a fateful thread of blue-grey smoke shot between the boat and the Alouette and by that smallest of moments both craft were indomitably linked together. The rocket's sustainer motor had barely reached full thrust when the grenade detonated.

At first, Rex thought the missile had missed its target;

that Gerard had bungled the shot, then, as an over-ripened fruit struck by storm hail the Alouette's shape distorted and was torn almost in half by the terrible force of the explosion. Simultaneously, the aircraft's fuel tank ruptured and a halo of burning Avgas engulfed the fuselage.

Like some macabre, twisting fireball the Alouette cartwheeled into the river. The flame-out was horrific; pools of burning fuel fled with the current and then, as if nothing had happened, the river again fell silent. Rex swung his attention back to those aboard the *Isabella*.

Lee pulled himself on board and whilst shielded from the mayhem, Karen threw him a second mooring line. In a matter of seconds the Alouette had disappeared; ripped away by a maelstrom of angry water, the debris and charred human remains taken down to the deepest parts of the channel.

In places, Bella's decking had been torn up by sustained machine-gun fire. Pasviri's determined attempts to annihilate the crew had been unrelenting, his obsession with the Empress Deep had at last boiled over.

Physically unscathed, Tendai stood with his hands still locked to the empty gun, his finger fully down on the trigger. His face was slack and as if he were still in the grip of deep sleep his eyes saw nothing. Alongside him, Gerard lay with his arms thrown wide open above his head; at the centre of his sternum, dark arterial blood soaked through his shirt and as theatrically as the scene itself had come and gone, so did a pool of that same dark blood spread across the decking.

Dumbfounded, Lee stared down at his friend and that dark morass of anger and sadness that comes from the loss of someone dear rose up inside him. He knelt against the decking and in the palm of his hand cradled Gerard's head, as if the act would afford the old man some comfort. Though he had seen the drama of dying played out so many times before on the battlefield, still that pattern of guilt and non-acceptance flooded over him. He spoke softly, for the words struggled and caught in his throat.

'That was you all over, old-timer. You should have waited for me.'

Karen left him alone with his grief. The pain of her own sorrow became the clenched fist inside her chest, but to Lee the pain was even more powerful, almost unfathomable. Only when he heard the sound of a second Artouste engine did he find the strength to look up.

From behind the guns, Rex stared down at him. Lee made no attempt to defend his boat. Wind from the Alouette's rotors snapped at Gerard's battle flag. Rex signalled the pilot in lower and Lee waved for Tendai to take Karen inside the protection of the wheelhouse.

Shielded from the turbulence, Karen looked on from the wheelhouse window. The Alouette hovered to within six feet of *Isabella*'s decking. Lightly as a cat, Rex dropped from the starboard hatchway; he waved the pilot away and the wind abated.

'Captain.' He nodded his head to Lee and raised his arms to show that he carried no weapons. 'I think we have both suffered enough; time for us to talk things through.' He looked down at Gerard's body and shook his head. 'You were warned of the consequences. Honest answer – was it worth it?'

'We both knew the risks involved.' Lee said quietly. 'He died under no illusions. Rather it happened this way than in some soiled prison bed with your CIO people getting off on his suffering.'

'More twisted ideas on how we operate, captain.' He pulled out a pack of cigarettes and held it out to Lee. 'Not all of us are infected with Pasviri's ideologies.' Lee

215

shook his head. Days had gone by since his last cigarette.

Rex fastened the pack away in his shirt pocket, lit his cigarette and inhaled deeply. The Alouette put down on the island, close to where *Isabella* was anchored. He watched it land and simultaneously acknowledged the pilot's hand signal. There was no one else; just him and the young Matabele. The others were dead, swept away by the river. No one would know what really happened, nor did he care. Pasviri's death suited his needs – provided the living with a way out. Even more to the point, Julius Pasviri's unfortunate accident would enhance his chances of influencing those who held in the palm of their hands, the control of Zimbabwe's future. His own needs were far more reaching, but his patience and timing would prove to be the key. He could wait – fate would make its own choices.

Lee crouched over Gerard's body and gently drew the old man's arms into his sides, settling his limbs before the onset of rigor mortis. His friend had gone, what was left would be consigned to a makeshift grave, eaten by insects, left to rot in a strange unfriendly part of Africa miles from home. The thought of leaving Gerard behind angered him. He looked up at Rex.

'I need to ask a favour of you.'

'What do you want?'

'You help me bury Gerard. Then we'll talk.'

'Then first I must ask for your word that this debacle is over; no more running.'

'No more running,' Lee promised. 'Help me sort this out. How much fuel have you?'

'Enough to make Buffalo Range; maybe another fifty miles.'

'That will do.' He walked to the stern railing and untied the nylon cord to Gerard's ensign. He freed the flag and carried it to where Gerard's body lay on the

216

deck. It was then that he realised how long it had been since that initial phone call had so easily started the ball rolling. Gerard, as always had been overly supportive, always there in a crisis. *'Twenty-five years with Her Majesty's destroyers, old boy. Whatever it is you want, I'm your man.'* Clearly, as though it were yesterday, Lee recalled that fateful night at the homestead and he cursed himself for it.

He laid the flag out alongside Gerard and looked to Rex for assistance.

'Help me lift him on.'

Between them, they lifted the body; already the limbs were stiffening, that rare phenomenon of cadaveric spasm triggered by sudden death. Gerard would have felt nothing, his heart and upper spine pulped by a single bullet. With thumb and forefinger, Lee drew down the old man's eyelids and even in that torrid midday heat he felt that first chill of death touch her lips to his fingertips.

Rex helped Lee slide a small inflatable dinghy down through the stern launching port. Using the dinghy's ten horse outboard they crossed to the island and lifted Gerard's body on board the Alouette.

*

Tendai and Karen remained aboard the *Isabella* and like the watchful mother hen, Tendai fussed over Karen's well-being, insisting that she rest whilst he set to preparing her food. He took out bacon, eggs, pork sausages and red-ripe tomatoes from the galley fridge, and though Karen's mood was melancholic, that less than subtle smell of frying bacon and the lure of sweet tea flooded her mouth with saliva.

She ate in silence, staring out from the wheelhouse

window she strained her eyes for one final glance of a helicopter pulling away above the eastern horizon, but the sky had already emptied and her heart ached, for now her grief walked hand in hand with her guilt. Somewhere on board the *Isabella*, Gerard, under Lee's instruction had stashed a fortune in gold bullion, though at that very moment, for the chance to turn back the clock, gladly she would have given it all away.

-57-

Close to the surface the currents were powerful, but at depth that stretch of ocean was drowsy, quietened by her reefs and deep trenches. Lee decided that it was here that Gerard would find the peace he had often spoken of; it was a place fit for a man who had given everything. Behind the Alouette stretched the chocolate-coloured remnants of a mighty river, and to either side, the Indian Ocean rolled warm and turquoise-blue upon Africa's ancient shoreline.

'Over there.' Lee pointed to a stretch of dark water; it symbolised a deep rift in the ocean floor. As a violet-coloured throat it swallowed the sunlight down for hundreds of metres. It was here the pilot held the Alouette on an even trim – one hundred feet above the ocean. Knowing that no one would hear him, Lee gathered together a few words and talked them into the wind. He laid his hand on the ensign.

'This is where you belong, old-timer. When you catch up with Pasviri, give the bastard hell.'

Weighted with stones from the river and wrapped in the white ensign, Gerard's body balanced precariously close to the edge of the Alouette's open cargo door. It took but the slightest, sideways lift for Lee to initiate the old man's final journey to the ocean floor.

Both men watched him fall; then a slight flurry of white water – a dolphin perhaps.

-58-

Karen prepared a second serving of bacon and eggs and watched the three men sat at the galley table wolf it down. Not before all the plates had been emptied did any one pass remark as to what had happened. Lee was first to break the silence. He glanced at the pilot, but Rex spoke for him.

'He is a Matabele, you have nothing to fear.'

'So, where do we go from here?' He frowned at Rex. 'I'm just a little bit confused, why are you helping us?'

Rex smiled, and that cold, non-committal expression of the Party politician disappeared.

'Not all as one-sided as it may appear, captain. Your helping me rid our country of men like Julius Pasviri will prove to be beneficial – for both of us.' He leaned across the table and his eyes sparkled. 'That is, providing you see sense.'

In those eyes, Lee saw that first glimmer of hope; a plausible future.

'What are you saying?'

Rex lit a cigarette and dropped the packet on the table.

'You, Karen and the gold go back with me to Zimbabwe – decide otherwise, captain, and on your head be it.' He inhaled deeply. 'Though if you go with the latter, there will be no coming back. The door into Zimbabwe and access to the Empress Deep will be slammed in your face and your assets liquidised. In effect, you will be locked out of your own backyard. The government will declare your family, *persona non grata* –

permanently.'

Lee listened to Rex's reasoning with a fixed avidity, and it took only a minute for his interest to water through.

'Besides your word, I would need written government guarantees of my major shareholding in the Empress Deep, as well as proof of deposit with my London bank for one half the value of the bullion; the rest to my company account in Masvingo.'

'A fair expectation,' Rex agreed, 'consider it done. Your fifty-one to our forty-nine percent share of company holdings, with yours truly as working partner. My government will demand on-site representation of interest or they will not agree to what you ask.'

'And I get left alone – no harassment?'

Rex nodded. 'No harassment. No more visits from the CIO.'

Lee looked across the table at Karen.

'What do you say, my sweetheart? Take the money and run or head back home?'

'Home,' she leapt at the chance, and then the sparkle fell from her eyes. She looked away 'Gerard should have been here with us.'

Rex shook his head.

'Gerard destroyed the makings of a tyrant, a man who would never have agreed to what I have told you. He reminded us all of our mortality and what it takes to rid the world of men like Pasviri. Without his efforts, all four of you would be dead. Even me, perhaps. Julius Pasviri would have gone on killing for as long as it took him to get his hands on your Empress Deep.'

'How do we know we can trust you?' Lee asked him.

'You don't, but ask yourself why I didn't kill you when I had the chance. From the helicopter, captain, you know yourself just how easy it would have been.' He extended his hand to Lee. 'You have the word of Rex

220

Khumalo, that will have to do for now. The rest I cannot give you before returning to Zimbabwe.'

'It can wait,' said Lee and accepted the hand, 'your word is enough.'

'Then we will leave as soon as we have transferred your cargo across to my helicopter.' He looked around him. 'What about your boat?'

'Tendai will take her back to Maputo. How will you cover for Pasviri's disappearance?'

'A terrible accident,' Rex rolled his eyes theatrically. 'Pilot error; caught the branches of a tree with his rotor blades. Over in seconds, nothing we could do to save the honourable, comrade minister from piling into the river.'

'And myself and Karen? How do we fit in to this grand deception of yours?'

Rex's eyes narrowed. 'Complicated, I admit, but not unsolvable.' He stubbed out his cigarette and leaned back into his seat. 'You were caught by the flood; your boat capsized a mile downstream from Mahenya and you lost everything. We found you on an island; midstream, soaked through and half starved.' He looked at Karen for her opinion. She shook her head and grinned.

'Habitual liars, the pair of you.'

Lee stood up from the table and nodded to Rex.

'Time we got a move on; a couple of million dollars in gold bullion will take some shifting.'

Twenty, ten kilogram bars of gold bullion were loaded into the dinghy and in a single trip, ferried across to the island. Their combined weight equalled that of two grown men and necessitated their even distribution over the Alouette's floor space; along with the pilot and three other personnel, the aircraft would be flying as fully loaded.

Rex gave Lee his final instructions; once the Alouette had uplifted, there would be no going back. Lee knew his commitment to Zimbabwe and the Empress Deep would be total and unequivocal.

'David, your employee will be waiting for you at your camp in Mahenya. You're sure he knows nothing about the gold?'

Lee shook his head. 'Nothing.'

'What about your manager? Byron Fuller?'

'Likewise. Byron hasn't a clue. As far as he is concerned I'm off on a fishing trip with Karen.'

'Your gold has already killed off over fifty men, captain.' Rex climbed in next to the pilot. Behind him, Lee and Karen had the seating to themselves. 'Let us hope for a more benign future. Compared to watching people die, I find gold mining far more appealing.'

'How long before I see you again?' Lee asked him.

Rex pondered the question; the thought of him travelling solo from Mahenya with a fortune in gold aboard an ageing helicopter was already giving him nightmares.

'Give me a week and I'll be in touch. Break camp at Mahenya first thing tomorrow morning. You should be back in Masvingo by nightfall. Everything should be as you left it so keep your returning home calm and uneventful. No shouting your reappearance from the rooftops. One day at home to settle in, then back to your office as if nothing has happened.'

'What about the Hippo Mine road block?'

Rex shook his head. 'I will put through another signal to the company commander. He will be expecting you. A stand-in major has already been brought up to date regarding the death of his predecessor and our run-in with Renamo bandits, but as yet knows nothing of Pasviri's accident. Keep it that way. A need to know basis only – no extras. Your involvement with Mozambique has been well covered up; you have been holidaying at Mahenya with your wife – nothing more.'

'And Ponte Sobre?' Lee reminded. 'The temporary base near the bridge?'

'Already disbanded,' Rex assured him. 'By tonight, all Fifth Brigade personnel will be back in barracks. Ponte Sobre is back to what it was – a bridge over the Rio Save and a place where Shangaan herd boys water their cattle, that is all.'

Rex gave the pilot the all clear for him to uplift. From *Isabella*'s wheelhouse, Tendai watched with mixed emotions, half expecting Gerard to clamber up from the galley with steaming mugs of over-sweetened coffee. 'Made us both a brew, old boy.' Absent-minded, Tendai emulated Gerard's proper British accent and looked back over his shoulder, but he was alone and the abandonment rushed in on him. High tide in two hours; just before sunset. He raised his hand and saw Lee reciprocate. The Alouette lifted clear of the sandbank and within that same minute, disappeared above the forest. Tendai checked the time on the wheelhouse clock. There was just enough daylight left for him to make the estuary and lay anchor for the night. Without his friend Gerard, it would to be a long and lonely ride back to Maputo.

-59-

Under Rex's guidance the pilot manoeuvred his Alouette into a tight three-sixty above Lee's fishing camp. On the sand bank, from the company of his small fire, David followed the aircraft's progress and on seeing Lee in the open doorway, immediately he relaxed. Smoke and ash from the fire swirled about him as a maelstrom of grey dust.

Lee was out through the doorway before the pilot had

chance to power down.

'David! You're okay? You had us worried. Rex told me about your swim with the crocodiles.'

Delighted by the sudden rush of attention, David related the horror of that fateful happening; he bowed his head and shook it vigorously.

'The devils were snapping at my head; for that moment I heard my father's father calling out to me.' He shook his head in wonderment. 'Never have I stood so close to death.'

Lee started to laugh.

'Then the bullshit passed and Rex was there to pull you out from the water; you haven't changed, you old bugger.' He reached out and playfully he squeezed David's forearm. 'You haven't eaten? Why is my once ferocious lamp room supervisor now smaller than a Bushman? If you were a chicken I would get nothing for you.'

David frowned his distaste for the river.

'Fish! Everyday fish, but they are small and my stomach growls like that of a lion for fresh meat.' He stared longingly at the Land Rover. 'I think it is time for us to go home, sir – before my wife's lover drinks all my beer and my children forget the face of their father.'

'First thing tomorrow,' Lee promised and gestured to Rex. 'Before you abandon us, let me make sure the Land Rover's battery still has some clout.'

He climbed inside the cab, the keys were in the ignition and there was a thin film of dust across the seat; comforting waves of familiarity washed over him. He turned the key and watched the dashboard gauges spring to life. The engine fired on his second attempt, it settled and drummed evenly. The fuel gauge showed half-tank and two full, eight gallon jerry cans were still secured inside their carriers behind the cab. He switched off and gave Rex a thumbs-up.

'What about food?' Rex asked.

'Enough for a couple of days,' said Karen, 'Tendai packed a cooler box for us.'

'Anything else? What about cigarettes?'

Lee shook his head. 'Gone this long without the cursed things...'

'He's given up,' Karen interrupted and Rex threw up his hands in mock surrender.

'I'll speak to you soon,' Lee added. 'Just look after my investment, outside of the Empress Deep, it's all I've got.'

Rex climbed back inside the tech's seat and spoke animatedly to the pilot. He turned to Lee and nodded his head. The trust was there, it showed in his eyes. Lee took hold of Karen's arm and led her a safe distance away from the downdraft. The turbo whined to full pitch; dust flew up and the Alouette, like the willing horse stood lightly to its wheels then uplifted from the sandbank. Mesmerised by what had happened over those last few days, they stood in silence and watched the Alouette shrink then blur to nothing against a late sky. Pushing all his negative thoughts aside, Lee shouted to David.

'Build up the fire, old man, time to pile some fat back on those bones of yours.'

They left David alone with his fire-building skills and, holding hands like lovers, walked along the water's edge to where the river fell at their feet from the high lip of a waterfall.

'I think your lamp room supervisor was pretty much glad to see you,' mused Karen.

'Just a little,' Lee chuckled. 'Love him to pieces; another couple of days on his own though and I reckon the old man would have hot-footed it back home.'

'We were lucky,' Karen whispered. 'There were at least a dozen times when I thought we wouldn't make it.'

'Likewise,' Lee admitted. His mood tempered and suddenly the weight of it all was too much for him to comprehend. 'Today was the worst day of my life; at least since the war. Gerard's death hit hard – really brought things home to me.'

'It was a joint decision,' Karen gently disputed the statement. 'No one was forced into going along with it, Gerard was just as taken with the crazy idea as you were.'

'Gerard had cancer.' Lee dropped the bombshell. 'Prostate; advanced stages, left it too damn late before seeing his doctor. He was dying. Told me about it the day he left for Maputo with the gold.'

'You never said anything – I'm sorry.'

'Made me promise not to. Left a letter for me with Byron; wasn't to be opened unless he didn't make it home.' He sucked in the warm air and wished he had a cigarette.

'I'm really going to miss him,' Karen whispered. She rested her head on Lee's shoulder. 'Any problems and Gerard was always there to help sort things out.'

'Still is,' Lee insisted. 'Nothing's changed. Gerard will always be Gerard; not some cancer-ridden wreck of a man soiling some hospital bed sheets.' He stood up from the granite and looked out across the pool. The water was still discoloured, but the anger had gone out of it and it swirled as soft eddies and quiet backwaters along the shoreline. A lone crocodile had found just enough exposed sandbank for it to lie clear of the water. Its mouth was wide open and a pair of toothpick birds worked the saurian's teeth for scraps of meat.

'Lesson for us both. Over there on the sandbank, a classic, symbiotic Zimbabwe-style relationship – the ancient art of give me what I want or I'll take your head off.'

Karen recognised the birds. 'Egyptian plovers – I

226

guess that's what we'll both be doing from now on, sharing our meals with predators.'

'We have no choice,' Lee told her. 'Either we adjust our thinking or lose the mine; from here on in we'll be picking the teeth of every government official in Zimbabwe, just to stay afloat.'

'What happens if Rex is double-dealing us?'

'Again, Hobson's choice,' Lee said. 'We have to go along with him. I trust the man; he could have taken the gold and left us for dead in Mozambique, no one would have been any the wiser. We'll know for sure in the morning when we reach the military road block at the Hippo Mine.'

He helped Karen up. 'Another half hour and it will be almost dark and I'm starving. Right now, all my dreams are made up of rump steak and a bottle or two of cold beer.'

-60-

They broke camp at first light. Without the Zodiac and its ancillaries, all that the trailer carried was Lee's old four-man tent, strapped to the cross-member. Neither was there an illegally-owned FN rifle and ammunition, nor a supposed cache of gold bullion to worry about, so that Karen found it easier to relax and took time to study the forest for wild game and local flora. An hour and a half after leaving their camp, as they came out of a tight right-hander, the same military boom was suddenly there; no more than fifty yards to the front. Lee was forced to break hard.

'Don't forget,' said Lee, 'too polite and they'll smell a rat. Just be normal; no obsequious remarks.'

Three soldiers manned the checkpoint. The tallest of

them carried a pistol strapped to his waist, and on his epaulettes, Lee recognised the black crown insignia of the company major. He slid back his window and nodded affably.

'Good morning, major. Comrade Minister Khumalo said you would be informed of our travelling through your check point.'

'Your papers, please.'

Karen had them ready and handed them across to Lee. Without so much as acknowledging Lee's government clearance, Major Josiah Masasiri stayed silent whilst scrutinising the contents of their documents.

Lee turned off the Land Rover's ignition and settled back to wait. Across the entire continent of Africa, attempts made by foreign travellers to speed up government formalities only made things worse.

Karen focused her attentions on a pair of ring-necked doves; perched amongst the topmost branches of a tall tree, they faced the sunlight, their feathers pink and grey, necklaced in black about the throat.

'Comrade Khumalo spoke of your ordeal.' The officer glanced over his shoulder at the redundant boat trailer. 'I believe the river took your boat, Mister Goddard?'

'We lost everything.' Lee stopped short, offering little chance of contradiction. Instead, he ran through the story that he and Rex had cobbled together, readying himself for the inevitable suspicion.

'Everything?'

Lee and Karen nodded simultaneously.

'Cameras, food, everything,' Lee lied convincingly. 'Would have been a lot worse if Comrade Minister Khumalo had not found us. We hadn't eaten for four days.'

Masasiri looked up from the paperwork; he nodded his head at the comment, his eyes were narrow slits from the morning's low angle of sunlight. His jawline clenched and released spasmodically, the actions were those of a man frustrated by some higher authority. Annoyed by a personal need for him to implement more in-depth questioning, he forced himself to relax the conversation.

'My predecessor lost his life to that same river; Major Ephraim Thebisa. His helicopter crashed some distance from our border.'

'I'm sorry to hear that.'

'You saw nothing of him passing over your camp?'

Lee almost took the bait, but rallied instantly.

'We were marooned on an island, major. The noise from the flood would have drowned out any sounds made by a helicopter.'

'Of course, how foolish of me.' Now he was smiling. He handed back the paperwork and nodded his head to the man on the boom. Counter-balanced with a heavy weight, the metal post swung up and away from the Land Rover. 'You are free to continue your journey. Any approaching military vehicles and you will please give way to them.'

'I'll do that,' said Lee and started the engine. He drove for almost a mile before either one of them spoke.

'Close, but no cigar, major.' Lee checked the rear view mirror, half expecting to see a buff-coloured army Land Rover bearing down on them. 'Had me worried, though. If Rex hadn't given us clearance, our jumpy major back there would have pulled us in.'

'Just keep going,' Karen pleaded and closed her eyes. 'Don't wake me until there's good old tarmacadam under our wheels.'

Slumped against Lee's shoulder, Karen slept solidly for two hours. It was late afternoon before Lee swung on to the gravel road leading to the homestead. The security gates had been left open so that he drove straight up to the veranda steps before killing the engine.

Karen stood on the driveway and looked on lovingly at the homestead.

'A sight so beautiful it must have been gazed upon by angels in their flight.'

'David Livingstone's first sighting of Victoria Falls.'

'And for what it's worth my sweetheart, compared to this, there's no contest. You can keep your seven wonders of the world and all the fancy frills that go with them.'

She started up the steps. The familiarity of the surroundings washed over her, even the smell of polished floors and the scents of commonplace flowering garden shrubs now seemed to her as heaven-sent. The patio doors swung open and Byron Fuller stepped onto the veranda; feather duster in one hand, cup of tea in the other. He beamed at Karen.

'Saw you through the window so took the liberty of making you a cuppa.' He placed the cup on a wicker-top table and then transferred his interest to Lee. 'Would I be right in saying you would prefer something a little more volatile, Mister Goddard?'

'Just a cold beer thank you, Byron. Have you sent for the kitchen staff?'

Byron nodded his head and pulled out a chair for Karen.

'On their way up to the house as we speak.' He sensed something was wrong. Lee picked up on Byron's canny, sixth sense and decided to put things to bed. All the way back from Mahenya, this was the situation Lee had been dreading.

'You had better sit down.'

Byron did as he was told and with wide eyes stared apprehensively at his employer.

'What's happened?'

Lee shook his head.

'Gerard's dead. The day before we left for Mahenya.'

'I don't believe you.'

'Gerard had cancer.' Karen edged back in, her voice thick with remorse.

'Nonsense I don't believe you. Why are you telling me this?'

'Because it's the truth,' Lee said.

Byron dropped his duster next to his chair and on shaky legs, stood up from the table.

'I'd better get back to work. There are things to do. The quarterly production figures.' Still in shock he looked to Lee. 'Will you be coming in tomorrow?'

'Early as I can.'

'There's a letter...'

'I'll get it tomorrow.' Lee said, and like a second storm, again the pain reared up inside of him.

-61-

The boardroom appeared untouched, as though he had never been away; just as he had left it. The long table shone as it always did, the grain beneath the wax alive and vibrant. Succumbing to old habits, ritualistically, Lee touched and lifted his fingertips to and from the tabletop, leaving small rabbit-like tracks across its surface. He waited for them to disappear before reaching for the phone. The action was slow and tentative and for long moments of uncertainty he stared at the key pad. It was through will power alone that he managed to dial Gerard Brownlee's home number.

'Moses?'

'This is Moses speaking, sir. Mister Brownlee is not here today. Perhaps he is here tomorrow.'

'It's you I wish to speak with.'

Moses recognised Lee's voice and his mood lightened.

'Mister Goddard, sir. How can I be of assistance?'

'I'll be down in half an hour, put the kettle on and make some strong coffee – for the both of us.'

He replaced the phone and re-read the letter Byron had left on the table. He read aloud, unsure of his voice.

Lee – looks like I've left you in the lurch old boy, hopefully gone to a better place and now it's time to sort things out. Told you about my son Robert, works for DeBeers Consolidated Diamond Mines in Botswana; Jwaneng, the mine's called. Resident geologist there. Let him know what's happened, if you would be so kind. More likely to be the cancer or hopefully, something a little swifter, never was the hanging around type. Everything; bank account, car etc. goes to Robert, but not the cottage. That goes to my servant, Moses. My legal people have the details. To you, I leave my daybook and associated bundle of loose papers. Sounds trivial, but read them all carefully; most important old boy, something to tantalise the mental taste buds. All of it is kosher and above board. Do this for me Lee, and for your grandmother, Isabella, a most cherished and dear friend.

I know you will have done things right regarding my disposal, whatever you decided, I know would have been your best efforts. Anyway, no regrets, old chap; knock the lid off the brandy – top of my wardrobe. Better give Moses a shot – never was any good with saying goodbye. Wish him well for me, and to you and Karen I bid you both a fond farewell. You were and always will, remain my best of friends.

God bless you both,
Gerard

A post script had been added:

The old leather case, next to the brandy. The daybook and personal papers are inside. Whatever happens don't lose the damn thing. Guard it with your life if need be.

232

Lee buttoned the letter inside his shirt pocket; he went downstairs and out through the main door. In the car park, the air was a comfortable twenty degrees and the sky was that pale, eggshell blue of an African summer's morning. Shadows thrown by the shaft headgear stretched across the corrugated roof of the compressor house; the demand for compressed air was at its peak. Three, Belliss & Morcom compressors and their drilling crews were full out. By lunchtime the rock face on three levels would be drilled, charged and primed ready for blasting.

David came out from his lamp room; the old man's hair seemed whiter now.

'Morning David, I take it you're glad to be back at work?'

David nodded vehemently and grinned at his employer.

'Most definitely, Mister Goddard, sir. I think for me there will be no more fishing at Mahenya.'

'For you and me both.' Lee chuckled and climbed inside the company Land Rover. Isolated from the outside world by the quiet of the cab, the joviality of those past moments abandoned him; spiteful recollections joined him at the wheel. He looked up at his own reflection in the rear-view mirror. Grief and lack of sleep had left him with pouches of flaccid skin below his eyes. Inside his head the old man's chipper voice was again the garrulous passenger. Gratefully, he picked up on Roy Orbison's Pretty Woman on the radio and then turned the ignition key. He let out the clutch and without touching his foot to the accelerator allowed the engine's tick-over speed take him quietly away from the car park.

That first section of road had recently been resurfaced with gravel from the waste dumps; a sugary mixture of quartz and mill tailings crunched under the tyres. He pulled over at the apex of that first bend, stepped down from the cab and let the sun's heat wash over him.

Far below his feet, the road wove its way across the hillside like a gravel thread, cut with pick and hammer and dynamite it writhed through tight turns and over hazardous ravines strewn with black ironstone, some of which still carried the scars and sockets left there by the driller's steel. Now the bridge supports were of reinforced concrete pillars, though originally, the ravines and gulleys were straddled with rough, native timber. Cut from the valleys by so many cursing men, the raw wood was hauled upwards over impossible gradients, sleighed by teams of mules thirty strong. Shaped and bored with red hot irons the timber was then pegged and lashed together before being slung across the gaps as makeshift bridges. Only then could machines and mining paraphernalia be hauled upwards and re-assembled. He pondered the dangers and difficulties faced by those who had built that road, how many men had died, how many wagons and trek mules had lost their footing and crashed to the bottom.

Haze fell as a shimmering wall across the valley so that anything more than a mile out appeared blurred and indiscernible. On steel pylons, silver-threaded and snakelike the incoming high voltage line walked its way up from the valley floor, humming with energy – there was power in excess for any future development of the Empress Deep.

He reached for his cigarettes, realised he had given up and returned his hand to his side. 'We'll need more men to open up the western reef,' he mused. 'And more air and water; another compressor even.'

Now at ease with his thoughts he climbed back inside the cab and re-started the engine. Twenty minutes later, as if emerging from a dream he found himself on the driveway to Gerard's cottage bungalow. Set amongst a grove of fruiting peach and irrigated vegetable gardens the tiny dwelling appeared idyllic. The sprays were on and as wide, flickering rainbows flooded the lawns and flowerbeds. Moses watched him drive up and already that austere look of the worried man was there on his face.

'Good to see you, Moses.'

The old man nodded and tentatively, managed a thin smile.

'It is good to see you also, sir, but in my heart I feel the news you have brought with you is not so good.'

He opened the Land Rover door for Lee and followed him up the veranda steps and into the cool of Gerard's living room. He made coffee, strong and black and overly sweetened with brown sugar, and in the silence both men sat and drank until eventually, unable to hold things off any longer, Lee was forced to clear his throat and speak.

'Gerard won't be coming home, Moses.'

The old man dropped his eyes to the table and out of a sudden need for distraction reached for more sugar.

'I have been expecting it, he was a sick man.' His fingers shook when he stirred the mixture and within the space of those next few minutes, the weight of ten more years settled heavily about his shoulders. Again, Lee coughed the hurt from his throat.

'It was not the sickness. Gerard did not die as a sick man, but as a warrior.'

The old man's face altered. He could not speak, though in his heart Lee's words burned more brightly than the sunlight. As Lee went on and still at a loss for words, Moses stared out through the doorway and listened avidly to Lee's full account of Gerard's final moments.

'He fought like ten men.' Lee elaborated. 'I owe him my life, nothing less.'

For that next hour each man related incidents and adaptations of their long-standing friendship with Gerard Brownlee, and the bottle from on top of Gerard's wardrobe fell quickly to the halfway mark. Moses chain-smoked and the blue cloud that he generated was now thick about their shoulders. Both men took solace from the brandy and gratefully, with every mouthful, the heavy burden of their pain became easier for them to bear.

From that same wardrobe, Moses lifted down a battered leather case and carried it through to the living room; he set it down on the table and gestured to Lee for him to unbuckle the single, leather strap.

Gerard's daybook had been deftly bound in leather, ornately stitched and deep maroon in colour. To Lee's fingertips the binding imparted feelings of long ago and reflected the thoughts of a man whose life's most poignant happenings were scattered there amongst its pages. Pressed beneath the daybook were stuffed envelopes and bundles of loose papers, roughly held with old string. The urge to open them was strong, but he resisted and closed the case. There would be time for them later, when he could take in their content through fresh eyes and unravel their meaning with a clear, uncluttered mind.

One last time, Lee read from Gerard's bequest, he pointed out all things relevant to the man in front of him and at the end of it, both stood up from the empty brandy bottle and through half-closed eyes peered around the room as though Gerard himself might well be stood there in the shadows.

'Time for me to get back home,' Lee said, his voice only slightly marred. 'Whichever road you choose to walk, I will always be there for you. We will talk again. Stay well, old friend.'

From the veranda steps, Moses watched the Land

Rover disappear inside the haze. He waited for the dust to settle, then went back inside the house and closed the door.

-62-

Days passed before Lee found himself mentally able to cope with an in-depth exploration of Gerard's personal papers. Eventually, armed with a steaming mug off strong coffee, he ventured back inside the storeroom and closed the door behind him.

The old suitcase was where he had left it – open and intimidating on the roll-top desk. He drew up a chair and started reading.

Candid references to Isabella Goddard, Lee's grandmother, made him sit up and smile; it was more than obvious that Gerard had carried a fiercely burning flame for her and from between the pages, old photographs of that same beautiful woman flurried out and stared back at him. Her hair, steel-grey and even without the flattery of modern colour photography it shone out brightly, brushed back from her forehead and, as Lee remembered all too well, it was held in place with that clasp of mother-of-pearl and raw gold from the Empress Deep's richest reef.

'I would never have guessed,' Lee grinned, 'bit of an age difference, gran, but so bloody what. Reckon you two will be doing a fair bit of catching up right now.'

Gradually, the mood of Gerard's writing changed; from memories of the calm and infinitely sedate to the more mysterious, so that Lee now found himself drawn in, unable to tear himself away. An hour later, motivated by a sudden need to share his findings, Lee stood up from the desk and went to look for Karen. He found

237

her outside, supervising the laying out of her herb garden. He waited for her to finish doling out instructions before calling to her.

'Something I want you to look at. Either I'm reading it wrong or Gerard had already lost his marbles when he wrote it.'

Karen followed him back inside.

'What have you found?'

Lee pushed the book across to her. 'Read from the second paragraph to the bottom of the page. Tell me what you make of it.'

Karen settled into the chair and with expectant eyes she started to read. Gerard's handwriting was faultless and easy to follow. She reached the last line and then, owl-eyed, looked up at Lee.

'That's incredible. It has to be true, though. Not in a million years would Gerard make up a story like this – not just for the hell of it.'

Lee nodded his head. 'That's why Gerard wanted me to have it. The repercussions from this being found by the wrong people are unimaginable.'

'What about Rex?'

Lee shook his head. 'Not until we've worked it all out. Then we'll tell him.'

'Damn it, Lee. This belongs to him. I don't think my nerves will stand the strain of waiting. Keeping birthday presents from the kids is bad enough, but this, this goes a million miles past anything we've ever dreamed of.'

'Not just to Rex,' he countered, 'it belongs to every man, woman and child in Matabeleland. That's why we must be sure of which side of the field Rex is playing for.'

*

Lee gave the rest of his morning over to studying Gerard's roughly bundled collection of memorabilia, and for all of that time, beyond a growing redoubt of empty coffee cups, nothing else existed. Without his wristwatch, any awareness of real time eluded him.

Karen touched his shoulder.

'Why don't you take a break? Byron's been on the phone, wants you to ring him back.'

'Did he not say what for?'

She shook her head. 'Just that he needs to speak to you, came across as a little agitated.'

He followed her through to the lounge, picked up the phone and dialled Byron's office number.

'You've been trying to reach me?'

'Have you read the paper?'

'Didn't get one. I'm busy, Byron. Get to the point.'

'Front page: *Government minister dies in Mozambique. Defence force helicopter brought down by Renamo rebels.*'

Lee felt his heartbeat quicken.

'What else? Names? Places?'

'No names, but doesn't look good.'

'For Christ's sake, Byron.' Lee snarled into the phone. 'Give me the full picture. What have they printed?'

Byron cleared his throat; in the background, shaft call bells crashed out the signal for 387 Level.

'*Minister for Mines detained by CIO. Investigation led by dead minister's wife; newly appointed Permanent Secretary for Indigenization and Empowerment, Comrade Jemaiha Miriam Pasviri.*'

'I'll call you back.' Lee dropped the phone in its cradle and stared at Karen. 'They've got Rex – CIO has pulled him in for questioning.'

The colour drained from Karen's face. She steadied herself against the mantelpiece. Pasviri's influence was still alive, her darkest nightmare had come back to haunt her; the snake had escaped the hunter's fire. From the

239

wreckage of a burnt-out Alouette, Pasviri's charred hands were reaching out for them.

'They'll come for us.'

'Rex will tell them nothing.'

'There are other ways to make men talk,' hissed Karen. 'You know that better than I do.' She paused to gather her thoughts; only days ago, her world had at last become her sanctuary, now like before they were being backed into a corner. Beyond the dayroom picture window the mine headgear was just visible. Almost hidden by new growth, only the sheave wheel and service platform stood out clearly above the treetops. 'This time we may not be so lucky. We could lose everything, perhaps even our lives.'

'It won't come to that, Rex knows how these guys operate. We just have to sit tight until we hear from him.'

Outside, the gardener and his sons were turning over Karen's herb beds. The sun still shone and the turned earth smelled of far forests and rain. Africa always stayed the same, raw and beautiful; only her governments changed, more often than not for the worse. Through extolling the virtues of socialism, all they had achieved over that last one hundred years was the indomitable destruction of a once, rock solid political infrastructure.

Past the homestead's main gates, as far as Lee could see, the gravel road was empty; no dust, not yet. They had come so close to very nearly perfect.

63

Tentatively, Lee lifted the phone to his ear; those last four days had passed without incident.

'Tomorrow.' Rex's voice was overly authoritative – out of character. Lee immediately realised that an unwelcome third party was listening in. 'I will be conducting an official tour of your underground workings. Comrade Minister Miriam Pasviri and I will be on site by late morning. You will make sure everything is in order, Mister Goddard. The new minister for Rural Development and Indigenization is a woman of high expectations. Do not disappoint her.'

'I'll organise overalls and safety gear.' He angled the phone for Karen to listen in

'Everything.' Rex insisted. 'The minister's safety is my foremost concern. One last thing, comrade. Minister Pasviri asked me to pass on her preference for lunching at the mine. She suggests your wife prepares something traditional.'

'My wife will be honoured, comrade minister. I'll have my people prepare the boardroom. I feel sure that Comrade Pasviri will find our executive amenities more than adequate.'

'Comrade Pasviri is also keen to view your extraction methods.'

Lee smiled at the forewarning. 'Consider it organised.'

'Until tomorrow, then; make sure you are available, Mister Goddard, your co-operation is of vital importance.'

Lee replaced the phone and smiled reassuringly at Karen.

'We're still in with a chance, my sweetheart. Rex has obviously bluffed his way out of trouble, but easy over the eggshells. Pasviri's wife is reputed to have the nose of starving hyena. One slip of the tongue and she'll have us manacled, trussed, and carted off to Chikarubi prison.'

'Something traditional,' Karen hissed, 'must admit I'm tempted.'

'Don't even think about it.'

'Grasshoppers meunière drizzled with termite sauce and a light sprinkling of grilled caterpillars?'

'Don't push it. Chikarubi won't suit you.'

'It would be worth every minute, just to see the expression on her face.'

'From your cell window?'

'I need a drink,' said Karen, 'what about you?'

'Brandy,' Lee nodded his head, 'a large one, my nerves are all over the place.'

He phoned Byron and prepped him for the ministerial visit.

'Best stock up the fridges for at least a dozen; plenty of beer. We'll gear up for a boardroom style barbeque so make sure the gas bottles are full and there's plenty of steak. After traipsing around the mine for four hours the little loves will be ravenous.'

'What time are they arriving?'

'Mid-morning. Remind David to have the visitors' lamps fully charged; and new overalls, different sizes. Go for big, extra large. Pound for pound I reckon our Comrade Miriam will have a butt on her like the back end of a bull buffalo.'

'Boots?' Byron queried.

'Those as well. New wellingtons – easier on the feet.'

'Will there be anything else, Mister Goddard?'

'Don't know, Byron. Use your imagination, that's what I pay you for.' Lee put the phone down, filled his mouth with iced brandy and coke and swallowed it in one. Like fire, the spirit burnt its way down, but the after feelings fuelled his resolve.

242

64

As he had done on that day of Julius Pasviri's first visit, Lee stared down from the boardroom window; the same ministerial cars were back in the car park, long and black and heavily armoured. The drivers parked abreast, the doors opened and six CIO men stepped into the sunlight. Like before, their suits were of that same, midnight black and their aviator sunglasses reflected that same portentous glare of a circling vulture. All of them topped six feet. All of them were broad-shouldered and even at that distance, Lee picked out the usual, prominent bulge of hidden weapons.

Miriam Pasviri was last to step out from her bulletproof limousine. She stood in open sunlight, feet apart, grey Armani two-piece suit and black stilettos. Lee guessed her height at a shade under five eleven – taller than Karen. Like those of her bodyguards, her eyes were hidden, well shielded from the sunlight. From behind her Ray-Bans and as the predatory leopardess, she tilted back her head and matched her stare to that of the watcher at the window.

Lee stood his ground, for him to step away from the window would destroy his credibility as managing director to the Empress Deep. Miriam dropped her gaze, smiled sardonically and made straight for the main entrance.

She was first through the boardroom doorway. On long legs she crossed the burgundy Axminster carpet and stopped directly in front of Lee; the elevation she enjoyed from wearing high heels brought her eyes to a level almost in line with his own. She removed the Ray-Bans and as a final touch to her felinity, allowed those exquisite, almond-shaped eyes to readjust. It was then Lee noticed the texture of her skin; that soft, enchanting hue of brown silk.

'Mister Goddard?' She stretched out her hand to him, openly amused by the confused expression on Lee's face. 'You appear surprised?' She smiled, her teeth a natural shade of white, no expensive enhancements. Lee liked her for it and having been spared the usual ministerial pressures, gratefully he returned the smile.

'You are not as I expected, comrade minister.'

Her eyes glittered. 'Not Valkyrian enough?'

'Different.'

'I'll take that as a compliment, comrade.' Quickly she appraised the man behind the suit. His grip was strong, that of a powerful adversary. His gaze never faltered and beneath the welcoming façade, she saw a man fully prepared to protect his territory. There was no need for open confrontation for already she had control, she would manipulate his vanity. From behind their aviator sunglasses the CIO security operatives watched and listened to every going-on; their backs pressed against the wall, their eyes on everything, their facial expression totally impassive.

Karen strode out from the boardroom kitchen – her head held high. She prayed for the morning to end quickly, to expect a relaxed, convivial atmosphere was out of the question. As if she had sensed Karen's brusque entrance, Miriam Pasviri turned to face her. She hovered there, snakelike, her lips heavily glossed and slightly parted, those of the mamba, the tip of her satin tongue flickering out from between them.

'You must be Karen?'

Karen matched her gaze and found the remark trite but predictable. She felt her anger come awake; she needed some sort of distraction and glanced around the room for an excuse to disengage from conversation. In that charged silence her anger was difficult to contain.

'Can I get you something to drink?'

Lee sensed a drawing of swords; tension crackled about the room as the imminent threat of confrontation kicked-up a gear. The event of Gerard's death was still fresh and like some prominent, priceless jewel it glittered maliciously. Karen's hackles were up. The slightest untoward remark from any one of Pasviri's entourage would unleash the venom in her. However, it was becoming apparent that Miriam Pasviri appeared to know little, if anything at all about the Mozambique debacle. Lee made pretence of Karen being needed in the kitchen and as they walked, whispered a warning to her.

'Easy on the minister, sweetheart, I'm pretty sure she's still in the dark over what we've been through. Play the jolly hostess for them or we might well be working down the mine instead of owning it.'

Reluctantly, Karen suppressed her anger and though still with a heavy heart took control of her emotions. She turned on her heels, crossed the room and faced the minister head-on. This time her smile was softer and her voice more genial.

'My apology for appearing somewhat frayed at the edges, comrade minister, a combination of month-end paperwork and sleepless nights hasn't done much for my bonhomie. Having a husband as your boss does have its disadvantages.'

'You are fortunate; your partner obviously knows what he's doing. My own husband was a fool of a man, though some have said he sacrificed his life for the good of Zimbabwe; chasing smugglers over the border into Mozambique, I believe.'

The remark almost caught Karen off her guard, but within that same moment the minister's face blossomed; her smile conciliatory. Like the diamond studs in her ears, her eyes glittered. Not so pleasant memories of her husband's shortcomings were with her, permanently.

'Forgive my little indulgence, Karen. Scotch and ice. Some one on one girl talk might do me a power of good right now. Julius was a drunken, wife-beating, philandering bastard. So no loss there, I feel like celebrating.' She winked an eye at Karen. 'Want to know something? As cold-hearted as it might seem, whoever killed the useless son of a bitch deserves a medal.'

Karen returned with a generous measure of Glenfiddich. She handed it to Miriam Pasviri and then sipped her own through the ice. It warmed her cheeks and she felt that first hint of stress-releasing euphoria begin to work the tension from her neck.

'Any objection to me calling you Miriam?'

'Infinitely preferable to comrade minister.' She pointed out the rear wall. 'Your rogues' gallery; talk me through it, I want to know all about your ancestral empire builders.'

'What about your tour of the mine workings?'

Miriam shook her head and frowned at the thought of going down the mine.

'I'll skip the underground bits. Rex can handle that; digging out rock is his forte. A quick walk round your surface installations will be more than enough. I'm a politician, Karen not some chunky outback geologist.'

She ushered Karen forwards; the boardroom's gallery of past events covered most of the rear wall; all of them were matched, professionally framed in black and heavily shielded with non-reflective glass – most were of a time that Miriam Pasviri new little or nothing about.

'The woman and the boy,' Miriam pointed them out, 'you may start with them.'

Karen moved in closer and unable to help herself, for the umpteenth time stared long and deep at a recorded vista of ripped earth, vast hillocks of plundered ground and gaping mine workings. Screened and washed of the more friable oxides, diamond-bearing gravel had been left piled and made ready for the sorting tables. Karen's eyes worked upwards. Black and thunderous and though forever imprisoned by glass, she sensed a torn sky where it howled in and wet and cold above the diggings.

'Just looking at it makes me shiver,' Karen whispered. She made space for Miriam and together they witnessed the likeness of a boy and that of his mother, both images so very lifelike. Standing shoulder to shoulder they seemed aware of the voyeurism and in mute retaliation stared back through the glass. The boy's fists were clenched determinedly at his sides and in contrast to those terrible surroundings, his mother's smile was one of wistful resignation. Behind them there gaped the dark maw of some devilish pit. Rigged with makeshift ladders and steel haulage cables it was a way inside the earth for those obsessed with finding the makings of a fortune, where they might chance upon those eight-sided, silky crystals of pure carbon. A single glittering stone, were it large and pure enough could set the cap of any man for life.

'Your family?' Miriam surmised.

'Both of them.' Karen touched the glass. 'Catherine Goddard, my husband's great-great-grandmother; the boy, Mathew is her son. Lee's great-grandfather.'

Miriam leaned in closer and read aloud from the picture's title; though the writing was barely legible.

'New Rush – 1892.' She shook her head and smiled sardonically. 'Things were pretty grim back then.' She looked to Karen for answers. 'Some sort of mine?'

'Kimberley diamond diggings.' The beginnings of DeBeers Consolidated, the world's biggest producer of gem quality stones; a mile across and over two hundred feet deep. Dubbed, The Big Hole, for obvious reasons.'

Miriam was openly impressed by Karen's wealth of personal insight and by the unashamed way in which she unravelled the one hundred year evolution of the

Goddard family's progress with their comparatively small, though successful mining empire. Hungry for facts, Miriam devoured every new word with growing interest.

Without rancour, Karen breathed fresh life into their conversation, plying Miriam with information relevant to the discovery and subsequent development of the mine. Twice Karen refilled their glasses and like the Scotch, the words flowed easily. Their differences appeared as if they were set aside, replaced instead by an easy mutual acceptance of both old and new ideologies.

On reaching the last row, Miriam pointed to one of a pair; a picture that by its creator had been afforded every attention to detail. She stepped up to the sepia-coloured photograph and wittingly, singled out the likeness of Cecil John Rhodes.

'This one I know well – my Party's *bête noire*. Victorian England's, Genghis Khan. He took so much and gave us back so little.'

'That's the way it was back then,' Karen said, the tone of her voice non-aligned.

'And not a lot has changed,' Miriam admitted. 'Winner takes all. Especially true of Africa, rules are bent to favour the conquering party. Guns and democracy make for poor bedfellows.'

Rex came into the room, accompanied by Byron Fuller. Miriam nodded her head to him and gratefully, he detached himself from Byron's droning intonations of his personal exploitations of the stock exchange.

'We are behind schedule,' Rex reminded her.

'Do we have to go on this ridiculous tour of yours? I would much rather stay here.'

'It's important that you show interest. There is much at stake.'

'And I suppose I'm expected to wear one of those coverall things?'

'Already on its way over.'

He looked across the room and smiled reassuringly to Karen; so far as he knew, the day was progressing smoothly, he still had control.

-65-

The milling and ore extraction plant had been erected less than a mile from the Empress Deep's General Office. Lee's company Land Rover headed the convoy; only a few minutes passed before the visiting government entourage stood parked up beneath an overhanging redoubt of mature acacias. Miriam Pasviri had insisted on Karen travelling with her. Still lightheaded from the whisky they chatted garrulously, like old friends unwittingly brought together by some frivolous school outing. The limousine's air conditioning held the temperature inside the car at a comfortable sixteen degrees, so that when the doors were again opened the air rushed in, hot and overpowering.

Built into the hillside, the Empress Deep's mill crouched bear-like over the car park; an alien metal structure grotesquely out of place against a backdrop of lush natural forest and towering ironstone cliffs. The roof and outer walls were constructed of corrugated iron, fixed to a giant inner framework of steel girders and partitioned throughout with rough cement brick to segregate each different stage of the complex milling process. All of it, the entire structure, trembled from a continuum of moving parts and growling machinery and even the very earth about its footings appeared to shake.

Tied to a rigorous seven day shift system, men and equipment were pushed for maximum output; only through dire need of repair were any of those thundering machines brought to a standstill. Then, gutted like some iron fish the machine was relieved of its broken innards, repaired and reconstructed within a space of a few hours and speedily brought back on-line.

Byron had gone on ahead to warn the workers of the imminent ministerial inspection, light-heartedly threatening those who failed to expedite their responsibilities with a slow and painful death.

Dressed in crisply laundered coveralls, government ministers, along with their minders followed Lee *en masse* between the mill's heavily meshed security gates; company security people saluted smartly and nodded to their managing director that all was well and that the relevant areas had been well hosed down and cleared of dust. For Lee to convey his explanations successfully, he was forced to shout above the crash of breaking rock and the metallic roar of live machinery.

'This is where the mined reef comes in from the shaft stockpile.'

A fifteen ton, Foden tipper was in the process of offloading rock into the ore pass; an avalanche of heavy gold-bearing quartz thundered downwards at a steep angle. Lee compared that initial stage to the diminishing sands of some giant hourglass. Inexorably, the precious ore was drawn further inside the rock plant's concrete gullet, then out and over the vibrating feeder chute and onto the endless rubber belt of a waiting conveyor.

Mesmerised by noise and the perpetual urgency of machinery, with fixed expression, the visiting dignitaries were compelled to follow the upwards flow of rock. Concentrating on the conveyor's steep angle of ascent, they willed the ore upwards and onwards to where the metre-wide rubber belt surrendered its load of rock to the growling steel jaws of the rock plant's primary crusher. Once again, Lee was forced to raise his voice above the pandemonium.

'From here, the broken ore drops onto another conveyor; then up to the secondary jaw crusher.'

Miriam Pasviri appeared nonplussed by the overly complex operation.

'Why do you need two crushers? Surely the first could be adjusted to do the work of both machines?'

Lee shook his head.

'Set the jaws with too tight a tolerance and they'll jam solid. We crush in three stages: primary crusher takes it down to minus four inches, secondary to minus one, ready for the tertiary crusher. After that, the ball mills crush the rock to minus one millimetre, ready for the concentrators.'

Without constraints, Miriam accepted the tactful lesson in crushing rock and gestured to Lee for him to move on. Rex saw his opportunity and aware that he was out of general earshot, drew level with their tour guide.

'Your gold is safe,' he told Lee, his voice barely audible above the background noise. 'Other than me, no one else knows where it is. You have my word on it.'

'Where?'

'Now is not the time. Wait for things to calm down – then I'll contact you.'

Lee accepted his reasoning.

'Pasviri's wife doesn't seem overly saddened by her husband's death?'

'She isn't. And don't let the polished demeanour fool you. She's good at what she does; by fair play or otherwise she always gets what's she's after.'

Lee glanced over his shoulder. Karen was talking animatedly to Miriam, gesticulating with her hands in order to make herself fully understood.

A double set of rubber-lined doors closed behind the tour stragglers, so the interminable roar of greedy crushers was left behind. However, though now of a

251

different, more fluid tone, again the noise levels rose.

In a straight line and mounted on immense concrete plinths, three, one hundred ton a day, ball mills commandeered most of the floor space. Rotating on massive bearings and geared specifically to an exact speed, the giant steel drums, having been loaded with a precise amount of iron balls, ground the semi-masticated rock to finer, more easily treatable slurry. Through inverted cone-shaped holes in their manganese-hardened liners, gold rich concentrates were forced outwards, down into their take-off chutes. Miriam Pasviri stood as close as the barrier allowed to the concentrator tables.

'You keep this area permanently sealed off, Mister Goddard?'

Lee nodded his head. 'For security reasons as well as safety.'

'Security?' Obviously perplexed, she waited for his reasoning behind the erection of high, meshed security barriers. The access points were double-locked.

'Malicious theft,' Lee added. 'Two key holders; myself and Byron Fuller, my production manager. No one else can get in there without me knowing.'

Her fingers, like cats' claws hooked at the mesh.

'Your workers cannot be trusted?'

'No more than your own,' Lee countered.

Her eyes narrowed. 'You have made your point, Mister Goddard. Do you have the keys with you?'

'Always,' Lee said and without hesitation, stepped up to the gate and dropped off both, brass padlocks. 'Be my guest, this is where all those hours of digging in the dark finally pay off.'

A row of nine James tables fronted the rotating crushers; three tables to each ball mill, all of them set to a slight angle, both horizontally and diagonally. Their decks were supported from beneath by flexible bearers;

rocked back and forth by a motion head, each of the tables discharged shallow rivers of spent tailings as well as a narrower, three inch wide line of black, gold-saturated concentrates. At the highest point of camber, through the table's asymmetric shaking motion, an inch-wide ribbon of yellow granules moved forward – millimetres at a time, thrown nearer to the table's bottom edge by each new bump from the motion head.

Miriam's eyes widened. She leaned in closer, mesmerised by that glittering stream of yellow metal.

'Now I can see why you lock the gates. Leave them open and your entire workforce will have their fingers in the cookie jar.'

'The temptation would be too great for them to resist,' Lee confirmed. 'Legally or otherwise, unlike diamonds, gold is the easiest commodity in the world for a thief to sell on.'

Miriam straightened up; she smiled affably.

'In one month – how much could you produce? Running seven days a week and after averaging out on breakdowns?'

Lee became aware of Rex's unease. Wide-eyed, Rex tried to warn him off; Miriam was assessing the overall value of the Empress Deep.

'Depends on the ore,' Lee went on, driven by vanity he was unable to resist feeding her interest. 'Some of the smaller reefs are running at three ounces to the ton of ore milled.'

Avarice bloomed in Miriam's voice.

'Then why not take it? Surely it makes more sense – a much more lucrative return for less work?'

Her gaze, like that of a greedy child fell back on the yellow metal; sunlight from translucent overhead roof panels encouraged the granules of raw gold to glow and glitter. Even in its raw unrefined state, the yellow granules signified the total embodiment of immense wealth, but to Miriam Pasviri gold was so much more the complete obsession. More desired, more coveted than even the diamond or the emerald that one day might well be mounted upon it.

Miriam moved closer in to the James table and with eyes for nothing else stared longingly at the potential wealth moving in front of her.

'You have not answered my question, comrade; why not mine the richest ore bodies while the price of gold is pegged to a worldwide all time high?'

Lee silently cursed his own stupidity; Miriam had cleverly drained him of sensitive information and his willingness to comply with her so-called mining interests suddenly dried up.

'Other than deplete my company's reserve funding, it would achieve nothing. Lining my pockets through personal greed would jeopardise the mine's longevity. We have vast reserves of low grade reef; on its own, mining it would fail to cover our basic running costs.'

Rex came to the rescue.

'So you mix the two together to produce a more average, overall grade. Has to be done or like Mister Goddard pointed out, a year, perhaps two at the outside and the mine will close.'

'But over the period of that single year,' Miriam overrode his reasoning, 'milling a hundred tons a day would yield upwards of two hundred ounces of fine gold per twenty-four hour cycle?'

Lee nodded. 'Possible, but foolhardy.'

Miriam turned on her heels and brushed past him; she looked at Rex for him to follow. At the far side of the room, shielded from the rest of the party by stacked timber and spare parts she tore into him.

'One week, comrade. I want a full collation of all the Empress Deep's underground assets; the whereabouts of every reef on every level complete with width, length of payable strike and current values.'

Her eyes flared; the pupils dilated, like those of the drug addict fixed to the chemist's window. Without warning, as if she suddenly regretted the outburst, Miriam shook off the moment and started back towards the entrance.

'I have seen enough, this noise is bringing on a migraine. Tell your Mister Goddard we're going back. I need a drink.'

Back in the boardroom and with the air conditioners set to maximum, a more congenial party-like atmosphere settled over the gathering; even the CIO men appeared relaxed and on occasion, smiled and tapped their feet in time with Mango Groove's, *Dance Sum More.*

Resigning himself to the inevitable, Lee found sanctuary behind the boardroom bar. Set into the wall, a gas and charcoal barbecue crackled its iron grill up to temperature. Specially designed and adapted for the benefit of visiting businessmen, the in-house grill was large enough to take a dozen steaks at any one time. Recurrent smoke was drawn away by powerful extractor fans, so that the air inside the boardroom remained fresh and untainted by the smell of roasting beef.

'Your boardroom is well-equipped, comrade.' Miriam watched Lee smother the grill with prime fillet. 'Enough to feed an army; old habits die hard, captain.'

Lee baulked at her veiled reference to his involvement with the military.

'That was a long time ago. Leave the war where it belongs, back in the past.' He swivelled around and looked straight at her. 'Rex told you?'

She shook her head and smiled wryly.

'You forget quickly, comrade. The CIO is at my disposal; I have only to snap my fingers.'

'I was a soldier with Smith's army, so what?'

She drained her glass and slid it across the bar for a refill.

'I agree. Your preoccupation with shooting people is of little consequence, captain.' She watched him intently, but this time as a woman. 'A weakness of mine, I get hung-up over men in uniform.' She glanced sideways; Karen was cracking her whip at the kitchen staff and there was no one else at the bar.

Lee carried on pouring her drink. Her breathing had softened. She was coming on to him and the old, pre-marital macho vanity was creeping out from its hiding place; the fox had awakened and the fantasy it evoked of Karen listening in brought out the devil in him. Still with his back turned, he took his time pouring the scotch. Miriam watched him in the mirror.

'Rex told me about him working for you, prior to the war.'

'Rex is a damn good mining engineer,' Lee said. 'More's the pity I lost him to an ideology. What else did he tell you?'

'That you actually went head-to-head in the fighting?'

Lee dropped ice in her glass, turned around and set her drink down on the bar. Without dropping her eyes from his, sensually, she sipped her scotch through the ice.

'He saved my life,' Lee said matter-of-factly.

Miriam almost choked on her drink. 'Correct me if I'm wrong, but I have always been led to believe that the objectives are the same to both sides – to eradicate the opposition.'

Lee's distaste for her intensified, Mango Groove broke out with, *Moments Away* and he took in the soulful harmonising of their music. It calmed him, made him want to get drunk and sit outside in clean air. From behind their Ray-Bans the CIO men watched his every move.

'You would not understand.'

'Try me.'

Miriam abandoned her bar stool, selected the nearest, high-backed lounger and like some exotic bird to the nest, settled between its red leather wings. She stared up at him for an answer, then crossed her legs. The act was enticingly slow and deliberate; long and slender, sensual colours – dark skin and white silk, her smile softened, her eyes limpid, those of the endearing fawn.

'I'm waiting, comrade.'

Meat juices ignited; yellow smoky flames. Lee swivelled side-on to the barbecue – grateful of the distraction he doused the flames with beer and flipped the steaks. The fillet was well sealed. Each, two-inch thick piece came off cleanly. Within that next minute all of them were seared-side up and with his face in close he caught the waft of perfect steaks and old times.

She let him finish. 'You were about to tell me why Rex saved your life?'

He wiped his fingers and dropped the paper towel into the pedal bin.

'Honour amongst thieves. My family put Rex through school and university, obviously before the war. To Rex it was his way of squaring the debt. We were both involved in the same firefight.' He reached up and pushed back a lock of hair from his forehead. After all those years the scar was still vividly white. 'Gave me this as a keepsake, then patched me up and used my own radio to call in one of our choppers.'

'He could have finished you there and then?'

'Could have done, but didn't.' The voice came from behind her. Rex waved his empty glass at Lee. 'Any chance of another drink?'

'Didn't realise you were listening in.' Lee grinned and reached for Rex's glass. The intrusion was well-timed.

'Be wary of the man with big ears for he is blessed with malicious intent to eavesdrop. Your boardroom

257

acoustics are too good, when the music softens your voices carry. Couldn't help but hear what you were talking about.'

Miriam straightened up in her chair. 'Been squeezing out information; seems like the pair of you go back a long way, comrade?'

'You make us look like a pair of pensioned-off war vets,' Rex chuckled. 'The man exaggerates – just a scratch; band-aid and drink of water and he was ready to carry on fighting.'

He changed the subject and focused on Lee. 'Your Mister Fuller brought me a message. Sally just phoned from Masvingo Airport. She'll be here within the hour. Best warn Karen; my darling wife will want an A to Z on your trip to Mahenya; every minute detail.'

'I'll talk to her,' Lee said.

Rex added to his list. 'I told her about the barbecue; hold back one of those steaks, or we'll both be in deep trouble.'

'How is she getting up here?' Lee asked.

'Hire car. Sally cajoled my secretary into organising everything over the phone; it was waiting for her at the airport.'

Lee turned down the heat on the grill and ducked beneath the counter hatchway.

'Back in a second.' He grinned at Rex. 'Karen will be over the moon and before I forget, you'll be staying over at the homestead tonight – no arguments.'

He found Karen loading up stainless steel salvers with her own specialities: a mountainous variety of salads, baked potatoes shrouded in steam and touched with salted butter and chopped parsley. An oasis of food and as always, more than would ever be needed.

'I need you to try the sauce,' Karen told him. 'Your CIO pals don't strike me as the salady-types.'

Lee salted and crunched a celery stick.

'Your buddy's on her way up from the airport.'

Karen stopped what she was doing.

'My buddy?'

'Sally.'

'This whole thing is turning into some bizarre get together. Car-loads of thieving, government officials are committed to stealing our livelihood and here we are giving them a party?'

'I thought you liked her?'

'I do.' She brushed a lock of hair away from her face. 'Sally's a sweetheart.' She glanced sideways, out through the kitchen doorway. 'Sally and Rex are fine, it's these other corrupt bastards I have issues with. I just don't know how much longer I can go on playing hostess of the year to this lot; not without eventually losing my cool.'

Her voice dropped an octave. Now the low growl, it matched her sudden mood swing. Her eyes settled on the back of Miriam's neck and the chopping knife in Karen's hand rose and fell like the guillotine's blade to an innocent bunch of spring onions.

'Gerard shouldn't have died out there – not like that. My pound to your shilling says the bitch will never know what happened. Nor would she care.'

Lee saw the hatred boiling out from Karen's eyes.

'Stay calm, you're doing a great job. Let's get this lot fed and watered and on their way back to Harare.' He leaned towards her and kissed her cheek. 'I'd better get back, Comrade Miriam has the hots for me – might get lucky.'

66

Sally Khumalo parked her hired, Peugeot 405 well away from the row of government limousines; even as the wife of a high-ranking government minister she was not immune to that sinister aura which enveloped them, and as carriers of Mugabe's executioners, she found the sight of those ominous, black vehicles both powerfully repugnant and intimidating. In the heat of mid-afternoon all four vehicles shimmered; their windows purposely blacked out, the bodywork was heavily armoured and reflected the Party's paranoid fear of attack.

At the head of each vehicle a driver sat with his back to the protective bole of a tree, facing the incoming road. They were always watching and, like the CIO operatives, all were ex-ZANLA guerrillas, heavily armed, chosen for their unequivocal loyalty to Robert Mugabe.

Sally closed and locked her car, taking time to familiarise herself with the environment. To her left, that steel giant of a mine headgear towered above the Empress Deep's main shaft.

Rex met his wife at the door and escorted her through to the boardroom. Lee's face lit up. Dressed in jeans and yellow silk blouse, Sally was, as usual, every inch the iconic fashion magazine's front-pager.

'Radiant as always,' Lee poured out the flattery. 'You had best go through to the kitchen, Karen's been on tenterhooks for the last half hour. I'll bring you a glass of red if that's what you fancy?'

Sally nodded her head. 'Red will be great, Lee.' She turned to her husband and kissed him lightly on the lips. 'Back in a minute. Do I get something to eat or have you lot wolfed it all?'

'Steak,' Rex said. 'Baked potatoes, salad, or whatever

you fancy?'

'Salad will be fine.' She saw Miriam Pasviri at the far end of the table, she was talking to Byron Fuller; in her grey suit and stilettos she was exactly the woman Rex had warned her about. As if she had sensed the scrutiny, Miriam glanced sideways and picked out the latest addition to her gathering of ministers and security personnel. Without warning, she swung away from Byron and followed Sally through to the kitchen. Karen and Sally were in the throes of a friendly embrace when Miriam walked in on them.

'It's been a long time, Sally.' Her eyes narrowed, enhanced by a recent touch of makeup they appeared artificially pronounced, threatening even; searching for something to harm. Too much Glenfiddich and the unexpected appearance of an old adversary had triggered her mood swing.

Sally's attempt to shield herself from the memory was quickly overpowered. Miriam twisted the knife and gloated openly over the control she still wielded over the grown woman in front of her. Her mind rolled back to their final year at boarding school.

'You haven't changed much, how's the arm?'

They stared at each other from opposite sides of the table. Miriam shook her head. 'Not much of a fighter back then, were you. In fact, you weren't much good at anything; the runt of the dormitory. Skinny little arm caught behind the door handle – I heard it break. Like a dry stick, remember?'

At arm's length and with both hands, Miriam tightened her grip on the imaginary limb and with her teeth bared, rotated her wrists – violently downwards.

'Snap!'

Sally grabbed for her own forearm and protectively she drew the injured limb across her chest. Now her eyes were wide; the trauma accrued of that long-ago conflict

261

was still there – it had settled in deep.

Karen realised what was happening, her abhorrence of the bully had like that of Sally's, followed her from boarding school. She stepped in front of Sally and confronted Miriam head-on.

'Leave her be. Why are you doing this?'

'Because I can,' Miriam gloated, 'and as wife of the soon to be, ex-owner of the Empress Deep, you would do well to show respect, or I will see you across the border at Beit Bridge with little more than the clothes you stand up in.'

'I should have known. I expected more of you.'

'You thought we were friends?' Miriam sniggered at Karen's naivety. 'I have but one, true circle of friends, Karen – off-shore bank accounts. Compliments of a once very wealthy and now very dead husband.' She moved in close and with her face just inches from Karen's. 'Be very careful, comrade, appearances can be most deceptive; we are not as civilised as perhaps you would like to think.' For a moment, that same, viperous tongue whispered between her lips. 'I might even fuck your husband, just for starters.' She turned on her heels and swept from the kitchen. The way she walked was enough to silence the boardroom. Lee reached over and killed the music.

'Time to go.' Miriam fired her voice through the quiet, drained her glass and growled at Lee. 'My people will be in touch. Prepare yourself, Mister Goddard.'

'What's wrong, you haven't eaten yet?'

'Your kitchen staff ruined my appetite – maybe next time.'

67

Showered, dressed in baggy shorts and one of Lee's shirts, Karen brought their coffee through from the homestead kitchen, percolated Brazilian from her personal cache. In the new Zimbabwe, good coffee was almost impossible to come by.

'The bitch is evil; loved every minute of it. She was toying with me – cat and mouse. The cow knew exactly which buttons to push.'

'She's gone,' Lee emphasised. 'Make the most of the quiet because you haven't seen the last of her. A week, two at the most and the wolves will be back.'

Karen set the cups down; alcohol was furthest from her mind. The simple, aromatic smell of ground coffee, everyone found to be pleasantly refreshing. Through open patio doors the scent of watered lawns and night blooming flowers drifted inside the dayroom.

'Must admit you worried me; the way you were tightening your grip on that chopping knife,' Sally recalled and everyone laughed, though just beneath that jocular mood there was now a more sinister, underlying atmosphere. Lee looked across the table at Rex.

'You do realize that being seen to fraternise with white colonists won't do your career much good?'

Rex smiled at the inference. 'Bit late to start worrying over that. Pasviri already knows I can't stand her. Makes her dead husband's antics come across as almost saintly.' He sipped at the coffee. 'More to the point, she wants a complete dossier of your mining operations on her desk within the week; tonnage mined, actual tons milled, grades, along with your actual production figures.'

'Gold banked?'

Rex nodded his head. 'That also. Got her mind set on a new approach – selective mining. If the fool gets her way she'll soon have us picking the eyes out of your Empress Deep; high values equate to high returns, no matter what the consequences.'

'The mine will fold,' Lee growled, 'the bulk of our ore reserves are of low to medium value. Told her twice; we need controlled extraction to create a sustainable average grade. Without it, the lower values won't be worth mining.'

'She knows that. Miriam doesn't give a damn; all she sees is a year's steady flow of bullion to top up her off-shore bank account.'

'I sometimes feel ashamed,' Sally mused and quickly Karen picked up on her angst.

'What made you say that?'

'The more involved I become with our government, the more I despair. Maybe old Smithy is right, we just don't seem capable of running our own affairs.'

Lee shuffled uncomfortably in his chair and spoke out in Sally's defence.

'You're suffering the after effects of what happened up at the mine – you're on a downer, beating yourself up over your run-in with Miriam will only make things worse.'

'Tribal mentality only benefits those in power,' Rex interjected, 'that's why it has to be changed, or Zimbabwe will end up like some of its siblings north of the border; a banana republic – nothing more.' He stood up from the table and crooked a finger at Lee. 'Your grandmother's storeroom, we need to talk.'

The smells, the dust and piles of antiquities were just as Rex remembered them, even the feeble glow from an incandescent lamp on the far wall. It was then that Rex suffered his first, involuntary shiver, for the awakened, zephyr-like fingers of old superstitions had already reached inside his collar.

'So you never did pluck up courage enough to go for a

clear out?' He looked around the room and smiled wryly. 'Just as it was all those years ago. When your time comes, captain, I'll convince Karen to put your mummified corpse in here and brick up the door.'

'Reckon I could do worse,' said Lee. 'Most of everything I hold dear is in this room.' He cast his eyes about the walls, over cluttered shelves and other, haphazard piles of Victoriana, then hurriedly he cleared his mind for fear of being overwhelmed by the atmosphere they were creating.

'Before we came in here, you seemed pretty agitated?'

Rex shook a cigarette from a pack of twenty. 'I had reason to be.' He took his time lighting up and prepared himself for the gravity of what he was about to say. Lee pulled out two chairs from beneath a linen dust sheet. They both sat down and faced one another from either side of an old imbuya table. With heavy, emotional undertones, Rex disclosed his plans, all of them dramatically grandiose, way beyond the limits of anything his attentive listener could ever have imagined. Lee, now somewhat mystified, sat there spellbound.

'The Matabele are a proud people, captain. Like their forefathers, they give well of their friendship, but only to those who reciprocate. As you have experienced firsthand, Robert Mugabe is at odds with everyone other than his own chosen few. Since that first day of Zimbabwe's independence the Matabele have been held to a permanent a state of submission by Mugabe's personalised warmongers.' He drew heavily on the cigarette. 'His race is almost run, captain. Soon, within this next year, you will witness the rising up of the new Zimbabwe. The existing Shona monopoly of my country will be at an end; those who do not comply will be mercilessly swept aside. Those who resist militarily will be eradicated.'

'You're crazy.'

265

Rex smiled at the inference, though it was what he had expected.

'A pot and black kettle spring to mind.'

'Not in the same league,' Lee countered. 'You'll never disband the Fifth Brigade nor will you kick out Mugabe's government; for starters, you lack the firepower. You, me, Karen and Sally armed with Lee Enfields might look good in the movies, but not rampaging through Harare.' He stood up and looked around him. 'This room has sucked you in, Rex. Wrong era; Rhodes and Lobengula are long dead. This is nineteen-ninety-six, or haven't you noticed?'

'Sit down, Lee, I haven't finished.' He scowled at the empty chair. 'The least you can do is hear me out.'

'You're talking treason, buster. Get on down to the authorities and hand yourself in, just don't expect me to share your cell.'

'I need your help.'

'The debt was squared a long time ago, I owe you nothing.'

'Sit down – please'

Lee succumbed and slumped back into his chair.

'I'm waiting – inspire me. But before you go any further with this impending calamity, have you mentioned this crazy scheme of yours to Sally?'

'Many times,' Rex countered. 'We stand together. Sally's support is unequivocal.'

Lee calmed himself. He recalled the howl of helicopter gunships wheeling overhead and the harsh crackle of machine-gun fire, the terror evoked from being hunted down, and yet, that normally dormant part of his psyche was slowly coming alive. What had started out as seemingly ludicrous was now a glowing ember of wild, inexplicable excitement.

'I still think you're insane, but go on, I'm doing my best not to run round the room pulling my hair out.'

Rex paused for a moment, and when he had rid himself of any last flutterings of uncertainty, he leaned forward with his elbows on the table. Through the sincerity of his voice he projected the truth that Lee was looking for.

'Firstly, nothing of what I tell you has in any way been taken lightly. They are not the ramblings of some disgruntled, deranged war vet. For upwards of five years, those of our government in favour of a united, Zimbabwe democracy have been planning and working together for the removal of Mugabe. Most are Ndebele, though you might well be surprised to hear that some are Shona.'

Lee shook his head at the enormity of what he was hearing. Any leak, even so much as a whisper to the wrong people and their lives would be forfeited. They would simply disappear; taken into the bush and disposed of.

'This is too much for me to get my head around. What about finance? Men and weapons to power a government takeover don't come cheap.'

Rex sat back in his chair. Lee's patriotic fervour had been awakened.

'Let us say our sponsors, for want of better terminology, are in a state of wait and see. Governments sympathetic to our cause still need to be convinced of our authenticity and though all of them are keen to see Mugabe removed from government, like the jackal and the wild dog they wait for the lion to strike the first, mortal blow.' He held back and reached for the ashtray. 'That is why, captain, for the lives of my people and for the future of our country, the aforementioned lion is here in your home, specifically to ask for your help.'

Lee held out both hands as a gesture of supplication. The look on his face was one of total bewilderment.

'You flatter me, Rex and I'm sure that Lawrence of

Arabia would have jumped at the opportunity, but I'm one man, not an army. What in God's sweet name are you expecting me to come up with?'

Rex's features hardened; there was a long and empty silence before he spoke again. When at last the words came out they were with the sincere commitment of a man dedicated to the offering up of all that he possessed, even his life if that is what it would take to ensure the eventual winning back of a country.

'Yours would be a pivotal role, captain. You have control of the largest, privately owned gold mine in Zimbabwe; you have the power of political procreation at your fingertips.'

The conversation intensified; talk of war and dark thoughts took their seats at the table. Through those last one hundred years, the room had piled its recollections, one upon the other, some of them catastrophic, all of them tumultuous. Onlookers crowded the table: Cecil Rhodes, Lobengula Khumalo, Nathan Goddard. Lee sensed them all – as if from a coming together of different winds, the fine hairs inside his collar trembled.

'Go on,' said Lee, 'I'm waiting. Get to the punchline, Rex; give me the full picture and then I'll tell you why it can't be done.'

'Before I can do that, I need you come with me to the ruins at Great Zimbabwe.'

'For what reason?'

'I cannot say, but I need you to trust me.'

Lee rolled his wrist to the light and checked the time on his watch.

'It will be dark in less than an hour?'

Rex nodded his head. 'Someone already waits to lead us in; the darkness will not be a problem.'

68

By the time Lee and Rex reached the Great Zimbabwe Ruins Hotel car park the sun had already set. They left the Land Rover beneath the jacaranda trees and went ahead on foot. The hotel's perimeter security lighting was soon left behind, blanketed by thick forest.

'I feel like a grave robber in some Hammer horror movie.' Lee juggled a Cadac gas lamp into a more comfortable position against his shoulder. Besides the gas lamp, both men were equipped with powerful, battery-powered mining lamps. However, so as not to attract the attention of tourists and park wardens, they decided against using them and found their way between the trees solely by the light of a full moon.

'Ghosts,' Lee mused, 'definitely not a good place to be at night. This place gives me the willies.'

'That's good,' said Rex, 'a little nervous imagination enlivens the mind – keeps a man focused. If I am right about where we are going, what waits for us will prove a lot more harrowing than any ghoul-filled graveyard. Prepare yourself, captain; what you will see tonight may well stay with you for the rest of your life.'

'Karen was well peed off with being left behind; pleaded with me to let her come with us.'

'Likewise with Sally, but believe me when I say they would not have thanked us for it.'

They followed the gravel road down through the Valley of Ruins to where the great temple enclosure reared in front of them, grey and ghostlike. Where sections of the outer wall had tumbled into disrepair, shadows now stood in place of stone and for hundreds of years, ancient trees had laced their roots deep inside the footings of the walls. Here, the darkness was at its most intense. Rex paused at the north-facing entrance and he listened, but other than sound created by nocturnal creatures hunting the stone labyrinth he picked out nothing else.

'If the authorities catch us doing this we'll be in for the high jump,' Lee intimated. 'Are you certain about the security personnel?'

'Relax. They stick to their daytime hours. The local wardens steer well clear – frightened of ghosts.'

He stepped through the portal and was immediately overwhelmed by deep shadow. Lee followed him through and inching forwards in single file, both men felt their way along a narrow corridor.

'We can use our lamps now,' Rex whispered. 'I was told to follow the outer, east-side corridor; our guide should already be waiting. Keep your lamp pointed to the ground until we're well away from the entrance.'

Moonlight lit up sections of stone walling. Warm air carried the scents of moist stone and rich black earth, and through a narrow gap in the corridor's uppermost ramparts, Orion the Hunter gazed down upon the intruders.

Tentatively, Rex moved forwards. With his left hand he traced the curvature of the great outer wall. He made good progress and within minutes, to his front, rising vertically from the natural earthen floor a thirty foot conical tower, built from that same grey granite reared up bastion-like in front of them. As guardian to the enclosure's innermost secrets, the tapered structure appeared to have that very night forced its way from beneath the ground. From base to the partially ruined apex, symmetrically it reached amongst the branches of the overhanging trees.

Though he had seen the tower a hundred times before, Lee still marvelled at its construction. Cloaked in moonlight, the aura it reflected fired his imagination.

'Never get bored of seeing this,' Lee mused and

reached out his hand for that familiar feel of rough stone. With his eyes he followed the structure's conical outline to where its apex stood out sharply. Plundered by Victorian treasure hunters the tower's highest extremities had, through the fossickers' rampant excitement been broken away.

'I feared you would not come, Khumalo.'

Both men were caught unawares and stumbled backwards from the tower as though the voice had sprung from out of it. To Rex it was the whine of some mischievous ghost or that of the witch's familiar. Either way, instinctively he balled his fists and readied himself for confrontation. Again the voice piped out through the moonlight.

'You see nothing, and yet you prepare to strike out?'

Reluctantly, Rex lowered his fists and listened – turning his head to source the voice.

'Where are you, spirit? Show yourself – step out from your hide!'

A moment of silence then yet again, the voice came at him.

'You are Rex Jando Khumalo, yes?'

'I am,' Rex growled. 'What of it?'

'Son of Philip and grandson to Thabisa, youngest and last wife to He Who Drives Like the Wind, The Great Elephant – Lobengula Jando Khumalo?'

'It has been said, spirit. Many people know this; what difference would it make if I were not?'

'Then both our journeys would have been wasted. If you are not who you say, then go now, other important matters await my interest.'

'I am that man,' said Rex. 'Enough of your games, spirit; show yourself and be fairly judged as we were.'

This time, the voice emanated from high up on the tower; silhouetted against a full moon, the creature started downwards. With the dexterity of a vervet monkey it rustled over the stonework.

'I am Pfupi, the last boy child borne of Mutiswa, the seer of all our destinies. My body is small, like that of a child, but do not judge me as such.'

Pfupi clung to tiny cracks and breaks in the rock; quickly he moved from one tenuous finger hold to another, his nails against the stone were scratching, furtive things and the sounds they made flushed the nape of Rex's neck with ripened gooseflesh. With trembling hands, Rex held the creature within the circle of his lamplight.

'This has to be a dream,' he whispered and like his comrade, watched the strange phenomenon manifest itself before them.

Some six feet from the base of the tower, Pfupi relinquished his grip on the granite blocks and with effortless skill, landed lightly on the balls of his feet, less than an arm's length from where Rex and Lee were standing.

'I am the one who has been sent guide you,' he told them and from the level of Rex's thigh stared up at the man who had first seen him. In that artificial light his features showed as awkwardly shaped; pitch-black and doll-like.

'We must hurry, Khumalo, there is little time. Like moonlight at sunrise, already the seer's life begins to fade.' From the corners of Pfupi's eyes to the comical protrusions of his leaf-like ears, the dwarf's skin was finely wrinkled. At the temples, his curled-up peppercorn hair was whiter than winter grass.

'How old are you?' Lee asked, and Pfupi's eyes twitched excitedly.

'You are *muRungu*, a white man, and yet you speak the language of the Makalanga.' Six times he held up all his fingers for Lee to count and as tiny metal bells his laughter rang from off the stonework. 'So many seasons, so many passings of the moon.' He looked upwards for the night sky, bewildered by the question. 'They come and go like stars! Bees to the hive, white man, so many days and nights; like the drops of a thousand storms, together they make the river, but as drops...' he wagged a tiny, wizened finger at Lee, 'I cannot remember.'

He turned to Rex and in the blinking of an eye, seized upon his little finger.

'We must start the journey, Khumalo; my legs are short and the way ahead, long and arduous.'

Rex steeled himself and nodded his head.

'Then you must take us where you will, though remember, before the sun rises I would do well to be far away from this place.'

For that next full hour, Pfupi led them down narrow trails worn by the feet of badger and the hooves of tiny dik-dik antelope and in the moonlight, on bowed, spindly legs, through Lee's eyes he became the fairy tale marionette from Carlo Collodi's, *Pinocchio*. With his hand still wrapped around Rex's little finger, purposely, he led them wide of their destination, avoiding roads and open areas adjoining the ruins where thrill-seeking tourists might brave the night to observe the unique, moonlit phenomenon of the ancient stone city. Surrounding the entire valley, stripped of their soil by centuries of natural erosion the hills and ridges showed as giants; asleep in soft moonlight, thickly skirted in deep forest.

When at last they reached the foot of the ancient hilltop fortress, Pfupi stood for a moment and afforded his tiny legs the chance to replenish their strength. Rex cupped his lighter to hide the flame; doubling their journey time had made him irritable and he welcomed the chance of a cigarette. He recognised redoubts of stone walling where they had been cunningly positioned along the high cliffs, some were built beneath rocky overhangs and without ropes they were unreachable.

Silhouetted against the starlit skyline, baboons, like living gargoyles stared down into the valley and watched the intruders.

Lee appeared uncertain of their progress.

'You're sure this is the place you told me about? Eighteen years is a long time.'

'No mistake, but for whatever reason, our little friend here has brought us around to the north side.'

Pfupi urged them onwards. Already the moon was halfway down the sky.

'We are close now, but from here the way is steep.' He looked up at the tall Matabele, imploring him to lift him across his back. 'We would travel faster, Khumalo.'

With one hand, Rex swung the dwarf across the small of his back.

'Piss on me, dwarf and I will choke the life from you.' Like a lemur settling to its mother's fur, Pfupi hooked his tiny fingers into the folds of Rex's shirt. 'And keep your foul breath away from my face, I have no desire to smell your innards.'

'There is the great tree.' Pfupi threw up his arm and pointed out their final marker. Silver and tall, the acacia leaned into the moonlight. Able to make better time, Rex pushed all out for the higher ground and within a span of fifteen minutes they were standing inside deep shadow. Rex lowered Pfupi onto the ground.

'Where to now?'

'No further,' said Pfupi and with gleeful anticipation hopped about amongst the trees. 'You have brought Pfupi home, Khumalo; once again the time has come for you to confront the wisdom of the great seer.' He stopped in front of Lee and with a lemur's giant eyes peered up at him, his face framed in moonlight. 'And to you, white man I give the task of seeking a way inside the mountain. Seek with the eagle's eye for what you see now is but a guise.' He moved further inside the

274

shadows and within that same moment disappeared. Lee switched on his miner's lamp and swept the area for signs of trickery. To his front, a wall of solid rock rose vertically from the ground.

'Show yourself dwarf, enough of your games. Come out from your hiding place or I will return with a thousand dogs and sniff you out.'

Lee heard the rustle of bare feet over granite. He used his lamp to source the making of the sound.

'Over there. The rock face,' he called to Rex. Bright orange lichens had colonised the surface of the stone and from within that multitude of colours, Pfupi's eyes glowed like those of a rabbit trapped in the glare of car headlights.

'I can see the little bugger's face; the rest of him has disappeared.'

Rex moved closer; it was then that he saw through the illusion of solidity created by a convex shaped overlap in the living rock; only by his more angular approach to the granite was the secret exposed. From head-on, the rock appeared seamless, camouflaged by natural folding and multi-coloured lichens the cleft was rendered almost invisible – undetectable from all but a few feet away. A slender line of shadow appeared in the rock, vertically from the ground; from it, Pfupi stepped out into the open and with thin, frog-like lips grinned at his followers.

'Without Pfupi to guide you, Rex Khumalo, no one, not even the descendant of a great Ndebele king could have found the way.' Again Pfupi disappeared from view. However, this time, Rex turned sideways-on to the granite buttress and like the dwarf, manoeuvred his way inside the fissure.

Grateful of the powerful miner's lamp, Lee followed him through and after only a few yards the cleft swung away at a right angle. Porcupine quills littered the floor and the air itself reeked with the pungent smell of rock rabbit urine.

'We're headed more or less due south,' Lee guessed.

'Makes sense,' Rex replied. 'Beneath the hill fortress, same as the last time, but from the opposite direction. Would have doubled as an escape route.'

Pfupi, on tiny legs scurried deeper into the hillside; emboldened by the strong light, playfully he reached out with both arms and ran his fingertips over the sidewalls. Both men had to widen their stride in order to keep pace.

'Pfupi does not need your light to find his way, Khumalo. Every step I know; even in the darkness I can find my way. My forebears were a people gifted with great skills, the magic they possessed was passed on only through the spoken word; I, Pfupi, am the last of their kind.'

Silently, Lee counted his own steps and at the exact spot of his sixtieth footfall, the passageway widened out. No longer formed of igneous granite, the walls were now of green serpentine, soft enough to have yielded easily to the miner's adze. The sudden change in rock formation caught the eye of both men; simultaneously they angled their lamps at the sidewall.

Rex stepped in close and scored the rock with the metal clip of his lamp; it left behind deep marks and a white, silky-smooth powder adhered to his fingertips.

'Talc. Soapstone; metamorphosed serpentine – the sculptor's dream.'

Lee did the same and traced the outline of the embedded rock. Levered from the sidewall, a single cubic metre of soapstone would provide enough material for a hundred sculpted pieces.

'The museum,' Lee whispered.

'What of it?'

'The carvings found in the ruins,' Lee went on. 'The

soapstone birds, the stele and some of the artefacts from Karen's excavations; don't you see? This is where the ancients found their raw materials, not from miles away like everyone thought.'

'What you say makes sense. Hundreds of tons would have been mined out when they dug this passageway.'

Pfupi called them on; to him the stone was of little use.

'We must hurry, Khumalo, or the moment will be lost forever. In their thousands your people will perish.'

The passageway inclined upwards at a slight angle, and again it levelled out and narrowed to less than a yard in width, barely wide enough for them to pass without the need for turning sideways-on. What Pfupi had told him rampaged wildly through Rex's imagination. Strange odours filled his nostrils, those of lamp fat and rotting hides, redolent of wild beasts. Both men sensed the change and readied themselves for the unexpected.

Rex stopped in his tracks; all the fears, terrifying images and fantastical happenings he had experienced eighteen years ago were coming back to him. Sounds, like those of far-off thunder rolled from out of the living rock, some of them a hundred times more harrowing than any he had heard before; the screams of women and children being put to the sword, the cursing and cries of men fighting for their lives and the crash of steel on steel. Pfupi saw the change come over him and reached out for Rex's hand.

'She knows we are close now, Khumalo; stay strong. Already my mother reaches out for you. Take hold of my hand and I will lead you to her.'

With trembling hands, Lee put down the gas lamp and held a lighted match to its mantle. Then, taking hold of the carrying handle, he walked with it low to the ground to shield his eyes from glaring, white light. Without a weapon he felt vulnerable to whatever forces waited up ahead; now the urge for him to turn back grew stronger with every step.

Rex urged him forwards.

'Stay calm, keep a hold on your senses, most of what you see will not be real, captain. Fear itself cannot harm you.'

'I'll be okay,' Lee told him. 'Let's get this over with.'

At a steady pace, Pfupi led them deeper into the hillside, his own shadow danced as that of a tall man to their front. Rex picked up on the smell of filth and human excrement, but overlaying these it was the foul odour of the witch that terrified him the most. The scent of snake, wood smoke and the corruption of human flesh; the sweet smell of balm and wild herbs. It was the mixing of the forest with that of a world of pain and dark happenings.

'We are close now.' Pfupi's limbs trembled, but not through fear; the dwarf appeared invigorated by the foul atmosphere and the presence of powerful magic. He gestured to Lee and pointed to the footwall.

'Leave the lamp, white man. The sound it makes is that of a snake, we have no need of it.'

Lee set the lamp down and adjusted the flame to a low burn. Further along the passageway, a less than potent flame beckoned from the semi darkness. Fed with rendered animal fats the lamp was nothing more than a flicker of yellow light.

From a niche in the sidewall, like that of a candle, the flame wavered and to the left of it the passageway widened unexpectedly. The soft, serpentine rock had been mined out in vast quantities and now the scale of the workings projected an aura of infinite space. At the edge of the hall-like excavation, Rex stood still and gazed about him, overwhelmed by the familiarity of it all.

'The same place,' he whispered to Lee and breathed in deeply, as if to fortify his mind against the horrors he had seen before. 'This is where I left Mutiswa. All those years ago, captain; even then I swore she was older than these ancient walls. Not even a witch could have survived this long.' He looked down at Pfupi and his face was dark as thunder. 'A fool's errand, dwarf; your mother is long dead, why did you bring me here?'

'Believe me, Khumalo, my mother still lives, but her time upon this earth has almost ended.' He pointed to the far side of the great cavern. Rex screwed up his eyes and peered into the near darkness.

On a low ledge and indistinguishable from the skins that were heaped upon it, Mutiswa's emaciated body appeared to Rex as neither that of a human being nor the remains of a wild animal. Then, through the quiet, he heard the creature breathing; each painful intake choked and guttural, as if drawn through thick slime.

'Since that last night, Khumalo, like vultures the seasons have come and flown, but now the carcass that lures the creatures in has been stripped bare. My life is over. More dark nights than I can now remember. Come closer, Khumalo and you also, white man, I have words for you both.'

'What would you have with us, old woman?'

'Come closer,' she insisted and again her voice crackled and hawked. Thick phlegm dribbled from her chin and amongst the infected strings of green mucus were those tell-tale smears of bright red blood, ejected by her ruined lungs.

Rex covered his mouth in a vain attempt to guard himself against infection. With the fingers of his free hand he twisted the knurled switch on his miner's lamp.

In that harsh light, Mutiswa's naked form appeared more grotesque than anything either of the two men could ever envisage. Stripped of flesh by disease and the inability to eat, her shape was that of the rotting cadaver. Through the permanence of living beneath the ground and the added debilitation of ageing, the ancient crone was now condemned to a state of almost total blindness, even in that bright light thrown by Rex's lamp, her eyes remained wide and unblinking; both were opaque; deeply clouded. The flesh that surrounded them had been all but eaten through by the invasive greed of her rampant facial carcinoma.

'I see only your lamplight, Khumalo, but I remember your face from long ago. Much has happened and though I am sightless, still I have the strength to see beyond these stone walls.'

Through his own feelings of total revulsion, Rex sensed the first, slight glimmerings of compassion for the ruined creature before him.

'You are already dead, old woman. Your spirit is set to fly; what I now see is nothing more than dry leaves awaiting the wind.'

'And I embrace it, Khumalo, but on that same wind are the voices of Mjaan, Gandang and Lobengula, the Shaker of Mountains, those even who died in battle at Bembesi and Shangani; that of your father. All of them are here Khumalo, look well into the darkness and you will see their faces.' Her dead eyes swung onto Lee. 'You also white man. Like that of the man alongside you your blood flows strong here.'

Though beneath the ground there was no real wind, still the oil lamp guttered and leaned as if a door had been flung open. A presence engulfed the cavern and the sounds that were now inside the granite hillside were real enough to make Lee lift up his hands to cover his ears. Rex screwed up his eyes, expectant of whirling devils and other spiteful entities that might confront him. Beyond the makeshift granite cot where Mutiswa was lying, shadows and shapes took on human form and as had happened before, voices cried out in anguish and still the spears rose and fell. Above it all, the clatter of modern weaponry and the terrible roar of ancient maxim guns echoed about the cavern.

Pfupi stood wide-eyed and watched the change come over the men he had brought here, though he himself was unable to witness the magic. Created by burning the pulverised leaves from the snake bean and those from the wild *mbanje*, the smoke hovered, mist-like; held as a single layer between the cavern roof and its footwall. For hours the fog had hung there undisturbed, floating chest-high it was the witch's final snare. As some pale, translucent trap it lay in wait; potently sweet and pleasantly aromatic, its hallucinogenic powers were well disguised.

Mutiswa sensed their agitation and hawked a ball of thick phlegm from her throat. Unable to spit it away, with her tongue she pressed the mucus from between her lips. Freed of the restriction to her airway she continued to speak. Whilst she did so and with what strength remained in her shrivelled arms, Mutiswa pinched another generous measure of herbs from the pouch about her neck and sprinkled the potent concoction over the embers of her small fire.

'Now is your time, Khumalo, the blood of kings runs in your veins – that of The Black Bull.' Her ruined eyes flickered and strained for his image. 'There is place enough for one lion at the waterhole. Are you that lion, Khumalo? Or are you now but one of a dozen jackal content to fight for scraps at Mugabe's fireside?'

Fixated by the witch's sightless stare, Rex stood silently, his mind in a state of drug-induced lassitude. From the fire at his feet, tendrils of pale smoke wrapped around his legs; as entwining, ghostly limbs they reached upwards for his face.

'I am that lion,' Rex whispered, 'but Mugabe's soldiers are many. How can it be that I am expected to stand alone against a thousand?'

'You are the peoples' champion, Khumalo. Your calling is to stand at the head of ten such thousands. Without you, all but a few will perish. Mugabe will at last be rid of your Matabele.'

Angered by the witch's prophecy he was no longer afraid.

'And how would I stop this?'

'Arm the people, Khumalo. To each man you will give the *isibamu*; guns Khumalo, do this and the spirits of Mjaan and Gandang will stand with you. Talk is worthless now. Look to the blade and the Kalashnikov, or your warriors will become as women and bend their backs to the cooking fires of Shona generals.'

'You speak in riddles, old woman.'

'Then I have judged you wrongly; you have the heart of a girl.'

Rex looked down at the pathetic creature laid out corpse-like before him. It would take a single blow with the heel of his boot to snuff out her life.

'For one so weak and close to death, you speak with a careless tongue, Mutiswa.'

She ignored the threat and turned her head.

'Where are you, white man?'

Lee moved one step closer and immediately, the witch locked on to him.

'What do you see, white man?'

'Death,' Lee told her. 'Like the *magora*, the vulture, it stands over you.'

Mutiswa's lips twitched; more the grimace than the smile, for through the malignancy of the disease there was little left of her features.

'It is indeed the bird of death. You see him at my shoulder and I shall not keep him waiting long.' Again, she retched the mucus from her lungs and minutes passed before the violent paroxysm abated. 'There is much for you to do, white man, as it was with your father's grandfather, I see in you the warrior's heart.'

Mutiswa lifted her arm and without dropping her eyes from Lee's, pointed to a shadow-filled alcove, less than a yard from where she lay.

'The bird, white man; reach the creature out from where it has nested, now is the time for it to fly.'

Reluctantly, Lee leaned across the stone cot and reached inside the alcove. Almost touched to Lee's chest, the witch's decaying body lay within a pile of her own filth and rancid animal skins; where her flesh was at its very worst, maggots tunnelled inside of it and in their hundreds fed ecstatically. The stench that rose up from her was thick with those vile smells of rampant putrefaction, forcing Lee to hold his breath for fear of emptying out his stomach. Cockroaches and other verminous insects scuttled between his fingers, but his nerve held and he felt his way deeper inside the dark orifice.

'Hurry white man. Take up the bird or it will be I, Mutiswa who will be the first to fly.'

Lee forced his arm full length inside the alcove and at its furthermost recess felt his fingertips touch against the ancient artefact. Again there were voices; strange intonations, seemingly from the air above his head. From within his own subconscious store of recollections, there poured out images of both himself and Rex standing before an ancient mural created of a hundred different colours and textures. Images of past battles, men of different race locked in conflict and above all of this, enhanced by the brightest of beaten gold and held aloft by some godlike entity was a likeness of the very bird that he now lifted out from the alcove.

The effigy, part crocodile, part raptor glared up at him; eighteen years had come and gone since that first time he had set eyes on it. Equal in length to that of his thumb, at an inch thick, the weight of it nestled comfortably to the palm of his hand. The purity of the precious metal was protection enough against the effigy being eaten away by any natural acids exuded by the rock, nor had the excrement of a thousand crawling insects tarnished it.

'Exactly as I remember you,' Lee whispered and like a purveyor of precious stones held the ancient totem closer in to the lamplight.

As he gazed upon it, through drugged eyes, he witnessed scenes from both times long-gone and those of his future. Men on horseback, slouch hats set at a rakish angle, deep forests and drizzling, *guti* rain and from the high Matobo hills the Matabele watched them pass, their spears and chests already wet from the killing. From within that same moment sprang images of modern cities, the gathering of dark storms and the bass growl of their thunder; as an ominous cloak the sky above Bulawayo hung black as ironstone, her city streets and wide avenues ran not with storm water, but with her gutters thickened with blood.

All these things he witnessed and the seeing of them held him spellbound. Through the innermost parts of his mind he saw the passing of a full one hundred years, most were fleeting moments, but others as poignant revelations were laid open and blatantly thrown before him; portentous and terrifying. Mutiswa's voice barely found its way through the chaos that flurried inside his head.

Summoning the last of her strength, Mutiswa reached out for him, her touch was that of hot embers against his skin.

'Stand together with the Matabele, white man. Alone, neither you nor Rex Khumalo shall find power enough to quell the evil infecting this land.' Her lungs, like ancient bellows laboured unwillingly, the beat of her beleaguered heart weakening by the minute. 'The bird you hold was borne of fire, here at Zimbabwe, the Place of Stones. Here, white man, upon this hillside, but the *ndarama*, the gold itself was brought from the Nyanda mountains, from the very place where you now dig beneath the earth.' Her hand swung over to Lee's and as if her senses were again strong enough for her to admire the refinement of the precious metal, she scrutinised the surface of the talisman with her fingertips. 'Your own forebear held this to the sunlight, just as you now hold it to the lamp. As a girl I saw in him the spirit of brave men, he gave me back my life and those who threatened to take it from me, were cut down and consumed by fire.'

'Why do you tell me these things?' Lee asked her and then, still without his understanding of what was happening, for a brief moment saw beyond those cancerous features to the face of another woman; one of unblemished beauty, clad only in sunlight and a miniscule apron of soft leather. At the very nip of her hourglass waist there hung that same belt of coloured beadwork, upon it were the blood-red feet of the Bateleur eagle and the claws of the king leopard. Behind her towered the granite walls of Great Zimbabwe, engulfed by fallen trees and strangler vines, the blocks of raw stone were barely visible.

'I was the flower,' she went on, her failing mind hallucinating; she had become enraptured by recollections of her youth. Rex realised this and stepped up to the alcove.

'The reasons for you bringing us here, what are they? Give us your inner sight, old woman, or these last moments of your being will stand for nothing.'

Mutiswa paused, long enough for her to gather her strength and then, with the deliberation of a much younger woman, in a single fluid movement swung her legs from the cot and stood four-square in front of Rex.

The sudden transformation shocked him and like a man swept before some ice wind he fought to keep his balance. Outwardly, her features portrayed the devastation of that terminal disease, but from within, her voice rose up strong and vibrantly clear, mellifluent even. Her eyes, though dulled by blindness followed his every move.

'Beware the black leopard, Khumalo. Like a ghost she will come at you from the dark.'

Caught off his guard, Rex opened his mouth to reply, but with an imperious sweep of her arm Mutiswa silenced him.

'There will be others; men of little stature, but devious of mind. Look for the trap and the snare, Khumalo, or you will be dangled by the throat that others might mock your dancing on the hanging tree.'

Rex stepped back and as his only means of defence, focused the powerful beam from the miner's lamp full-on to Mutiswa's ravaged face. He felt his gorge rise; but for a few yellowed wisps of hair, nothing other than mottled skin encased the fragile dome of her skull. Live vermin clung to her cheeks and even at that distance, Rex was aware of their scuttling back from her face, fearful of his lamplight.

'You are already dead, witch.'

'And others will be more than quick to follow, Khumalo. Already Mugabe rallies his soldiers; with the lion's eyes he watches only for the chance to rid the land of all but the Shona. The Matabele, the Shangaan and the white settler – all of them he will sweep away.'

'The world looks on,' Rex countered, 'what you foretell could never come to be.'

Her head, like a piked skull wobbled upon a neck thinner than a child's wrist. Clothed in nothing more than her belt of coloured beads, as a living corpse taken from those terror camps of Auschwitz or Dachau, she struggled to remain standing. Stripped of healthy flesh, the skin that remained barely covered her bones. Threadlike veins and arteries entwined her limbs and from deep, ulcerated pustules, the engorged young of the maggot fly fell as ripened fruit at her feet.

'I am the seer, Khumalo. What I lay before you will one day be judged as truth or folly, but I tell you this much, you have but one chance to lift the people's eyes to your own, one chance to strengthen the hearts of this nation, for Matabele and Shona alike have already lifted their faces in search of fresh winds.'

Lee raised the beam from his miner's lamp. Mutiswa's ruined eyes reflected the light.

'You would have the nation revolt against their leader?'

'There is no other way, white man. More the tyrant than the leader; Mugabe sees himself as invincible. The Catholic priests who raised him created more than they had bargained for.' Her chest heaved and constricted for her to hack the choking sputum out from her throat. With the back of her shrivelled hand she cleared her lips of the filth. 'The man who now stands as leader of the people sees himself as second only to the great *Mwari*, the Supreme Spirit.'

Lee shook his head at her supposed insight. Logistically, to implement what she had proposed needed upwards of a king's ransom, motivating those sympathetic to the ousting of Mugabe's government would eat up millions of dollars.

'Even if the people were willing, to raise an army would empty even Mugabe's coffers, old woman. Where would such wealth come from?'

Mutiswa shuffled forward; Pfupi closed in next to her and though he was no taller than a child, easily his fingers fully encircled his mother's wrist. Lee backed away, repulsed by the things that moved towards him. Alongside the abomination that was Pfupi's mother, on

287

agitated, tiny feet, the dwarf scuttled insect-like about Mutiswa's legs. In the light from Lee's lamp, Pfupi's teeth were deep yellow, forced outwards by a deformation of his lower jaw. Buried deep inside his skull, his eyes glowed needle-sharp, black and piercing. The sight of him alone was more than enough to induce in Lee the need to destroy both creatures that now stood in front of him.

'Your eyes are still strong, white man, and yet you see nothing; those of Mutiswa are long dead and though she never leaves this world of darkness, every day she watches the sun rise and the stars follow.' Again, Mutiswa hawked up phlegm from her lungs and squeezed it out from between her lips. 'The day will come when the rivers run red; men and women will lift up their hands and fight to the death. Not even Mugabe's soldiers will stop this.' She turned to Rex and this time her deportment altered; she shrugged off her son's supporting arm and what had once been the infected voice of a dying crone was again the clear, bell-like invocation of the young girl.

'Go now, Rex Khumalo, now is your time to fight; look to your father's guardian for the wherewithal. Look to the eagle and be wary of those who would take it from you. Look for the words and wealth of a king through the writings of another.'

She fell silent, waiting for her tortured lungs to charge with air. This time, the deep bass voice of a man boomed through the cavern. Again, Rex staggered under the weight of fearful superstition; where once he had been able to counter the horror with logical explanation, now there was an overpowering resurrection of ancient tribal beliefs. From every recess of the cavern there came out the whisperings of dead men.

'Leave us, Khumalo! Return to the Great Wall, there lies your answer. Now is the time!' Rex covered his ears and closed his eyes to shut out the chaos. The voices rose about him, those of warriors, women and children; a thousand urgent intonations, even that of his dying father, spoken on that fateful moonlit night so many years ago. 'The bird, my son, guard it with your life!' After what seemed to him as the passing of an entire lifetime, the noise abated; left in its place was the gentle, keening voice of a small boy. Warm air filled the cavern, making the lamp above Mutiswa's stone cot waver. Rex lowered his hands and looked about for the witch.

'Where has she gone? I can see neither one of them.'

Lee swung the beam from his miner's lamp back and forth across the cavern, but the walls were irregular and roughly shaped, much of the rock cloaked in deep shadow.

'I've seen enough, Rex. Leave them to it and let's get out of here.'

'Over there.' Rex focused his lamp on the sidewall. A second alcove had been cut from the rock, much deeper and wider than the first. Lamps had been lit and from their stone niches cast down pools of yellow light. Here the smell of herbs and rendered animal fats were at their strongest, like before, the cot was thick with pelts of leopard and jackal and upon them Pfupi had dragged the still form of his mother. Alongside her, Pfupi sat cross-legged and in his outstretched hand there balanced the earthenware bowl of an oil lamp.

'You should leave us, Khumalo. Keep to the passage and it will lead you out of here.'

'Your mother...'

'No longer lives,' interrupted the dwarf, and his eyes were heavy with grief. 'You and the white man, you must leave.'

'You cannot stay here alone,' Rex countered. 'Come with us, there are those who will take care of you.'

'I have all that I need, Khumalo.' Pfupi smiled at the

kindness and then drew aside the silken pelt of a young otter from about his torso.

Wrapped about his waist and now in an aggravated state of aggression, a full grown female adder fought to free herself from where she had driven her fangs full length into the soft fold of the dwarf's groin. In the full glare of Rex's lamp, her diamond and fallen-leaf markings were exquisitely repugnant, the colours of a far forest floor mottled in shadow and sunlight. Her girth was that of Rex's forearm and with powerful little fingers, Pfupi needed all of his strength to control the reptile; holding her in place, he increased the pressure on the base of its spatula-shaped head. With the heel of his right hand he rocked the adder's upper jaw against his flesh, milking every drop, pumping its powerful haemotoxic venom directly into the femoral artery.

'There is nothing here for me, Khumalo. Go now, and take the portent with you. You both know what has to be done. Walk away or you also will be consumed.'

It was then that Rex saw the dwarf's reasoning behind his holding the spluttering lamp at arm's length, for the alcove in its entirety glistened with tallow. The pelts that enwrapped Mutiswa were smeared with it, and even the dwarf's own skin shone like wetted ironstone from a rubbing of that same, warm fat. Dry grass and timber, a metre deep, surrounded them. The dwarf, like some misshapen Buddha nestled alongside the wasted corpse of his mother. Mutiswa's death had been well orchestrated; Pfupi had merely to add his own, final macabre touch to the spectacle.

Mesmerised, Rex was powerless to intervene. Pfupi's eyes flew wide open and for the smallest of moments he stared at the man in front of him. His fingers opened and seemingly, in slow motion, as a final gesture of supplication the lamp slid from his hand. As if it were meant to be, the spluttering lamp found its way deep inside the stack of dry kindling.

At first, the flame, disturbed by the fall spluttered and shrank harmlessly, then, the tiny flame steadied and grew; with renewed commitment it found the mixture of tallow and tinder and greedily it took hold.

Like a child in the throes of fitful nightmares, Pfupi shuddered violently and slumped sideways, his body convulsed and arched like the hunter's bow, his eyes were wide open and within the vice-like grip of his right hand, still he held on to the adder.

Unable to tear their eyes from the spectacle, both men watched the fire lick across the alcove walls and upwards to the stone roof. Buffeted by the inferno, Pfupi's doll-like form writhed and withered like that of the snake. Blackened and featureless, his tiny limbs were laid open, ravaged by that terrible heat. Completely entombed by the pyre, slowly, Pfupi's charred corpse succumbed and nestled deeper in to the fire's heart.

Now a fearsome, impenetrable wall, the fire spread outwards from the alcove, incited winds snatched away the smoke and airborne sparks. With them went the sweet and sickly stench of roasting pork.

-69-

'Shouldn't you be telephoning the police?'

Lee shook his head, his face drawn and still heavily streaked with soot. He smiled through the filth.

'They wouldn't believe me.' He pushed his empty cup across the table. 'A refill, my sweetheart and then a shower, I smell like the barbecue chef from hell.'

It was half past six in the morning. Outside, the gardens were awash with first sunlight, birds were singing and the gardener was ferrying a barrow-load of bedding plants to the rear of the homestead. To Lee, those happenings of that previous night were no longer real; the remnants of some faded nightmare.

'There would be an enquiry,' said Rex, 'and a titillating piece in the Sunday papers.' He spread his arms to accommodate an imaginary broadsheet: 'Government minister and white mine owner cremate innocent mother and child. Authorities suspect ritual killings. Magic and devil worship not ruled out.'

'They'd throw away the key,' Lee mused. 'Comrade Miriam Pasviri would have a field day.'

'What happens next?' Karen asked.

Lee swivelled in his seat and held out a clenched fist to Karen.

'Brought something back for you; old acquaintance of yours. I'm sure you'll like it.'

Karen scowled at him. 'If it's alive I'll kill you.' She looked to Rex for clues, but he held up his hands, feigning ignorance.

'Don't ask. I'm staying well out of this one.'

For best effect, Lee positioned the talisman upright on the table; side-on to incoming sunlight. As had happened all those years ago on that fateful night of Bella's dinner party, everyone fell silent.

'My latest contribution to your museum.' Lee restarted the conversation and not without excitement, watched for the change on Karen's face.

Karen recognised it immediately, the urge to reach out now powerful and demanding, throughout her entire lifetime never had she witnessed anything more beautiful. Avidly she listened to Lee's explanation as to how, for a second time, he had come by it, but there was something not quite kosher. Intuitively, Karen realised her husband was holding out on her – half the story was missing.

'There's something you're not telling me.'

'Nothing that can't wait, my sweetheart.'

She shuffled to the edge of her seat and looked across the room at Rex, demanding information with her eyes. Rex cleared his throat. Unable to escape and from the periphery of the discussion, guiltily he explained the reasoning behind their secrecy.

'If word gets out, every government minister in Harare will want in on the find. Your Empress Deep will be turned into an archaeological peep show. Miriam Pasviri will be selling tickets at the shaft head.'

'Go on,' Karen invited, 'What else?'

Rex poured out a detailed description of the ancient mural they had found in the old workings.

'We had it sealed off.'

'For almost twenty years!'

'Eighteen,' Lee foolishly corrected her and stood up. 'Think I'll take a shower – Rex can fill you in.'

'Stay put,' Karen growled and like some chastened schoolboy, Lee looked to Rex for moral support.

'We were going to tell you, just that the timing wasn't right.'

Karen let them stew for a while, but driven by burning curiosity, she capitulated.

'I can't believe you kept it from me, but from a professional point of view, I would still like to see it.'

Simultaneously, both men breathed a sigh of relief.

'First thing tomorrow morning,' Lee promised, 'once the shaft has been cleared for maintenance. I'll have Byron lay on a special cage for ten o'clock.'

Her excitement resurfaced and she stood up from her chair.

'I'll need my camera and spare batteries.'

'And bacon and eggs before the men in your life die of hunger,' said Lee.

'When you have both showered,' she shot back at him. Now unstoppable, Karen plucked the gold artefact from the table and left them in the dayroom. Her mind raced; already it was filtering through a hundred possibilities of what she might find. There would be other artefacts to catalogue and photograph, notes to be made of their exact location below ground. A myriad of things the men had missed were waiting for the trained eye – a chance like this was a one-off, the discovery of a lifetime.

*

Back in the dayroom, showered and shaved, Lee re-aligned his thinking and swung the focus of his attention along more demanding lines.

'The gold you brought back from Mozambique. What's happening to it?'

'It's safe,' Rex assured him. 'Tomorrow, once we're back out from underground, we'll talk about it. I may well have a proposition for you.'

'What about Pasviri?' Lee went on. 'How much do you think she knows?'

'About your Mozambique debacle?'

Lee nodded his head.

'Her husband killed, two choppers and a couple of fixed-wing aircraft trashed, ostensibly on some sort of training exercise?'

'I know, I know. Word must have got back to Harare. Miriam's CIO friends aren't stupid. Someone, one of Pasviri's soldiers could have passed on what he saw.' He shook his head. 'The fiasco at Ponte Sobre; could have been that.'

'What about your chopper pilot?' Lee reminded him. 'He actually helped us load the bullion into the helicopter.'

'No worries on that front,' Rex insisted, 'He answers

directly to me. Any purposeful slip of the tongue and he knows I will cut his heart out.' He looked out through the window and watched a pair of yellow-billed kites hunting the ridge above the homestead.

'Miriam Pasviri is our number one problem. She says nothing because at present, her husband's disappearance from the political scene suits her purpose, her way up through the ruling party ranks is wide open.' He turned back to Lee and reached inside his pocket for cigarettes. 'But when the time comes for her to make a move, she will use whatever means she has at her disposal.' He flicked the wheel on his Zippo. 'Your company's moment of truth, captain; and as things stand, neither one of us can stop her.'

'There's always a way,' Lee argued.

'That depends,' Rex added, 'on just how hard she pushes and just how far you're willing to go to protect your business interests. The woman has already set her sights, captain. As you once pointed out, gold is more negotiable than even US dollars and through her diplomatic immunity, easily shipped abroad. There isn't a politician or banker outside of Zimbabwe who would not jump at the opportunity to get his hands on that amount of bullion.' He nudged the ashtray with his cigarette. 'To Miriam Pasviri, the Empress Deep's gold production is a means to funding her own private insurance policy. Her pension plan for when there's nothing left in Zimbabwe for the Party to hoover up.'

Karen came back from the kitchen; her Pyrex bowl filled with scrambled eggs and topped off with thick rashers of grilled bacon. She smiled at the men, her mood buoyant; still on a high she dropped a heat-proof raffia mat on the table and plonked down the Pyrex bowl.

'Sally still asleep?'

Rex nodded. 'Leave her be; compliments of yesterday's

run-in with Miriam Pasviri. The lie-in will do her good.'

'Salt, pepper, toast or just more coffee?'

'All of those would be much appreciated,' Rex thanked her and stubbed out his cigarette. 'There's something else.'

Karen stopped what she was doing.

'You've lost me?'

'We should have told you about the mural on 387 Level. Just that the war and everything else sort of got in the way.'

'Dead and buried,' Karen said. 'Rather late than never and I'm grateful for that.'

'There's another one.'

'Another what?'

'A second mural,' Rex admitted. The silence went on; even the birds outside in the garden went quiet.

Once again, Karen's interest piqued. 'Go on, I'm listening.'

'Not as simple as it might sound,' Lee said.

'Try me.'

'Eighteen years ago,' Rex recalled what happened, 'the night my father and me were abducted.'

'What are you getting at?'

'Beneath the Hill Fortress,' Rex added to her confusion. 'That's where it is – the second mural.'

Lee tried as best he could to dampen his wife's interest.

'Let it lie. Now is not the time for us to go snooping around Zimbabwe's premier national treasure.'

Like a buffalo watching from deep undergrowth, Karen fixed her eyes on him.

'What else haven't you told me?'

Lee shook his head. 'I didn't know about it. Not before last night.'

'It can wait,' Rex insisted, 'Going back there would be a mistake – too dangerous. One step at a time, whether we like it or not, from here on in, Miriam will have her people watching our every move; we must play her at her own game – keep her in the dark and out of the way as much as possible.'

Lee replaced the telephone and raised an eyebrow at Rex. Dressed in overalls and boots, both men were already equipped for going underground. The expression on Lee's face dispelled any hopes of a smooth, integration with the government's acquisition policies – he was in for the rockiest ride of his life.

'Miriam Pasviri is on her way down from Harare.'

'Flying?'

'Private charter; she left Harare half an hour ago.'

Rex glanced at his watch. 'A couple of hours at the outside and she'll be hammering down your office door.'

Karen breezed into the room, like the men, she had changed and kitted out to cope with conditions three hundred and eighty-seven metres below ground.

'Why the long faces?'

'Pasviri's flying in from Harare. Byron's just phoned me.'

Karen rolled her eyes and stared at the ceiling. Up to that moment her morning had been almost perfect.

'What else did he say?'

'Just that she was pretty off-handed and insisted on us being on site when she gets here.'

She cursed under her breath and stared out through the window; her eagerness to see the mural already evaporating.

'Just as well Sally chose to stay at the homestead. So what do we do now?'

297

'We comply,' Rex told her, 'take whatever she throws at us, at least for now. Stay dressed as you are and I'll convince her I'm doing a safety audit.'

'We have an hour at best before she gets here,' Lee reminded them.

'Something's wrong,' Rex realised. 'Either Miriam has decided to blow the whistle on her husband's incursion into Mozambique, or someone has tipped her off about the reef on 387 level.'

Lee shook his head. 'Other than you, no one outside of my family has ever seen the old workings.'

'Just how rich is the reef?' Karen asked.

'Very,' Lee said. 'Drilled and proved over one hundred metres; six feet wide at best and most of it riddled with visible gold.'

'Secondary enrichment,' Rex explained for Karen's benefit. 'Very often that's the way it is with the uppermost sections of oxidised gold reef. The main difference being that with this one, instead of the more common, smaller pocket of extraordinary high values, here the enrichment is on a much larger scale.'

From memory, Lee made a rough mental calculation of average values across the entire upper section of reef; his forebears had taken out only a small section of the oxide zone before sinking their shaft to access the lower parts of the ore body. At present day gold prices, the amount in hard currency was staggering.

'Fifteen million American dollars give or take, before the values drop off at depth. In the harder sulphides the values stabilise; sort of level out. That particular section of reef has been left alone; an emergency stockpile should the company fall on hard times.'

'And I suppose the mural just happens to sit slap-bang in the middle,' Karen pre-empted.

Rex nodded his head.

'That's not our only problem.' He lowered his voice.

'The gold I brought back from Mozambique.'

'What about it?' Karen cut in.

'It's on 387 Level, all of it. I had no choice.'

The blood drained from Lee's face.

'Jesus Christ, Rex. That's all I need.'

The door opened and Byron blustered into the room. His face was blood-red; the stress he suffered from repeated ministerial visits was getting to him.

'She's just phoned from the airport. Forty minutes – as soon as the hire cars have been fuelled and cleaned they'll be on their way.'

'What else did she say?' Lee asked him.

Byron brushed a bead of sweat from his nose and with an already sodden handkerchief, mopped his forehead.

'Wanted to know if you were on site; told her you were en route, that was about it.'

'Organise a ship load of ice, Byron, and get the kitchen to knock up some sandwiches. Equal mix of brown and white bread – The Dragon Lady gets annoyed if anything comes across as pro-colonial.'

The boardroom's air-conditioning maintained a comfortable eighteen degrees. Lee sat at his desk and stared long and hard at the incoming road; now at full strength he sensed the heat outside pressing against the windows. Karen brought him a second glass of orange juice and ice.

'What about something to eat?'

Lee took the glass from her. Pasviri could have phoned him directly, what was she after? Forcefully, he abandoned his paranoia for second guessing and instead smiled reassuringly at Karen.

'No thanks – see if Rex wants anything, my sweetheart.'

'He's downstairs waiting for Miriam.'

Karen screwed her eyes at the haze beyond the office window and like her husband, focused intently on the incoming gravel road.

'Someone's coming.'

Lee stood up from his chair and moved in closer to the window.

Slowly at first, from the ground upwards the haze was changing shape; leaning away from the road a thick, ochre-coloured cloud of dust manifested itself against the skyline. From out of it, two white Nissan 4x4s thundered towards the Empress Deep. Nose to tail – both vehicles were travelling at high speed.

'It's Miriam.' Lee told her. 'Couldn't be anyone else, only her CIO boys would be crazy enough to drive on a hillside gravel road at that speed.'

Rex stepped out from the foyer and slowly made his way down thirty-one stone steps to the car park. He adjusted his sunglasses to cope with the sunlight and on reaching level ground, stood to his full height; arms folded across his chest. Both vehicles swung wide and then drew up side by side in front of the steps. The doors of both Nissans opened simultaneously and Comrade Pasviri's usual bodyguard of four CIO men were first out. Quickly, they secured the immediate area, in turn, each man raised his arm and nodded to the drivers, only then did Miriam step out from the protective armour of her vehicle.

'The one and only, Rex Khumalo,' she purred, then donned her Ray-Bans and frowned defiantly up at the harsh sunlight; her makeup was immaculate. With reptilian stealth she moved to within an arm's length of the government's most powerful mining man. 'I see you're dressed for hard work, comrade?'

'Safety audit,' Rex lied. 'You were here less than a week ago, why the sudden urgency?'

'Love the overalls; very manly.' She ignored the query and with her hand on his elbow encouraged Rex towards the steps. 'Drinks first, business second, I thought you knew me well enough by now.'

Once inside the boardroom, Miriam took centre stage at the bar. Lee watched her movements via the mirror tiles behind the optics; her eyes, though still guarded by tinted glasses were everywhere.

'Single or double?' Lee watched her reflection.

She took off the Ray-Bans and with a slight nod of the head, acknowledged his pleasantries. 'Large one, please. Fill up with ice and whatever space is left with soda. First decent drink since we left Harare.'

Karen came in from the boardroom kitchen, her disposition businesslike, distasteful memories of their last meeting still very much alive.

'Chicken, roast beef, and cheese for anyone who wants them.' Without so much as glancing at Miriam she left two stainless steel salvers of sandwiches on the bar. Miriam ignored the food and stuck with her scotch and soda. She swivelled sideways on her bar-stool and without any hesitation, followed Karen through to the boardroom kitchen.

'You're looking well, Karen, why the overalls?'

Outshone by Miriam's haute couture, Karen suddenly felt dowdy and heavy-waisted. Being caught off guard by the minister's irregular attitude swings confused her; disarmed her mentally. The reply flurried out, contrite and unintentionally light-hearted.

'High fashion; goes with my once a year daredevil descent into the bowels of the earth for a conducted tour of God knows where.' She frowned at her own reflection in the stainless steel work surface, silently cursing herself for parading in front of Miriam Pasviri as the frumpish also-ran. 'A failing of mine; never was able to generate much enthusiasm for crawling around in the dark.'

'You and me both,' Miriam retorted, 'not too happy with tight spaces; rather like being in prison, I should imagine.' Again the coin flipped and what was only seconds ago the warm, conciliatory sparkle quickly fell from her eyes; like those of the addict, they were now devoid of any emotion. 'Not that anyone such as you would know what I'm talking about.'

Karen maintained her composure.

'Nor do I intend to find out; quite happy to stay on my own, boring side of the fence.' She reached for Miriam's empty glass. 'You're running on fumes, let me top you up.'

Karen made her way back to the boardroom, refilled Miriam's glass and joined her at the far wall.

'I see you're back with your favourite personality.' Again, Karen waved the olive branch; following Miriam's lead she showed interest in the boardroom picture gallery. Miriam ignored the contentious likeness of Cecil Rhodes and swung her attention onto a more modernistic gathering of men stood to the hull of a sleekly lined, charter fishing boat.

'This one's interesting. Your husband's fishing boat?' Without waiting for an answer she slid her finger further along to where the craft's name emblazoned the pristine, white prow. '*Isabella*,' she read aloud, purposely accentuating the discovery. 'A name one would not easily forget.'

Karen's blood ran cold. Miriam sensed the change in her and like some blood-sucking insect, probed deeper.

'The man stood next to the sailfish. A family friend?'

'Was.' Karen said and knew then that getting in first was her only way of surviving. 'Gerard never told anyone he was dying of cancer. Rode the storm without treatment. The pain must have got to him – took his own life.'

'I'm sorry.' Miriam said, but more as a matter of course than out of genuine sentiment. She paused, allowing Karen free rein.

'Somewhere off the coast of Mozambique,' Karen went on, 'his helmsman was below. Heard the shot, but he was too late. By the time he reached the upper deck, Gerard had already gone overboard.' She turned away from the photograph. 'I would rather we didn't discuss it.'

Miriam backed off. She had hoped for more. Annoyed by her failure to find fault with Karen's explanation, she turned on her heels and made for the bar. Rex saw her coming and as a deterrent, attempted to strike up meaningful conversation with Byron Fuller. However, like a Border Collie cutting a sheep from the herd, Miriam stepped between them.

'What happened in Mozambique, Rex?'

Rex took his time draining his glass.

'You must be getting desperate, Miriam. Didn't realise we were on first name terms. What exactly are you talking about?'

The whisky had sharpened her features; like the unsated female spider, she moved in close enough for him to sense the threat.

'Don't play games with me, Rex. Both you and my husband were involved in something nefarious.'

'Like what, Miriam?' He projected disinterest.

With the malicious intent of live steam the words hissed from between her lips.

'Be careful, comrade. I know about the gold.'

From the slightest characteristic tightening of his jawline, Miriam knew she had broken through.

'Three days ago. CIO people picked up your pilot friend.'

'I am at a loss, comrade.'

She ignored the pretence. 'I watched them work on him.' Her eyes glittered. 'It took a long time, but in the end he told me everything.'

Rex summoned every last ounce of willpower to beat

back the devils that now roared inside his head; vengefully they screamed for him to retaliate, urging him to drive his fist through Miriam's face. Revenge was now the new obsession, the young pilot had trusted him; Emerson Ndhlovu was little more than a boy. Without breaking eye contact, Rex took his time lighting a cigarette. He forced back his anger and slowly the calm returned.

'Where is this vast fortune supposed to be hidden, Miriam?'

Miriam waved her empty glass at him, her voice now that of the shrewish remonstrator.

'Stop lying to me, Rex, or within the space of this afternoon you and your colonial accomplices will be discussing your futures with the CIO.' She reached out and plucked the lighted cigarette from Rex's fingers. 'And I have decided to take up smoking.' The venom dropped from her voice and she smiled as though nothing untoward had happened. 'I'm told it will take the edge off my appetite and inches off my waistline.'

Rex's mind flew back to him looking down from the tech's seat of an Alouette gunship, fixated by what was happening aboard the *Isabella*; gunfire roaring in his ears, Gerard's body folding in front of him and then, discarded doll-like it lay there, broken and motionless; a single bullet through the centre of his chest. Unlike Gerard, Emerson would have died less than forty-eight hours ago, on the backroom floor of the CIO's Chaminuka Building in Harare; his face disfigured, bones broken by brutal, indiscriminate hammer blows, his body hurriedly wrapped in black plastic and dispassionately got rid of; dumped beyond the city limits, in amongst a hundred other, shallow unmarked graves.

'Who else knows about this?'

Miriam pulled on the cigarette; naively, as a first-timer

she mouthed the smoke, squashing it from between her lips as she spoke.

'At the moment – no one.'

'Why should I trust you?'

Miriam shook her head and laughed. Cigarette smoke made her eyes water, her eyelids flickered and blinked at the irritation; she coughed to clear her throat.

'Because you have no choice. Look around you, Rex. From now on this will be your home; for as long as there is gold in the Empress Deep, comrade, this is where you will work, live and breathe.' She lowered her voice to a whisper. 'Like they say in the movies, we need each other. Alone, neither one of us will survive this. A wrong word, comrade and I will have you dragged back to Harare in time for your wife's funeral.'

Rex kept his cool, but the lethality of his intent was now the raging fire in his eyes.

'Harm Sally and I will kill you.'

'The gold, Rex – where is it?'

He took a deep breath. 'You said the pilot told you everything?'

'He did. There was nothing there. Either he was lying or you moved it.' She lost interest in the cigarette and dropped it into the ashtray. 'Before he died, your pilot was pretty forthcoming; he told me about the old workings, I want to see them.' Like those of a leopard, her eyes were on fire. 'You can't win, Rex. An offshore bank account has already been registered in your name and a substantial transfer in Hong Kong dollars was made this morning, by someone who will stand up in any court of law and swear on the authenticity of your mutual business interests.'

'You're setting me up.'

'Couldn't have put it better myself, comrade. Clever of me, don't you think?' Again, she waved her glass at him for a refill. 'You can talk while you pour and don't look so glum, my friend. Two years from now and we can both retire to some exotic, Far Eastern paradise and live out the rest of our lives like gods.' Her eyes narrowed. 'Hand in glove, comrade. Business partners – perhaps closer, even. Think of how much fun we can have and with regards to your darling Sally?' She tossed her head and laughed. 'I just don't give a fuck.'

-71-

Lee fixed the battery onto metal hooks riveted to his belt and draped its metre-long umbilical lamp cable over his right shoulder. Angered by Miriam finding out about the gold, he glared through the doorway.

'Where is she?'

'Visitor's change house, Karen's helping her kit-up. Brace yourself for an interesting couple of hours, I know her all too well. The bitch is playing us for fools.' Rex jerked the slack out from his boot laces. 'So help me, I could choke the woman with my bare hands and feel nothing.'

'You'll have to stand in line, old son. Like it or not, she has us by the balls.'

'We're not done yet,' Rex countered. 'Stay calm. Keep your wits about you and don't start winding up on the woman, or we'll end up with nothing.'

'What worries me is how much of this has leaked out.'

Rex shook his head. 'No leak. We would have heard by now. Comrade Miriam is the only government minister we have to contend with. She plays her cards close to her chest; wants it all.' He donned his safety helmet and started for the change house door. 'We'll wait for her at the shaft head. Don't forget, keep your cool, maybe we can squeeze something workable out of this mess.'

306

'The woman's insane,' Lee said. 'One phone call to the PF hierarchy and her number would be up.'

'And ours with it,' Rex cut back with the stark improbability of it ever happening. 'She knows she's safe; don't underestimate Miriam Pasviri. Some of the younger Party members already refer to her as the black widow. The woman is lethal.'

Lee followed him outside. They crossed the General Office frontage and stood in deep shade below the shaft headgear. Rex leaned with his back to the steelwork and casually smoked a last cigarette before going underground. His eyes were locked to the visitors' change house door. As things were at that moment, Miriam was now in full control and he cursed her for it.

'Here she comes,' Lee growled. 'Don't let me lose my temper, or I swear I will send the bitch to shaft bottom – minus the cage.'

Miriam was talking to Karen, as if explaining the rudiments of an annual routine inspection, a cursory going-over of a pre-selected section of the mine's underground workings. Once she came within earshot, Miriam's face hardened and her step was suddenly that of the disgruntled overseer. She focused on Lee.

'I must assume that everything is in order, Mister Goddard.'

Lee nodded his head. 'The conveyance is on its way – give it a couple of minutes to reach surface.'

She swung her attentions to Rex, her gaze unwavering.

'You are aware of the consequences, should there be trouble?'

Impassively, Rex stared back at her for a long time before turning away.

Karen picked up on the discord, immediately aware that things were not as they seemed she looked to her husband for answers.

'What's going on?'

Lee shook his head; apart from bravado-driven talk, Miriam had as yet, committed no offence. However, should she choose to blow the lid off things, at best, he would be facing life imprisonment.

'Miriam knows about the gold.'

'Has done for some time, comrade,' Miriam retorted.

The shaft bells clamoured. The conveyance settled, the banksman shot back the locking bolts and flung up the roller shutter safety door. Lee gestured to the onsetter.

'387 Level, Jack. I'll phone from the station when we're ready to come out.'

The conveyance hung motionless; a rodeo bull poised to break free of the bucking chute. Miriam's eyes widened and she moved in closer to Rex.

'Is this thing safe?'

'Most of the time.'

She glowered at him. A miner's shovel clattered against the steel floor. Miriam grabbed for Rex's arm and visibly shrunk from the noise. The onsetter rang his 'clear to descend signal' through to the winding engine driver then pulled down the safety door and kicked in the locking bolt. He switched on his cap lamp and looked to Lee for reassurance.

'Everything alright, Mister Goddard?'

Lee nodded. 'The *madala-side*, Jack; the old workings – anyone been down there lately?'

'No one that I know of. Ghosts and dust, that's all there is on 387. You be careful, Mister Goddard, bad ground. Would be worth your while to stay away from the old stope. All those years without proper maintenance, reckon the hanging's ready to come down.'

Miriam fumbled her lamp on. The conveyance shuddered and her grip on Rex's arm was vice-like. The driver had engaged his powerful, thyristor-driven controller and for a brief moment the cage lifted an inch above the shaft bank; then, like a serpent eager to reach its lair, the steel rope uncoiled and sent the conveyance deep below the surface of the earth.

-72-

Fate had brought Lee full circle, back to where it had all started. Now he was about to face the repercussions of all his grandiose scheming; the gold bullion was now the grasping other woman, about to flounce her skirts and dance away with everything he held dear. Rex saw the doubt in him and drew him out from the silence.

'Confirm you have the key with you?'

Lee nodded his head. 'The lock could have seized. It's been a long time.'

'Should be fine. If not, we can always access the stope from surface via the old adit, the same way I did.'

'How far in is this place?' Miriam demanded of them, her eyes still wide. The drop to 387 Level had left her shaken and unsteady on her feet. She walked with her shoulders hunched as if in readiness for a quick escape, for she was all too aware of those thousands of tons of living rock that were pressing down on the walls and roof of that ancient tunnel.

'A few hundred metres,' Lee told her, 'might want to watch your step though; this part of the mine was abandoned over forty years ago. Any chance of a rock fall and we'll find out soon enough.'

Lee was first to climb out from the cross-cut; over heaps of fallen rubble he worked his way inside the mined-out stope. The others followed his lead. Fine dust fled as glittering smoke from their footfalls and the smell of long abandonment was thickly spread around them. Lit by their powerful lamps, a grey wind worked its way downwards through the stope then disappeared inside the gaping mouth of a derelict ore pass. Miriam stared in abject horror at the emptiness; like that infamous black hole of deep space, the ancient inter-level ore pass sucked down everything that was airborne, even the sound of human voices and light from their lamps appeared to disappear inside that dark abyss.

'This way and stay close in to the sidewall.' Lee waved his lamp at Miriam. He took hold of Karen's hand. Taking no chances, he guided her well away from the six feet diameter hole in the footwall. The steel grizzly that once covered the shaft opening had disappeared. The ore pass sides had deteriorated enough for the grizzly's own weight to have freed it from its mountings, sending it hurtling downwards for the old draw point, three hundred feet below on the mine's deepest production level.

Rex brought up the rear and now, matched to his every step was his loathing for Julius Pasviri's widow. Her CIO men had refused to accompany her underground, superstition and fear of old mine workings had kept them from what they saw only as self-entrapment; openly and without embarrassment they shunned this world of lost souls. Their fear of the spirit world suited Rex; desperately he searched for ways to turn the situation around. Miriam had them caged and like unwary fowl, all had been earmarked for slaughter. Once they were back on surface it would all begin. The act of stripping the Empress Deep of her gold would be swift and merciless. Not an ounce of accessible, high grade ore would be left unmined.

'Give me a hand here, Rex.' Lee stood in front of the steel security door. Almost twenty years had passed since he, along with a crew of ten men had cut and strengthened the rock for it to support the heavy door. 'The lock has opened,' Lee explained, 'but the door won't move.'

'It moved before and it will move again.' Rex cursed their run of bad luck, then stepped away from the door. 'Give me a minute,' he said and on the strength of some faint recollection, dragged the toe of his boot through thick dust where it had collected inches deep along the base of the sidewall.

'A long shot, I know,' Rex grinned and after feeling beneath the dust lifted out a two metre long, steel bar. 'From the last time we were here and exactly where I dropped it.'

At its widest point of access, Rex forced the flattened tip of the steel barring tool between the door and concrete framework. Again, he nodded to Lee and made place for him on the bar.

'Everything you've got, my friend. Put your weight to it.'

The steel bar bent under their combined weight and squealed against metal and seasoned concrete. Gradually, a millimetre at a time, the gap widened.

'Keep the pressure on, it's starting to move. One more time should do it.'

Both men doubled their efforts and threw their all at the lever; the door groaned and shuddered. Disturbed by the ongoing work and that sudden change in airflow, tails of silver dust appeared through the gap and spirited away for the ore pass.

'She's opening, Rex! Don't let up.' Each renewed lunge at the bar served to weaken the grip of oxidised metal and quartz dust, until at last, the armoured door shrieked on dry hinges and swung outwards; in its place there gaped the beginnings of a dark cavern. Both men waited for their senses to readjust before stepping inside.

Without warning, Miriam brushed passed them. Excitedly she swept the cavern floor with bright light;

311

panning the beam from side to side. Metre by metre she probed the darkness. The floor was strewn with fallen rock; dust rose spectre-like about her feet and hurried past her. Oblivious to any danger she moved forwards, but Rex reached out and caught hold of her arm.

'I could let you fall, comrade. Watch where you walk, remember where you are.'

Miriam snatched her arm away. Dust had found the sweat on her forehead. In the lamplight, she appeared wan and ghostlike and in her eyes, Rex saw the re-surfacing of what had come to be her wildest obsession. Through her sudden, irrational need for great wealth, Miriam Pasviri was poised to cross over from normality to a world of the borderline insane.

'Where have you hidden it?'

'Another thirty yards,' Rex told her and with the light from his lamp pointed the way for her.

Alone and unaided, it had taken him almost half a day to bring in the gold via the ancient adit, one bar at a time; twenty, ten kilogram bars of almost pure gold – every one of them a dead weight.

The change in Miriam Pasviri was catalytic; what niceties she had exhibited earlier were gone – dissipated by greed. Only a few hours before, with the panache of a wealthy debutante had she swept through the boardroom and commandeered the attentions of the Empress Deep's hierarchy with confidence and authority; now, dressed in overalls and wellington boots and with grey slime smeared about her face, she epitomised little more than some panicky treasure hunter; her once immaculate coiffure was now the unkempt, tangled mass protruding from beneath her safety helmet, thick and braid-like. To Rex, hers was the head of the mythical Medusa, her hair a nest of viperous, writhing snakes in his lamplight.

Four powerful miners' lamps lit up the cavern's central floor space. Miriam looked on slack-jawed at the sheer enormity of wealth confronting her; now in a state of total euphoria, she crossed those final few yards and, reaching out, ran her fingers over the topmost, butter-coloured ingot. Though still in that semi-raw state of its first casting, it was the imparted feeling of warm silk that thrilled her to the core.

'Seems like my husband's eagerness to catch up with you was justified, Mister Goddard.' From the brink of her other world she looked back at those who stood behind her. She focused on Rex and smiled sardonically. 'Your pilot friend was right, comrade. A king's ransom at the very least.'

The smile disappeared. 'You will remove it from the mine. In the meantime, comrade, you will make doubly sure no one else has access to this place.'

'No one else has a key.' Lee told her.

Her eyes narrowed. 'You are sure there are no duplicates?'

'Ninety percent sure,' Rex added, goading her with the uncertainty. Karen's anger rose serpent-like from the pit of her stomach. In her eyes, Miriam had become the voracious vampire poised to drain the Empress Deep of its lifeblood. A year, two at the most and every ounce of prime ore would be milked from her deepest reefs. Recollections of dark storms, mangrove swamps and the ape-like Roberto stood up alongside her. More than anything, the hellish clatter of Pasviri's guns when he killed Gerard; left bleeding on the deck of their beloved *Isabella*, the expression she had seen on Gerard's face would never leave her. They were handing Miriam a fortune in gold without so much as a fight. Once they were back on surface, Miriam would, without the slightest hesitation call in the CIO. The gold, the Empress Deep in its entirety would be hers to exploit, whenever it suited her. Gerard would have died for nothing.

'Why are you doing this?' Karen growled and both Lee and Rex were quick to pick up on her new hatred.

'Because I choose to.' Miriam lashed back at her. 'Because of what I stand for. Because I am part of the new elite and you and yours, settler bitch, are nothing more than pathetic hangers-on – colonial leftovers.' She dismissed the futile attack on her reasoning and again, turned to the bullion, worshipping the stack of yellow metal through a lover's eyes.

At first, Miriam's determination to lift away the topmost ingot was thwarted; smooth contours and sheer weight made it impossible for her fingertips to find purchase. However, undeterred she redoubled her efforts and by pushing the ingot sideways to where it over-reached the bar below, found strength enough to lift it clear of the pile.

Lee watched her, fascinated, but even more than that, like Karen's, his strongest feelings were those of virulent anger and disgust. Only by the smallest of margins did he come up short of snuffing out Miriam's life. Her thieving epitomised the Party's blatant disregard for Zimbabwe's minority and total lack of concern for the country's future. In the face of worldwide media, corrupt government officials were being left alone to steal and persecute at will. What Miriam had come upon was more than her mind could comprehend, so that her hands trembled and those first bright drops of spittle dribbled out from between her lips. Without her realising, like the hyena over the stolen kill, she was salivating.

'I could kill her,' Karen hissed under her breath, but

through that same sense of morbid fascination she was being forced to watch the spectacle unfold.

Rex stepped forwards; Miriam struggled to stand erect, the unbalancing effect of the weight in her arms threatened to topple her over.

'What are you doing?'

'Taking this with me, what does it look like?' Miriam backed away from him and with a huge effort gathered the ten kilogram bar of gold against her chest.'

'You'll never make it to the shaft station,' Rex warned her.

'Touch it, comrade and I will see you in hell!'

'You still have to climb back through the stope.'

Miriam steadied herself and pointed with her chin. 'You will walk in front. I have seen enough, take me back to the shaft station.'

'The onsetter will know what you're carrying.'

'Then distract him. Make sure that he knows nothing.'

With malicious intent she turned on Karen.

'When we are back on surface, your husband will be issued with a verbal notification of acquisition.' Her face contorted and she sneered triumphantly at Karen. 'Something for you to think about, settler woman. It will prove interesting to see just how hard you try to convince me otherwise.' She nodded her head to Rex. 'Lead the way, Comrade Khumalo, I have need of sunlight and something to drink.'

Once the steel door had been closed and locked, a strange silence came over the old workings. Lee found himself likening it to that time he had spent with Rex, staring down to where Gerard's weighted corpse had plunged beneath the surface of the Indian Ocean. Both places, though so set apart by their own diversity were indomitably linked, the open sea and the darkest parts of the mine were to Gerard, equally deep and powerful, as exciting as they were foreboding. In his own peculiar way he had loved them both.

Lee reached out and touched his fingers to Karen's shoulder, and when she turned to face him he saw in the light from his lamp that silently, his wife was crying. The trauma she was suffering as a result of Miriam's continuous harassment incensed him, his mind was in turmoil and desperately he racked his brains for a way out of their impossible situation.

Miriam stumbled on ahead, downwards at a steep angle. The physical strain from her carrying such a heavy weight was beginning to show, but like a mantis clutching prey to its chest, relentlessly she clung to the gold bar, determined that no one would wrest it from her.

Lee steered Karen towards the access point for the main cross-cut, it was then that Karen reached up for him and gently kissed his cheek. 'Do not try to stop me,' she whispered to him and before Lee had chance to prevent her, slipped her hand from his fingers. Armed with a determined mindset, she increased her pace and made her way forwards.

Rex still led, his mood sombre; his expectations those of a betrayed soldier condemned without trial to be thrown in front of the firing squad. Constantly, he analysed their situation. Miriam had no illusions over his empathy for the Goddards, once they were back on surface she would be quick to fire her accusations. Everything he had planned for was falling apart. The future reeled in front of him and he saw the world he had hoped for turn its back on him and rush away on dark wings. To his rear, the only sounds were those of boots on broken quartz and the soft moan of far-off ventilation fans.

Karen moved closer in to the sidewall. Her breathing roared in her ears and twice the rock wall to her immediate right scuffed the skin from her elbow.

However, she was now indomitably committed to a head-on confrontation. Ignoring the instability of broken ground and steep angle of decline, she increased her pace and quickly she gained on Comrade Miriam Pasviri. Her thoughts turned to dark things, fuelled by that sudden rush of adrenalin, her fists balled and her teeth clenched. Propelled by a mother's instinct to destroy the curse that threatened her family, Karen swept down through the gloom; the lioness in pursuit of the scavenging hyena, her fear of any repercussions already evaporated for she had nothing left to lose. The drawn out pretence of bonhomie was finished with, rather one last all-out fight, one more deal of the cards before her family's very existence crashed and burned.

Without concern for her own safety, she shouldered Miriam out of the way. Miriam lurched sideways, thrown off balance by the dead weight she was carrying. With one hand to the rock wall she kept herself from falling, the lamp on her helmet now turned full-on to Karen's face.

'Push me aside again, comrade and I will kill you.'

Gleefully, Karen rounded on her. It was the catalyst she had been waiting for; driven by her own terrible rage she lunged forwards and wrestled for a hold on the heavy bar.

Like some fairground contestant locked in a tug of war, Karen threw herself backwards, at the same time, driving hard down with her heels. Lost to that sudden rage, Karen screamed obscenities at the woman in front of her and with the violence of a hardened street fighter she fought to rip the gold from Miriam's hands. Her movements now were powerful, more coordinated; she threw her weight from side to side – the terrier worrying the rabbit.

Lee moved to break up the fracas, but the unstable, rocky ground slowed him down.

Suddenly thrown off balance, again, Karen stumbled and relinquished her grip on the gold bar. Miriam saw her chance and, driven backwards by her own momentum, instinctively she felt with her feet for firm ground.

It was for the smallest of moments that Karen witnessed the triumphant look in Miriam's eyes and then, as if by some macabre sleight of hand, still with the bullion clutched to her chest, Miriam disappeared – swallowed up whole by the dark.

-74-

Rex looped an inch-thick hemp rope about both axles of an upturned cocopan, creating a makeshift pulley system. Lee took up the loose end, anchored it across his shoulders and drew out the slack to a point where he felt the rope draw tight and hold against the axles. With the rope tied around his waist, Rex inched his way backwards and leaned out into the void. Forty feet below him, the glow from Miriam's lamp was still visible. The redundant steelwork straddled the shaft walls; jammed at a tenuous angle, the steel grizzly had broken Miriam's ultimate sickening, three hundred feet fall to shaft bottom. Her lamp, still attached to her waist by the battery's power cable, hung between the latticework of steel bars and like the fateful arc of a pendulum, the light from it swept from side to side.

'I can see her!' Rex shouted to Lee. 'Give me some slack, I'm going to try and get down there.'

Lee glanced at his watch. Karen had been gone for fifteen minutes; by now, she would have made it to the shaft station and phoned their situation through to Byron's office; besides the rescue team, Lee wanted at least one CIO man on site. They needed a witness; his word alone wasn't enough to safeguard them from the inevitable accusations.

Rex braced himself for the climb down.

'Miriam! If you can you hear me, hang in there I'm coming down.'

Like a climber preparing to abseil the face of a sheer cliff, Rex inched backwards and let the rope take his weight. Balanced against the balls of his feet he took in one last, deep breath and then started downwards.

Karen showed up through the dark and called out to him. Her run from the station had left her winded.

'Rex, wait! Byron said to wait for help – no heroics.'

Rex ignored the warning and continued downwards. His own lamp lit up the shaft throat and from far below him came the sounds of loosened rock striking the shaft wall. He shouted up to Karen.

'She's landed on the old grizzly. We can't wait any longer.' He looked up and signalled to Lee. 'Keep the rope coming, captain and watch your footing. Nice and easy, now. Even tension on the rope or we'll have a runaway.'

Inch by inch, Rex moved closer in to the grizzly. Miriam lay on her side and from the awkward placement of her right leg, Rex knew that it was broken. Half a metre from her right hand, driven in hard by the fall, the gold ingot had wedged itself between the steelwork and the shaft wall; like some giant butterfly valve the dislodged grizzly bridged the ore pass. However, any sudden movement could cause the heavy screen to shift position and tip sideways.

'Miriam – can you hear me!'

Miraculously, Miriam still had strength of mind enough to turn her head and look about her, seemingly unaware of her injuries. Waving his lamp, Rex again signalled to Lee for him to stop paying out rope and instead of climbing in closer to the grizzly, concentrated his efforts on communicating with Miriam.

'Raise your right hand if you can hear me!' He heard a commotion coming from above and then Lee called down to him.

'They're here, Rex. The rescue team are rigging a stretcher and lifting gear. They want me to pull you up.'

Miriam raised herself on one elbow. Her behaviour changed; exhibiting all the signs of trauma peculiar to a victim of concussion, she now appeared confused and disorientated.

'We're going to lift you out!' Rex encouraged her. 'Don't move. Keep still or you'll fall.'

Standing as close as he dared to the lip of the ore pass, a CIO operative strained to listen in.

'Miriam!' Rex kept on trying to get through to her. 'Talk to me, Miriam!'

'Rex listen to me, we're going to pull you up.' Lee's voice reverberated inside the shaft, but Rex waved his lamp as a warning – holding him off.

'Not yet, give me a few more minutes; I need to get through to her. She has to be aware of what's going on.'

For a moment, as if emerging from a dream, Miriam stared up at the light, then, like an animal going to ground she flattened against the grizzly, but it was not through her fear of falling that made her do this. With her leg fractured below the knee, still she pulled herself across the steelwork; she had seen the gold bar and now, seemingly oblivious to what had happened, with her good leg driving from behind, slowly she inched towards the shaft wall.

'For Christ's sake leave it, Miriam!' Rex shouted to her through the now constant flow of voices pouring down on him. The rescue crew were rigging their lifting tackle, swinging in heavy sheer-legs and rope blocks above the ore pass, the noise from it all drowned him out; his

320

efforts were wasted. He heard them lowering a chain ladder, it reached to where he hung suspended above the grizzly, and then, like some iron snake it passed him by and slithered away inside the darkness.

The steel ladder rattled against the grizzly bars and it was then that Miriam's eyes flew wide open. Alarmed by the sudden clatter of metal on metal, Miriam made one final, desperate attempt to reach the gold. Just as her fingers touched the ingot and without so much as the smallest of sounds, like a child's see-saw the grizzly tipped and prised itself free of the shaft wall. The steelwork fell away; silently at first, then it sparked and rang when it clipped against the rock and intermittently, Miriam's lamp became the distant, falling star.

Lee heard it strike shaft bottom; that coming together of steel and stone. Everyone knew what had happened and that Miriam could never have survived a fall of that magnitude. Devoid of any compassion, Lee's mind raced ahead of the situation; Comrade Minister Miriam Pasviri had, through her own endeavours been taken out of the equation. To retrieve Miriam's body, the ore pass would have to be accessed from the lower level. She would be unrecognisable, broken and ragdoll-like, what was left of her would be zipped inside a body bag and dispassionately carted to surface. After going through the motions of an enquiry, the government would be quick to draw a line under it. As of that moment, like vultures to a fresh kill, the Party faithful would be wheeling in for a crack at the latest vacancy and over the rudiments of some impotent investigation, Rex, as Minister for Mines would be afforded the final say. Miriam had just become the latest ministerial statistic for the Party's registrar of deaths.

First-aiders milled about the ore pass, robbed of their chance to shine they buckled up their canvas bags and prepared to head for the shaft station. Three hundred feet below, a ten kilogram bar of gold bullion lay mixed in with the mayhem; Lee knew that he had to recover it before the authorities found it and started their witch hunt. Cold crept in through the souls of his boots; Karen was sobbing and the rescue crew was stripping down their equipment from above the ore pass. The CIO man was already on his way back to the shaft station for an early ride to surface; beneath his overalls his own clothes were sweat-soaked.

From off the chain ladder, Rex hauled himself clear of the shaft collar; his legs were shaking, softened by those last few weeks of easy living and riding in government limousines. Gratefully, he accepted a cup of heavily sweetened coffee from one of the rescue team then moved away from the ore pass, crossing the broken ground to where Lee and Karen were waiting.

'It's over, captain. Before you know it, all of this will have been forgotten.' In that half-light the two of them exchanged the first hints of wry smiles. Rex nodded his head to Lee. 'Couldn't have happened to a nicer person. I'll send flowers and our mutual condolences to the crematorium.'

'Bastards, the pair of you,' said Karen, badly shaken by what had happened; her eyes were still fixed on the mouth of the ore pass. Rex shook his head at her sentiment.

'Had it been the three of us down there, Miriam would be dancing a jig over her good fortune. It was an accident, Karen. Nothing sinister happened here.' He draped his lamp cable across his shoulder. 'There's nothing more we can do. I need a cigarette; time we were back on surface.' His eyes sparkled. 'As of right now I'm on a week's hard-earned, compassionate leave.'

As on most evenings, Lee watched the mountains lose their colours to the twilight. Within those next ten minutes, like fireflies from the far forest, stars rose up and filled the firmament with tiny, glittering lights. Karen touched his arm. Dressed in loose jeans and favourite sloppy shirt, for the first time in several months she came across as comfortable, relaxed even.

'Penny for them?'

Still watching the oncoming darkness, Lee hooked his arm about her waist and picked up on the faint scent of Chanel. Karen leaned her head against his shoulder and together they watched the sky, for only a faint sliver of light remained – then it too was drawn beneath the western horizon.

'Getting my head around these last few months,' he answered. 'So much has happened.'

Rex and Sally came out onto the veranda. Rex had dressed in shorts and polo shirt, but wore nothing on his feet. Sally, like her husband had chosen shorts, but her blouse was pure white Armani silk.

Rex slapped the palm of his hand against his stomach. 'Too much food and drink. Got to stop. Too damned fat.'

'Leave your diet till after the holiday,' Lee suggested. 'Your security people phoned Byron, so if it's exercise you're after I'll be needing help clearing the old draw point on 587 Level.'

'How much rock would you say is still inside the ore pass?'

'Ten, maybe twenty tons. I'll give Byron a couple of days to organise half a dozen good men and whatever equipment we might need.'

'The royal, we.' Rex chuckled. 'Thought I might have

gotten away with this one. God only knows what we'll find in there.'

'A bloody mess,' said Lee. 'Literally, but it has to be done and the sooner the better. It's hot inside that ore pass; the putrefaction bugs will have a field day. Three or four days and the smell will flood the entire level.' He crossed to the veranda door and pushed it to. Insects, attracted by the living room lights were already tapping at the glass. 'Our CIO friends want the body back in Harare by Tuesday night at the latest.'

'So much for a week's R and R.'

'Byron is convinced the authorities are planning another surprise visit.'

'Why would they bother?' Sally joined in. 'Not like our infamous killing brigade to worry their tortuous little minds over recovering a corpse.'

'Unless they know about the gold,' Lee suggested. 'What about the pilot? The men who killed him; they would have been witness to what he told Miriam.'

Rex put their minds at rest. 'Miriam was alone with the pilot when he told her where I offloaded the bullion.'

'How can you be so sure?' Karen asked him.

Rex lit a cigarette and inhaled deeply. 'Because she told me. Miriam wasn't stupid. She killed the pilot herself before the CIO could get to him. No one else knows about it.'

Karen was horrified. 'She actually killed him?'

'Single shot through the back of his head – took great delight in telling me exactly how she did it.'

Karen gulped her drink. 'Makes my coming to terms with her falling down the shaft a whole lot easier.'

'Miriam was no pussy cat.' Rex went on. 'Trained by North Korean instructors in Mozambique. Both she and her husband were active ZANLA guerrillas. Miriam saw killing as a perk. She was part of the cadre that led the attack on your Musami mission in seventy-seven. Seven

Catholic missionaries; none of them were spared.'

'I remember the newspapers,' said Lee.

'She was fifteen years old at the time.'

Karen picked up empty glasses from the table. What she had seen in Miriam's eyes just minutes before her death now made sense. Perplexed by what had happened she fought to rid her mind of the nightmare. The thought of having stood so close to a psychopath turned her stomach and for a moment, beset with gooseflesh, she shivered violently.

'It's getting cold,' she told Lee. 'I'm going inside.'

Sally followed her. Like Karen, she favoured a more convivial atmosphere. They left the men alone on the veranda.

*

By midnight, the moon had reached its zenith and like besotted hounds Lee and Rex stared up at it. They conversed without dropping their eyes from the moon's pock-marked pattern of craters that for tens of thousands of years had held the whole of mankind within its thrall. Karen and Sally were already asleep and the homestead, now flooded with moonlight, was silent.

'There's something I want you to take a look at,' Lee said. 'An unbiased opinion, see what you make of it.'

Rex blew a perfectly formed smoke ring and on the stilled air of the enclosed veranda it floated halo-like above Lee's head.

'Sounds intriguing.'

'You look bushed. If you prefer, we could wait for morning?'

'Too late, captain.' Rex stood up from his chair. 'I wouldn't be able to relax. What do you want from me?'

'Confirmation or condemnation of a theory. Truth or

untruth, you be the judge of what you see.'

'Why do I feel the sudden need for a certain key?' Rex went ahead and reached behind the austere likeness of a hippopotamus. Carved from local soapstone and waxed to a dark olive green, for more than forty years it had stared down from its high shelf, a lone custodian of the homestead's storeroom door.

'You do the honours,' Lee insisted and waited for Rex to insert the key, throw the lock and push back the door. Rex reached inside for the light switch.

'Most things change,' Rex whispered, 'but not this, not your grandmother's storeroom.' He stepped through, but this was more than just another door, it was a way inside another world.

'Over there, on the old man's desk,' Lee pointed it out. He followed Rex between stacked tea chests and neat, sheet-covered rows of his grandmother's Victoriana. Rex went straight to the Bakelite on-off switch beneath the standard lamp's heavy brocade and tasselled shade; he turned on the power. A warm, somnolent glow fell upon the roll-top desk. Lee pulled another chair alongside his own and gestured to Rex.

'Sit close in; saves me stretching.' He shuffled aside to make room for Rex. 'You never met Gerard?'

Rex shook his head. 'Saw him knock down Pasviri's helicopter with a rocket-propelled grenade; that was all I knew of the man.'

'Brave man and a good friend,' Lee emphasized and held off those dark, melancholic clouds that he knew were always quick to gather around him. 'Wouldn't be here if it weren't for Gerard Brownlee. I shall miss him.'

Rex gave the moment chance to dissipate; the storeroom had long since become a shrine to past champions of the Goddard family empire. He drained his glass and was grateful of the cigarette he had brought with him. He leaned against the desk top; restless from the waiting, he nodded his head to Lee, urging him to speak.

'Put your ghosts to bed, captain – let's get on with this, the suspense is killing me.'

Lee shook off those morbid recollections and reached for Gerard's old suitcase.

'Steel yourself, Khumalo. You're about to have your proverbial socks knocked off.' He flipped back the lid and drew out a large, nondescript manila envelope; its gummed flap torn and curled back. In the right-hand corner, a strip of old Rhodesian stamps, complete with Fort Victoria post office franking marks.

He handed the envelope to Rex.

'Cast your mind back almost twenty years; driving back from the Mines Office in Fort Victoria – you and I both joked about a certain aspect of so-called, Ndebele folklore? Time for a serious re-assessment, my friend – your family history is a lot more complex than we realised.'

Rex balanced his cigarette on the lip of the ashtray and with his curiosity piqued, eagerly he reached inside the envelope.

Most of the papers were brittle to the touch – almost parchment-like. Stored in close to Gerard's corrugated iron roof, the sun's heat had baked them yellow and the edges had years ago turned in on themselves. Rex drew out the tied bundle in its entirety. Gently, he slipped the knot, pulled away the string and settled his eyes on the text.

Not wanting to influence Rex's interpretation of what he was reading, Lee stayed quiet. One o'clock came and went before Rex pushed the papers aside and rocked back in his chair.

'I want to carry on reading, but no chance.' With his finger and thumb he massaged the ache from his eyes. 'Enough. I'm shot. Too much brandy and too many

327

damn cigarettes.' Owl-like he blinked at Lee. 'I'll finish them later. Got to get some sleep or my head will burst.'

'So, before you hit the sack. Going off what you've read so far, the condensed version – what do you think?'

'I think the old man was just as crazy as you are. Where did he get this stuff?'

'Two separate sources,' Lee explained. 'The typed-up geology bits came from Gerard's son, he works for DeBeers Consolidated Diamond Mines in Botswana. The bulk of the report is a facsimile of his university thesis; sent it to his old man several years ago.'

'For his doctorate?'

Lee nodded his head. 'Witwatersrand University. Got his PhD and then took up a job offer as resident geologist with DeBeers. To hell and gone out in the Kalahari.'

'What about the handwritten stuff? Looks like something out of a Dickensian ledger. I pictured old Scrooge sat in his office scratching away with a goose quill.'

'That Dickensian ledger, my old son, might well be the key to your salvation.'

Lee reached across the desk for the single sheet of paper, and though he had read the transcript several times, still the sight of it excited him.

'Have you read any of this?'

Rex shook his head, his eyes already half closed.

'I tried, but I'm too damned tired. The writing jumps up and down, too spidery; I'll read it in the morning. Finished the thesis stuff – that was okay. A lot of grey areas but put that down to lack of sleep on my part.'

Lee glanced at his watch. It was going on for two in the morning; the moon, like yesterday's sun was ready to slip below the horizon. Within that same minute, Rex's eyes closed and he fell asleep in the chair.

To stay awake, Lee forced himself to check the time by

the half hour. Constantly he mulled over the contents of the documents, then his mind began to cloud and reluctantly he gave up on the task. He dug out a blanket for Rex from the linen cupboard and for himself, fresh coffee and hot buttered toast from a quiet kitchen. Leaving Rex asleep, Lee went out onto the veranda and pulled a chair in close to the coffee table. The air was thick with the scent of watered gardens and woodland. All the homestead lights were off and with quiet eyes he stared up at the sky. The first faint glimmerings of dawn were already there above the horizon. From the ridge above the homestead there carried the raucous cries of Swainson's Francolin. As always, Lee found the familiarity of their weird cries strangely comforting, so that his listening wandered in and out of choked ravines where he knew the birds had roosted.

Dulled by the oncoming light, the stars, like anemones left behind by a receding tide lost their colour and one by one they disappeared. Baboons stirred and barked down from their cliff-top fortress, and then gradually, the sounds faded and the toast and coffee were left untouched on the table.

-76-

Lee woke up with the sun shining directly onto his face. Karen kissed him lightly on the cheek and pushed a mug of steaming coffee against his fingers.

'Coffee then shower and shave, my darling – you smell like a goat.'

'How do goats smell?'

'Not funny – where's your drinking partner?'

Lee straightened up and swivelled in his seat; his neck hurt and mosquitoes had been at work on his softer body parts.

'I covered him up and left him asleep in the storeroom.' He reached inside his shirt and scratched. 'Reckon I should have done the same.' His hand shook when he lifted the cup to his lips. 'I could eat a rat.' He cursed himself for missing dinner the previous night and looked to Karen for sympathy; he found none.

'Careful what you wish for buster, after abandoning me for the entire night, rats are pretty high up on your menu.'

'I suppose over the top, sex in the shower before breakfast is way down on your wish list?'

'Right first time.' She waited for him to finish his coffee and took the empty cup from him. 'I've promised Sally a visit to the Ruin's museum. You and Rex will have to fend for yourselves, at least until lunchtime.' She started for the door. 'We'll await the arrival of our intrepid adventurers in the cocktail bar.'

'The Ruin's hotel?'

Karen nodded. 'Or we might still be down at the museum – and bring your cheque book; you're paying for lunch and a bottle of very expensive red.' She changed tack. 'Last night, did you make any headway?'

'Didn't finish,' Lee admitted, 'too tired.'

'Too tired, or too drunk?' Karen chastised him. 'Go take shower, and wake up Romeo before Sally finds out where he is and emasculates the man – bacon's on the top shelf of the fridge, next to the eggs.'

77

Karen and Sally chatted like old friends, they followed the gravel road leading from the hotel, down into a park-like valley and eventually, via a few granite steps climbed upwards to a small, innocuous looking stone and thatch building set amongst a grove of Jacaranda trees. The entire site was lorded over by tumbled granite walls. Centrally positioned so as to be within easy walking distance of any part of the Great Zimbabwe Ruins, the building itself, though outwardly in need of some minor restoration, epitomised the cool and airy; a refuge from the dust and heat outside.

'The old museum is not much to look at, I'm afraid.' Karen explained apologetically. 'She could do with a new roof and a good old fashioned lick of paint.'

'Needs some money thrown at it,' Sally agreed, but that aside, rubbed her hands together in anticipation of what she might find. 'Let's get in there, Karen, our heritage calls.'

Split into sections, the museum was complimented with glass-panelled display shelves and larger, open alcoves, and where once there had been displayed a plethora of ancient artefacts, now the shelves were only half filled. Only items of mediocre interest and of low value had been left for visiting tourists and amateur archaeologists to ponder over. Other than Karen and Sally, there was no one else there.

'Again, not much to see,' Karen apologised. 'The interesting stuff has all gone.'

'Gone?' Sally appeared shocked. 'Gone where?'

'Done quite openly,' Karen went on matter of factly. 'Hustled away to Harare in ministerial cars and auctioned off to foreign collectors.'

Sally shook her head in disbelief. 'Our country's

heritage sold off?'

'From the cleaner upwards, they're all involved. Eighty percent of what we excavate. I've gotten used to it.'

A door opened, and as if emerging from a cold winter's hibernation, the museum curator poked his head inside the room. He recognised Karen and though the smile held, from his mannerisms and thin underlying tone to his voice it was obvious that he resented her being there.

'Karen. You're not due back for at least another week?'

A single, gold filling picked up light from the window. Dressed in banker type, pinstriped trousers and open necked shirt, on thick legs the curator lumbered hippo-like into the room. A sugary crumb of flaky pastry clung to his chin. His eyes swung onto Sally and like overexcited insects they scurried over her, assessing her curves and the expensive cut of her clothing. The smile changed, became engaging and placatory. He stood to his full height, wiped the palms of his hands across his stomach and turned on the charm.

'Jonas Masasiri, the museum's curator.' He stretched out his arm, but forewarned by sticky, sugary lips, Sally made no attempt to accept the handshake. She waded straight in.

'Why the empty shelves, comrade?'

The hand withdrew and just as quickly the smile disappeared; now suspicious of the impromptu visit, Masasiri dropped the niceties. Defensively, he folded his arms across the great mound of his stomach.

'We have international loan arrangements with selected universities and museums, a percentage of what we find is always, how should I put it – on the move.' He glanced meaningfully at Karen. 'Our excavation people struggle to keep pace with demand. Perhaps if our resident archaeologist was more forthcoming with her finds, my shelves might well be overflowing with relics

332

of greater interest.'

Karen ignored the accusation; she had long since become used to in-house political wrangling over who took what and for how much. It was the how much part which conjured up the most attention though. To those who did the wheeling and dealing, Zimbabwe's cultural heritage meant less than nothing. US currency was what they were after; off-shore bank accounts were commonplace amongst the government's hierarchy. She fired back at him.

'How much did you make from my last find, Jonas? A thousand? Two? Or correct me if I'm wrong, wasn't fifty thousand American the price I heard banded about after our last meeting?' Karen stared at him defiantly; challenging him with her eyes. Any previous apprehension over personal repercussions now replaced by a liberal pouring out of her frustrations. Her entire excavation team knew exactly what was going on, unable to react, they were emasculated and could stand only as silent, limp-wristed minions in the face of united Party autonomy. This was Zimbabwe. Those with any political clout used their infinite powers of bribery, or the threat of outright terror to control those beneath them. With only one thought in mind they worked together – and to the detriment of the ordinary man in the street they were now unstoppable.

Jonas kept his calm; the woman was no threat to him, she would be looked upon as just another disadvantaged colonist; arrogant and provocative. Any investigation of his supposed motives by some higher authority would be ruled in his favour. Without any hesitation they would safeguard their own agenda against any imperialistic move to discredit one of their Party's loyal supporters. With regards to any World Heritage witch hunt, most of the organisation's co-ordinators were naive and easily manipulated. Black market demands for the more unusual artefacts were on the increase and for the appropriate wad of American dollars, Zimbabwe's treasures were easy pickings; the ruins themselves were now regarded worldwide as open hunting grounds for the avid collector.

'You will regret what you are implying, comrade. I shall report your insinuations to the authorities. I can assure you, Karen, as of this moment your position of resident archaeologist for the Great Zimbabwe Ruins hangs literally, by a single thread.'

Before Sally could step in, Karen raised her hand to within inches of Masasiri's face.

'Then this perhaps will change your mind.' She thrust the object closer, forcing him to step backwards for him to focus on what she was holding. 'How long would it take for you to find a buyer, Jonas? How long, before an artefact of such importance suffers the same fate as its predecessors?' She moved forwards. 'Look closely, Jonas, outside of this room nothing like it exists – the only one of its kind. Never in all your time here as museum curator have you come across anything so beautiful, nor would you be offered this chance again.' She went on with the tirade. 'How much is it worth, comrade? I would guess at upwards of a half a million US. Even shares, I think you will agree would be a fair way to split the spoils.'

Cloaked in natural light, the slight trembling of Karen's fingers served to enliven the precious metal.

'Where did you find it?'

'Here, amongst the ruins,' Karen goaded him. 'Lost during the final defence of these ancient walls, you could tell your buyer.' Again she thrust it closer to his face. 'The smell of blood is there Jonas. What horrors did this creature behold? How many men would kill to possess a totem such as this – what fortunes would they part with?'

Masasiri's eyes bulged; tiny droplets of sweat stood out from his forehead.

'May I see it?' He held out his hand; the aggression that he showed to Karen a moment ago had dissipated, replaced by awe for the half reptile, half bird that now hovered just inches from his face.

Karen hesitated, but only momentarily before she placed the gold talisman in the palm of his hand.

His fingers closed around it.

'An exact likeness of our country's armorial bird. What you have brought here has in truth always belonged to the people of Zimbabwe.'

'And even if I were of a mind to let you keep it, within a single week, comrade, you will have sold it on.'

He ignored her sarcasm and like a child with some long-awaited toy, Masasiri drew the talisman close in to his chest.

Through the awakening of his mind's eye, he visualised the vast fortune it would bring the seller. He would simply disappear – no one would find him. His mind raced through a thousand ways for him to spirit away with this most precious work of art. As Karen had already pointed out, Far Eastern collectors would kill without hesitation to possess such a relic.

Sally saw the change come over him; no longer the responsible protector of Zimbabwe's heritage, Jonas Masasiri now stood entranced. With a wolf's hungry eyes, he stared longingly at the priceless artefact.

'What you have uncovered is beyond any monetary value. I have heard it spoken of by tribal elders and until now, dismissed their stories as mere fireside superstitions.'

Stepping in close to the window he held the totem aloft for better effect. Enwrapped by raw sunlight, the metal took on soul and held precedence over everything in the room.

'But this,' he whispered, 'this is far beyond my wildest dreams. How many men have held the weight of a treasure such as this one?'

'Not very many, comrade.' Dressed in Wrangler jeans and white shirt Rex stepped through the doorway, more the casual tourist than government minister. Lee followed him in and stood next to Karen.

Masasiri balled his fingers about the talisman.

'Who are you – what do you want?'

Rex smiled sardonically.

'Who I am is something you will find out soon enough. What I want is for you to return the artefact to its rightful guardian – now.' He took his time lighting a cigarette, never once did his eyes drop from those of the man in front of him. 'Or I will take it from you by force if need be.'

Reluctantly, Masasiri handed the talisman back to Karen; hatred bled from his eyes.

'You have not heard the last of this. As soon as you leave I will inform my associates in Harare.'

'Rather you give me their names,' Rex growled, 'I will tell them in person; face to face. And before I forget, as of now and on behalf of my government and the World Heritage, Comrade Karen Goddard has just taken sole charge of the entire site; including all current and future excavations and the running and revitalisation of this excuse of a museum.'

'Which means that you've just been fired.' Sally grinned delightedly. 'Go clear your desk, comrade. As of today your access rights to the ruins will be limited to those of the visiting tourist. On your life, comrade,' the grin turned venomous, 'ignore the ruling and you will continue to live out your days as custodian – only this time, to some government prison vegetable garden.'

78

For more than an hour, Lee sat quietly whilst Rex gathered in the threads of that previous night's revelations. Most he had fathomed, apart from the contents of a single sheet of paper torn from the spine of some old ledger. In black Indian ink the writing was rigidly formal and upright, the punctuation spartan, and yet the writer had woven his story through with skill and many veiled enticements. Thoughtfully, Rex tapped against the paper with his cigarette lighter.

'This is the piece that puzzles me the most; doesn't make sense, reads like an excerpt from Rider Haggard's, King Solomon's Mines.' He pushed his chair back and out of frustration, lit another cigarette. 'None of this is real – some sort of prank. You say Gerard's son is one of DeBeers top geologists?'

Lee nodded his head. 'Robert Brownlee.'

'Then why, if this is kosher, hasn't he followed it up?'

'I spoke to him a few days ago; tracked him down via the company switchboard in Orapa. Gerard's son is more in the dark than we are.'

Rex refocused his attention on the handwritten paper.

'So where did it come from?'

'Look at the signature.'

'Already done that. Who the hell was John Jacobs?'

'John Jacobs was your grandfather's personal advisor and go-between. He went everywhere with him.' He waved the document in front of Rex's face. 'He wrote this – there's nothing hanky-panky about it.'

Lee paused to collect his thoughts; the excitement of what he had found set his pulse racing.

'Don't you see? Jacobs was the royal bean counter; he documented Lobengula's entire fortune. Gold sovereigns, ivory, diamonds brought back from the

Kimberley diggings, everything. By the time Rhodes' mob marched on GuBuluwayo, your grandfather had already amassed and hidden a vast fortune.' He looked down at the inventory and quoted verbatim, ignoring anything he saw as irrelevant.

One thousand and seven stones all of the first water. All are larger than the first joint of my middle finger.

Lee grinned at Rex. 'I would hazard a guess at nothing smaller than five carat, cut and polished. A king's ransom, old son. Find them and there will be enough money to fund whatever revolutionary ideas pop into that crazy, Matabele head of yours.' He jumped up and started for the door. 'Grab your hat, Rex Jando Khumalo and bring those papers with you – we're going to see a man about a treasure.'

*

Moses watched them in through the driveway gates, his expression at first, deadpan, then his face broke with a wide smile when Lee and Rex came within useful distance of his failing eyesight and he ushered them both inside.

'Good to see you again, Mister Goddard.'

'You too, Moses. We need your help, old friend.'

'Will you be having something to drink, sir?' His eyes twinkled.

Lee shook his head and smiled. 'Just coffee, you old devil, I need to keep a clear head.'

They sat down and from the battered envelope, Lee drew out Gerard's papers and daybook and dropped them on the table.

'This one gives me the biggest headache.' He separated

the single handwritten sheet from the rest. 'Think carefully, Moses. Have you any idea where it came from?'

Moses reached out and took it from him, a wry smile already materialising.

'I know it too well, Mister Goddard. How could I not? He pointed to the signature. 'My father's name. These are his words, all of them. John Jacobs was an educated man, he has written many such letters.'

'John Jacobs was your father?' Lee pushed back in his seat, totally flabbergasted.

'Now you are thinking that what I have told you would not be possible, and yes you are right to doubt me, the letter was written when my father was but a young man; many years before I was born.'

Rex lowered his voice and displayed the respect conveyed by a younger man for his elder.

'How many years have come and gone for you, *baba*?'

For a moment, Moses wrestled with dates and years; when he fell upon the right numbers his eyes sparkled.

'In July, I will be eighty-one years old. July twenty. Yes.' He nodded and chuckled delightedly at the recollection of his father's image. 'I am sure.' He clapped his hands, titillated by the facts. 'That is very old; perhaps already I have outlived both of your lifetimes.'

Rex looked across the table at Lee.

'It fits. Puts his father somewhere around the forty-seven mark when Moses was born.'

Lee nodded his head in agreement.

'What of your mother, Moses? Do you remember her?'

The old man's smile faltered; he stared out through the open doorway, his eyes on the far hills.

'I hold no memories of my mother, she died before I felt the warmth of my first summer.'

'I'm sorry,' Lee said, 'perhaps now would be a good

339

time for you to bring out that bottle, old father. Your brandy might ease the pain. We have much more to speak of.'

Rex shook out two cigarettes from a full pack and rolled one over the table. Moses plucked off the filter and flicked it away through the open doorway. He waited for Rex to thumb the wheel on his lighter and though his eyes were small and rheumy, indomitably, they held the gaze of the younger man sat across from him.

'You are amaNdebele, this much I see in you.'

Rex nodded, but momentarily his tongue was thick and silent for now there were powerful forces pulling up chairs to the table. Like smoke from ancient fires, that of their cigarettes moved about the room and from inside of it there came out whisperings and soft sounds.

'Like your own,' Rex told him, 'my father sired me when already he had crossed the line from youth to old age. The final roar of an old lion.'

With his eyes, Moses urged him to go on.

'My father was little more than newly born when the soldiers cast our people out from GuBuluwayo.'

'It was a bad time,' Moses agreed and dragged hard on his cigarette. 'My father, John Jacobs, was forced to flee, but not before he completed all that the king had asked of him. There was much for him to set down as letters such as the one you have shown me.'

'You have others?' Lee asked.

'First the bottle,' grinned Moses and shuffled his legs from beneath the table. 'Glasses.' He pointed to where they were kept, 'Top shelf; easier for you than me to reach them down.'

The brandy was South African, the glasses worn and clouded, straight from the fifties; Gerard always preferred the barrel-shaped colonial style tumblers. *No need to change what don't need changing* he always told Lee.

340

The old man poured; each of the tumblers he filled to the brim.

'I have ice in the freezer?'

Both men shook their heads and in unison the three of them drank down that first, fiery mouthful of raw spirit. The moment the liquor exploded in his stomach, Moses shuddered appreciatively and without waiting for the feeling to pass pulled deeply on the cigarette. Purposely, he held in the potent mixture of smoke and brandy fumes. Tears of pure pleasure squeezed from between his eyelids and when the fire in his belly had eased, like a hot wind robbed of its strength, his breath exhaled and those first euphoric waves induced by nicotine and raw spirit came over him.

'Better!' he croaked and within that same moment, quickly he refilled his lungs with smoke and his mouth with hard liquor.

Rex cleared his throat and in earnest, started his search for answers.

'Did your father speak of what he had put to paper as a truth, or merely perhaps as stories with which to delight his grandchildren?'

'All are true,' the old man assured him. 'What John Jacobs put to paper were only those things which he himself had witnessed. No other man or woman was skilled enough to read his writings. Some of it, not even the great king himself, Lobengula Khumalo, was ever party to.'

Lee spun the lid off the bottle and topped up their glasses. The brandy was kind to the taste though harsh on the throat and there was a faint, underlying sweetness mixed with the spirit-burn of pepper and wood smoke.

'In the letter,' Lee went straight to the crux of them being there, 'he speaks of diamonds and gold coin. 'John Jacobs, what would he say to the man who might well be charged with their safe keeping?'

341

Moses drained his glass and cocked a doubting eye at the rhetoric.

'The hoard belongs to the Matabele, even if I knew of its whereabouts, why would I pass on those secrets to anyone carrying less than the full blood of a king?'

Lee looked across the table at Rex, urging him to come clean.

'And if such a man were here now, how would you look upon him?'

'With the eyes of a sparrow for the eagle, but that is not possible. All would have perished with him. They would not have deserted their king, not even in the face of death.' He frowned and looked about him. 'There were many stories; old wives' tales. Stories that were told through the flames of a thousand fires.' He shook his head and laughed softly. 'All, I think were untruths. Those of the king being carried by his warriors to the land of the Makololo beyond the great waterfall – another of his youngest wife, a woman with the king's unborn child already in her belly. There were those who swore of her living out her life amongst the Makalanga, many days march to the east of GuBuluwayo...'

He pulled up short. As if a door into the past had been flung open and a chill wind had come out from it, Moses shivered. His gaze swung on to Rex and as though the old man were held in the thrall of powerful magic he was unable to tear his eyes away. Then he continued on with his story telling – still with his eyes on the man across the table.

'As decreed by The Great Elephant, for her safe keeping, the king's Induna took Thabisa to be his own.' He fell to his knees and with both hands covered his face as a show of deep respect.

'She gave him a son; your father. You are the one, *Baba*. I see this now. You are the Great Father of the Matabele.'

Rex's mouth dried up. In the old man's eyes he was now descended of the divine spirit of Lobengula Khumalo, The Shaker of Mountains; the thunder of the storm as yet to come upon the earth. He reached for his glass and drained it in a single gulp.

The old man trembled in awe of his own stupidity.

'Forgive this old man. Only now do I know you are the son of all sons; descendant of the house of Mashobane. The grandson of He Who Drives Like the Wind. From that last sown seed of The Great Elephant.'

Rex reached out for him and lifted him up from the floor.

'Take it easy, old man, you have nothing to fear. Rex Khumalo will do just fine for now.' He set him down, back in his chair and lit a cigarette for him. Rex refilled the old man's glass and allowed him time to calm himself.

'You said that you had more letters?'

Eventually, Moses relaxed. Allowing them to scrutinise his father's work pleased him. He stood up from the table.

'There are pictures.'

'Pictures?' Lee echoed. 'What are these pictures of?'

'I will fetch them for you.'

They waited in silence for the old man to return.

Moses reappeared and placed a cardboard shoe box at the centre of the table. Long ash drooped from the end of his cigarette. On the bridge of his nose now perched a pair of ancient reading glasses and Lee guessed that Gerard had passed them on to him.

'Even with these spectacles, my eyes are not so good,' Moses chuckled at his own failings. 'When I was young, from as far away as one mile I would pick out young girls washing their *magaro* in the river. Now that would not be possible, even if they were using my hosepipe and stood no further than the bottom of my garden.'

He lifted the lid on the shoe box and tipped out all of the contents. Two faded, sepia-coloured likenesses topped the pile. One was of John Jacobs, standing alone and stoically regimental-like in front of a mud brick building. The name: *Dawson Brothers* in rough, painted lettering showed from above the doorway.

From records of his own family history, Lee recalled the traders' names and the influence James Dawson wielded over the Matabele.

'The king trusted this man Dawson,' Moses continued. 'He would bring news from across the Limpopo River. Dawson was always the first to warn the king of any soldiers or settler wagons entering his kingdom.' He changed the subject and sorted a second photograph from the pile. He dropped the picture in front of Lee.

'Lobengula stands between my father and the king's *Induna.*' Thoughtfully, he ran his finger over the likeness of a tall Matabele. 'I do not remember his name. Perhaps this man and the protector of Thabisa, the child's mother are one and the same.' He tapped his brow with the flat of his hand. 'Sometimes my father's stories fly as frightened fowl inside my head, though only the king's most trusted could claim the right to stand in the king's shadow.'

Both Lee and Rex were transfixed. Unable to tear their eyes from the warrior at the king's right hand, they studied the picture as though it were a lost Monet or Turner's, *Fighting Temeraire.*

'I need more time to make comparisons,' said Lee and looked at Moses for permission to take the shoe box and its contents away with him.

'Take them.' Moses complied. 'When you have found what you are searching for, then you will bring them home.'

79

Lee was first through the storeroom doorway; Rex followed and just as eagerly found himself staring down at the same, dog-eared photograph. Three men stared back at them. With careful fingers, Lee lifted the photograph from the desk and angled his wrist for the picture to catch the full light from the standard lamp. He faced the room's west wall. His head thumped from too much brandy, but his hand was steady. Only the beat of his heart had quickened.

'No doubt about it, Rex. Your mysterious protector is back in the frame – literally.'

As if by fate, Rex was drawn to make his way between rows of boxes and stacked chairs; he stopped within a few yards of the west wall. Through the placement of the portrait, he was forced to crane his neck to scrutinise the likeness of a powerfully built Matabele Induna. Committed in richly melded oils it was a picture that Lee's grandmother had brought to Rex's attention so many years ago. From within its gilt frame, the same austere face peered back at him and even the battleaxe rested between his feet was as near as humanly possible an exact, artist's reproduction of the weapon in the photograph.

'Mhlangana Khumalo,' Rex whispered, 'I should have guessed you were involved. Where in the name of all my people are you leading me this time?'

'Over here, Rex. Come take a look at this.'

Rex made his way back to the desk and pulled up a chair. Lee had been busy, already he had sifted through more handwritten records, one sheet in particular had grabbed his attention. Like before, the writing was precise and coal-black.

Word was brought by messenger that white generals were readying soldiers and many wagons at the place they call Victoria some four days march to the east of GuBuluwayo. I saw that Lobengula was greatly troubled by this happening and indeed within that very moment, the will to stand and fight abandoned him.

On the king's word I have accounted for all his wealth and already a sum of ten thousand gold sovereigns has been spirited away to a place unknown to those other than his most trusted followers. With this hoard went twenty wagons loaded with the teeth of slaughtered elephant. Perhaps this forsaken treasure has at last found sanctuary amongst the great stone dwala of the Matobo, but the reality of these facts, rely only on my own, perhaps flawed suppositions. One thing I am sure of, the diamonds brought from the Umgodi Makhulu, The Big Hole, called so by those white men who live far beyond the Crocodile River, were counted by my own hand. Over one thousand of these were stitched into the belly skin of a yearling calf. The king's man, a man who he himself carried royal blood in his veins was charged with their concealment, and indeed this one man, namely, Mhlangana Khumalo assured me of their safe keeping. For seven days the stones were carried southwards and only on that last day, a place deemed worthy of such a treasure was found and put to good use. The king's man told me this himself and I trust him as a fellow brother and protector of The Black Bull to have in truth carried out this task. No one but the king's Induna and I know of this happening and with respect to the dispersing hordes of Matabele, would prove greatly fortuitous to the entire nation for it to remain so.

Upon his return the Induna, like me, found the king's kraal and the entire city of GuBuluwayo in flames. The said, Mhlangana Khumalo shared my camp for a single night before, with his son Ndumiso, he insisted on following the king's wagon spoor. This I am sure he did with strong and loyal commitment to his king and since that day no further words have passed between us. The king fled northwards whilst I, John Jacobs took of that same speed and fled southwards towards the great Crocodile River.

346

All these things the king bade for me to write down and as decreed, only those of royal bloodline will, after the protective veil of time has been lifted and through the guidance of noble spirit, chance to come upon this fortune in gold coin and precious stones. On that same day the kingdom of the Matabele will again be made whole.

Lee's finger slid to a second, underlying page. Here the ink was weak and severely yellowed by age. From a small drawer in the roll-top desk he took out a jeweller's loupe and with his forefinger, opened out the lens.

'Most probably something and nothing,' he mused and pressed the loupe to his right eye. He strained for fresh strength of vision and struggled with the text, hovering close in to the spidery writing he concentrated all his efforts to deciphering every single letter. At last, he dropped the loupe against the desk's leather inlay and rubbed his eyes.

'The thesis for Robert's PhD, what was the subject matter?'

Rex's head thumped, the brandy had left him with a dull ache behind his eyes.

'Something about the Matobo hills.' He reached across and searched for the copy of Robert Brownlee's post graduate studies of a twelve hundred square mile granite batholith.

'Okay, I've got it.' He read from the cover. 'Intrusive hydro-thermal solutions – the formation of limestones, resultant caverns and sinkholes relevant to the Matobo granites.'

'Geologist-type rhetoric.' Lee chuckled.

'So there could be a link between old Jacob's stuff and Robert's thesis?'

Lee shrugged his shoulders and breathed on the lens.

'Could be. Stay objective; no romanticising. Pound to a penny, Moses isn't aware of what we have here.'

He cleaned the lens of his own fingerprints and with the back of his hand, smoothed out the sheet of paper; this time he read aloud.

The hunter whom Mhlangana came upon was equal in height only to that of a small boy still in his third year as herder and protector to his father's cattle. Not dark-skinned like others directly descendant of the Matabele, more the colour of burned clay, a mixing of yellow and brown, more like my own, that of the Cape half-caste – neither black nor white but through God's insistence, in-between the both.

The words that follow are those of Mhlangana Khumalo and are not the fanciful concoctions of my own imagination. I can only pray that they are first looked upon by a man whose courage is great enough to face the rising up of whatever terrible force awaits him. From here on, I therefore write as Mhlangana speaks. The fire about which we sit has burned to a low flame. Above us, the sky is filled with stars and for Lobengula Jando Khumalo, king of the Matabele, my heart portrays a great sadness.

With much regret and thoughts of what might have been, I write for you the name, John Jacobs, the year of our Lord, 1893.

Rex leaned in closer, his mind fired up by these fresh discoveries.

'He said there was more?'

'There is more,' Lee promised. 'The final couple of paragraphs are just about readable. From what I can make out, these are more or less the actual words spoken by your buddy up there in the painting.'

Lee rested his weight on his elbows and moved in as close as the lens would allow for him to focus on the writing. He cleared his throat and with staccato-like precision, read out those all-important last few lines to the man sitting alongside him.

On that last night of my journeying amongst our sacred hills, the

rain came and did not stop before the rising of that next sun.
Water sprang from every crack and hole in the mountain sides and
where the waters joined as one river, with the voice of a thousand
angry storms it thundered beneath the earth. Guided by the spirits
of our ancestors I went onwards and stood close to where the water
was swallowed inside that terrible hole. Above me, as a rabbit
crouched to the high rocks, the hunter, N'go looked down from a
place where neither my spears nor axe could reach him out.

As guardian of this sacred place, N'go led me deep inside the
earth to where a million creatures fell upon us and it was here that
I feared my life would be forfeit. Only through the Bushman's skill
and magical powers was I able to escape this darkened underworld,
rising up from a place of terrible suffering to one of silence and
great beauty.

At the feet of a great king I cut free the leather bindings of the
isikhwama, and in that sacred light, the cursed stones that I
carried so far filled that place beneath the ground with the voice
from a thousand stars.

Neither one of them spoke and for a long time sat
back in their chairs, staring across the room as though
the entrance to some fanciful treasure cave were there in
front of them, let into the far wall.

Based on John Jacob's account of that lost hoard, Lee
took a mental stab at its present day value.

'Got to be over thirty million British pounds. Fifty
million US dollars, but there again, maybe it's all made
up? Old John Jacobs could have set himself up for one
last laugh at whoever's expense.'

'It's kosher,' Rex realised. 'Read the thesis. Gerard
must have picked up on both references to an
underground river and tied the two together; his son
mapped every major limestone cave and sinkhole in the
Matobo Hills. One of them in particular, I found to be
of interest. Due south of Bulawayo, give or take seventy
miles as the crow flies. He mentioned the start of an

underground water course – and what he claims were bushman paintings close in to the entrance.'

Lee nodded his head. 'If the diamonds are real, that's one hell of a lot of political clout if we find them.'

'Not if, captain – when. I'm getting too old for this. Finding the old man's treasure will stand as my swansong.'

Rex looked across the desk at Lee and the smile that he smiled almost covered the width of his face.

* * *

8607151R00209

Printed in Great Britain
by Amazon.co.uk, Ltd.,
Marston Gate.